The BITTERSWEET BRIDE

Advertisements for Love Series

To Shaii,

Thank you for your support.

Be blessed!

NR

The BITTERSWEET BRIDE

Advertisements for Love Series

VANESSA RILEY

Entangled Publishing, LLC
2614 South Timberline Road
Suite 105, PMB 159
Fort Collins, CO 80525
Visit our website at www.entangledpublishing.com.

Amara is an imprint of Entangled Publishing, LLC.

Edited by Erin Molta
Cover design by Kanaxa Designs
Cover art from Taria Reed/The Reed Files and Shutterstock

Manufactured in the United States of America

First Edition January 2018

Chapter One

You Have Mail & Memories

London, England, September 7, 1819

Theodosia Cecil dipped her head, hoping her gray bonnet would hide her tall form amongst the crowd of Burlington Arcade shoppers. Her heart beat a rhythm of fear as her brow fevered with questions.

Could it be him?

Why was he haunting her now?

She spun, praying her wobbly legs would support her flight from the ghost. Spying a path between a chatty woman and her admirer, Theodosia claimed it and swayed toward the open door.

Safe in the shop, she put a hand to her thumping heart. Seeing the face of someone dead… It shook her, forced too many memories. The image of Ewan, her deceased first love, had to be a figment of Theodosia's conscience, nothing more. Why would this vision rear up now—questioning her resolve to be in town garnering letters offering matrimony from strangers?

Her hands trembled, puckering the stiff seams of her new kid gloves as she stuffed the sealed papers into her reticule. What if she'd dropped them in her mad dash? With all the people milling beneath the sparkling glass roof of the Arcade, the responses would've been lost, and with them, her dream of protecting her son. Hope in her plan slipped from her grasp, even with her onyx mitts. This time, there would be no kind Mathew Cecil to pick her up and wipe her clean.

She missed her late husband and his endless patience. He should be the only dead man in her head. Yet, there stood Ewan Fitzwilliam's ghost, vividly in her imagination. Perhaps it was her heart crying out at this unromantic way of finding a new husband.

"Ma'am, may I help you?"

Theodosia lifted her gaze from her gloves to a small cherry-red face.

"Our store has much to offer," the young girl said. "Did ye come for something special, Mrs. Cecil?"

Startling at the girl's use of her name, Theodosia raised her chin, then scanned from side to side at the pots. She took a breath and smelled sweet roses and lilacs. "What is this place? A perfumer?"

"Yes, Mrs. Cecil, and we use Cecil flowers to make the best fragrances."

The girl knew who she was, and the lilt in the young blonde's voice made Theodosia's lips lift. Respect always felt good.

A little less jittery, she nodded at the girl then turned to the walnut shelf and poked the lid of a greenish jar. The scent of lavender filled the air. Pride in her and her husband's accomplishment inflated her lungs. "Cecil flowers are the best."

The calm ushered in from the soft, sweet scents allowed

her thoughts to right. Ghosts didn't exist. If they did, then it would be Mathew visiting her, guiding her, pushing her cold feet forward whenever she felt she couldn't do something, as he'd often done during their five short years of marriage. He had died almost a year ago.

The shop girl came beside her, dusting the shelves. "Would you like some of the lavender, Mrs. Cecil?"

That beautiful name, the only last name she'd ever possessed—the repetition of it inspired questions. "You know me from the flower fields? Have we met?"

"Everyone knew Mr. Cecil. God rest his soul. And all the flower girls know you. If a Blackamoor... Sorry, if a shop girl could be more, then we all can."

Theodosia, dark skin and all, an inspiration to others? If those shop girls knew the whole of things, they would be scandalized. Horrified at the things she'd done, Theodosia became teary-eyed. She'd received unmerited favor catching Mathew Cecil's eye and his mercy.

"Sorry, I didn't mean nothing."

Theodosia nodded and tugged at her sleeve, hitting her reticule against her buttons, which clinked like serving bells. Her fine clothes hid the past, the fatigue and hunger of living on the streets. She forced a smile. "Becoming more is the beginning."

"Yes, ma'am. Quite a good 'ne."

From the outside, it must look like that, but some secrets were best kept in the grave. She turned from the almost-hero worship look in the shop girl's eyes and counted the brightly colored decanters in hues of salmon and cobalt blue lining a near table. "This is a lovely place. Have you done well since the shop's opening?"

"Some days. Some mornings, we're good and busy. Others, slow and easy. So much different than selling on the streets."

That worn-out heart of Theodosia's started moving within her chest. She caught the girl's shy gaze and said, "Slow days mean no money, but they can give ease to the back." With her palm, she cupped her mouth. "I meant selling flowers...long days." There were worse things for the back than an honest day's work selling flowers. Her mother's work at a brothel—that had been hard.

The younger woman nodded, but frowned as a shadow engulfed her.

A thick, portly fellow wearing a heavy burlap apron stepped from behind them. "Do ye belong here, m-m-miss?"

Theodosia blinked then stared at the man who stood with arms folded, disapproval flexing each meaty muscle. "Are you sure you're supposed to be here? Black servants don't come unattended. Blackamoor or whatever you are?"

"Sir, this is Mr. Cecil's widow," the shop girl said as her gaze dropped.

The man gawked as he glared at Theodosia. After an eternity of seconds, he said, "Oh...that Mrs. Cecil."

The pride she'd felt at hearing the Cecil name slipped away. It fell to the floor, ready to be trampled by her own short heels. With silk ribbons trailing her bonnet and an onyx walking dress stitched with heavy brass buttons, he still saw her as low. Was he thinking, as she often did: *mistress, half-breed, by-blow, whore*?

No matter what Theodosia felt about her past, she'd not let the sour shop clerk, or anyone else, stuff her into one of those names. She was a widow to a good man. "I'm not a servant, sir. In fact, you are one of the many vendors who use my family's wares for your livelihood." She took a step closer to the man. "I'm your business partner."

The man turned a lovely shade of purple, darker than fallen bee orchid buds. The veins on his neck pulsed.

As wonderful as it was to make him uncomfortable, it

was never good to leave a bull enraged. Mathew had taught her that. She jangled her reticule, letting the *tink-tink* sound of clanging coins speak for her. "I'd like to be a patron."

The man harrumphed over his glasses. "We have many items." He pivoted to the shop girl. "Sally, go dust in the back. I'll take care of Mrs. Cecil."

The young woman nodded. "Good meeting you, ma'am." She offered another smile then pattered away.

Theodosia forced her shoulders to straighten and paced around the man. As a free woman and a proper widow with money, she could shop here. A glance to the left helped her settle on a practical item. "I'd like to purchase some soap."

The man nodded and pointed her to a table skirted in crimson silk. He dogged her footfalls, following close behind, as if she'd steal something.

She sighed. Hopefully, she wouldn't have to become used to this treatment again. The last year of grieving had protected her from outsiders, and the years of having her late Mathew's guidance had almost made her forget.

Almost.

She pressed her gloved fingertips against a jar colored lapis blue. "What type of soap is inside?"

The clerk pushed up his thick spectacles that had slid down his condescending nose. "A fine lavender. Very expensive, about four shillings a piece. Not so much for Cecil's widow."

Though she had the money to buy most things, years of thrift and haggling still pumped in her blood. She poked at the glass, tilting its heavy lid. The fragrance, honey-like, wafted from the pressed bars, stroking her nose. Surely, they had been made from Cecil spike lavandin—for nothing else could hold such strong perfume.

This had to be a sign from Mathew. He must approve of her actions to marry again in order to protect the son he'd so loved. She must buy the soap. She stroked the jar. "I'll take two pieces, and wrap it in paper. Make sure the scale is clear of fingers. I'd hate to pay more than what's necessary."

The man picked up the container. His head bobbed up and down as if it had taken this long to see past her face to her wealth. "I'll weigh this out…ma'am, without a finger on the scale."

Half watching the clerk, half watching the window glass, she decided the store front was more interesting than the man's balding head. She filled her vision with the sea of sleek top hats and crisp bonnets passing through the Arcade. None of them an apparition. She sighed again, the tight grip of apprehension further loosing from her spine. The vision had been her nerves.

Slowly, carefully, and in full view of the clerk, she dipped her fingers into her reticule pulling out the foolscap letters she'd retrieved from the stationer. She flipped to the first, a thin sheet of light gray paper, and mouthed the address. This was the second correspondence from a man with the rank of squire to her marriage advertisement. Though his crisp writing of her name, Mrs. Cecil, denoted elegance, their meeting last week had been far from elegant. It had been dull, lifeless, and made worse by his obvious discomfort in talking with her. He hadn't even had the courage to hold her gaze.

Surely, between the folds sat a polite *no*, and for that she'd be grateful. Theodosia was in want of a man's protection, but a new husband needed to be like Mathew, a Boaz protector. Yes, one of those gentlemanly fellows who cherished family above everything and who'd never be ashamed to be seen with her son.

What if it was a *yes*? She tapped the second letter to her bosom. If she had another offer she'd get her friend Ester to help pen a rejection to the squire. Ester's chaste brain had to be filled with clever ways of saying no.

Chuckling silently, she switched to the next response.

This one addressed her advertisement number not her name. A first correspondence. New air filled her chest.

The primrose-colored paper felt thick beneath her fingers, and the thick glob of red wax sealing the note held an indentation of a crest. Could it be from a gentleman? Maybe someone titled? Maybe this could be the man who would stand up for her boy. The notion of such decency lifted her lips, even the bottom one she chewed when nervous or frightened.

"Mada...Mrs. Cecil." The shopkeeper's impatient voice sounded, cutting through her woolgathering. "I've more paper in the back. Another minute."

The heat from her kid glove made the wax melt a little. She should open it now and read the particulars, his age and situation, but having her dearest friends' dueling perspectives would help make sure she wasn't getting too excited. All the money in the world could not make a man want to father a sickly child and wouldn't help fight for the boy's interests.

Loud voices sounded from the backroom. The door opened and a shaking Sally came out. The blonde twisted her hands within her long apron. The stocky clerk passed in front of her and stood behind the counter. "That will be eight shillings."

Theodosia shoved her letters under the crook of her arm and fished out a half guinea.

The bright shine of the gold coin reflected in his widened eyes. They bulged like greedy hot air balloons. "Is there anything else you wish to buy?"

She shook her head and waited for two shillings and sixpence change. Everything her late husband had told her was true—money trumped questions. Pity all men weren't like her honest Mathew, or dreamers like her apparition. No, most were manipulative, lying as soon as they opened their mouths.

She picked up her package, shifting the treasure between her palms, and looked at the hurt painting the shop girl's face. She looked like Theodosia had used to look, contemplating the wrong choices. That couldn't happen. She flicked the edge of her parcel, making a hole. "Sir, might I have more paper? I don't want to lose these."

The man slapped the counter. "Aye. Picky. Seems money makes you the same as the rest."

Theodosia bit her tongue, then her lip, to keep a tart reply inside her mouth. She needed a moment alone with the girl.

As soon as the clerk headed into the back, Theodosia came alongside her. "Sally, was it? If you ever need an honest job, where you will be paid fairly for a good day's work, come visit Cecil Farms. Tell them Mrs. Cecil said to hire you. Whatever you decide, come to our Flora Festival in a few weeks." She dipped into her reticule and gave her three shillings to pay for transportation. The farm was a post ride out of London.

Amber eyes smiled at her. "Thank you, Mrs. Cecil."

The man returned, harrumphed, then settled the jar between them on the shelf. "Here's your paper, ma'am."

Theodosia took the blue material and carefully wrapped her soaps. Feeling good at being able to help another, she turned to the door. "Thank you, sir." Keeping another woman from making mistakes would honor Mathew's memory. Even Ewan's ghost would smile, if the shop girl could find a way to dream.

As she stepped back into the crowded throughway, her letters slipped and landed near a man's boot. She bent to retrieve them, but the fellow grabbed them first and held them out to her.

"Thank you." The words crawled out slowly as her gaze traveled up his bottle-green waistcoat and broad chest, past his lean cravat and thick neck, to a familiar scar on his chin.

She didn't need to see his thick, wavy, raven hair. She stopped at his eyes, the bluest eyes, bluer than the sky stirred clean by a thunderstorm.

"It *is* you, Theo," said the man.

Her heart ceased beating. Theodosia looked down to see if it had flopped outside of her stiff corset. Ewan Fitzwilliam stood in front of her. He wasn't dead. Didn't look the least bit distressed or deceased from the war. And he was no ghost, unless hell made apparitions look this good.

. . .

Six years had passed since Ewan Fitzwilliam had seen this beauty. The last time, the locks of her long, straight hair—a gift from her father, an Asian junk sailor, who'd been portside long enough to purchase companionship—had been free about her shoulders. Her deep bronzed skin, a blessing of the negress mother she'd barely known, had been exposed at her throat from a hastily put-on blouse. Her wide almond-shaped eyes, onyx pools of decadent wonder, had been afraid, like now. "Theo, the Flower Seller."

Chewing on her bottom lip, she nodded and blinked her lengthy, silky lashes, hiding the largest irises he'd ever seen. Before, those eyes had captivated him. He'd thought them passion-sated, but now, he knew them to be big with avarice, another of her deceptive guises. "It's been a long time, Theo."

She nodded and maybe took a breath, but still said nothing.

One look at her expensive frock, the tailored obsidian-colored walking dress that sculpted her hourglass form, and any doubt of her greed left his jaded heart. The sands of time had been good to her curvy form, and Theo had used her womanly wiles to attain wealth. Despite her humble background, she was no different than the ladies Ewan had met at the balls his mother forced him to attend. All were young women seeking advancement or larger purses, something a second son didn't possess. "Six years and you have nothing to say to me?"

"You died." Her alto voice dropped lower. "You are dead. An apparition."

"Very much alive. You look to be breathing, too. Barely."

She squinted and shifted the ribbons of her bonnet. "Whatever you are, can I have my letters? Then you may return to being dead."

Playfully, he waved the sealed papers fanning his chin. "Can you, or may you? A woman should know her capabilities. You know, like the ability to deceive."

He waited for her to respond. His Theo would offer a stinging retort, something with fire.

But this woman stood still, her fingers hovered inches from his as if she were afraid to take the letters. This wasn't his Theo.

Nonetheless, when she bit her lip again, he knew the folded notes held some importance for her. Out of habit, he swept them farther away, tucking them close to the revers of his tailcoat. Would this new Theo reach for something that was hers?

The woman glanced to the left and then to the right, but did not move. Part of him soured even more. Yes, she'd been shy when they'd first met, but never this cautious, not with him. This wasn't the girl he'd ruined himself over. Perhaps she had never existed, just a novel characterization his playwright mind had invented. "Are you sure these belong to you? Let me check for a name."

He read the markings on the folded papers and burned at the written name, Mrs. Cecil. "It doesn't say Theo the Flower Seller, but Mrs. Cecil. Is that you?"

She put a hand to her hip. "Yes. Give me those letters."

He waved at her again, fanning the pages near her cheek. "Then take them from your old friend. I don't bite. Well, not unless provoked or dared. Remember, Mrs. Cecil—my dearest Theo?"

She snatched the letters and stuffed them into her reticule. As she looked up at him again, her henna-colored cheeks darkened. "Too well, Mr. Fitzwilliam. How are you not dead? They said you died in Spain."

He extended his arm to her. "Perhaps we should get a bit of refreshment and have a long chat. You seem rather faint. Let's go to your shop. I recall you *scheming* to get a flower shop."

"I…I have no shop."

She did look faint and the part of his heart that should know better made him take the tissue-wrapped package from her lean fingers and support her palm atop his forearm. "There's a coffeehouse, Theo. Let me buy you a sweet. That will give you time to recover."

"No. No, I must go. I can't be seen with you."

She pulled away, leaving him holding her parcel. With elbows flying, reticule swinging, the daft woman dashed into the hustling crowd. He stood there watching until her form disappeared beneath the triple arch at the south entrance on Piccadilly Street.

She'd gone from the Burlington Arcade. Where? Where did she lay her head at night? And, whose pillow now possessed her?

He wanted answers. But chasing after Theo shouldn't be done. His pride wouldn't let him. However, he was holding the schemer's bag.

Like breathing, his fingers automatically sought to fist, but her bulky pack sat in his hands. A few nosy pokes released the strong bittersweet scent of lavender. The flower had meant something to him once, not a sop for the soul, but of being caught in a thunderstorm. The scent came to him in his dreams. Isolated in one of his father's carriage houses close to the Tradenwood flower fields, trapped with the business-minded flower seller who hadn't talked about bouquets when he'd finally taken her lips.

Who was this Cecil who had them?

Did he know lies lived within each kiss?

Or had Theo lied only to Ewan?

Craning his neck toward the skylights above, he warmed his chilled blood with the sunshine. Yet more questions filled his breast.

Why did Theo think him dead? Was it another of her falsehoods?

Slinging her package under his arm, he spun in the opposite direction she'd fled and marched out the north side of the Arcade onto Burlington Gardens. Seeing the past twice in one day would be too much.

With each step, Ewan stewed a little more. His gut ached. The words of his father's letter, recounting how Theo had run away with another man, mocking Ewan's choice for love, burned as badly now as it had when he'd first read them, laying near death in Spain. *And this Blackamoor harlot you wished to make a Fitzwilliam.*

Blood started to hiss and boil in his veins. He plodded down Bond Street, taking the long way back to where his brother's carriage awaited, all while repeating his father's slur.

Before a footman could jump down, Ewan gripped the pearl-black door and flung it open. Dragging himself into a seat, he prepared himself for questions and hoped his mind could swallow up the bitter dregs unearthed from seeing his past.

"Are you all right, Ewan?"

The concerned, low-pitch voice of his brother Jasper

Fitzwilliam, the Viscount Hartwell, startled him.

Ewan gave himself a shake and dumped Theo's package onto the dark tufted seat. Theo. How could she still have a hold upon him? Hadn't he poured out all his anger at her lies into the lines of his latest play? He'd used his mad muse to re-create Theo as the perfect Circe, the goddess the playwright Homer had created to turn men into swine. Risking everything for Theo had made him low, like his father's hogs. No, he wasn't a fool in love anymore.

"Hello, in there." Jasper leaned over and thumped Ewan's skull. "Not creating your next masterpiece, are you? Have you tried selling the first?"

"Not my first, but by far my best. My first would have been exhibited at Covent Garden six years ago, if not for Father's influence on the manager. He made Thomas Harris renege on his commitment to buy my play."

His brother poked his lips into a full grimace, so different from the man who loved to laugh. "Please, not that again. There are more things afoot than six-year-old misunderstandings."

The way Jasper said *afoot,* made the writer in Ewan sit up straight. He leaned forward to give the man his full attention. "I'm listening."

"I asked you to help me with these newspaper responses, but there's more I need to involve you with. You've been in London these past three months and haven't come out to Grandbole, yet. Why haven't you seen him?"

The *him,* their father, the Earl of Crisdon, hadn't yet summoned Ewan, and he hadn't had the energy to volunteer for another dressing down. *A Fitzwilliam doesn't write plays. The theater isn't a profession for a Fitzwilliam.* "Jasper, please. It's difficult enough to visit with Mother and listen to her constant complaints of how I was cheated of Tradenwood. But I was not cheated. Only bad luck."

"Well, the report of your demise did make your uncle designate a new heir, who was not your mother. Their feud never ended."

Ewan stared up at the ceiling. Counted to ten. Yet, in his head, he heard his mother's soft-voiced lament of his uncle changing his will to leave Tradenwood and all its fields to a distant cousin—all because of the incorrect report from the battlefield. He shook his head, banishing the loss. "Another subject. Your mystery woman had already picked up her mail. Our clever note is on its way to the intended victim. And since you corresponded as one of Father's lesser titles, Lord Tristian for his barony, your identity is safe."

Jasper rolled his beaver dome between sweaty palms. "Who else should borrow but his heir? Being the eldest has its privileges."

"And its headaches." Ewan shook his chin, wanting nothing to do with his father's grooming or any of the ways the man sought to control Jasper. "But you seem to manage."

His brother nodded as his smile shrank. "It's my humor. It comforts me. So, no peek at what the grand woman looked like?"

Beautiful as ever, but Theo wasn't the lady his brother was asking about. "Pardon?"

"The newspaper advertisement owner. The woman who placed the matrimony request in the paper."

"The new shop clerk hadn't seen her. I waited past the usual time you said the widow checked for correspondences. Sorry, old boy, your stationer has things wrong. Don't let Father know a Fitzwilliam failed to obtain secret information. That would bring the earl such misery."

Jasper dropped his hat and folded his arms about his jacket, a hunting garment with oversized sleeves. It was hard to make someone so big look even bigger, but the man achieved the impossible with dozens of tiny diamond shapes running north and south upon his copperplate printed waistcoat. "That's what I get for sending a writer to do a spy's work. Should've sent Father."

The unflappable Jasper seemed nervous, a side of his half brother Ewan had never seen. With his brow rising, he felt his quill finger cramp as if preparing to write dialogue for a new play. "I am surprised the earl's encouraging you to find a bride like this. Maybe he *has* changed after all these years."

Jasper shrugged his shoulders. "He doesn't know that I am. I'm taking a turn at being the rebellious one and doing something Father wouldn't approve of."

"How is that working?" Ewan chuckled.

"A few disappointments. Mostly, I've exchanged letters with women of the wrong temperament or situation." His brother shuffled his boots. "You don't know how I've missed your assistance. You visit with your mother in Town, but what of us?"

The *us* was Grandbole and all that came with the grand house. Ewan did miss it. He missed the land and walking it to clear his head. He missed all the Fitzwilliams under one roof. "There are many things to remember, many things to forget."

"If I hadn't spied you at the countess's party, would you have let me know of your return?"

"I missed your wit whilst I soldiered in the Peninsula, even the jokes at my expense. But I didn't miss the arguments with the earl. It is he that gives me pause, not you."

Jasper looked down again, as if a humbled posture could wipe away the vitriol of their father's famed rants.

Ewan had given up on the earl. The pressure of never measuring up would build inside, until his lungs exploded. He was glad the scars on his chest bound him together, kept the rage from showing.

He took a small breath. The pressure released. He wasn't that weak-minded person anymore. Hadn't the bad memories, the disappointments, become part of his sharpened sense of humor, the kindling wood for his farce comedies? Tweaking his cravat, Ewan sampled a little more air and sank into his beloved sarcasm. "Jasper, I would love to be the genesis of this rebellion, but take it from me, start small. Borrow the earl's hunting dogs without permission. Then work your way up to…oh, I don't know, petty larceny. Then you'll be ready to take a bride without his approval."

Jasper sat back and drummed the black leather seat beneath his thick fingers. "I haven't picked the lady yet, for it is so important to do this well. Once a gentleman proposes, there's no taking it back. What if she doesn't like children, as she says? What if this one is like the others, not as young as she stated in her advertisement?"

"If you are fretting, go about finding a bride the old way. Pick a chit during the Season and propose. Lady Crisdon will help."

His brother's face grew more serious with his jaw firming, his eyes drifting to the right. "I can't bear to hear how none of them are like Maria. I *know* that."

The man quieted. If his eyes moved more to the right they'd fling from his skull. It must be hard losing a good wife. From the letters the brothers had exchanged over the years, Jasper had cared for her himself until the stomach cancer had taken its toll.

"I'm sorry, Ewan. It will be a year next month." Jasper tugged at his sleeves, readjusting his cuffs over his thick wrists. "Have you asked for your mother's matchmaking assistance? That might get her to come back to Grandbole. We should be unified now."

Unity? At what cost? Ewan pushed at his temples with fingers that now reeked of lavender, Theo's lavender. He put his palms onto the seat, gripping the edge, as if that would ground him from the memories of a fleeting romance with one of the Crisdon flower sellers. No luck. She'd be in his head tonight, tormenting him. "I've no time, or the finances, for a wife—not until one of my plays succeed."

Jasper rubbed at his chin. "What of that ginger-haired girl you danced with at your mother's dinner last week, the one with freckles? She didn't seem to mind the absence of a fortune."

That was unusual in London, to be sure. Mother must've whispered nonsense in the girl's ear. "She'll become enlightened by her own matchmaking mama. The second son from a second marriage can only do so much, particularly one recovering from banishment."

Jasper sat forward, folding his arms. "Father's irascible, but he only did what he thought was best. I will admit he is often misguided, but sometimes... Sometimes he's right."

Yes. The earl was right in the worst ways. He'd said Theo was after Crisdon money. He'd said she wouldn't remain faithful. Groaning, Ewan looked down again at his hands, his fisting hand. "The earl also does wrong. Lording his money over our heads, doling it out when we do as he wants. But then, he stops us from gaining the means to be independent. Not this time. My new play will succeed."

"How would Father put it?" Jasper held his nose up and made his voice strangled and low. "Fitzwilliams do military or religious service. We may go to the theater, but not perform in such. Ewan, use your writing talents for sermon making." He laughed and wriggled his nose. His voice returned to its normal energetic pitch. "That would've made Father very pleased."

Ewan's stomach churned, thinking of both the difficulty of doing as the old earl wanted and the image of himself being struck by lightning behind the pulpit. He spoke very slowly. "The black sheep can't wear white frocks, and I've already done my military service. Five and a half, almost six, years of service in Spain and the West Indies. My Fitzwilliam dance-card-with-bullets is jotted in full. I should be able to live as I want. I have stories to tell. They should be on the stage, no matter what the old man thinks."

Jasper dropped his hat as his shoulders slumped. "This new one is very good. It was a pleasure to read, but I hate being caught between you two. I'm not sure what has seeded the ill will, but this is a new day. We need family to pull together."

Not wanting to argue or mouth aloud Theo's name, Ewan sighed. "So, how do you intend to tell the old man of your plan for a new wife?"

"If advertisement number four lives up to the promise made in the newspaper, he won't mind adding another fortune to the family."

Ewan couldn't disagree with that logic, even if it felt wrong and unromantic. "Perhaps, but I still think you should give the traditional way a chance."

Jasper ran a hand through his curly, reddish-blond hair. His frowning lips turned up. "My rugged features do pale against yours, but I have three girls who will require dowries that my modest income will not profer. I don't want their fates to be under the earl's control. I need a young heiress who will be a good mother to my brood and add to my coffers. That can't be had at Almack's."

Maybe this finding-a-bride-by-newspaper-advertisement was a safe way for his brother to start living again. "A lovely brood, from what I can remember. Your wife gave you all she had. That is to be treasured."

Smoothing a wrinkle from his waistcoat, Jasper nodded. "I'm done with sentiment. You're only allowed one great love in a lifetime. The next will be a marriage of convenience."

That couldn't be true. His heart shuddered at the notion of only loving once. It would take a great deal of vanity for

Ewan to convince himself that what he'd felt for Theo in those heady days before he'd left for war, was less than love. Oh, if only he were that vain.

What had started as an innocent, well, almost innocent, flirtation between the errand boy for the largest flower grower of greater London and a sassy street vendor had changed everything. Wanting Theo had cost Ewan dearly. He'd been disowned, dispatched from the family, and had almost died in the war. He grimaced, allowing his gut to knot and twist with the horrid truth. Seeing how things had turned out: she'd apparently married a wealthy man, he'd written a farce of Theo's love that would draw all of London. Perhaps she had been worth the sacrifice. Yes, his humor had matured.

"Pay attention over there." Jasper smiled. It was his infectious weapon. "Do you remember your nieces? You should see them. My eldest is now a petulant ten."

He stuck a hand in his pocket and shrugged. Staying away had cost more than time. Deep down in his heart, he missed his family, that sense of belonging. "Perhaps you can bring them to town. My flat is small but clean." *And not under the old man's control.*

Jasper raised his brow. "You should come see them today."

Ewan shook his head. "No."

"But I will need your plotting abilities. I could pay you to help write my correspondences to number four of the *Morning Post*. If this woman is indeed young, with a fortune, and not so bad on the eyes, there could be competition." He shuffled his boots. "And if you are not courting, who's the package for? Smells like lavender. What secrets are you keeping from your elder brother?"

"No. I bumped into a woman in Burlington Arcade. She left it. I'll toss them away."

"Pretty expensive wrapping. A pity to disregard. When

did you have time to make a new acquaintance? Did you miss my mystery woman when you were flirting?"

"I'd hardly call a pleasant exchange flirting." But what would he call running into his past? Though Theo wore expensive garb, she could be like him, all outside trappings. These perfumed soaps shouldn't be abandoned. Perhaps he should return them to their owner and have that final chat. He whipped off his top hat. "Our mission is done today, Jasper. Drop me back to my residence."

"No, you must come with me for dinner with the girls… and Father."

Ewan slumped in his seat, wrinkling the vest he'd labored to pick out for an evening of cards at his mother's house in Town, not for seeing the earl. What type of mood would he be in after seeing Theo and his father in the same day? He shook his head. "I'm beginning to feel tired. Yes, very tired."

Jasper groaned, loud and long. "The chest wound?" His brother's voice raised an octave. "Does it still bother you?"

"Only on wet days…and during thunderstorms."

"Come to dinner, Ewan. So much has changed. The family needs to pull together. Don't be stubborn like Father."

Like the old man? His brother might as well have punched Ewan in the face to utter such horrid words. "I'm nothing like him. Stop the carriage. I'll walk."

Grabbing his arm like a madman, Jasper kept him from leaping out of the carriage. "I'm sorry, but it is true. I won't say it again. Have one meal. Get his complaints off my shoulders for a day. See my girls."

His brother had always tried to keep the old man at bay, even slipping Ewan a fiver upon occasion. "One quick meal, but as soon as he starts in, I'm gone. I'll steal a horse and return to London. In fact, give me money to stable a stallion now. For you know it won't take long for Father's harangues to start. It's about three jokes before he fumes."

"Fine, that will take care of one problem. For the second, you must also agree to help me with my potential newspaper bride, lady number four. I want to know more about her before I ask for a meeting. She'll respond to your quip. We'll need a clever note to follow. Help me write something to keep her attention. You're the clever one."

"You want to see her true character, then ask a question of substance. Let me think on it."

"Well, come up with something to match your riddle, Ewan. Maybe it will be so good you'll use it in your next play."

Avoiding the temptation to roll his eyes, Ewan nodded. "All right...I'll help."

"You think you'll find the owner of the package, or do you think my girls might like it? Is it too personal?"

Anything regarding Theo was too personal. Yet, returning this package intrigued him. She had obviously purchased this in the Burlington Arcade. Perhaps, the perfumer knew where Mrs. Cecil resided. Ewan eased his head onto the seatback, preparing to sleep all the way to Grandbole Manor. Since she'd be in his brain, he piled up all the questions he wanted to know of Theo. Perhaps, he'd ask them the next time he saw the flower seller. "It should be returned to its rightful owner."

And there would be a next time. Fitzwilliams were good at finding things—weaknesses and secrets. Nothing else brought a smile to Ewan's jaded heart than the thought of improving his characterization of his play's villainess by visiting Theo, his personal Circe.

Chapter Two

Family, Friends & Enemies

Theodosia's carriage rumbled forward. With each passing second, her lungs constricted a little less. Her driver and horse team didn't know she'd fled a ghost. Surely, they assumed she needed to hurry back for her dinner guests. She wouldn't correct them.

By the time she'd passed Tottenham Road, the jarring and swaying of her ivory seat had jostled every bone in her body. The ache, however, didn't compare to the pain of seeing Ewan again. All these years, and the man was alive. *How could he not be dead?*

Six years of mourning him, of feeling ashamed for living and finding some happiness with Mathew, all while thinking a bullet had felled her poor dreamer.

How many times had she looked in those fancy glass mirrors at Mathew's Tradenwood, the home they'd shared, and had seen a traitor to the future she'd envisioned with Ewan? The man with the crooked smile that had set her heart pounding. Today, that crooked smile had crushed the useless muscle in her chest to dust.

Wait.

If Ewan didn't die in the war, where has he been?

Why did he stay away when I needed him?

Her stomach soured, thinking and rethinking their foolish dreams. His plays would be performed on London's grandest stages, and her flower shop would provide roses, the best ones—without a single thorn—to his actresses. And Theodosia's Ewan wouldn't be tricked by those ladies' beauty. He'd said he only had eyes for *Theo, his Theo.*

Lies.

Dreams were lies.

Ewan had gone to war and hadn't come back to her. The life they had whispered in secret was nothing but deceit, lines from a play he hadn't yet written. Her heart burst all over again.

Had he laughed with his brother at getting her to love him? Did he smile to his circle of friends about taking her virtue? Had he said pretty words about loving her to lower her guard, making Theodosia forsake her vow not to be like her mother? Theodosia had given Ewan all of her, and then he'd left.

She'd become Theo the Harlot because of him.

Her pulse raced and whirled so loudly, her ears hurt. Almost panting, she forced air into her hurting chest and gripped her reticule to her bosom. Her eyes were already weak from sitting at her son's bedside till well past midnight. Crying now about lies would only make them sting. Ewan Fitzwilliam wasn't worth another droplet.

Her hand clenched. Her nails dug into the fringe of her reticule. That ache should have died six years ago. Ewan and his lies were no more. He couldn't affect her future or destroy the life she'd built for her son.

Another two hours of ridiculous fretting occurred before

her carriage passed the Fitzwilliam flower farm. Squinting from her window, she could see their house, Grandbole Manor. The cold gray stone looked small at this distance, but it overshadowed the lilac-colored flowers in the orderly fields. Hard to believe it neighbored Mathew's warm Tradenwood, with its pinkish stacked stones. Tradenwood wasn't as grand, but she believed it held more peace and much more understanding. Things Ewan had always complained were missing at Grandbole.

She slumped onto the seat. Ewan couldn't be staying at his father's estate. She would've seen him at least once these six years if he'd resided there.

The urge to know why he'd played her false might cause her to be rash, to do something crazed. No, Theodosia Cecil didn't look for trouble anymore. She glanced at her rows of flowers. She thought of walking in those fields, of finding answers and strength there. She'd found Mathew there, or he'd found her. If she were to go out there now, she might find peace, the peace he had so often talked about growing, like buds in those fields.

Her carriage began to slow. Peeking out the window, she saw the grooms and proud horse teams of vehicles lining the drive of Tradenwood. Her dinner guests awaited her inside the parlor. They couldn't see her so broken. The ladies were there for an early meal to discuss the Flora Festival, the grand picnic Mathew had started as a reward for his workers, one that had evolved to also include every one of his vendors and their workers. She chuckled, wondering if the perfumer she'd met today would come. She prayed the girl Sally would, and she wondered if she would seek employment with Cecil's Farms.

The carriage stopped and one of her attendants came to free her from her stewing. Marching through the doors of Tradenwood, she slowed her steps and stopped at the console.

Her butler stood near.

Pickens, with his starched livery of dark crimson and gold braid, held out his hands. "Welcome back, Mrs. Cecil. I'll take your bonnet and bag. Your guests are waiting for you in the parlor."

She unpinned her hat and gave it to him, but held on to her reticule. She wasn't prepared to relinquish her letters.

Pickens's brow raised, but he didn't try again for her bag. Six years had given them a routine and, hopefully, a measure of mutual respect. If memories hid in the wizened creases of his forehead, he knew Theodosia held on tight to things that were hers, only relenting when she was good and ready. "Thank you, Pickens."

He pulled a folded paper from behind his back. "This came for you while you were out. The footman said it was important. It's from the Fitzwilliams family. The earl himself."

Swallowing her newfound reservation upon hearing the name Fitzwilliam, she slid off her gloves, stashing them on the console, then clutched the thick parchment. "Thank you."

Emotionless, always about his duty, Pickens bowed his graying head and pivoted toward the long hall leading to the parlor. "And Mr. Lester is visiting. He's in the nursery with Master Philip."

Lester. The name sent shivers of fear and hate up her spine. Who knew Mathew's faithful steward would turn into a vengeful frog the moment he understood the powers Mathew's will had given him.

The tapping of the butler's footsteps moving toward her dinner guests sounded like a muffled drumbeat, but the decision to go to the birds in the parlor or to the vulture near her boy, wasn't a question.

In as dignified of a manner as she could muster, Theodosia's short heels clicked hard against the polished marble with its shiny cranberry veining. The moment her foot dropped upon the first mahogany tread, her false calm shredded. Visions of Lester taking her sweet boy and shaking him for a response froze the blood in her veins. She lunged up the steps and sailed on fretful wings to the door of the second-floor nursery.

She didn't see the leech in the hall. He had to be inside with little Philip. How long would it be before he discovered the boy's illness?

Theodosia couldn't blow into pieces like a dandelion in strong wind. She steadied herself, clasping the molding. The stupid parchment crunched against the raised wood before relenting and curling about it. With a strangled breath, she pushed open the door.

Scanning to the left and then to the right revealed nothing out of the ordinary. Polished pine planks on the floor and a thick jute rug of blue yarn warmed up the pale beige walls. A huge closet hid enough space to house a small family.

In the middle of the wide room, swimming in a pinafore of cream and blue threads, sat little Philip alone with his governess, Miss Thomas. No Lester.

Fanning the paper, hoping to chase away the fear fevering her brow, Theodosia took a few steps inside. A hungry panic of losing Philip was stirring, growing, pressing at her temples.

Lovely, honest Mathew had protected Theodosia and Philip, writing his will to withstand the challenges his young family would face in his absence. But a dead man could only do so much from the grave. Her own wit and a new, trustworthy husband, someone as honorable as Mathew — that would have to be enough to keep vultures like Lester away. Where was the pushy brute?

Coughing from the growing knot in her throat, she moved closer to her son. She wanted to look in the closet or under the bed for Lester as she would hunt for a ghost. Lord knew she'd happened upon enough apparitions for one day.

Little Philip scooted forward, pressing his lean fingers against a carved block. His eyes were on the wooden toy, not looking at her.

That was good. He shouldn't see sadness on his mother's face.

She put a finger to her lips to keep the governess from announcing her. One heavy step after the other, clomping, stomping, she made her heels pound as loudly as she could as she approached his weak side.

The five-year-old didn't flinch. Never turned.

Her heart clenched.

The boy didn't hear her approach. The physicians, the old ones with gray on top, the young ones, trying to run experiments on the mulatto boy, even the ones who wouldn't see him until they heard his surname Cecil, all their words had been true. Philip was deaf on on his left side and losing his hearing on the right. This was the most painful consequence of her many sins.

Looking up to the ceiling, she counted her wrongs. Trusting Ewan—wrong. Holding on to pride too long—wrong. Not becoming a mistress to Mathew sooner, not trusting him sooner—wrong. Of keeping Ewan on a pedestal for so long, it had made it difficult for a good man to reach her heart—very wrong.

She lowered her gaze and looked at Philip. The boy jostled the toy between his small fingers. He still hadn't caught up to the size of other five year olds.

This punishment of barely hearing, of perhaps losing all of it, tore her up inside. Would he forget the sound of words? Would he remember an impatient giggle? It was too much for an innocent boy. Living as she had, speaking lies, listening to her dreaming heart, were the reasons her child suffered. She cleared her throat. "How's my Philip?"

The governess tapped the little boy on the shoulder and pointed. "We had a good day today. No more fever from last night."

Philip spun toward Theodosia and showed a toothy grin. Her worn-out heart stirred. His bright blue eyes opened wider. He rushed to her, stepping onto her feet, embracing her legs. A smile she no longer thought she possessed lifted her lips. "Love you, son."

She scooped him up. His pinafore bunched in the crook of her arm as he wiggled his way to her cheek, placing his face there. His pulse pushed against hers. She wove her fingers into his dark, straight hair. She'd do anything for Philip, the only person in this world who was truly hers. For the first time today, she breathed easier. Maybe her withered heart had a little more living to do.

"*M-mmm-m*," he said, before giving her a big, wet kiss.

The boy offered another hug about her neck. Theodosia needed to keep him safe, to keep his world secure and beautiful, even if that meant selling herself in a new marriage.

Footfalls sounded behind her.

She spun with her precious cargo, tucking him deeper within her stiffening arms. Anger rose inside seeing Wilhelm Lester, her late husband's steward, smirking at the threshold.

"Well, isn't this lovely? Mother and son. The usurper and her spawn."

Theodosia leaned down and gave Philip back to his governess. "Come with me, Mr. Lester."

She squared her shoulders, tightened her grip about the paper, and waltzed past the scourge who had dared to be Mathew's confidant. She kept moving until she stood yards from the nursery.

The beast followed too closely. Was it onions and mutton on his breath?

"Theodosia, what was it? How did you bewitch old Cecil

and convince him to make his mistress his wife? Usually only fools do that and Cecil was no fool."

"Maybe the same reason you've been asking to marry me? You didn't even wait for my dear Mathew to be cold in the grave."

The tall man laughed and flipped back a reddish-brown curl from his flat forehead. He would be handsome, if not for all the ugly evil spouting from his thin lips.

"No, can't be the same, my dear." His voice sounded like a fat cat's purr, one that had eaten its mouse. "You were penniless then. Now, you are a wealthy woman sharing the Cecil fortune. Yes, fifty-thousand pounds annually is more than enough reason to marry you, Theodosia."

"It's Mrs. Cecil to you. And I told you, you are not welcome in the nursery. Stay in the parlor."

"Can't. Your gaggle of hens is down there. Where did you find more educated dark ones?"

Ester and Frederica? Knowing her friends were near gave Theodosia more strength. "You heard what I said. Go downstairs."

"Then come with me." He held out his arm for her.

The thought of touching or being touched by Lester made her skin itch. It'd be like fiery ants who had stung her hands in the fields when she hadn't been careful cutting flower stems. Around him, she needed to be extra careful. She scooted past him and started down the treads, but he fell in step with her.

"The boy? Is he breeched yet?"

"No, he's five."

"Well, Cecil wasn't that tall of a man, but this one seems a might scrawny. As his guardian, I will need to make sure you're not coddling him too much. He might need to be sent away, if you're not taking good care of him. That's a guardian's job to make sure his ward is well protected."

She lifted her chin as she cut her gaze to the fool. "Philip is fine. Growing well. Don't threaten me."

Lester grabbed her and yanked her close.

Her reticule swung around her elbow swatting him in his midnight blue waistcoat. "Let me go, you bounder."

His grip didn't slacken. He leaned near her ear. "Things would be better for the boy if we worked together. You're not so bad with that mouth of yours closed or given to a common purpose."

She shook free and stared into his beady blue-gray eyes. "Don't touch me. Some of the coloring of my hand may slap onto your sallow flesh. It will leave you black and blue. You wouldn't like that."

He clamped her shoulder, shaking her. "The hellcat protests too much. And I'm an improvement over an old man. It's been too long for you, hasn't it, dear? It's almost been a year since his death."

She made herself stone, forcing away the disgust threatening to spew vomit from her mouth. "How dare you? I'm not even out of my mourning for Cecil, the man you claimed to love. What would he say to you if he saw this?"

Lester's sneer shifted into a frown as if for a moment a bit of humanity filled him. Mathew's endless kindness had made him a weak spot for many. Theodosia had noted Lester's affection for Mathew during her husband's illness. At the man's first threat, she'd invoked Mathew's memory, Lester's Achilles heel, but how much longer would it work?

The blackguard lowered his hand and yanked the parchment away from her fingers. "This looks important." He ripped it open and held it to the light. "Another offer to buy our flower fields. You're not considering this?"

Theodosia put a hand to her hip. "All the fields are mine and Philip's. Cecil left you an income to be an advocate." She softened her tone to keep the man's fragile ego intact. "It's hard to consider something I haven't had a chance to read, but you know I will consult you."

He ripped up the offer into bits, balled them up, then stuffed the pieces into her palm. Lester stepped very close, his shadow falling upon her. "The Fitzwilliams ruined my father's business and took his lands. Land is everything. I won't let that happen here, and I've taken steps to ensure it." His brow rose. "The earl must think you stupid for such a low offer, though I think you know low."

He moved out of slapping range. "When you're done playing a lady and see that our interests align, mine for the Cecil business, yours for nurturing the heir, send for me. I'll come to you, Theodosia."

Lester grinned again, more evil than the first, and headed out to the hall. With a final smirk, he grabbed up his coat and cane. "See you soon, Mrs. Cecil, dearest woman. It will be good to see you out of your mourning garb. Maybe you and the lad shall come with me to Holland. Your head for numbers might come in handy."

No. Never would she go anywhere with him. Holding her breath, she made her response soft. "This is our first overture to those growers. You must go alone and represent us. I need you to do that."

"Yes, you are right. You do need me."

Even as he exited, his smirk stayed etched in her brainbox. Full of arrogance and condescension, it was a familiar response a Blackamoor woman faced in business. Exactly what she counted upon to be rid of him.

The footman closed the front door. The sound of the heavy thud made her hands tremble. If only Mathew had known Lester was vermin, worse than vine-rotting aphids. If he didn't go to the Dutch farms alone, her plan to outwit him would never work. How would she protect Philip then?

Pickens came near, squinting, creasing his brow even more. "Ma'am, do you need something?"

Yes, Mathew alive and here to keep me and Philip from harm. She shook her head and moved at the world's slowest pace down the treads. "How are my guests?"

"They are well. Enjoying your treats. I will go see if they are ready for more refreshments." The butler turned and left for the parlor.

Once she reached the console, Theodosia dumped the paper pieces onto the mahogany surface. Her reticule slid from her elbow down the length of her forearm, but that didn't stop her from arranging the torn pieces. She swirled the paper with her pinkie and made out the sum, ten thousand pounds. The devil was right. The offer was far too low for anything she and Mathew had worked so hard to build. The earl, Ewan's father, must think her daft. She put the paper into her reticule. Later, she would toss it in the hearth and watch the bits burn.

She started to reach inside the satin and peek at her newspaper responses but decided against it. With a room of guests to attend, she needed to complete the planning for Mathew's Flora Festival down to the tolling of the small parish bells. He had so loved this event.

She folded her arms, her fingers clanging the brass buttons of her dark sleeves. These mourning shrouds had become her friend, a comforting hug, like now, when she was weak. It was a show of respect for a good husband gone too soon. Was marrying again the only answer? "Madam?" The butler stood beside her. Woolgathering, she'd missed his solemn footfalls.

"Your guests are waiting. Mrs. Cecil never keeps her guests waiting."

It wasn't censure in his voice, but something thick and noble, almost like understanding.

She nodded. "Cecils do what they must."

Pickens nodded. "Yes, even when things are difficult."

He bowed, back as straight as a new fence post. "I'll go see if Cook's pastries have run out."

The loyal man proceeded down the hall. She watched his steady, easy gait until he disappeared around the corner.

Easy. Why did she think getting a husband by advertisement would be easy?

Go to the stationer's, pick up the latest response to her *Morning Post* advertisement, then return home safe and smiling with a suitable offer of marriage—all before dinner. Easy.

Easy, my eye. She took a breath, but it rattled within her chest until it found the right pipe to escape. She coughed, wiped her mouth, and tried to think of anything but fleeing. If Tradenwood wasn't safe, where would she and Philip find safety, find acceptance?

Still a little shaky, Theodosia commanded her wobbly legs to move toward the parlor. The meeting for the festival needed her attention. Tucking her reticule under her arms, she ordered her lips to form a smile. Once everyone left except Ester and Frederica—the Brain and the Flirt—she'd rely on her friends to keep her steady and follow through with their newspaper advertisement plan. Or... Theodosia would gather up all the coins she could muster and escape with Philip to the Continent.

$\cdots$

Dining at Grandbole Manor after six long years wasn't as horrible as Ewan expected. His nieces grabbed ahold of him from the moment Jasper pushed him across the threshold.

Oh, how much time had slipped past? Three girls, three beautiful little girls. Only two had been here that last summer at Grandbole, before he'd joined his regiment. His heart burned, roasting with the memory of proud Jasper bundling two small girls in his arms as he escorted his pregnant wife to their carriage. Maria hadn't wanted her laying-in here, but at her mother's home in Devonshire. Dutiful, appeasing Jasper had defied everyone, even shouting down the earl to please Maria.

Ewan had never been more proud or more jealous of his brother. He hadn't yet experienced the burden of that type of love. Ewan hadn't yet met Theo.

Anne, a ten-year-old with blonde-like-her-father locks, put a palm under her chin. She appeared to be the head inquisitor of the three girls and chose to ask questions rather than peruse the long cedar table that held more food than a regiment of a thousand men could devour. "Uncle, so what temperature is the West Indies?" she asked.

"Very hot, my dear."

Lydia, nine years old and very much math inspired, drummed the table with her little fingers. "Is it hotter than Grandbole on a summer's day or an autumn day?"

"Very, very hot—hotter than both."

The little one whose name also started with an L, Laura, no Lucy, cast a big frown. "That's not very descriptive, Uncle."

Ewan looked at the cute upturned nose and the strawberry-blonde hair and released a smile. "You are right. I can do better. The heat of the day starts warm and inviting. By noon, it's enough to positively boil the tea. There. Will that do?"

Lucy closed her eyes and nodded. Ewan smiled again. He'd discovered the dreamer in the mix.

Jasper chuckled and finished dumping a piece of bread into his mouth. "Girls, save your questions for later or Uncle Ewan won't come back. We mustn't frighten him away, and no tricks, not yet."

It wouldn't be the three angelic moppets who'd make Ewan flee. No, it would be a curmudgeon whose chair at the far end sat empty. With a sip from his glass of cool water, he couldn't exactly measure the disappointment roiling in his gut alongside the succulent duck they'd had for dinner. Scanning the dark polished floors, the high walls strewn with family portraits of Fitzwilliams through the ages, a dormant sense of pride wet his tongue. Though he'd never mention it aloud, Ewan had missed Grandbole and his family, even the earl.

A servant came and whispered in Jasper's ear.

His brother nodded. "Father's finishing up business. He wants to meet with you in the library."

Ewan chugged more water and wished the wetness possessed the tang of liquor. He'd been formally summoned. With a slow motion, he stood, bowed to each of his fine nieces, then turned to make the long walk through the quiet corridors. He filled his lungs, savoring the scent of polish, noting the absence of flowers. It seemed that the family livelihood stayed outside.

After several turns guided by the swords strewn across every inch of the dark paint, he made it to the library. He pushed on the heavy door, folded his arms behind his back, and marched inside, entering a room of fine emerald-colored silk walls.

He was alone. Again, a sense of disappointment stirred. Turning to the exit, he decided against retreat and sank upon the inflexible straight-backed sofa centered upon the wide gold rug.

The grand walnut bookcases still towered as they had six years ago. Both were filled with books, among them Aristotle, Bacon, and Descartes, titles meant to sculpt the Fitzwilliam men's minds. But did not the shelves also hold the gilded pages of playwrights Hensley and Broome? How was Ewan to know those ideas were out of bounds?

Not able to help himself, he popped up and moved to

a perennial favorite, Shakespeare, and poked at the torn spine. One he'd probably injured. No smile pressed his lips. Memories of dressing-downs filled his head.

The door opened like a lid to an ancient coffin, slow and moaning. His brother entered and behind him, their father.

Archibald Fitzwilliam, the Earl of Crisdon, had aged. A thousand more white hairs rimmed the balding spot he'd long tried to cover with powders. Now, that battle had been lost. However, the sneer over his glasses, the condescension that only his narrow dark blue eyes could bring, none of that had changed.

"Good of you to come for dinner, Fitzwilliam, finally," his father said. His head dipped up and down as if scanning a rose for an aphid bug. "About time for you to slink back here. At least you've seen your mother in Town. Haven't totally abandoned family."

Ewan released a low, tight breath, then straightened to his full height. He refused to look at his brother who, obviously, still served as a trickster. "I was told you wanted to see me. Surely, I've been mistaken." He turned to the heavy door. "I'll see you in another six years, sir. You, too, Jasper. Oh, don't mind me taking your carriage back to town."

Before he could touch the knob, his Judas brother leaped in front of him with hands outstretched. "Father, you know you wanted Ewan here. And Brother, if you were truly against visiting you'd have jumped from my carriage earlier. You're both too stubborn. I tire at being caught between you."

Ewan had no desire to feel his peacemaking pain. In fact, he wanted to be numb. He wandered over to the sideboard, moved the false panel book that hid their father's prized brandy, and poured a glass of the amber liquid. Perhaps, if he drank enough, quickly enough, the anger trapped in his skin would evaporate. "I'm here. Tell me what you want me to know, Father."

The earl came up beside him and filled another glass. "Your service to the Fourth West Indian Regiment ended three months ago when it disbanded. Why didn't you return to Grandbole?"

"Did you pay for it to disband? Of course, you did. Something I was begrudgingly good at must have been horrid for you."

The tall man patted his thickening middle. "Son, you are being ridiculous."

Ewan took another slow swig, holding the honey on his tongue, missing the sweet rum of the Caribbean. "Well, you've done your best to stunt anything I've wanted to pursue."

"Your judgment has made me suspect."

Blinking, Ewan remembered how his actions had been judged in this room by the earl. *Your life will be a waste. She's a dalliance, nothing more.* With another slurp, his humor returned, for who couldn't laugh at the man being right? Theo's love hadn't lasted, but the memories of her, of shy, business-minded, insatiable Theo, had formed the play that would make Ewan a fortune, one independent of his father's. "You are right as usual, sir. I don't know why I came, either. That questionable logic thing is hard to outrun. The beefsteaks were good. Give my compliments to the cook."

Looking at the blank stare on his father's countenance reminded Ewan that his father had a poor sense of humor, another thing they didn't have in common. "Time to leave. Father. Brother."

The earl coughed, then said, "Sorry."

Ewan froze for a moment. Then put a finger in his ear to unplug it. "Did you say something, sir? My eardrums could be lying."

His father gritted his teeth. He partially opened his mouth, exposing the canine fangs that had sunk into Ewan's hide and that of any man standing in the way of accomplishing something the earl wanted. "I said sorry. I shouldn't have demanded you to go to war to prove your merit."

The old man apologizing. Something wasn't right. The repeated word, "sorry." What did that mean? Shouldn't there be thunder crashing, maybe a flurry of villainous violin notes, as would happen in the theater? "What is this?"

"Your mother hasn't told you?"

Only a Fitzwilliam fool offered information freely, and Ewan was done being a fool. He didn't blink or move.

"Your mother blames me for you not inheriting Tradenwood."

Oh. The nonsense about inheriting his uncle's lands. "My uncle read the same letter you did about my demise. Pity he passed on before he learned the truth."

The earl frowned and stood uncharacteristically quiet. There must be something more.

But Ewan didn't want to submit to any of the man's games. "I am quite resolved, Father. For what would a soldier or a playwright do with all that land, anyway?"

Pushing at his forehead and the deeply etched frown lines, the earl gulped down his brandy and poured himself another. "Not the theater nonsense again."

Jasper jumped between them. "This is not a time for family to be fighting. We need to come together. Crisdon lands are under threat. The competition for flowers is more than ever. And Tradenwood is withholding water. They're building dams on the springs. If that continues, we'll lose it all."

"We?" Ewan folded his arms and kept his gaze level, resisting the call back to the sideboard. "You need to pay the new owner more money. Who is the lucky fool to have the land you wanted?"

The earl wrinkled his nose beneath his brass wire frames. "That blasted uncle of yours left everything to a distant cousin. The new owner passed away, leaving his widow with control of everything. If she doesn't take my latest offer I may have to..."

Ewan spread his feet apart, slightly enjoying the concern rattling the earl's grumbly voice. "You may have to what? Offer full value to my cousin-by-marriage, or is that once-removed?"

Jasper moved from blocking the doorway to perch on the large desk near the window. His face was strained, more serious than Ewan had ever seen.

"Father's done twice that on the last offer. I think she wants to ruin us. For a woman, she's a savvy one."

Back at the sideboard, the earl tapped the brandy stopper, but this time his hands shook. "Might have to resort to direct negotiations. It's been difficult, with her observing full and now half-mourning rituals."

There was something not being said by the old man. Something was in the air, heavier than the smell of dusty books or the warm cigar ash—the scents that stayed in his head embodying this library. "You've never had a problem being direct." Ewan lifted his gaze to the candles burning in the corner, counting flickers, counting direct slights.

No more playwriting nonsense. I didn't raise you to be a fool.

The regiment will make a man of you. Maybe even a good one.

If you serve with honor, then I'll turn my eye from your dalliances.

One dalliance was his first play. The second, Theo.

"Sir, I remember very well how you've made your opinion known. What's stopping you?"

His father nodded and downed his glass. "This situation is difficult, but Mrs. Cecil has a price. I have to figure out what it is."

Cecil? Ewan's pulse started to tick up.

His father stared at him as if hunting for something, but Ewan didn't know why, unless this Mrs. Cecil was the same Mrs. Cecil he'd met at the Burlington Arcade. Ewan's legs started him moving, even before he was ready to. He circled around the grand desk to the window. From the wide glass, in the tiptop corner, he could see the edge of Tradenwood. Could that be where Theo lay her head? Had Theo gotten herself a rich husband, a cousin to his mother? And now she owned Tradenwood?

Ewan pulled the curtain closed, keeping him from looking for her again. When he turned and saw the guilt painting the earl's face with those cocky brows flying high above his quizzing eyes, Ewan knew Mrs. Cecil was Theo. Making sure the shock paining his chest had drained away, he cleared his throat and forced his tone to be even and steady. "I'm sure that a fair offer will get the response you deserve."

With a tug to his waistcoat, the earl sank onto the stiff sofa. "What do you intend to do now, Fitzwilliam?"

Was it too beneath the earl to ask his son to reason with an old lover? Perhaps. He scratched his nose and sniffed strong lavender. Theo's smelly paper package that he'd left in the carriage still stained his fingertips. Just like her to stay with him. "I...I'm working on a new play."

"Not much money in theater, Son."

Ewan jerked, tensing at the hint of a slight, then remembered his facade of not caring. "It's more than enough because it's earned by my hands, not yours. Except for the purchase of my commission, I haven't needed you—or your assistance."

Jasper chimed in. "This one is very good. He's created this villain. She's outrageous. London will adore this play."

"Ewan, you must stay at Grandbole and work on it. Become reacquainted with the land you once loved. The flower fields and its fragrances are in your blood, from your mother's family as well as my side. And you could be a help to Hartwell."

"My brother knows I welcome his help, but I can do more to manage Grandbole, if you let me, Father." His brother's voice sound unusually strained. "Your nieces would like to know more of Uncle Ewan, too. And they are getting started with their questions."

"Stay a while. Then, tell me of your desires. Maybe this time you can convince me of your passion for the theater."

Could the years have moved the earl from his harsh stance on the arts? Or maybe this war with Theo had changed him. Well, Theo had changed Ewan. "I turned down Mother's request to stay with her in London, I don't think—"

Jasper came alongside him and filled a glass with brandy. He drank one and then another in quick succession. "You're the perfect story crafter for the girls and for those whom *you* write."

Ewan sighed at the not-so-subtle hint at helping his brother with the newspaper bride stunt. With a shake of the head, he ignored the two faces waiting for his yes. It wasn't that easy. He set his glass down and again drew his hand along the bookshelf. These leathered spines written by playwrights had caught ahold of his imagination, never letting go, until he had spied a young woman gathering roses in the fields. Now, the thought of his Circe injuring his family wouldn't let go. Their common problem was less than a mile away. "I've missed a great deal. My nieces are fine girls. They make for a tempting offer."

Jasper clasped Ewan's elbow. "We need reinforcements. The girls outnumber us and with their pranks, we need you. Perhaps, we could have a chance at being a united family. Isn't that so, Father?"

The earl moved to the door. "Please stay, Son. You are

welcome. Your room has been refreshed. Might even find a change of clothes to your liking."

He glanced at Ewan, dead in the eyes. It felt like an apology, but that was how it was between them, only going so far, never crossing the line. Respectable, distant, passionless. Yet, he'd never know if things could be different, if he turned away now. Ewan planted his boots apart and braced. "I'll stay for a few days. My flat and Mother's errands will keep."

The earl nodded. "Well, she's seen you enough these three months in London. If you stay, perhaps she will abandon her parties and return to Grandbole, too."

Being a pawn between his parents was an old game. One he'd hoped they'd stopped playing when he'd gone to war. Ewan shoved his hands into his pockets and shrugged. He'd let the earl fight that battle. Ewan would focus on his Circe and the package of smelly lavender that needed to be delivered.

Chapter Three

The Return of an Impassioned Ghost

Once Theodosia waved good-bye to her planning committee, she walked back to the parlor. Of all the rooms in Tradenwood, this one she liked the best. From the doorway, she scanned the gold-papered walls crowned with dented white trim. It felt regal and clean and held the largest fireplace she'd ever seen. Still better was the access to the private patio, a cobblestone wonder rimmed with flowerpots and overlooking a multitiered garden below. Majestic—it was the best place on earth. There, Mathew Cecil had made her an offer she couldn't refuse.

In this very room, he had offered her a name and his protection. The lowest moment of her life had become her best. Tonight, when everyone was in bed, she'd go out onto the cobblestones, smell the clematis they'd planted together, and listen to the night. Her lovely memories of a life with Mathew would stop her from fretting over her present troubles…and Ewan.

For a moment, she closed her eyes and clutched the heavy

door. The bittersweet memories she'd tried to forget returned. Ewan's voice teasing her, as she had cried upon his shoulder after being cheated out of a guinea. How they'd snuck behind the coaching house and had danced in the rain. Even now she could the feel the strength of his arms as he'd twirled her till she'd lost her breath.

Theodosia tensed. She shook as if it were yesterday when she'd found out that the love of her young heart had died. The news had been tossed to her like trash. She'd fallen to her knees behind that coaching house sobbing until she'd become breathless, mourning his loss—Ewan had died in some foreign land. She never thought she'd see his face again, or bump into him at the Burlington Arcade.

His return could be a problem *Oh, who am I kidding?* His return *was* a problem. Could she pretend he was still dead and go through with her plans? She touched the letters in her reticule. There must be one decent offer from her newspaper advertisement, one that would keep her heart and Philip safe.

Pickens and a few grooms passed her as they returned the desk she used for business. In another moment, they exited the room with the excess chairs from her meeting. The butler bowed as she stepped into the parlor. He started closing the door then paused. "Will you need anything else for the evening, ma'am?"

"Nothing more tonight."

"Then good evening, Mrs. Cecil."

As if her surname was a magical elixir, a mixture of relief and wonder flooded her middle. Mathew would be proud of her planning. The meeting had gone well. The Flora Festival was one step closer to being perfect—with chimney sweeps and bell ringing, like when he'd lived. "Thank you, Pickens."

Once the door shut, she offered a smile, a small one for her two dearest friends. "So glad this dinner is over. Thank you for staying."

"Like w-we'd leave before hearing the news of your trip into town." Frederica Burghley popped another chocolatey bonbon in her mouth. It made her perfect pronunciation sound stuttered. "Did you get another answer to the advertisement?"

Theodosia patted her reticule, made her way across the room, and sank into an emerald chair by the fireplace. "Yes, but let me enjoy this moment. The last tradesman's wife has boarded her carriage." The faithful and the curious had had their fill of her hearty and expensive rabbit stew, a sixpence and a farthing a bowl. Then they'd eaten the best rainbow-colored jellies that could be had in all of England. "They had a good meal and surely enjoyed dessert. A shilling each."

With her short brown nose pressed in a book, Ester Croome put her feet up on the chaise. Her silky pale blue slippers peeked from beneath the creamy hem of her gown, like pollen stamens within a lily. The points of the Vandyke lace edging the pleats of her bodice matched the slim bonnet she used to cover her hair. Like a mobcap, she wore one all the time, each one more intricate and delicate than the next. "Theodosia, I see you counting with your fingers."

"You know I like knowing costs." Lord knows, life and death had taught her this. "But I think we did well. I saw many of the merchants' wives smiling with approval."

Ester, lovely, relaxed, always sketching—the brainiest of them all—turned another page in her book. "So how much did you spend on people hoping you'll fail?"

A little over one and sixpence a plate, but that wasn't her friend's true question. Theodosia sighed. "It's for Cecil's festival. I must honor him. His widow has to do this. I will not have anyone saying this wasn't done well or *she* didn't do it well."

Frederica wiped her mouth of crumbs, then smoothed her blush pink bodice. "Of course you must, but let's end the torture, Theodosia. Did my plan of a newspaper advertisement catch you a husband at the Burlington Arcade?"

Typical of her friend to get right to the point and take credit for things they'd all had a hand in, but Frederica meant no harm. Her heart was too big for that.

"I caught something." Theodosia unhooked her reticule from her wrist. The pouch sank to her lap. She didn't quite know how to explain about the ghost from her past. She couldn't even stop from chewing her bottom lip with all the uncertainty this day had brought. "The letters are in here, but I can't look. Not another surprise."

"Another? What is that supposed to mean?" Frederica sprang up from her chair. The blush-colored tail of her gown, layered with lace appliqués that looked like new growth leaves in spring, rustled as she paced back and forth in front of the oversized bookcase. "Did you get an offer or not, Theodosia?"

With a hand on her hip, Frederica stopped. Her perfectly coiffed sandy-brown curly hair bounced and fluttered as her large hazel eyes lifted. "It's not good for one woman to tease another. That's a man's job."

Despite everything—a ghost, a guttersnipe, a gaggle of guests—Theodosia laughed. "Frederica, the flirt. You're always good for a giggle. And I need humor today. We have letters, but the danger to Philip grows daily. I could lose my boy."

"No. We won't let that happen." Frederica crossed to her and held her palm out. "This plan will work, and end your suffering and ours, too. You look so drained. Let me read the letters."

Five years of friendship had surely taught Frederica to wait for Theodosia to bend. And she would for these women. No one knew her better, but none knew of Theo the Flower Seller, the waif who'd made horrible choices, doing things she'd sworn she'd never do, becoming what she'd sworn she'd never be. Only a ghost, whom she hoped to never see again, knew Theo. With his family up the hill, it would only be a matter of time before she saw Ewan again.

She pushed the letters into Frederica's hand. "Take them. If they are bad, burn them like weeds. My cup is full."

"Don't. Do nothing of the kind, Frederica," Ester piped up, though she hadn't put down her charcoal. "We are stronger than weeds or words on paper. We will give a proper response, fitting a respectable widow. Agreed, Mrs. Cecil?"

The magic of the name worked again, stirring up the dormant hope Mathew's kindness had planted and watered over the years. It couldn't be gone. The strength he'd given her had to live beyond the grave. Theodosia lifted her head. "Yes. A proper response."

Frederica nodded and waved the letters. She sorted them, flipping from one to the other. "Two responses. The squire sent one, and we have a new one. We'll start with the squire." She tore into the man's fancy gray paper, then mouthed a few words.

Seconds ticked by. The grandfather clock moaned from the corner. Anticipation built in Theodosia's chest, giving a little lift to her deflated lungs. With Lester's threats growing worse, the boring squire might be the answer, if he wanted to marry. Their meeting two weeks ago had not gone terribly. He'd sat very quietly through much of the coffeehouse visit and had not looked her in her eye. Had he been shy? Or had he been uncomfortable with her race?

"It's a yes. The squire wants to marry you." Frederica's voice didn't sound happy. In fact, it held shrill notes. "That's good, I suppose."

With wide eyes, Theodosia popped up and stared over Frederica's shoulder. "This is the answer. My boy can be protected by the squire. But you don't like him." She took a step back, lowering her desperate sounding voice. "What is it? What is wrong?"

Her friend started to pace again, this time with a hand to her hip. She frowned something awful and looked as if she'd toss the letter into the hearth. "He wants you to pay for the license. Does he have to be so cheap about it? This is not the man for you."

What else could a desperate Blackamoor expect? At least, he hadn't cursed at her or not sent a response after their meeting. Theodosia rubbed at her brow, but squared her shoulders. "I'm not perfect. None of these men are. Only my Mr. Cecil was. He was so generous. One of a kind."

Her flirty friend wrinkled her nose. "One of an old kind. Very old. Shouldn't a second marriage right that scale? Or are you afraid of young and virile?"

"Now you sound like that toad, Lester. He's almost forcing himself on me, even as he threatens to take my son."

"Well." Ester's voice rose, though, again, she didn't raise her pretty olive-colored face. Her gaze remained buried in her drawing. "Some men bluster because they fear rejection."

Theodosia moved to the patio door. She parted the curtains to allow the moonlight inside. She didn't need someone fearful. Her old love, Ewan, the one she thought had died, had feared his father more than he'd feared parting from her. No. No. She despised anyone who wasn't brave, even herself. "We've planned this Holland visit for Lester. It will give me enough time for banns to be read. Before he returns, I'll be a properly married woman with a husband who can advocate for Philip."

"So an old and cheap husband is fine for you?" Frederica's laugh grew louder. "Not for me."

Focusing on the patio, Theodosia let her eyes soak in the darkness dancing beneath the reflections of stars. Her arbor, holding the wonderfully growing clematis, let patches of moonlight onto the stone floor. This planting was Mathew's last great indulgence, so expensive to tend, yet so lovely. A cheap second husband couldn't be the answer. How would things fair when Philip's doctoring bills increased?

Despairing, she turned back to her friends. "If I had a choice, I'd choose another man, but only a man can fight for me at the Court of Chancery. A man will keep Lester from using his guardianship to take my son. Lester wants to control the Cecil money. By controlling me, he controls the fortune."

Frederica rubbed her palm along the back of the floral chaise, making the nap of the fabric darken. "It's such a lovely fortune." She chuckled again. "Very lovely."

Frederica was not shy about her want of riches. Though she'd been provided an extravagant allowance by her wealthy father, the Duke of Simone, the woman seemed to be on a quest to gain more. Her relationship with the duke was as well as one could expect between a father and his acknowledged bastard. Perhaps this need for coins was a way to attain her own security. Theodosia stepped close and put a hand on her shoulder. "I want honest and brave."

"Yes, but money is important. It gives us a say in this world, even if it's only a peep. You know it's a requirement for your next husband."

Theodosia picked up the poker and stabbed the logs in the snowy hearth, before leaning back against the heavy marble mantel and facing her friends. "I have enough. Cecil made sure of that."

With a clap of her hands, Ester lifted her face from her sketch. "This is so grand. We've been at this business for three months and we have our first offer."

She'd been selectively listening as usual, but she was right. At least Theodosia had an offer. "The squire is in his late forties and seemed honest. I need someone beyond reproach to protect my son. Philip Cecil had a good man who loved him. Is it too much to ask for another one?"

Nothing but silence and smiles of pity greeted her request. Maybe it was. Theodosia shook herself. Woolgathering was not to be had now, not with another letter to open. "Maybe the other letter will be better. There might be time for a new prospect, if we can get him up to scratch before the festival. The banns could be read, everything in place, before Lester figures out what I've done."

Frederica wiggled her small fingers under the wax seal of the second letter. When it broke open, she dipped her head and again her full lips moved. This time she put the letter on the table. "I don't know what to make of this."

Unprepared for another note filled with false praise, a request for funds, or addressing the wrong advertisement, Theodosia dropped onto the chaise and locked arms with Ester. "I need you to read it. I can't."

Ester put her feet on the floor. "What's going on Frederica? What is it?"

"It's a riddle of sorts from a man of good character, or so he states," said Frederica. "But he's a peer—a baron, I'd guess."

Ester slipped from Theodosia and pounced on the letter. Her brow creased more deeply. Surely, this was not a good match. Her friend waved the paper. "It's a riddle. This baron is either too clever or it's a test to figure out your character. We must be very careful in our response."

Stopping from biting her lip, Theodosia took the letter and became confused by what seemed like a poem. She laid it back down. "So we should take this seriously?"

Frederica shrugged her shoulders. "Why didn't he ask for a first meeting, Theodosia?" she asked. "I'm never afraid of first meetings."

Ester's forehead crinkled with more lines. With hands lifted, as if putting Frederica into her sights, she said, "I wouldn't be either, if my father was a peer, and my complexion was light like yours, Frederica."

Being caught between worlds was a sore spot for Frederica, not light enough for some, not dark enough for others. Lips in a full pout, the flirt sashayed over and scooped up the letter again. "Let me see if I can figure out what the brain cannot."

"Ladies, please. No fighting. I've had a horrid day."

Ester mumbled something that sounded like *Sorry, Frederica.* Her smirk-laced smile had turned to a frown. "What happened? You weren't at a safe store? The Burlington Arcade is very public."

The rise in Ester's voice would be followed by a scold of going without Phipps or another male servant. Theodosia didn't want to depend on someone else fighting for her. Like today, she'd been careful to pick shops that hated skin color less than they loved money. It was Ewan who had ruined things, but she couldn't say that. "No. Nothing untoward happened. I was able to shop, but I lost my expensive soap. It would have made for a nice bath, but nothing will wash this day away."

Frederica fanned herself with the stationery. "Oh, Theodosia. That's terrible. If you purchased them from the Burlington Arcade, I know it cost you."

Smile restored, Ester crossed her fingers. "Maybe we can discern what this new man is looking for in an answer. That is, if it's not a joke."

"A farce, like in the theater. That is what this sounds like." Frederica nodded then traced her pinky over the paper. "A baron? Could be a courtesy title. *Hmm.* That means he'll inherit something when his father dies. If he's looking for a wealthy bride, he could be either mouse poor or in a family given to scandal. That might not be good."

A title sounded nice, but how much worse could things

get with family scandals? She'd had enough of those. Scandals caused families to split. The arguments she'd witnessed between Ewan and his father had been horrible—terrible like thunder. The day the earl had caught her and Ewan in the carriage loft, his anger had flashed. His words had killed her, and he'd made Ewan leave her. She blinked and closed off that stupid part of her heart, the part that remembered that fleeting summer love. "Is it worth the risk to think that this poet wants a marriage and not just games? I could spend my time getting used to the squire."

"I'm a hopeful cynic." Frederica waved her hand as if music played. "A baron could be a more impressive advocate to the courts. With my shock of his approach gone, I think he is a poetic, romantic man. He put effort into this. Listen. 'Some say their love of children is unending, but how can that be proven to be permanent, unbending? What say you?' How very sweet."

Ester leaped up on her short legs, her gown swishing as she went to stand next to tall Frederica. "I get it now. He does not want to meet yet. He wants you to respond about children. Why is that important? Maybe your advertisement sounded too good to be true. What did we put again?"

Theodosia started to reply, but movement on the patio caught her gaze. Something sparkled in the evening light. A misplaced teaspoon or fork from her dinner guests?

It had been a long day of seeing undesirable things. She didn't need to look for more. She rubbed her eyes. "We said, 'Respectable young widow of means looking for honorable family man of good character for matrimony.'"

The grimace on Frederica's supple features was comical. Her nose wriggled as if she smelled dead fish. "Oh. I forgot we went the mind-numbing route. We should write back with more color. Something clever."

Trying not to turn back to the patio, Theodosia crossed

her arms. "What should I have said? Blackamoor beauty with babe and loads of baubles, needs beau?"

Ester smiled wide, like Philip's governess did when he did something right during his lessons. Over the years, Ester's tutelage and Mathew's guidance had taken a barely literate street seller and taught her to sound as if she'd been brought up under the love and care of genteel parents, not a poor urchin with no last name. "Maybe this poet baron will have a wonderful last name. I hate giving up the surname Cecil. I've grown so accustomed to it. And maybe this flamboyant man won't mind the company I keep. The squire or baron must allow my friends to visit."

Now, Ester's face held a frown. She started twiddling her thumbs. "Well, if he allows you to continue to shop Croome's fabrics, I know my parents will be thrilled."

Frederica came over to Theodosia and Ester, linking hands—light, olive, bronze. "I remember the shy girls I met at a party thrown by my father. They held their heads high amongst all the whispers, like the day l went from obscurity to the acknowledged by-blow of one of the prince's favorite dukes. People will always talk or try to isolate us, but we are more than that. In fact, I now feed the gossips things to say, like what parties I will attend and which of the Croome's fabrics I will turn into the latest design."

"'Tis true." Ester's voice boomed with pride for her family's business. "We have the best silks of all the tradesmen. The best woolens in all of Cheapside. We probably supply some of the mantua makers in that fancy Burlington Arcade you went to today—but enough of this silliness. We have a proposal and a provocative response. I say we answer the new mystery man and delay the squire. Two offers definitely means more choices."

Considering all, Theodosia turned toward the doors that led to the patio. It made sense to have another option. One path was something to avoid. Again, she noticed movement outside. Something stirred in the dim light near her favorite rosebush. She was sure of it. *Could it be the wind?*

She rubbed her temples. "Anyone can write flowery words. Or lie with beautiful ones to your face. But you two think we should waste another week and delay a solid offer? Time is so short. Delay doesn't sound like a shrewd decision. It could be costly."

Frederica yawned as she rubbed her arms. "Business-minded as always. If the second letter is from a gentleman with a courtesy title, *he* can defeat Lester at the Chancery. The squire is riskier. And marriage, this second one, should be forever. You are young. Your math mind needs poetry. Listen to this line again. 'Love of children is unending, but how can that be proven to be permanent, unbending?' It's poetry. I know you are tired, but a couple weeks delay will harm nothing and could mean everything. You deserve a chance at someone who could love you and your son, forever."

Her dear friend possessed a generous heart, so Theodosia wouldn't correct her about love or marriage lasting forever. None of those sentimental things lasted. "Very well. I'll write something at my desk tonight. You'll be able to edit it in the morning before you head back to Town. Now go on to bed."

Ester wrapped an arm about her. The shorter girl reached up to Theodosia's shoulder, though her wisdom was taller than most. "You do deserve poetry and joy. Don't stay up too long. Get rest. The lines under your eyes are from staying up with little Philip. He'll not get better if you are not well."

Pulling away, Theodosia moved to the curtains and fingered the burnished gold cloth. As she was about to close them, she stopped. Someone hid by her rosebush. Dread mixed with anger in her stomach. She knew she wouldn't be able to rest tonight, not until she dealt with her ghost. "You ladies go on. I'll stay here and take care of business. I'll have the response ready for review in the morn."

Ester reached up and kissed her cheek. "Promise you will go to bed soon."

She nodded. "Go on."

Frederica dropped the baron's letter onto the chaise, picked up her goblet of madeira, along with a final bonbon, and headed for the door. "Do sleep, Theodosia. With the festival and your newspaper groom options, you need a clear head."

"Good night, dears," Theodosia said, hoping they'd hurry.

Frederica and Ester passed a shrug between them as they left. For this, Theodosia was grateful. She needed to face her latest problem alone. Once their footfalls disappeared, she locked the parlor door. She took a deep breath, and with a hand steadied on the brass knob of the patio door, she opened it. In a low voice, she said. "Come in, Ghost. Commence your haunting."

• • •

Ewan stepped from the shadows of the big rosebush. What had started as a simple quest to walk past, maybe drop her package off with a footman, had become an overwhelming desire to see the usurper in all her ill-gotten wealth. This was his uncle's house. Theo had married into his mother's family, *his* family. Outrageous.

His boot heels drummed on the cobblestones until he stood six inches from Theo—grabbing-her-and-shaking-her-for-answers or kissing distance. "I'm no ghost. I thought we established that earlier."

Her eyes widened. The dim light caused the pupils within to dilate even bigger. "Still a ghost to me. Nothing'll change that."

"I am quite alive, breathing the same fragrant air as you, Theo the Flower Seller." He pushed past her and scooped up the note lying on the chaise. "So this is why you were at Burlington Arcade. Collecting your next swindle?"

Theo's henna cheeks darkened. He wondered if she'd fall over and faint, but as he moved closer to steady her, he didn't see weakness, but strength in her straightening posture, the leveling of her shoulders.

She reached for the paper and missed, almost slapping his chest in the process. "How dare you listen to a private conversation?"

"My apologies. But what makes the wealthy Widow Cecil seek a husband by newspaper?"

"It's none of your concern how I gain a husband. We both know that waiting for a man to profess his love for me but who then begs off of an elopement because of his father doesn't work. Does he know where you are? You should hurry back. Lord Crisdon might be snapping his fingers for you, or his dogs."

Now this was the woman he remembered—sharp-witted, expressing the precise sentiment to twist someone up. Shoving a balled fist behind his back, he shook his head. "That's not how it was. You know we had to wait until I served a year. That was all. But seems to me you don't know what it means to wait, Theo."

She bunched up her collar in the most prudish manner conceivable. "My friends call me Theodosia. Liars from the past, they call me Theo."

He gave her the letter, taking full advantage of clasping her hand, feeling her rising pulse. "Liar? I'm a liar because you thought me dead? I think you are mistaken. Perhaps liar doesn't mean what you think it does."

She slid her hand away from him, pulling back as if it hurt to touch him. "I've learned quite a few words since then. Like trespasser and bounder. Since you have no purpose here, other than to steal my peace, I suggest you leave."

"I have a purpose. Your soaps. Too feminine of a fragrance for me." He returned to the large rosebush where he'd dropped the parcel the minute he'd heard them read the lines he'd written for Jasper. Now, he saw his brother's brilliance in using the obscure courtesy title. Yet, the fool assignment of helping Jasper woo a newspaper bride had led to Theo. This was Ewan's luck, bad luck. "Here."

When she bit her lip, he knew the rawness of being face-to-face knifed her insides, too. A small part of him wanted her to suffer as he had, knowing she'd abandoned their promise. The other part of him was too busy concentrating on her delectable mouth.

"The soap was expensive, Ewan. But I can't risk you being here, can't be seen with you. Take it and leave."

"I told you. It's not my scent." He held the package close to her silky cheek that even now glowed in the soft light coming from the house. That creamy complexion had grown more beautiful. Kept women surely had an easier time of staying lovely. "It's yours, Theo. Or maybe I should say, Cousin Theo, since you've slept your way into my mother's family. Take it, Cousin."

Finally, her palm lifted. She touched his hand again before pulling the package to her bosom. "Please go."

She turned. The fine dark dress swathed her hips in a fashion that only Michelangelo could sculpt.

Ewan couldn't help but follow her inside.

Putting the package and the letter on a low table by the chaise, she faced him and winced. "Why are you still here?"

Her eyes were glossy and wet, not like before. *Is she crying?* Ewan wanted to kick himself for caring, kick himself for allowing her to still have a hold on him. "You don't think I'm owed an explanation? My father says you've been in mourning for Cecil for a long time. You're in gray—half mourning—that's months of paying respect for the dearly departed. You barely waited a few weeks to grieve little old me. And now you are hunting for a new husband. Why?"

"I owe you nothing, save a footman's coin for fetching my package. And is it so hard for you to think that maybe there is another man like Mathew Cecil who thinks I'm the marrying kind? Perhaps I'm longing for someone else who will treat me with respect."

His brow rose of its own volition. He leaned near her sweet ear. "Was respect required before or after you became a mistress?"

She stepped back, eyes widening, breath sputtering. "I've spent too much on you today. Leave."

Even as he said the slight, he knew it was wrong, but it turned her sullen eyes the color of flames, rich and dark, full of heat. Her fire was still there, merely trapped under neatly attired wrappings. And that heat made him press closer. "For six years, I wrote scene after scene in my head, why there was *us*. I didn't have money or titles or land. Was I practice? Was my teaching you to read enough to pretend to like me? Enough payment for an affair?"

"I was young and stupid, Ewan. So were you. Too much time has passed to do this now. They said you died. No one said you lived. Until today, you never came back."

"I was shot on the battlefield not even thirty days upon landing in Spain. It was bad. Names were mixed up and the regiment sent word I'd been killed. It took nine months before my full strength returned. Father wrote you'd run off with another man. I saw no need to return."

She blinked her long silky lashes. "I'm glad you're not dead. Maybe you can go live the life your father approves of and leave me be."

"Well, I am. You're in my latest play. I hope I've captured

your appeal, your exotic heady beauty, your underhanded dealings—"

"Why must I be exotic? Because I'm not pale or white as a sheet? Mathew Cecil thought me pretty."

"Well, you do clean up nicely in such fashionable trimmings. But what rich man's fetish wouldn't? I suppose you saw an opportunity and seized it. Business-minded to a fault."

"Do you want to hear that I grieved you? I did. Your father said you were dead, before he ran me off. They... He said you were killed in honor, something a wench like me could never understand. But you are not dead. Probably not even a scratch and you are mad at me for continuing to live. You should be relieved that you didn't have to return to these fields to wed the ignorant flower seller. Can you imagine figuring out how to feed mouths while still waiting for your father's approval?"

He came alongside her, took her free palm, and flattened the fidgeting thing against his chest, sneaking it under his waistcoat to the smooth linen of his shirt, making sure her fingers covered the raised scars on his chest. "Do you feel those scratches? The physicians call them scars."

Her hand stilled a moment and a world of emotions twirled in her eyes, across her trembling countenance. She shrank backward. "I'm sorry, Ewan."

Her face became streaked in silent tears, and though Ewan wanted to provoke her, he didn't want her to cry. He coughed, clearing the knot of humanity that lodged in his throat. "I didn't come here for pity. I took a mortal wound but managed to live. Knowing you became a hot little piece for a rich man, that about killed me all over again. Didn't know you'd chosen my cousin."

She wiped at her face, then steadied her shoulders. "So after six years, you've come back to haunt me about things that can't be changed?"

He sat on the high part of the chaise's arm, still marveling at how much she had and had not changed. Still beautiful. Still determined, but with a new sense of calm or reservation that gave him pause. He smoothed his cravat back into place. "Father was right about so many things, including the military. I was good at it. I served in the West Indies until these past three months. I came back because I am a Fitzwilliam. Part of me missed family."

She folded her arms and turned toward the fireplace. "Family is important."

"And I was helping my brother, the viscount, with an errand at Burlington Arcade. I had no idea I would see you today."

She stormed to the patio door, opening it wide. "Well, now that you have, leave me alone. Go live your life, Ewan Fitzwilliam. Be that successful playwright you dreamed of becoming."

"I intend to, but not your way. Success won't be had by scheming, lying, or selling myself."

Theo stopped biting her lip and pointed outside with both hands. "I may not be happy with my choices, but I own them. No one else. I did what I needed to do to survive. I have no luxury of a father to blame or surname to tarnish, for that matter. Now, leave. Don't sneak back here. And if you see me in passing while staying at Daddy's, call me Mrs. Cecil. That is my name. One I love."

He stood up and walked toward her. He wasn't in the habit of staying, if a lady requested him to leave, but Theo was no lady. She was a usurper intent to harm the Fitzwilliam family. "I will, if you stop threatening us."

She squinted at him as if he'd said lunacy. "What are you talking about?"

"I know you are threatening our farms by cutting off the

water to our plantings. Relent and I'll do you a favor. I'll take your name out of my latest play."

"You've written a new play?" The hope in her voice suddenly dropped to nothing. "And you've put me in it?"

"Yes. This one centers on a woman who uses her womanly wiles to seduce and gain riches until all her schemes become announced to the world. Then, she's left with nothing."

Her frown deepened. She slunk backward until she clutched the doorknob, her beautiful tawny fingers pressing so hard against the brass, they almost blended. "And you've named this villain after me?"

"Yes, Theo the Flower Seller. I told you, I wrote you in every scene. How do you think you'll fare when that name is circulated?"

Her chest rose, up and down, as if she struggled to breathe. "Ewan." Her voice became airy and choppy. "My name, laughed at in London... You w-wouldn't be so cruel."

He rounded back, took her cold palm, and pressed his lips to them. "Ghosts are supposed to be cruel."

This time she did strike his face. It was a hard slap that jerked his head backward. His Circe wasn't a pushover. He'd always liked that about Theo.

"Go home to your daddy, Ewan. And never come back."

"Time is ticking away. The play is being circulated. Once it sells, it will be too late. Stop threatening the Fitzwilliam part of the family, Cousin."

He marched out of Tradenwood. With one foot over the low wall forming the edge of the patio, he took a last glance at her. Her back was to him, but her shoulders shook as she hugged herself. He'd surely left her crying.

If she were heartless and opportunistic, his threat should anger her, not make her hurt. It should be an opening for her bartering, something at which he remembered her excelling. Why did it still punch him in his gut, as it had so many years ago, when she cried?

He trudged back to Grandbole, reminding himself that this was the same woman who'd sullied herself with his distant cousin. She was a greedy woman who could only be made to heel with threats. This kind of female, as Lord Crisdon would say, only responded to money and power. Ewan lacked funds, but his pen was mighty, and he'd use it to protect his family.

The wind whipped a little, bringing the lavender smell imprinted upon his hands to his nostrils. It felt horrid to threaten someone he had once cared about. Lifting his gaze to the stars, they winked at him, reminding him of his humor. He remembered all the ways he'd coaxed a young flower seller into his arms. None of his teasing or affection had had anything to do with threats. He wasn't the earl and should only rely on such tactics as a last result.

Determined, Ewan walked a little faster. With a little poignant teasing, he could get Theo to relent about the water rights and not have to ruin her new name. She was family now, after all. He chuckled to himself, contemplating the joy of wearing her down. He'd need to do so quickly. His play could be bought in a fortnight.

Chapter Four

Love & Regrets

Theodosia sat in the parlor, pushing a translucent sliver of onion across her breakfast plate. The silver fork scraped and clanged, and she lifted her gaze to Ester's wide eyes.

"Dearest," her friend began, with a lilted voice dripping with the perfect blend of condescension and amusement. She lifted her pert nose from the parchment Theodosia had labored all night writing. "You get shifty and bothered when I review your correspondences, but there is no need to fret. I've corrected your letters these past four or five years. I know what to expect."

Theodosia nodded and began again her battle with the onion. This letter had to be worse than the others Ester had edited. Theodosia surely wrote nonsense after what Ewan had said. How could it be otherwise when he accused her of harming the Fitzwilliams, a family that had wanted her dead?

Why did he view her as a threat to his family? Hadn't the Fitzwilliams been the source of all her problems? They were a seed pod for stinky flowers, the perfume of her every regret.

Regret. Such an awful R word. She caught herself stabbing the plate, the fork tines making an awful screech. "I tried very hard. I wanted it to sound personal."

"Everything should be personal, or at least sound as if it is." Frederica's voice held too much cheer, as if she hadn't a care in the world. Characteristically forty-five minutes late to breakfast, she sailed into the parlor with her eggshell-colored skirts floating about her thin ankles. The fabric moved about her as she danced to the window glass of the patio door. Her fingers tapped to an inaudible tune as she spread the curtains wide.

What would it be like to live in peace with violin music playing only for her? It must be great to awaken without anxiousness or doubts or that awful R word.

A noise from the patio, a branch twittering across the stones, startled Theodosia. Her gaze leapt to the spot where Ewan had stood. Then she remembered her hand pressed against the scars of his muscle-hardened chest. He had suffered. Maybe he had died. Maybe he *was* a ghost.

"Theodosia?" Frederica's tone sounded of concern, but one look at the minx's eyes foretold mischief. "Are you well? Did you get much sleep?"

"A little."

"Oh. That's good, very good." Again, the tone echoed like a purr. "I think you pattered on your patio too late." She popped a piece of toast, one she'd slathered in butter, into her mouth and grinned.

Her man grin. The one she wore when she received a note from an admirer.

Had she seen Ewan? So, he wasn't a ghost, only a former lover set on revenge. Was that better? She set down her fork. "What were you doing up so late? You couldn't sleep?"

Frederica cleared her throat and patted her lips with the starched linen napkin. "Too many bonbons. I regret that I had one too many."

Regret. If only Theodosia's were candies. She regretted loving Ewan. She regretted discounting Mathew's love, even as he'd held her hand during Philip's birth. She released a pained breath, one stinging from the jagged pieces of her broken heart. "Ester and I are working on a response to the riddle. I want the words to show *me*, what's true inside. This man needs to understand what I am, so he can either abandon these letters or move quicker to ask to meet."

"I knew it," Frederica said as she sweetened her tea. "You do need poetry, and this man will be better than the squire."

Ester's brow wrinkled as she dipped her quill into the ink. "You have hope in this suitor? Why? Is Fredericka-the-Flirt right about poetry, from a man?"

Something in the rhyme. Something in the inked signature. Something in Ewan's reappearance. It all reminded her of a soft spot hidden behind her lacy tucker, near her bosom where she stashed her hopes. Theodosia picked up her fork again and pricked a potato chunk until it smashed. "There's something in his words, in his way of asking the question. And a baron would have more influence than a squire. Silly thoughts?"

Frederica reached over and clasped Theodosia's hand midstab. "Put the fork down. What has that Wedgwood plate ever done to you?"

Releasing the silverware turned hapless weapon, Theodosia chewed her lip. "I'm not myself."

Flipping the page, Ester never looked up. Her matronly lace mobcap fluttered. The otherwise stylish girl kept reading.

Frederica sipped from her cup. "What—is his letter missing a comma? Is missing punctuation a poor indication of character. I think not."

Ester waved the baron's letter. "The gentleman has a rather nice hand. Clever penmanship. He's educated. I'm glad you are answering him and not settling for the squire."

"I so agree. Options may be everywhere. Even next door." Frederica, picking through the platter of fruit for the ripest berries, stuffed a big one in her mouth. "Your landowning neighbor, the Earl of Crisdon. He has two sons?"

Theodosia's feet grew cold. The need to escape filled every inch of her lungs. She couldn't eat. If she picked up her fork again, she'd jam it through the table. "He has two. Lord Hartwell who is a viscount and a younger son, but they all hate me. They hate that I married Cecil, that I and Philip own Tradenwood. They mean to destroy me. The younger son, who happens to be Cecil's distant cousin, came here last night to tell me so."

Ester gasped.

Her smile gone, Frederica slammed her cup to the table. "No. I won't let that happen. I'll get my father—"

"To do what? To defend Cecil's mistress wife? The duke's a peer like the earl. He'll stay out of it, and I couldn't ask you to do anything that will put strain between you and your father."

Folding her arms about her, crushing the Mechlin lace of her bodice, Frederica shook her head. She picked up her fork and poked at another berry. "I would try for you or Ester. I could make the duke understand."

"No, sweetness. His world won't see I am an honorable man's widow. If I can't find a new husband to fight Lester for Philip's guardianship, I'm doomed." She lifted her dark palms, which still held stains from the past. "Why can't I take Philip and leave here? I could take care of us. Cecil left me money. I'm sure we could make a new start. I'd let you all know where we settled so you could visit. And you'd have to. You two complete my life."

Ester dropped her quill. Frederica her fork. "No," they both said.

Pushing back in her chair, Frederica stared ahead. "We have to give this plan a chance. You have one offer, a cheap one, but it is still a squire. Then there is the poetic baron. He might be the one."

"Mathew Cecil was the only man I could trust. They aren't him."

Blowing a curl from her eye, Frederica's light skin looked quite red. "Ohhh. You say this speech all the time. Might I remind you of all the hard work you and old man Cecil did to make these flower fields produce? Do you wish Philip to lose his inheritance? Cecil loved that boy. He'd want him to have everything."

This was true, and how could she deny what Mathew wanted, after all he'd done for them? "If Cecil knew how treacherous Lester was, he would have never left him as a guardian." That had been his flaw. He had trusted too deeply.

Frederica frowned. It looked so misplaced among her lean cheeks and a pert nose given to wiggles. But could she know that Theodosia feared ever finding someone who saw her as equal?

Ester put down her quill. "First pass, done. Dearest, it's not that bad. Quite improved. You impress me."

Impressions were momentary things, like a boy loving her...until his father changed his mind. And how would things fare when Ewan's play, the one he'd boasted of last night, played at the theater, offering lies and half-truths?

Even if, somehow, Ewan and Mathew shared blood, Ewan was a Fitzwilliam and Fitzwilliams were nasty, evil people. How could she stop them?

Theodosia looked down and rubbed at her wrists. She'd gripped them too tightly with her full-on fretting. Resigned, she smoothed her thick cuffs and steeled her spirit with Mathew's words.

Theodosia, you are a light rising from obscurity. When

you focus on helping others, the darkness you think you have will be like the noon sun.

"I need to get this letter sent as soon as possible, so I can focus on the festival. The workers and vendors will have a day like Mathew Cecil would give. I couldn't give them their due last year with Cecil so sick, then dying."

Frederica's brow lifted as she patted berry juice from her lips. "You both need to stop fretting. Ester, stop killing us with your slow edits."

Ester again waved her hand and frowned. "Final pass almost done. This can't be rushed, and Theodosia should know my opinion won't change because of a misplaced comma."

Starting to pace, Theodosia paused and decided to tell her truth. "Would your opinion change if it were made public that Mathew Cecil's widow had been an ignorant street beggar? That she made herself a harlot to survive and somehow managed to marry a wealthy man?"

The foul statement consumed all the air, burning up all the noise in the room like a greedy flame. Yet as she caught Frederica's gaze, her hazel eyes weren't filled with pity, but something akin to defiance. "Why stop at such a small insult? You and I are lucky by-blows and Ester's people would still be in Africa, if not for being such great sailors, coming before the slavers invaded." She stood up, marched to Theodosia, and gripped her shoulders. "We are misfits. And never good enough. With true friends, true lovers, none of this matters. You are decent, decent to us, to everyone. That's what matters."

As much as she wanted it to be true, it wasn't. The Court of Chancery would take her son from her and give control of his health to mean, horrible Lester. Unspent tears built in her throat, thickening it and drowning all hints of that R word. Sniffing, she nodded.

Ester's face lifted and a droplet rolled down her cheek. "Done. This letter is done. It's very good. We should still work on your spelling, but your teacher is proud of the formerly ignorant street girl, as you say. Frederica is right. You are a beloved friend. Theodosia Cecil is a kind soul, with a head for numbers, though not so much spelling and punctuation."

Holding her arms wide, Theodosia stood. "You're both such dears."

The chair screeched as Ester slid out, and she and Frederica rushed to Theodosia and embraced.

"I don't know how I'd do without you all," Theodosia said, still fighting a full-on cry.

Ester held her a little tighter. "You're too hard on yourself. If it were numbers, you'd best Frederica and me."

"You can't leave us," Frederica said, with a voice that didn't sound steady or cultured.

The love in their voices spoke to Theodosia more than words. She still had those who cared for her, and shoulders to cry upon when things became worse.

And they would worsen with the Fitzwilliams coming at her. She rubbed her jaw, smoothed the lace at her neckline, and decided to tell the newest threat. "The Fitzwilliams are threatening to scandalize my name if I don't agree to their terms, but I won't sell this place or the fields. You all are right about what my husband wanted. This is my son's home, his legacy. I'll do what I must to protect it, even marry a squire who can't hold my gaze."

Frederica moved and picked up the cut of foolscap that Ester had stewed upon. "You wrote this, Theodosia, because you know the squire is not for you. Your next husband could be swayed to sell the pieces of the business not entailed to your son. And what if evil Lester bribes him into siding against you? Philip's care could be in jeopardy. Don't accept the squire out of fear. Fear is the wrong motivation."

But the R word and humiliation were. Their power seemed greater than a vise, worse than horrible thunder coming for her. She mopped at her brow. "Let's get this draft ready, while I can still hope."

In silence, her friends nodded. They retook their seats and resumed their routines: berry selecting and reading.

Frederica leaned forward. "Well, maybe you'll attract someone at the theater next week. My father has agreed to let us use his box, if we promise to be discreet. And before you say no, Theodosia, you can go in gray or black. You should get used to being out again. Nothing's better at discretion than a dark theater."

Ester's nose wrinkled. "If it's dark, who will see us, or us them?"

Frederica twirled a strawberry on her plate. "We'll see them and enjoy the music, even if we must sit at the back of his box. It's not important to be seen, but to be there."

Theodosia nodded, but couldn't come up with a reason not to go. Outside of Tradenwood wasn't always welcoming. She'd have to find an excuse. The risk of leaving Philip alone at night was too great.

Her fingers tightened around the note to her fantasy suitor, coiling it within her palm. In her heart, she knew she'd met her new husband, the squire, for he'd already asked to marry her and she had a feeling he'd go through with it, unlike Ewan Fitzwilliam. She'd tell the squire after the festival, before Lester or the Fitzwilliams, especially her ghost, took her choices away.

• • •

Ewan pulled Jasper's gig close to the mews at the rear of the family's London townhouse. He stepped out and handed the reins of the fine beast to a groom.

The boy pulled the gelding into a stall and hitched him. The horse, pewter colored, with a high gait and a finely arched back, marched inside, as if this pen was something he owned.

Marvelous. Ewan almost envied the horse as it pawed at the earth, acting every inch the thoroughbred, not an animal with a layman's job. Maybe the horse knew something the *ton* couldn't conceive, that dignity and a profession weren't scandalous, but cleansing to a man's soul, even a jaded one. Not that he wished to be neutered. Ewan had big plans to be productive, with a wife and loving family—as he'd planned with Theo. Her handprint on his jaw, even the sting, had remained as he'd slipped into Grandbole. He could still move her. That would prove useful.

"Mighty nice horse, sir," the groom said as he brushed down the gelding. "Shall I wipe down the seat, give 'er a nice cleaning?"

"Yes." That would be a good thing to do for Jasper. Though Ewan had the money now to buy one of his own, the upkeep and stabling would consume his meager pension. A gig would be an indulgence he'd procure after his first author's benefit night. He'd be able to tell by the crowds if his play was a success.

Theo had taught him to be frugal. She had always calculated hidden costs, thinking about things others didn't notice. The way she reacted to his threat last night had the makings of a hidden cost. The sooner Ewan could figure out what that cost was, the sooner he could get her to relent.

He dug into his pocket for a coin and showed it to the groom. "There's an extra bit for a good job."

The boy smiled then went back to brushing the silvery coat.

No payment in advance of seeing the work—another Theo lesson. Ewan started down the alley toward the street. His nose wrinkled at the stench, the sourness in the air, the horse leavings. The city was nothing like the fields of Grandbole or those of Tradenwood. And every morning Theo awoke to the scent of fresh flowers.

He didn't have time to be jealous of her. No, he'd stewed most of the night on why? *Why hadn't mother told me?*

He waited for the butler to answer the door to the townhouse. The wind brought the smell with him, like it gave chase. Stewing, his gut knotted. What if Mother thought him incapable of handling another disappointment? Yes, he'd lost out on inheriting Tradenwood because of an inaccurate field message of his death. He could live with that, but losing it to a cousin who had made Theo its owner—that was tough. His stomach turned again and not from the stench of the road behind him.

The door opened and an older man in shiny blue livery stood there. "Mr. Fitzwilliam."

"Yes, I am here to see the countess."

"She's taking breakfast in the salon." The man turned and pattered down the gilded hall, stopping at a heavily trimmed door. He ducked inside and then popped back out. "She'll see you now."

Ewan fumbled with his jacket button, one of the garments his father had stashed in the room he wanted Ewan to stay. It had stung, sliding it on after hearing Theo's accusation about him not being his own man, but he needed to hold his mother's full attention. Buttons and baubles easily distracted her and gave her the opportunity to meander away from facts. He needed truth. He needed it badly.

Entering the bright sunlit room, he stopped and saw a smiling cherub in a pale pink morning gown.

Mother touched at her lacy mobcap, then extended her hand. "Ewan? To what do I owe the pleasure?"

Stepping fully inside, he met her at the large breakfast table. "I came to see the best lady in the world."

Her dimples spread and made her lapis blue eyes sparkle. "Then I forgive you for missing my party last night. Sit down, sweet boy."

Ewan stumbled. *I am a man, one who fought death and won. How can I still be a boy to her—to Theo?* He sighed as he plopped in an open chair to her right.

"I wasn't too mad at you. Although Mrs. Whilton's niece was disappointed."

"I'm sure they both will live and find another impoverished playwright to pass the time with. Perhaps a better card player."

Her nose wrinkled. "So what has you out and up so early? Have you accepted my offer? Will you leave your horrid flat and come stay here with me?"

"No, Mother. That's not why I am here."

She put a flaky, pale biscuit that smelled of fine butter and orange bits on his plate. "I have plenty of room. I'm sure you could write dozens of things. It's so nice here, not so dreary."

Dreary? Was she comparing the small townhome to his flat or to Grandbole? He broke his biscuit up into bits. They would be easier to swallow once he steered the conservation to the street address he sought. "I'm content where I am."

Her chin lowered and she swirled her teacup. "I understand, but it's easier here."

Unease settled in his gut, mixing with the cinnamon of the biscuit. Her residence in Town sounded more permanent than staying for the Season. He caught and stilled her elegant hand. "I'm happy with my own flat, but you, you are the Countess of Crisdon. Even you must return from the ball at the stroke of midnight. Grandbole is at a loss without you."

"You look nice, dear."

"I take it you don't want to talk about Grandbole?"

She touched his coat, smoothing the lapel. "These full revers look best on you. I would love to send you to the tailor for more. I want to treat you."

The coddling he had enjoyed, as a protection against his father's temper, had never stopped. It hadn't stopped after being breached at six, going to war at twenty, or returning now as a man. Probably would never stop, unless he did something. Patting her fingers away, he leaned close. "This is the earl's tailor. He's quite good. I borrowed it so I don't feel obligated or more leech-like."

"Your father's doing?" The small fine wrinkles that dared to touch her creamy countenance deepened as she seemed to stare through Ewan. "Well, you should've worn it last night. I had a very disappointed young lady here. It was awful moving things about to find her a new card partner. You hampered all my plans."

"Jasper changed my plans."

She set another biscuit in front of him, but he hadn't eaten much of the first.

Another distraction. He pushed the plate away. "Jasper took me to see—"

"You know, I introduced Jasper to his wife. God rest her soul. Maria was a dear. I only want you to be as happy."

"He was happy, but happiness is fleeting. It seems Grandbole is gloomy with her loss and now yours."

She picked up the pot of tea and poured him a cup. Mint floated to his nose, beckoning. Another distraction.

Mother set the silver service down. "Jasper won't let me introduce him to another lady, one with a bigger dowry than Maria's. I can do the same for you."

He shook his head. "I'm not hunting for a wife or a dowry. And you haven't asked how I know Grandbole is dull."

"Jasper told you. He doesn't lie. He's nothing like your father."

"I know. I saw them both last night."

Her lips thinned. Perhaps she was trying to think of

another street to take him down, but he wouldn't be swayed. He needed to hear from her lips about Theo possessing Tradenwood and why his own mother thought him too weak to know. "Mother, why? Why didn't you tell me?"

"I thought you weren't going to see the earl until Yuletide. I have him considering wintering in Town."

"Jasper convinced me I needed to see Grandbole and Tradenwood."

She tossed her handkerchief onto the table. "Then I suppose you know."

"Mother, I've seen you once a week for the past three months. You lamented over your brother's passing, told me of Tradenwood going to a distant cousin because Uncle rewrote his will, thinking I'd died." He paused as his voice rose, almost shaking with the injustice rocking his windpipe, his soul. He'd lost everything—Theo, a fortune that would've funded his pursuit of plays—gone because of that false report from the battlefield. It had hit him hard, harder than he thought, seeing Tradenwood. Knowing another man had possessed Theo's curves, the henna-bronzed loveliness Ewan had thought only for him.

He took a breath and forced his tone to lower. "We've sat through dinners, or private moments like this, and no mention of my cousin's bride."

"It wasn't important. Tradenwood was lost to us. Nothing else mattered. Nothing could be done."

"The fact that I nearly eloped with this woman is not important?"

"No. No, it isn't. I don't mention her. The usurper who led you astray now has my Tradenwood." Her face twisted as tear-stained eyes drifted to the right. "I was raised in that home. I left for my come-out from those grand steps. Your father proposed on that patio. That she-devil and your cousin put up a trellis on my patio." Mother shivered, as if the covering were horse leavings. "Tradenwood should never have left the family."

"Technically, it's still in the family, in a distant cousin's hands. Well, now his widow's. How did that come about? Was she grieving me? Does grief make strange bedfellows?"

The crystals in Mother's eyes shattered, shaking in fury. "You can joke of this? That harlot made you wild, and you almost paid with your life."

Ewan chuckled to himself, for Mother didn't know wild. Wild was what he called his stint away. He'd been a dutiful soldier on the field, but he and his fellow officers had caroused, finding comfort in the towns and villages they'd encamped in Spain and the West Indies. Lots of willing arms had seemed to be enticed by his bright red regimental.

His mother's voice became more harpy-like. "The marriage should not have been allowed to happen. She's not worthy of Tradenwood."

"Their marriage was not legal?"

"That's not what I mean. Cecil's widow is a slut. A Blackamoor whore."

Ewan sat back and spun his teacup, covering the punch the slur made to his chest. "If she were a white harlot, that would be better?"

Mother leaped up with fists shaking. "That loose woman should be cleaning the floors, or cargo on a slave ship, not making menus and being hostess in that great manor."

Anger makes people do or say things they shouldn't. Yes, that would be the excuse he'd make for his mother. He'd coddle her stupidity as she'd always coddled him. He caught her hand and tugged her back toward her chair. "It must've been hard grieving me, then Uncle, then the loss of your family home. I am sorry. Don't let grief push you into saying cruel things. I'm making peace with the past. You must, too."

Shaking and nodding, lace fluttering, she dropped to the

seat. "It wasn't fair. My baby, my only baby was gone. You went to war because your father made you—because of her. He should've made her go. Then all would have been right. You'd own Tradenwood, not that harlot, Theodosia Cecil."

He lowered his voice to a whisper, but made his tone firm, resilient in Mother's tornado winds. "If I had stayed, her name would have been Theodosia Fitzwilliam. Would you have supported me or would you have called her names and torn down our love?"

"She wouldn't have loved you, never like you deserved. The creature is incapable of it. Hopping from bed to bed, gaining deeper pockets with each leap."

"Well, she didn't have a matchmaking mama to point her to the right pockets. But you are right. Mine are not as filled as Cousin Cecil's."

"You keep making jokes. You write funny plays, but it hides your pain. How can you stand to see her traipsing in your fields? Letting her heirs inherit it, not us."

It wasn't easy, but nothing changed the past. He closed his eyes and drank the mint tea, hoping to get his gut to utopia so it would match the noise of forgiveness he was about to utter. "It doesn't matter. She's the new owner of Tradenwood. It's lawfully passed to her."

"It doesn't make you angered that it's not yours? I could help you make it great again, like when it was my home."

He didn't have the heart to tell her it was great and well-manicured. Theo had not, in any way that he could see, dishonored it. But nothing would console Mother from thinking she'd been cheated, just as when she realized most of his father's courtship of her had centered on her large dowry and the hope of getting closer to Tradenwood. Gut settling, he took a final sip of the cool mint. "You've always wanted that house. I'm sure it's a great loss. I suppose welcoming her to the family is out of the question. That would resolve the watering rights issue that has the earl all worked up."

"Your father has tried to buy it for me, but his offers are too cheap. Maybe you can work on him."

"Weren't you happy with my not seeing him?"

"I didn't want you distressed over being reminded of what going to war cost you. You'd have had Tradenwood. You'd never want for anything. You could write all the plays you wanted."

"Well, I will make my own way, by writing all the plays I want."

"I'm sure you shall, but head back to Grandbole. Convince Crisdon to get Tradenwood for me. Tell him I'll return, if he does."

"I'm not going to get in the middle of your spat."

She pouted and frowned.

Feeling guilty at causing her pain, he nodded. "But I'll mention it to him. If there is a price at which the Widow Cecil will sell, he'll find it."

"Tell Lord Crisdon I regret our argument. I realize that there is no sacrifice greater than Tradenwood."

Overly dramatic as always, Lady Crisdon wasn't going to be the route to find information about Theo and Cecil. No, he'd have to get that from the source, his new cousin, the widow Cecil. He rose and kissed Mother's hand, but she leaned up and clung to him, as if she was again sending him to war. Well, maybe she was. He marched from the drawing room to return to Grandbole, readying to battle his difficult father and an ornery widowed cousin-by-marriage.

Chapter Five

The Cost of Revenge

Theodosia waited for Frederica to climb into the carriage. Ester was already tucked inside, probably with her eyes stuck in a book she'd found in Mathew's collection.

Clutching her bonnet, Frederica popped inside then stuck her head out. "We meet two weeks from now at the theater. Don't make me come back here to retrieve you. Theodosia Cecil is good to her word."

"Yes." That was all Theodosia could muster. That and a wan smile.

Frederica nodded then took her seat.

The carriage started to move. The onyx vehicle with the Duke of Simone's golden crest jerked and jostled down the long drive. Two pairs of handsome horses headed them back to London and Theodosia's heart dropped. Saying good-bye to her friends felt so final this time. It shouldn't, but it did. Maybe that's why fleeing stayed on her mind.

She pushed at a curl falling from her mobcap and took a huge breath of air. The sweet aroma of roses overtook her, cheering her spirit. She hugged herself and that feeling of being unprotected and alone fled. Her friends said they would stand with her. She'd believe in them until she couldn't.

Like she had believed Ewan would marry her, until he didn't.

Clutching her elbows as if that would latch in her courage, she looked up into the darkening sky and saw a streak of light. Then the sound that always brought dread pounded through her. Thunder. Fear filled her heart. It pimpled her skin all the way to her ankles. She couldn't have a panic in front of her pickers or tenants. The Court of Chancery would not look kindly on a mother so fearful of a storm. She would not be considered a good choice to raise a boy independent of his male guardian. No better than a harlot would.

As that feeling of again losing someone she loved swelled inside, the need to hold her son overcame her. She bolted for the portico.

Pickens held the door open for her, as if he'd been watching and had seen her panicked stride.

She ran on, lifting her heavy ash-colored skirts, and made it inside before the rain began to fall.

"Ma'am." The butler's voice made her stop and stand up tall.

"Yes, Pickens?"

He closed the door, shutting out the sound of the approaching storm. "Your letter has been sent to the Burlington Arcade."

Though he may not know what was on the inside of those sealed papers, he surely knew how important they were. She nodded to him. "Thank you."

In six years, Theodosia had learned the ways of Tradenwood, the roles and responsibilities. Yet, it always felt daunting. Thank goodness, Pickens was a stalwart butler who had served generations of Mathew's extended family.

The staff Mathew had hired were all good people to her, ones who wouldn't cheat her and who knew how to help without making her feel ignorant. "I've lived here six years and I still feel lost sometimes."

"You do fine, ma'am. You are quite capable."

She didn't feel capable, especially when thunder boomed. It reminded her too much of growing up in the harshest parts of London, trying to see the beauty of roses from the papered-up windows of a brothel. Again, she wrapped her arms around her and went in search of her son, her happiness.

Philip always made her happy, like the fluttering big-winged butterflies in the fields. He must've seen the door open or heard her slippers with his good ear, for he turned to face her. He lifted his arms and came to her. She picked him up and swung him around until his little face exploded with giggles, silent ones at first, then full belly-jiggly ones.

And Theodosia lost her cares and laughed, too.

"Mrs. Cecil. It is time for Master Philip's lessons," said the governess. The spinster lady with dull red-and-white hair sticking from her cream-colored mobcap clapped her hands. "Master Philip?"

Theodosia pulled his little body close and completed three more turns. His little palms were about her neck, and she kissed "I love you" on his forehead. "Ready, Philip. School time."

Putting him down, she kept his hand within hers and walked to his governess. "Here's your student."

The woman smiled and pointed the boy to his shiny maple desk that she'd retrieved from a deep closet. "It is time to begin."

Philip pulled at his pinafore and made his way to his seat. He fingered the book laid upon his table. The governess went to him and kneeled close to his right ear, his good one, and read the page, sounding out each animal's name.

When Theodosia heard Philip's pitchy squeak reciting the word "chicken," a tear welled. She straightened her shoulders, approached, and kneeled to their left, like a pile of gray silk.

"H-o-g," said Philip, and her heart skipped a beat. Swine had never sounded so good.

The governess had been highly recommended to work with children with difficulties. She was worth the thirty-three pounds in wages, almost twice what she would pay a good housemaid. Philip needed someone to pack as many words into him before his right ear gave out, like the doctors said would happen.

"Is he doing better?" Theodosia asked when they finished the repetitions.

The governess looked over her glasses at Theodosia, as if she spoke in a foreign tongue.

Stopping the impulse to chew her lip, she tried again. "I mean, is he learning?"

Shoulders drooping, the woman's gaze lowered. If her head bent any further, it might fall off and roll around like a cabbage. "I don't want to get your hopes up. He's good at mimicking. I've gotten him to write his name, but it's hard. He's not like the other students I've worked with. He doesn't hear my questions sometimes. He can't—"

"Try using the mimicking more. If he follows what you do, that will be helpful. I know he's copied my figuring on paper, when I balance my ledger books."

The woman nodded and kneeled closer to Philip. She popped her chin atop the crown of his shiny black hair. "I'll try, Mrs. Cecil. That is all I can promise."

Theodora picked herself up, as if the governess had kicked her in the teeth. She backed up to the entry, waving and getting that last silent smile from Philip. Closing the door, she let her forehead bang upon it. Something had to help. Something had to get him to learn. He couldn't start in this world ignorant, as his mother had.

Her guilt shook her over the hurts she'd caused this sweet child by her choices.

A noise sounded from the hall. Her butler's voice alerted her of a guest arriving. It couldn't be her friends back this soon. She smoothed her hair, putting her lacy cap in her pocket and hoped her eyes weren't as red as the guilt rotting in her gut.

Then she saw him standing in her threshold in broad daylight. The ghost.

"Good afternoon, Cousin Cecil," Ewan said. His smirk was wide. He dipped his chin. "I'm sorry to appear without a note, but I am here to see about family."

As steadily as she could, she managed to come down the steps without falling. "Pickens. Can you show Mr. Fitzwilliam into the parlor?"

The butler's smile bloomed, a ready harvest of charm. "And bring a tea service?"

Ewan wasn't worth the shilling for the ounce of leaves. How could she politely ask to bring some that had been used two or three times? There wasn't a way, especially for someone announcing he was family. "Yes, Pickens."

She followed the men into the parlor, hoping this haunting would be brief and stay contained to the lower level. Philip's lesson did not need to be interrupted, especially from evil men or liars. Which category Ewan fell into, she wasn't sure.

• • •

After leaving London, Ewan purposed to come to Tradenwood, not slinking around in the dark, but as a man given to ending all the trouble Theo had caused.

"Why are you here?" she asked.

Not liking the wariness in her dark teak-colored eyes, he turned to the fireplace and poked the log. Orange and red embers danced along the wrought iron stick. He fanned the raindrops from his coat. The shower outside had slowed enough for him to leap under Tradenwood's portico. "I came for a number. You are very good at numbers, from what I remember. Good at a lot of things."

When she looked away with darkening cheeks, he knew she wasn't immune to his jokes or their good memories.

The door to the parlor opened and Pickens came in with a tea service. After the cup he'd drunk with his mother, Ewan had had his fill, but he'd partake with Theo. Keeping this meeting more social might move Theo more than bullying. He hoped.

"Thank you," she said to the old man, and with her graceful long fingers she pointed to the low table. "You brought biscuits, too? I don't think Mr. Fitzwilliam will be staying that long. He's no doubt needed up the hill at Grandbole."

"It's cousin now. Right, Pickens? And I'll take a cup filled to the brim. I intend to enjoy Madam's time."

The butler raised a furrowed brow. "Sir, do you still take only sugar?"

"Yes." Ewan couldn't help but smile. Pickens hadn't forgotten him. And maybe he hadn't forgotten that Tradenwood belonged more to the Fitzwilliam side of things than to the usurper flower seller. "It's good you remember."

Pickens moved close to the door, and he seemed to stare through Ewan. "Ma'am if you need anything, do not hesitate to pull the bell."

"Thank you. Thank you for everything." Theo smiled, maybe the first one he'd seen on her face since he'd returned. Deep brown skin, crinkling eyes, full kissable lips. She was a beauty when she wasn't fidgeting or sad. That charm had swayed his cousin and the butler, too. It had disarmed him once, but now he needed her to be relaxed, so he could act as if they weren't enemies.

Pickens left, closing the door with a thud. Ewan circled her as she sat calmly looking toward the patio doors and the falling rain. "I'm glad to find you about today. A woman with late night visitors might be inclined to lie around, becoming lazy."

Her gaze stayed fixed on the patio, not on him. "Why are you here? Skunks hunt at night. Pigs, too."

He stepped in front of the golden curtains, hoping to force her to look at him. "I need a number to take back to my father. What will it cost for you to sell Tradenwood?"

She laced her fingers together, creased gray cuffs enveloping her slender wrists. "Your play must not be any good."

"What?"

"You're already back here with a change of plans. A new scheme to coerce me, Ewan? It hasn't been a day and you're already altering plans. Oh wait. That is what you do."

Was that her game, to make everything that had happened his fault? Though he wanted her to own her unfaithfulness, to say it aloud, that would show his hand. He couldn't sweet talk a woman who was set against him. He moved close and sat directly opposite her chaise, in the chair by the fireplace. "There is nothing here that I want other than to restore peace to my family."

She didn't move or blink or breathe. "You mean the family who haven't been so supportive of you?" Her low tone magnified. "The one that keeps you around only when you are useful. That family?"

Maybe Pickens wasn't the only one with a good memory. Ewan had shared his Fitzwilliam frustrations more than once during their brief courtship. He ran a hand through his damp hair. "You can understand what it means to bring peace to all sides."

"So, for your peace, you offer to buy me off, to take the only home…to take *this* home from me."

"I can make sure my father pays you enough so that you can buy another. This was my mother's home. I remember spending yuletides in this parlor. Years and years of memories. You'll have what you wanted—money."

Thunder rumbled, deep and bone vibrating as the rain came down harder.

Theo looked frozen, almost doll-like. Moments passed but he dared not utter a sound.

He risked a slap, but he reached out and put his hand over hers. He sang, "Twinkle, twinkle little star. How I wonder what you are."

Those beautiful eyes of hers widened. Her shivers slowed. All these years and she was still afraid of thunder, and his ridiculous tunes again brought her from the darkness. If she were his, he'd hold her in his arms and sing to her again. But she wasn't his. Theo was his cousin's widow. "The storm will pass. You are safe."

She said nothing but picked at the plate of biscuits. Then Theo put one on a plate and handed it to him.

Surprised, he took it. He meant to set it down, but it had a deeply caramelized crust, probably the deepest brown of the pile. His mouth watered, and his heart softened further. She remembered those were his favorite. "Thank you, Theo."

He took a bite and the crunch melted on his tongue with that sweeter-than-honey taste. He wiped his face and hands on the napkin she stretched to him. "You were always so neat."

Another pound of thunder made her jitter on her seat, but she didn't turn from him. "And you, Ewan, were always a hearty eater in want of a handkerchief."

"I recall we were friends once. Can we be that again?"

"I don't know, Ewan. You did know how to make me feel safe." She gazed at him, her eyes soft, maybe longing for yesterday, too. "Never once did you belittle me for such a childish fear."

"Never, Theo. You were always brave. Do what is brave now. Sell this place so my mother can have her childhood home. Restore her good memories, and we can all live in peace. I know deep down peace is what you want. It's what you've always wanted."

She dipped her head and uttered no response. When the storm quieted, her voice returned. "I have memories, too. One of a man who pledged he would protect and honor me. Of reciting vows by that mantel. Of being welcomed into this house, which I shared with Mathew Cecil. My memories count."

If she had leaped up and slapped him as she had last night, that would have stung less. Hearing her talk of his cousin, of treasuring their love, pierced. It was easier thinking her money-hungry than loving another.

She moved to open the patio doors. A breeze swept inside and her cheeks flushed, turning a deeper shade of mahogany. "I want you out of here, Ewan. Run home to your parents and tell them no. I will not be run off. I have been civil to you. Something that your people have never been to me. Even when I begged."

"What are you talking about?"

"Ask Lord Crisdon how I was treated when you left."

Knowing how vicious his father could be, Ewan balled his fist. What had she endured when he wasn't around to make sure she wasn't harassed? He eased his palm against his knee. "Is that why you turned to my cousin? To get even with the earl?"

"You never understood me, did you, Ewan? Why else

would you be here pretending to care, as you try to buy me off?"

"I knew you quite well, Theo."

He came close and took her hand away from clutching at her collar. Looping his finger with her fine ones he dipped his head close to hers. "Your mind is sharp. Your will is strong, but even you know that this feud with the Fitzwilliams is wrong. It won't end well."

Her eyes grew darker, the flecks of gold disappearing in the flames of her pupils. He could hear her heart beating. His heartrate picked up, too. "You don't want to be the center of this conflict. You and that next lucky fool who'll be your husband don't want that kind of constant tension. End this for me, for what we once had. I'll make sure they never bother you again."

A breath crossed her lips, then what started out sounding like a sob became a full-throated laugh. "You don't know me. Maybe you never did. If you had, you wouldn't come here and plea to me to think of your people, your senti...sensibilities. I will not sell. I need you gone."

He released her hand. Now she sounded like a Circe, one who would use her power to destroy the Fitzwilliams. The kindhearted woman whom he had cared for was gone. This was the earl's work. He'd known his father to be horrible to enemies. Yet Theo, strong Theo, had bested them all. She'd won. She had Tradenwood and control of the water rights.

He rubbed at his face. Her lavender scent sat on his fingertips. "We can't change the past, but we can set about a new future. Name the price to lease the waterway as before under your husband. The water is drying out."

"Water lease? Drying out? I'll check with Mr. Lester, Cecil's former steward."

Truth righted in his head, making his pulse race. "Perhaps, he is cutting off the water. Not you."

The sound of gentle taps of the rain on the stone floor of the patio was peaceful, serene, like the calm before a big storm. What was Theo readying to do? "It doesn't matter. If it was done in Cecil's name, it is my doing."

He came up behind her. He was close enough to hold her within his embrace, wrap his fingers in the curls in her chignon. "It wasn't you hurting my family. You haven't changed that much from the girl I once loved."

"I changed, Ewan. I had to."

"Theo, you can stop him. You can restore the peace."

"There will be no peace, not for free. You want a number. Ten times what Lord Crisdon paid Cecil. It will cost the Fitzwilliams something. I will be well compensated for their next revenge plot."

"Twenty thousand pounds is exorbitant. You don't need to be so vengeful. I won't let them hurt you."

She glared at him, with nostrils flaring. "I don't believe you. They'll be no different than the man who wrote a play to hurt me. You took your gift and made it a weapon."

He wanted to take her in his arms and shake her, but maybe he needed to shake himself. The play was his only leverage, since his charm seemed hopeless. Why wouldn't she think him trustworthy? "I wrote it thinking you long gone from here, not married to my cousin. I can easily take your name out to protect you, if you will only be reasonable. I remember when you were reasonable. When you were quite content to be reasonable with me."

Her lip trembled and her fists balled. "I remember believing that we would leave in the morn to marry. You changed your mind faster than I could pin up my hair. You say you'll stay, but you'll go away again. Then the war will begin anew. I'd rather stand my ground and collect the penalty money. When I tire of the war, when I say it is over, and go into exile, I'll take the bulk of the Fitzwilliam fortune with me. You'll never be able to hurt people again with your money. Do you know how many have starved because of the Fitzwilliams's need for revenge?"

Ewan could not answer, nor did he want to count. It hadn't mattered, for he'd wanted no part of the business. "I will be around this time. I'll show you. I'll haunt you to get you to be reasonable, to be better than my father."

She pointed to the doors. "Words. Words are the playwright's lies. Twenty thousand pounds. Take that to Daddy."

Thunder clapped and she shivered. Powerful and vulnerable and lovely, a Circe in the eye of his storm.

This wasn't how this moment should go, with her hating him, pointing out all the sins of his family. It was hopeless to make her see the difference now. He'd have to prove his resolve. "I'll be around, getting both sides to seek peace. You'll be sick of me, Theo. You may even grow to like your good old cousin again."

"I do know that I will never trust you. I see your flaws now. I wish that I'd known the truth while Cecil lived."

"Why?"

"I would've loved him more."

He watched her bosom heave. Waited for the knife to his gut to stop twisting. "Good day, Cousin."

That was all he could manage without arguing and showing how deeply her words had cut into his flesh. Ewan plodded down the hall and out to his gig, wondering why a woman he was done with still made him gnash his teeth.

When he climbed into the gig, the seat was wet, but maybe the soaking would quench his fire. Theo had loved Cecil. It wasn't his money that had drawn her. His family's treatment had pushed her to his cousin. How could he stop her from ruining his family when he truly couldn't blame her for hating everything Fitzwilliam? Knowing what they were capable of, he hated them, too. For believing they'd take care of her while he was gone, he hated himself.

But he was here now, and she'd see he wasn't going away. She'd see and even rue his attentiveness. He'd make her want peace just to be rid of him.

Chapter Six

The Haunting Begins

Theodosia couldn't pace around the parlor to the nursery to her chambers and back again, and not upset her rattled household. Her prior thirty treks surely had worn a path through the rugs and dragged scratches across the polished floors. The doctor would arrive to Tradenwood in another three hours. One hundred and eighty long minutes to wait. Then she'd know if Philip's earache was a tooth thing or more progress in his hearing loss.

As she came from the narrow hall, Pickens stepped into her path. A grin that said *caught you* disappeared from his aged, battle-hardened cheeks. "Ma'am, Cook has been asking for your final approval. May I tell her you will see her after your next round of pacing?"

The festival... How could she concentrate on that after rocking Philip, hoping and praying that his tear-stained eyes would finally close in sleep? "Can... May it wait until tomorrow?"

The butler nodded. "No delay longer than tomorrow.

She'll need to inform the butcher of cuts you'll need for the celebration at month's end."

Yes, festival preparation. Another thing to fret about. She wrung her hands then dropped them to her sides. "Thank you for keeping me on task. I'm not moving so fast today."

Pickens's brow rose. "You could outpace the fittest Olympian. You should take a drive. I've taken the liberty of having your gig pulled around. Visit the fields. You'll be refreshed by the time the doctor arrives."

"But Philip? He might need me."

"The boy is sleeping. The laudanum will keep him out of pain until the doctor is here." He picked up her gloves and hat, handing them to her as he shuttled her to the door. "Have a pleasant ride."

She started tugging on one glove then the other. They were close-fitting kid gloves, soft and thin. She'd be able to feel the power of her mount. Then she could pretend to be in control of something. "I'll hurry. I don't want to be late and miss being needed."

The butler handed her a knit shawl, acres of creamy stitches. "Master Cecil always said, it isn't about speed. It's about how you run the race."

Pickens was a dear and he must've studied Mathew, for he knew how to nudge her in the way she should go. His steady force, his apt words, had helped guide her these months without Mathew.

Waving off a groom, Pickens held the reins as she took her seat. "Go, Mrs. Cecil. Enjoy your ride. We'll see you in an hour or so."

She nodded. "Thank you. I'll stick to the paths so if I need to be... Thank you, Pickens. I will run this race the best I can."

He set the thick reins into her palm. "That's all anyone can ask, ma'am. It's all Mr. Cecil expected. Have a pleasant afternoon."

He turned and went back into Tradenwood.

Theodosia closed her eyes for a moment, then whipped the leathers, forcing the gig forward. The small buggy was her favorite. With one horse, her fastest one, she could fly through the fields.

Breathing the fresh air, free of ointments and laudanum tonics, she let her heart smile. The doctor would fix Philip. He would be well. Theodosia had to hold on to that thought, as she did the reins.

Her horse, Willow, leaped over a gully, making the wheels bang hard, but Theodosia didn't care. This was as close to freedom as she could grasp and she relished it.

She'd have to do something nice for Pickens. He was such a dear. If a platonic marriage of convenience could be had with the butler, she was almost tempted to suggest it. Pity Pickens was as old as dirt and his position wouldn't have any sway with the Court of Chancery. Maybe she should get his opinion on the squire or the new suitor, the baron. Well, the baron hadn't replied yet, but he might. Finding someone as understanding as Mathew or Pickens—the hope of it was all she had.

Settling into her gig, she flew over the hill and through the fields. The glass greenhouses she'd had Mathew install glistened in the sun. No one could grow more exotic plantings than Cecil Farms. Zipping up the trail, she waved to a few of the tenants still out picking.

The morning was the best time to gather the flowers, unless you were slow or sickly. Theodosia used to be good at it, and she'd get on her small gig, the one financed by her mother, and make it to the Covent Garden area to sell flowers to the *ton* by ten. Those harried days had been so long ago.

A smile freed her lip from being chewed, and she slowed to enjoy the contours of the blooming fields. Rows of lavender waved, alongside sweet pink roses. The air felt crisp, tingling her cheeks. The day after a storm was the best. Everything felt cleansed.

Though yesterday's argument with Ewan had drained her, it had been good to admit to him that she'd loved Mathew and that Mathew had loved her. The poison Ewan's family had spewed about her had to have marred his thoughts of truth. It did make her chuckle, thinking of the old earl turning beat red over the outrageous sum of money she'd asked to be paid to continue the water rights on her land. He might've been more outraged at that than his son wanting to marry a Blackamoor.

Sighing, she let her *R*'s, her numerous regrets, be overtaken by a mix of lavender, roses, even manure. The blend of scents made a rich perfume. The Cecil fields would always possess abundance. Mathew would like that. Good. The first time today she thought of Mathew and not Ewan. She needed to be in the fields to cleanse her of thinking about Ewan and thunderstorms and his little nursery rhyme songs. Or even how much her son would enjoy them if he could hear the lyrics.

She wanted to strike at her chest and banish this foolishness. She should've given Mathew all the room in her heart, but she hadn't. Ewan was still in there.

Despairing, she pointed her gig to the tributaries that fed all the fields—Tradenwood's and Grandbole's. The main artery to the Fitzwilliam's flowers had been dammed with limestone bricks. Ewan hadn't lied and Lester was a bigger skunk than she'd realized.

Shutting off the water was wrong, no matter what they had done to her. Lester had no right to do this without her permission.

Driving one fist into her palm, she decided she must do something. But what?

Nothing. If she went against him, he'd take Philip. Lester was his guardian. His word would overrule hers in the courtroom of men. She couldn't fix this until she and Philip were free.

The same sense of helplessness that made her check on her son every hour for fever invaded her soul. She bit her lip, to hold in the frustration she'd wanted to yell out last night, and stared ahead at the lonely limestone wall. It was as isolated as a widow, as a woman trying hard to hold on to everything.

"Coming to inspect your handiwork?"

She lifted her head and saw Ewan walking toward her. She hid her dismay behind a smile. "Morning. Needed to see this for myself. Fitzwilliams are proven liars, don't you know."

"That is ungenerous, Cousin."

"Good day, Ghost."

She turned her gig around and kept an even pace. Not slow enough to be caught but not fast enough to show fear. Ewan was a minor complication to her plans, a thorn in her floral arrangement. Lying must be contagious because now she was lying to her soul about Ewan being anything minor to her.

Willow neighed and clomped to the highest point, the place where Theodosia could see all the fields, hers and Philip's.

Her breath froze a little in her lungs as gratitude fell upon her. These fields had saved her life. She'd met Mathew here when she'd been broken and scared. He had protected her, fed her starving body.

To prove her love, she'd protect his fields as he had protected her and Philip. No ghost or Lester would wrest this place from her. Mathew had wanted it to be Philip's. Theodosia needed to make his last request come true, for he'd been the instrument to make her hopes true. "I'm sorry. Mathew, I—"

"Morning again, Mrs. Cecil." Ewan's sultry voice sounded again, heavy and soothing. "I hate to see a beautiful woman alone in such a picturesque place."

Her heart skipped a little. Then she remembered. They were at war. He swung a walking stick as if he were on a carefree stroll. But his top hat had been smashed onto his thick black hair. He'd run to catch up with her. She almost laughed, but she didn't know how she liked the thought of him pursuing her again.

"So what brings you here? Thinking of poisoning the Grandbole fields? Oh, I know. You are looking for that next husband. Am I interrupting a get-together?" He cupped his eyes and scanned. "Your new love is late? You must have quite a few advertisement responses to choose from not just... Who was it? Just a baron? My new wealthy cousin must have others writing to her. A duke in bad straights. Maybe a pauper prince in need of a healthy fortune?"

"Will you forget about my newspaper advertisement? It has nothing to do with you or us."

"It has everything to do with us. We are family now, Cousin Theo."

She bit her lip, hating that he knew of her gamble to find a husband. "Stay to the left, Ghost. You don't want to be on Cecil land. I'd hate to add fines to your fees."

"Grumpy? Only ghosts should be grumpy. Maybe you need a walk to refresh yourself. You have shadows under your eyes. That conscience you're suppressing is rattling you. Or is it my ghostly chains?" He held a hand to her as if to help her down. "You need to walk. I don't bite, much."

He *would* notice that she hadn't slept. How could she, with Philip in pain? But to take Ewan's hand, and depend upon his humor or anything he offered, that couldn't be. "I'm safe—I'm fine here."

His brow rose a smidgen, followed by a broad smile that

someone stupid would think charming. He pulled his arm back and wiped his fingers on his bulky black jacket, very different from his smart cut of yesterday. "Yes, you are, and scared of me, too."

"No, I am not, Ewan."

He stuck his palm out to her again. "Prove you're not afraid of ghosts."

It was dumb to accept his challenge and clasp his fingers. Dumber to let him lift her down to the ground. The dumbest thing was assuming he'd be a gentleman. He crowded her against her gig, with nowhere to run but deeper into his arms.

Brushing a fallen curl from her temple, he made his crooked grin bigger. "Cousin Cecil, have you thought of a more reasonable extortion? Maybe you do have some sense of charity."

She lifted her hands to push away from him but that would be touching him, something stronger than she. Instead she lowered her hands and braced for whatever he had in mind.

"So tense, Cousin." He gave her tired shoulders a little press. "Give me a reasonable offer so I can bring you relief. I could present it today and end this little family problem of the water. I'll assume selling Tradenwood is still off-limits."

"Yes, and why don't you rescind your blackmail? I might be more inclined to charity without your play nonsense."

He clasped her fingers. His other arm came up behind her, smoothing each bone in her wilting spine. "You need to relax, like you used to do." Changing the pressure of his fingertips, he spun her like a top as he used to do in the rain. "Has your dancing improved? I hear Cecil was rather old. He might not have had time for such trivial things."

"Let me go, Ewan. This is ridiculous with no music," she said, between twirls.

Her gripped her about the waist and waltzed her around

her gig. "Always music in my head, when I'm with you."

Willow neighed and kicked her hooves, making a rhythm that Ewan seemed to adopt. For a moment, she let the memories, the ones locked away in her heart, leach out. Closing her eyes, they were young again, sneaking behind the coaching house. Ewan had purloined a bucket of oats for her old mare and had made her sit in the shade as he read her Shakespeare. It was her favorite remembrance next to hearing Ewan's heartbeat, his lips mouthing *I love you*.

"Your dancing has improved, Cousin," he said as he kissed her hand. "But it seems we are at an impasse. I call blackmail protecting my family from the woman bent on destroying it. You call it fines. What would the late Mathew Cecil think of you allowing the agreement between the two sides of the family to dissolve into bickering? I didn't believe you to be so petty. I remember you caring about people."

He dared to bring Mathew into this foolishness. She moved away, as if she'd done something naughty dancing with him, and scampered back atop her gig.

"Oh, Cousin, you don't have to run off. We were getting along."

Picking up the horse whip, she rolled it between her fingertips, then let the temptation to strike him and his teasing settle down. The old Theodosia didn't think, always forgot about consequences. She placed the snappy pole across her knees. "I think Daddy's been feeding you lies. Doesn't look like he's fed you much else. You look a little thin."

His lips pursed. Those blue eyes, big and full of stories and dreams tucked behind his long dark lashes, winked at her. "Ghosts need to be thin. That's how we slip about. But you've eaten well, if your rounded cheeks are any indication."

Ewan stood on tiptoes, and his hot gaze roamed over her. "And you still fit well in my arms. I suppose getting a rich *loving* husband was good for you."

He peered at her again and his gaze seemed to penetrate through her thick shawl. For once, she was grateful for the heaviness of her mourning robes. "You possess a very well-rounded figure. Yes, my cousin must have been very pleased with you, an apt mistress you made. I'm not ignorant to how this love began with Cecil."

The way he put it made her feel dirty. "Must you be crude? Or maybe that's what you bounders do. You convince a woman of your love, only to deflower her. How wrong I was to believe the words of a playwright. *I love you. We'll elope after the storm passes.*"

He looked down and kicked a rock with his boot. "I shouldn't make fun of such things. It is so hard to imagine you—vibrant-spirit-filled—with my cousin. They say he was very old. Very old."

Ewan took the reins of her gig from her. "The strap is not slack enough at the rein ring. You'll do too much work pulling. The horse won't go any faster. I'll adjust it for you, like I used to do."

She watched his fingers work the straps, sliding fastenings, loosening sections, until it was at whatever tautness he felt was perfect for her, looking after her like he always had. Six years and Ewan still remembered. He had taken care of her, not with flashy things but in the smallest ways—a bucket of oats for her horse, adjusting her gig, a comforting rhyme.

He put the leather in her hands. "Was Cecil good to you?"

An odd question but he sounded sincere. How much did he still care?

A scream came from deep in her fields.

Ewan turned, cupping his hand to his eyes. "I think someone's fainted."

He started moving into her lavender fields.

Theodosia jumped down and followed. Which one of her workers could it be?

They pushed through stalks and fresh clippings and came upon an older woman. It was one of her tenants. Dropping to her knees, she fanned the woman's cheeks. "Mrs. Gutter, wake up."

Ewan bent and grabbed the picker's wrist. "She has a pulse. You know this person?"

Ignoring such a stupid question, Theodosia took off the picker's bonnet and waved it faster and faster over the stricken woman's countenance. "I know all my workers, and Mrs. Gutter's a stubborn one. She should have waited another week or two. She's been very sick these past few months. She should've started early morning when it's cooler."

Mrs. Gutter sat up and yawned, as if she'd taken a nap. Her ruddy cheeks seemed even redder upon her ashy gray skin. "I thought I was fine, Mrs. Cecil, but I do have a thick head so I don't listen." She tried to sit, but fell back. "I'm so sorry, ma'am. Give me a minute. I don't mean to cause no problems."

Theodosia took off her gloves and stashed them in her pocket. "Silly, who means to faint? May I see if you have a fever? I'll have to touch your forehead."

The old woman nodded and allowed Theodosia's dark hand to brush her pale forehead.

Mrs. Gutter felt warm, warmer than merely picking under the bright sun. "You do have a fever. Come with me. Mr. Fitzwilliam, help me get this woman to my carriage."

"Nonsense," Mrs. Gutter said. "I just need to catch my breath."

Theodosia grabbed Ewan's hand and put it under Mrs. Gutter's shoulder. "We need to get her back to Tradenwood and get her something to drink. I need your help."

Ewan pumped Theo's fingers. "I will always be here to help you. My return is permanent. You can count on me." He held Theodosia's hand a moment longer then turned to Mrs.

Gutter. "Ma'am, Theo—Mrs. Cecil is right. You need to go with her."

"Let me take you back to the main house." Hating the pleading tone in her voice, she shook free from Ewan. "The doctor is coming today, Mrs. Gutter. It would be no trouble for him to see you, too."

Ewan captured Theodosia's elbow and hovered over her as if to detect weakness. "Doctor? The shadows under your eyes. Are you well?"

She looked down to the rich soil, away from the bluer-than-blue eyes that had sent prickles up her skin when she'd first seen him, first spoken to him, in Grandbole's fields. Like they had this morning, dancing on the hill.

"Cousin Theo, you would tell me if you were not well?"

Must be the concern in his voice that sent a shiver now. "Fine. I'm fine. Mrs. Gutter is the one who is not. Help me get her to my gig."

Mrs. Gutter wheezed, but shook her head.

"No, my angel. I'm fine now. My son will be back any moment now with my cart." Mrs. Gutter gasped and sucked in a huge mouth of air. "He went to water the horse."

The lady was too big to pick up and carry to her gig. Theo needed to depend on the one man she couldn't. Swallowing doubts and bitter pride, she asked, "Please help me, Ewan? I need you."

Ewan didn't move, and his gaze upon her felt heavier than before. "You heard the lady, Mrs. Gutter. I'm not accustomed to denying one's request."

Did he see her as a lady now, not some lucky mistress, or was he talking about six years ago when she'd been stupid and had loved him more than herself. Theodosia put a hand to her bosom. Her cheeks felt heated like she'd leaned over flames. "Mrs. Gutter, I need you to allow Mr. Fitzwilliam to put you in my gig. Your son can meet you at Tradenwood."

"Fitzwilliam? Never. Leave me to dirt. I'm not disloyal to you, ma'am."

She couldn't stop the smile growing. Maybe Ewan would realize how awful his father would be to the tenants, if she sold to Lord Crisdon. She tucked the woman's hat under her arm. "Mrs. Gutter, you couldn't be disloyal, ever."

Ewan's eyes told another story. They still seemed to be on Theodosia and they held fire. "Consider this an act of chivalry, not disloyalty. I'm sure Mrs. Cecil could tell you the difference." He lifted the woman in the air as if the portly picker weighed nothing, maybe a shilling's worth of foolscap.

Theodosia stopped gawking and, in her haste, her shawl dropped from her shoulders and tangled in the bushes. As she yanked it free, it wrapped around her feet.

His chortle from behind grated. "Do you need a little help, my dear cousin?"

She sped up, intending to get out of his reach, but the shawl dragged more and this time she stumbled.

Before she hit the ground, Ewan grabbed her arm, jerking her up. Then he seized her about her waist, pulling her into his chest, steadying her. His baggy jacket hid pure muscle underneath.

He didn't release her, forcing her to absorb his heat, his light scent of musk, the entire way back to her gig, all while supporting Mrs. Gutter in his other arm.

Back on the smooth dirt road, Ewan released Theodosia then swung Mrs. Gutter into the seat. Then he worked a strong hand about the middle of Theodosia's back. "Now it's your turn."

The ghost levitated her in the air. Hard, lean, chiseled hands hoisted her onto the platform to drive.

"Thank you." It was all she could muster. He was too close, too strong, and the heat of the day had surely made her weak. How could she keep contempt for Ewan in her head when his arms felt of safety, something she'd missed since Mathew's death?

All smiles, as if he knew he'd addled her brainbox, he leaned over the side. "Even a ghost can be helpful, but we return to haunting, if agreements aren't met."

If not for her pride or Mrs. Gutter's watchful eyes, she'd let him know that ghosts needed to die painful, horrible deaths. But that would be impossible to do to a true ghost or the wily Ewan Fitzwilliam. He had to be tough, if Napoleon hadn't done him in. "Nice to know you finally found your strength. Six years too late. Go home to Daddy. Tell him of your big adventure."

"No, I'll keep it a secret, but I will take the liberty of checking on Mrs. Gutter. I want to know this doctor's report, Cousin."

She gripped the reins tightly and rippled them, forcing Willow into a full run. The horse left him swallowing dust with each high kick.

"Dear, don't let a Fitzwilliam bother you. They think they own everything and they love to get into everyone's business. But you're Mrs. Cecil and everyone knows you to be fair and honest, just like the great man."

She nodded, but kept her eyes on the lane. Six years could change things. From a mistress to a wife. From a thief stealing flowers and food to one who owned the flowers and food. What had the six years changed in Ewan?

And would he change again if he knew the doctor's full report about Tradenwood's inhabitants? That must never, ever happen. Her son couldn't be caught in any more of these rows. "We'll be to the house soon."

Mrs. Gutter smiled and closed her eyes.

How was Theodosia to keep Ewan from popping up and finding out her greatest secret? As he had done in his play, he'd use it to destroy her.

. . .

Ewan rapped at Tradenwood's front door and waited for entry. The day had slipped away. Only a few hours of daylight remained, and from his frequent trips to the patio off Grandbole's library, he couldn't get a good view of the comings and goings down here, which meant he couldn't tell if a doctor had arrived or if one had left. All he knew was that the not-knowing had become maddening.

Before he knocked again, he stopped, lifted his top hat, and raked a hand through his hair. A piece of demolished porcelain Dresden fell to his boots, a parting gift from Jasper's girls for rushing off from Grandbole more quickly than they wanted.

His nieces, blessed demons, had started an endless series of pranks. The cuteness and questions offered with cherub smiles was an act. They were little masterminds, pranking anything that moved. Starting with swapping the sugar for salt, to more dangerous things like falling Dresden.

He touched his head again, searching for blood or scars. He had enough of both.

Satisfied that he had no new injury, he again knocked at Tradenwood's door.

Why was a doctor visiting? Six years could change a great deal. He now had a chest full of scars, aches that followed him into the cold winters. What could be wrong with Theo?

For a final time, he took up the brass loop on the door and knocked. No answer still. Should he look to get in by climbing a tree as Jasper and he had done when they were kids?

The door opened and Pickens came outside, pulling the massive frame shut, as if Ewan would sneak inside behind him. "Mr. Fitzwilliam, I need you to go away. The family is having no visitors today."

"I am family. I came to see my cousin, Widow Cecil."

"Is there something I can help you with, sir?" Pickens came down a step. His hushed tone continued. "She's not taking visitors, sir."

"Nonsense. She'll see me."

The butler's frown deepened as he shook his head. "No. No, she won't. She left specific instructions."

He felt like a caricature of his youngest niece parroting words. "Left?"

Gripping his lapel of his liveries, the powdered-haired man nodded. "No visitors."

Ewan turned and started down the steps, but he couldn't taste any satisfaction with these answers. Not a pinch. Something was wrong. He stopped and faced the butler. "Pickens. Did Mrs. Gutter need more help? Is that why Mrs. Cecil went?"

The older man stared at him, maybe even huffed. "Mrs. Gutter is well. A bit of punch and she was as good as new."

Something did not add up, and the way that Theo liked numbers, he knew things were amiss. Drawing up his coat as the wind shifted, Ewan's temper grew hotter. "I ask again to see Mrs. Cecil. Why are you pretending she is not here?"

"I'm hoping you'll tire and go back up the hill. The mistress is getting some much-needed sleep, but you'll wake up the late Master Cecil with your ruckus."

The butler was trying to get him to leave. Why? Much-needed sleep. It was obvious. She had shadows under her eyes. "Pickens, is she well?"

"You need to go home." The butler turned and marched back to the top of the steps.

Ewan had to stop him, had to know about Theo. "Pickens, you worked for my uncle and my mother's father. You remember who I am. I should know about this. This is family."

The man stopped but didn't turn. "Yes, I remember you, Ewan Fitzwilliam. You were your uncle's favorite. He grieved hard when he thought you'd died, but he was also quite fond of Mr. Cecil. Cecil knew what family meant."

"My concern for the widow is true. I am her family now, even if it is by marriage. I should know."

Pickens peered over his shoulder with a look of scorn. "Does a Fitzwilliam know the meaning of family, unless it's convenient?"

Ewan hadn't expected that moment of truth. There wasn't much to rebut in Pickens's words. He shifted his stance. "I see you've adopted Mrs. Cecil's quick tongue."

"Sir, I've worked at Tradenwood for many years. I've seen more than I'll ever admit to remembering. Your family was not kind to Mrs. Cecil. They did not even acknowledge the master's death."

The tension and the truth becoming utterly unbearable, Ewan put a hand to his neck. "They do hold grudges. I don't think they approved of her marriage."

"The new mistress of Tradenwood is worth the title, and she deserves her privacy. If you *remember* anything of the widow from six years ago, she does things when she is good and ready."

The way he said *remember* indicated Pickens knew more. Did she tell that wizened-face butler that Ewan had ruined himself over Theo before she had attracted Cecil?

"The Mistress of Tradenwood is stubborn. I do remember that. It is still sort of galling to call her that, knowing how my mother, Lady Crisdon, wanted this estate."

"Your uncle chose not to leave it to her, but to Cecil. Now, Tradenwood is the widow Cecil's. Hers and her heir's."

Heirs? Could that be it? Was this sickness and doctors about Theo being with child? If so, she hadn't been devoted to Cecil any more than she had been to him. Had she hopped into bed with the next fool and was now with child? That had to be why she needed a new husband—to hide a pregnancy. "Her heirs?"

"Yes. Cecil didn't want the extended family to harass his wife."

The concern Ewan had started to feel for her was for naught. She hadn't changed her ways, despite the teasing fun of dancing with her or the warmth her claiming his hand in the fields had generated. His insides sickened, twisting with new frustration. "So much for hoping she'd changed. Good evening, Pickens."

That furrowed brow of the old man rose. "I hope she doesn't change. Never was a kinder or gentler soul. Good day, sir."

The door thudded closed.

Ewan walked away. Anger pressed on his lungs, making him pant as he paced. The lecture from the butler maligning his family was probably true. The fact that Tradenwood was Theo's, that was true. The jealousy and angst he felt over Theo, of not knowing of her health or if she carried another man's child, was true.

The reason for his current misery—unfinished feelings for Theo—that had to be a lie. If only he could convince himself that he was as over her as he had in writing his play. He took a few more steps and fought the urge to return, to find that tree, and see if it would hold his weight. He needed to stop lying to himself. He wasn't finished with Theo. That was his truth.

Chapter Seven

Pranks & Prose

Ewan stormed to his bedchamber door at Grandbole Manor, swiping at the cold liquid dripping from his face. He'd visited Tradenwood several more times in the past week only to be turned away by Pickens.

Theo didn't want to see him. He had no way of knowing if she were sick with an illness or suffering from the sickness that came from the changes pregnancy brought. He dabbed at his forehead, which felt sticky and ridiculous and blue.

He was wrong to expect the woman he had tried to buy off and scandalize in a play to tell him anything of a personal nature.

But that didn't stop him from wanting to know. It also didn't stop him from remembering the feel of her in his arms. Why did she still wind him up so tight? And who had Theo become these six years—the landlord whom all her tenants and servants loved? Was she the frugal business woman who knew all the figures? Was she an honorable widow?

The way she had forgotten herself when they'd danced—

had she felt as he did, excited, wistful, or lonely? He swiped at his sticky fingers and tried to stop thinking about *her heirs*. Had that sense of isolation made her break her customary twelve months of mourning? Had it caused her to take a secret lover? She didn't look as if she was going to pop, so a new birth would be well beyond the time a child could be claimed as Cecil's.

Only a legitimate child could inherit. Lord knew, his mother and the earl would protest. Why would she be so reckless? He put a hand to his eye, his blue hand to his blue, now stinging, eye. He'd created a complete story for Theo without any shred of facts. His playwright mind needed to slow. And his face needed to stop stinging.

"Uncle?"

Blinking, Ewan turned toward the low, squeaky voice. "Yes, Lucy."

She fingered her snowy dress, which had indigo droplets on the hem and ribbon-trimmed bodice. "Are you much hurt?"

"No. You and your sisters didn't kill me this time."

She looked down and held her arms behind her back. "Does this mean you won't go away?"

There was a sad quality to the voice. Someone that small should be dancing to angel music. He stooped low to catch her gaze. "I have a place in the city. But you haven't frightened me so much that I will be gone forever."

A smile burst between two cherry cheeks. "I don't want you to go. No one visits anymore since Mama left and Lady Crisdon won't come back."

His playwright mind didn't need to write this story. It was obvious. The children were lonely and misbehaving for attention. In true Fitzwilliam style, their fits could be extremely pain-filled and somewhat lethal. "Come here, little one."

He offered a hug and she held tightly, even if he were squishy and blue. "Your uncle is pretty tough."

He released her and she now had indigo splotched all over. "But don't keep trying my patience. Let your sisters know."

The moppet nodded. "At least you are not frowning. Your lips have been sad for a week."

He stood up straight. "Well, sometimes being an adult is sad."

"Then I want no part of it." She swung her head side to side, her blonde locks bouncing as she walked away.

Maybe Theo was as sad at this adult business as he. Maybe this love she claimed for Cecil was an act or a very good exaggeration. Would her pride let her admit it? Well, a baby for the widow would be a statement to the contrary. That made Ewan chuckle. Finding humor at her predicament was wrong, even if it proved Ewan right. No, he wasn't good at this adult thing.

What would it take for her to confess her regrets? Just one. And if she did, would that change the war between the families, or his feelings about her?

As surely as the muck drenching his collar, he couldn't take another day not knowing the truth. Maybe he should be more like a ghost and stop asking permission to haunt.

He grabbed the doorknob but stopped. The girls could've set another trap. He bucked up his spine, refusing to be terrorized by children, and females at that. He'd been to war, taken a bullet and metal shards to the chest. Yet, here he stood, as anxious as a rat in a field of wild cats. What if a pail of dye or dung awaited on the other side to drop upon him?

Shaking his head, he threw the door open, waited a minute, then barreled inside.

"Brother?"

Jasper's voice startled him and Ewan spun with fists raised

to see the man sitting in his window with his feet up. "I needed to talk with you in private. Didn't mean to spook you."

"No, you have your daughters for that." Ewan moved to his basin and dipped his hands in the water until they were clean. "So you are sitting in my room waiting. I mean, this room Lord Crisdon has let me use?"

Jasper rolled two pieces of sealed paper between his large fingers. "Yes. I hold a message from Mr. Brown. He's waiting to see your play today. He sent a rather impatient note. Is there a reason for your delay?"

The theater manager. Ewan had forgotten about that, so involved with Theo and the water wars. "I could see him today, but not blue. I'll need to change and borrow your gig again, if you don't mind."

"Of course not. If you are willing to return, you can borrow it as much as you like." The big man chortled with too much glee. "With your enhanced coloring, it's no wonder if my children's behavior doesn't push you out the door."

Ewan walked over to the chest of drawers looking at his choices in shirts, ones the earl had made for him. "Your girls are a handful. Aren't they supposed to be, as Southey said, made of sugar and spice, not antics?"

His brother chuckled as he picked up a glass that sat near his hip and took a sip. He waved the second letter as if his brow had fevered, then took another hungry gulp from his crystal goblet.

More liquor? And so early in the morning?

As if Jasper could read his thoughts, he put down his drink. "You mean Southey, the poet laureate. Ah, you and your love of poets. The girls are trying to get your attention. They will settle down once I've secured a stepmother for them."

Pulling off his ruined coat, Ewan shrugged, then untied his cravat. "Seems to me they need your attention or discipline more. Have they had it?"

Jasper's gaze lowered. He seized his glass, sloshing it with a rapid swing of his arm, but he didn't guzzle. "What are you implying?"

"I've noticed..." Ewan wanted to say "drink," but couldn't, so he softened and started again. "You disappear a lot. Maybe they act out to get more of your time."

Putting down his brandy, Jasper harrumphed then slapped a hand on the sill, the movement causing the folded note to jostle. "You've deduced this after two weeks? Your attention to family care doesn't speak well. Not sure I should be taking advice from someone who's been away almost six years. You don't know them."

Ewan wanted to say something ungenerous, such as, his brother didn't seem to know them very well either, and he'd *been* here the past six years. Instead, he pulled his shirt over his head and said, "I'm merely wondering at their behavior. Their pranks could hurt someone."

His brother took another long drink. Then he slammed down the nearly empty glass. "Didn't you snicker when they swapped Father's sugar for salt? The man blanched over his ruined tea."

"Their antics were amusing, at first. Who doesn't love seeing the earl turn beet red? And it was a joy seeing you move at the speed of a fleet stallion to prevent another Fitzwilliam prized Wedgwood from falling to the ground." Ewan pivoted away from his brother whose lips formed a droopy frown.

Reaching into the closet, Ewan smoothed his fingers over the nap of a smartly cut jacket and matching waistcoat of dark blue. "Lord Crisdon has fine taste. His bribes are the best."

"He wants you to be comfortable as you stay. He also wants to know if you've made any progress in your negotiations with Cecil's widow."

Ewan spun, his shirt barely clearing his head. "He knows I've been trying to see her. Has she sent any papers for the water lease?"

His brother's grin returned, making him the happy-go-lucky fellow everyone knew. "She hasn't sent anything. And Father hasn't said anything of a meeting. But your willingness to stay at Grandbole and the now-missing lavender package set my conspiratorial mind to work. A lucky inquiry to the merchants at the Burlington Arcade, the ones who sell that particular type of lavender soap, produced a familiar name, Cecil. I took a guess that you returned the parcel to Widow Cecil, our family's nemesis."

Jasper's eyes narrowed as if he were trying to see through him.

Then Ewan realized, with his shirt askew, the ten-inch nest of scars to his chest were visible. He started to yank the linen down as if covering nakedness, but he stilled his hand. He was half dressed, decent enough for a brother. "Yes, I returned the package. We spoke several times. Now she's refusing to see me. She's stubborn."

"Those look terrible."

The wounds from the field surgery were horrid, jagged, and bulbous. He'd grown used to them but not to how others reacted. Must be a shock for Jasper to see the aftermath of war. Probably more so for Theo. He'd pressed her finger to them, and she'd known his chest to be smooth.

It was days ago, but the anguish in her voice at his pain nested in his chest, alongside his wounds. She had truly thought him dead. But none of that sentiment would matter once a rich man caught her eye. They mattered even less with her new predicament, or she'd allow his visit.

"They are terrible, Jasper. All scars are."

His brother nodded and raised his glass in an invisible toast. The sun through the window cast amber diamonds onto the deep chestnut-stained floors, sad rainbows on the gray walls. "Sorry, Ewan."

Tying a new, starched cravat, Ewan stood straight. "Rather terrible than dead. Brother, why do so many pickers and tenants rave about Cousin Cecil? And his widow?"

Jasper set down the empty goblet, then shifted his feet along the floor. "Father is all about business. Cecil gave better terms to lease, and he also allowed women to pick his fields at advantageous terms. And those glass hothouses they've installed, well, they outdo us with exotic flowers available all year 'round. They've even grown pineapples in there."

Being better at business didn't answer all Ewan's questions. It certainly didn't explain all the love that seemed to shroud Theo now. Maybe being married to a demi-god had made her one, too? How would she fare with all her secrets exposed? "It seems to be more than that."

"Perhaps. But why don't you tell me how you know Mrs. Cecil other than a happenstance meeting at Burlington Arcade?"

Ewan put his back to his brother and finished dressing. "Why don't you tell me? You're the one with all the good guesses and conspiracies."

Something tugged at his collar, righting it. A scent of brandy took possession of the air. His brother now stood behind him fussing and pulling at Ewan's borrowed jacket. From the smell, Jasper had been drinking a lot, but he still seemed steady.

"So what is she to you, Ewan? An old acquaintance?"

"For a big man, you're light on your feet, even when sotted. I'll have to remember that."

Jasper settled a large palm onto Ewan's shoulder, but not a chuckle sounded. "I was away with Maria's laying-in for Lucy. They say you became involved with a low woman. Is Cecil's widow that Jezebel?"

Whatever Ewan thought of Theo, he didn't like Jasper calling her names. He gripped his brother's hand hard and flung it away. "She wasn't low when I knew her."

He turned and caught Jasper's brow cocked, one eye raised. "Ewan, she's a Blackamoor. From all accounts, illegitimate, with no money or connections at the time you were involved with her. What were you thinking?"

"I wasn't thinking. Not a thought about you, the heir in-waiting, or of anything Lord Crisdon held dear. I thought about me, about someone valuing me and what I wanted. And it didn't matter her origin or her connections. Only her love. Well, I thought it was love."

Jasper's lips parted then closed. He nodded and stepped backward. "I see. And she knew you were without fortune?"

"Yes. Not a dime to my name. Just a play to peddle. She didn't seem to care. We had a silly notion of building a life together, once I returned from war."

His brother went back to his perch in the window, picking up the folded letter by the edge, as if it were too delicate to sit upon, and leaned back. He eyed his empty glass as if it was the goblet's fault that it sat drained. "What happened?"

"Like everything else. The announcement a month after deploying that I had died set off the actions that changed everything—the loss of Tradenwood and her. She didn't mourn me and seems to have become Cecil's mistress before news of my living could spread. You'd think she'd have grieved a month or two, the way she appears to mourn Cecil."

Scooping up his ruined shirt and jacket, he sighed again. "I left her to go to the war. She didn't wait for me to return. This isn't a new story for a soldier, even if I am a Fitzwilliam."

"You must ask her why."

Dropping the clothes back onto the floor, Ewan locked his arms behind his back. "It doesn't matter her reasons. She found a rich man, my cousin, who made her wealthy."

He gazed at Jasper, hoping the man would stop. He could be as bad as their father when hunting for information.

Ewan moved to the mirror at the edge of the canopy bed and whipped a hand through his hair to right his blue-tinged locks. "Hopefully, the theater will be dark tonight. I'd hate to lose this opportunity because of stained hair. But I've done my mother's bidding; I asked for a price to sell Tradenwood. Mrs. Cecil won't. I've also asked for a new lease. She's come back with 20,000 pounds per annum, a ridiculous amount. I suspect once my play is purchased, she'll see the light. She won't want her good name ruined."

Jasper slapped his knee and leaned on the window as he erupted in laughs. "She's in your play? You've written her in as one of the hilarious characters? Oh no. She's that Cleo, no Theo the Flower Seller. Oh, what a clever form of blackmail. Lord Crisdon will be proud. He'll pay for the theater, maybe even handbills, to watch her disgrace."

Ewan rubbed at a spot of paint on his knuckle, dabbing it with a handkerchief. "Don't say anything of her being in my play. Let him know I will get her consent. If she agrees to my terms, I want to live up to my end of the bargain. I am a man of my word. The earl would still want to ruin her name."

"True, but I'm surprised you care. You still do care, don't you?"

Not wanting to search too deeply into his scarred soul for the answers, he scooped up the letter. "I suppose you need my help with a new marital prospect from the newspaper. Your matrimonial chase continues. Another woman to court?"

"No, the same one. The one we sent our rhyme. Seems she's had time to respond."

Oh, no. Theo had responded, giving Jasper new hope. If his brother found out this advertisement was Theo's, his spirits would be crushed. Ewan should tell him straightaway, but the look in his eye—slightly desperate, slightly hoping—would become more troubled. That could not happen. He'd find a way to spare Jasper any more pain. "So what does the mystery woman say?"

"Go on, open it."

Ewan did. The letter wasn't a short few sentences. It was three paragraphs. "Well, it seems our advertisement bride has answered with a resounding yes. She loves children and details how they need good, moral examples." *That is rich coming from Theo.* "She sounds like she liked our little rhyme. I'll take credit for that. She admires that we would even take a child's needs into consideration."

Ewan stumbled at the third paragraph. It pierced his jaded heart.

Jasper rocked and coughed, as if to draw Ewan's attention. "What else does she say?"

"She talks of the sacrifices that one should make for a child, especially a sickly child." If Theodosia wasn't pregnant now, then those doctors were for her heir, a child who lived now, out of the womb. So maybe she wasn't scandalous but a blasted dutiful wife and mother? Had Theodosia borne Cecil a babe? And was that child sick?

He rubbed at his eyes and paced a moment, hoping to have read something wrong. He'd been in Tradenwood. She'd never introduced him to her child. But, why would she? He'd threatened her with scandal in his play. He'd accused her of trying to ruin his side of the family with the water leases. "She must have a child, one that's not well."

Jasper folded his arms, as if he was in deep thought. "That wasn't what I hoped for. Sometimes people don't get well."

A chill set in Ewan's skin. It wasn't what he hoped either. He'd rather Theo prove herself scandalous than with a suffering child, but a child to an old man could be sickly. She should've grieved a little longer and not taken up with old Cecil. Now she seemed like a good woman who'd fallen for his cousin and gave the man a child. No, that is not what he wanted at all.

He pounded his palms together as if that could warm him. "I still don't know why a woman of means would seek a marriage of convenience by newspaper?"

"Companionship. And as I need someone to mother my girls, she may need someone to father her child."

Still made no sense, nor warrant all the secrecy and doctor visits. Ewan closed his eyes and allowed memories of Theo to haunt him, unvarnished by his own disappointments and jealousy. She had been shy, except when selling flowers. It had taken time to make her comfortable, to see her laugh. They were supposed to elope and had gotten caught in the thunderstorm. She had been skittish and so unsure of herself. But she'd trusted him and had given into the love that bound them. Then his father had discovered them and their plans had changed.

Had Cecil seen her and pursued her, too? Had he been patient and found a way to make her love him? He'd never thought of that possibility. He'd believed Crisdon when he'd told him that she'd become a mistress and disappeared. Fitzwilliam half-truths had struck again. He moved to his desk and fingered the pile of papers, the play that branded her a harlot. Ewan felt shamed.

His brother interrupted his musings. "I hadn't thought of being a father to anyone else's children. Is that selfish?"

"Jasper, I'm no one to judge selfishness." He dragged his thumb over the edge of the pages.

Theo had to have truly cared for Cecil to give him a child. Maybe she'd loved Cecil as she claimed. That stung more than it should. Fuming on the inside, surely his guts turned black. Ewan read the third paragraph again, and again. "It definitely sounds as if she is a mother and to a sickly child. Do you want that? To father a child who is not well?"

Jasper took the letter back. "I've done sickbed duty before. It's not something I want, but I can't let this lady go.

You must help me win her. I think she's the one. This is what I need for the girls. You've seen them. They need a caring mother. I'm failing them, Ewan. That's why they act out."

Ewan loved his brother, but he needed to give him a dose a truth. "The girls don't need a stepmother. They need more of you."

Looking to the ceiling, maybe counting the dark beams, Jasper was quiet, neither agreeing or disagreeing. Then he said, "You are always good at noticing things. You want to take care of things, but there is no more of me. Half of me is in the crypt with Maria. I'm doing what I can. Ewan, please stay at Grandbole. Come back here when your business in Town is done. Help me win advertisement number four. Ask her to meet. I am ready to paper this deal with solicitors."

A marriage contract? Ewan couldn't have that. As bad as it had been for Theo to marry his rich cousin and have a child with him, it was worse thinking of Theo with Jasper. Though her money might even make the earl welcome her with open arms, Jasper couldn't be what she needed. He still grieved Maria too much to be good to Theo. She needed more. But how much more?

One thing he did know, he had to make sure his brother never met this newspaper bride. "Jasper, you still don't know if you will like her. She could be playing on your sympathy. I'll pen a response and deliver it to her box today. You shouldn't meet with her until you are sure of her. The girls need you to be sure. If she writes back again, then you know she has passed all our tests. What she looks like won't matter so much, if her character is beyond reproach."

Vanity surely winning, Jasper nodded. "You are right. I still don't know what she looks like. She could be a rich hag. Or not so rich and more so hag. What will you ask her?"

"It will come to me, Brother."

Jasper moved to the door. "You are the best. And you

will return here?"

"Yes, after delivering the note to Burlington Arcade, a dash to my own residence to gather my own clothes, and a meeting at the theater. Mr. Brown, the theater manager, needs to read through my play before making a decision. He said he'd know in a week. Once I've dropped it off, I will return here. Then we will wait for your widow's response together."

Smiling, Jasper handed him the letter. "I've missed you, Ewan. You've always had a way to make things not seem so bad, calming and reassuring, for a younger brother." The man stepped back, picked up his goblet, then wobbled out of the room.

Ewan's conscience roared, stabbing a bit at his gut. He'd do his best to make things good for Jasper, but his brother couldn't have Theo. Shaking his head, he looked at the foolscap again. This was her hand, steady with a curly E. Someone may have helped her. From what he remembered, she could read a little and write short notes, like, *I love you, Ewan. I'll meet you, Ewan. I'll wait for you, Ewan.*

But six years and means changed things. Why did she need a newspaper groom? She could still be all these things and pregnant.

He shook his head of foolhardy conspiracies and determined to draft something cute to appease his brother, but something that Theo would never answer.

It would have to be something difficult. Something transparent, something that singed her fingertips with its nakedness.

Then it came to him. He needed to hear of her regrets. Proud Theo wouldn't dare answer.

But what if she did?

Would she tell a stranger from a newspaper advertisement the answers to questions she'd never offer to him?

Chapter Eight

A Field of Truth

Theodosia bristled on her patio. Her weeklong list of busywork tasks had come to an end and with it the excuses to miss the night at the theater with her friends.

Her quick morning jaunt and several gold coins had secured the parish bells to ring for the festival. Hopefully, the wives of the merchants and pickers whom she'd hosted in her parlor would keep their word about inviting musicians and other cart vendors. Perhaps Mathew would hear the horns from heaven. How nice that would be.

With her shears, she trimmed the clematis and tucked each of the new runners about the trellis. The blooms were secure, the female and male plantings held hands as Mathew had ordained.

Maybe if she repotted her rosebush that would eat up more time. She could check on Philip. Then she'd check on him again. He was well, learning from his governess. No pain today for him, probably none tonight.

Not a single reason to delay this outing. Deep down she

wanted one, something to stay close to Tradenwood. Even the faithful gray storm clouds appeared too small. The short rain storm hadn't lasted, leaving nothing but humidity. She took a breath of the heavy air. It wasn't enough to beg off, much too little to stop Frederica's pouts.

Theodosia wrenched at her neck, smoothing the lace of her high collar. She had a light gray gown of the nicest silk with starched Mechlin lace about its hem to wear tonight. It would be perfect with her onyx cape. She'd be demure, half mourning, maybe invisible in the dark of the theater.

With a sigh, she decided to focus on the good things in her life. A son who had no pain today. Plenty of food. Blooming clematis, purple and blush petals, vines holding hands, united in growth. She took another long breath, reveling in their fragrance.

She had been blessed. It had been a whole week since Philip's last earache. He'd been pleasant and without pain. Her heart had lifted when the doctor had said his hearing seemed to be at the same place it was when he'd last measured. Still not great, but no worse. The same pitiful hearing-from-only-one-side as before. She slumped against her patio knee wall. Nothing had yet been found to treat him or to keep these aches from returning. Nothing. Would he go fully deaf this year?

And a whole week without Ewan pestering her. What was he doing? Had he given up and gone back to town? Her stomach soured. It was a good thing for him to be gone, but that didn't stop that small part of her heart from beating fast when she thought him near, or the stupid part of her brain that leaped knowing he could visit any moment. She stomped her foot at her foolish, begrudgedly-missing-him heart.

A knock on the hall door made her pulse tick faster. Had she wished Ewan into visiting? Smoothing her skirts, she stepped back into the parlor. "Enter."

Pickens came into the parlor with a letter in his hands. "The footman retrieved this from Burlington Arcade. It looks important."

Her heart soared. The fancy paper with the bluish tinge. She opened her hands to receive it. A thrill coursed through her fingers as she saw the mark. The baron had replied. "Thank you, Pickens."

He dipped his chin but stared as if something made him cross. "The theater, ma'am. Might I suggest you start getting ready for the outing. It's a two-hour journey to Town."

She fingered the wax on the letter. What did the baron think of her answer? She flipped the paper over. "It's a long ride, too long of one."

His bushy brow rose. "You'll need to leave soon, so you'll not be late."

"I was thinking of not going. Philip might have another bad night. He'll need me."

"Master Philip has not had another upset. He will be well for this one evening." Pickens's face smoothed, showing the confidence that she'd come to depend upon. "I know how to contact the doctor. Your friends are counting on your presence."

She swiped at her brow. Fretting and humidity didn't blend. "It's not selfish to go? To leave Philip alone?"

"Ma'am, you've barely gone on your rounds. You can't stop living, waiting for the next upset."

It wasn't merely panic over Philip that made her hunker down in Tradenwood. Ewan had kept up his haunting. The man appeared everywhere, always wanting a moment of her time, but she couldn't give him any. He'd twist her like he'd done with Mrs. Gutter in the fields. She'd started thinking of him, missing his laugh. Why had she held his hand in the fields? That was how everything had begun, with him seeking her out. Would he stop by again tonight? No more being controlled by fear. She fanned the letter. "You are right. Miss Croome and Miss Burghley will be disappointed. I will go, but send for me if anything changes. If I am needed, I'll leave in the middle of the singing."

The butler chuckled, and then said, "Mr. Fitzwilliam stopped by again."

"What?" Her voice squeaked. "You know that I don't want him here."

Pickens's chest became big, as if he sucked in all the air of the room. "I know, ma'am, but this time he asked to meet your heir."

Theodosia blinked so hard it hurt. She must've seemed like a mad woman. Well, maybe she was, for everything felt as if the walls were closing in upon her. "What did you tell him?"

The butler took a cloth out and dusted the crystal knob. "I told him he was not welcome."

She coughed and let her heart start beating again. "Thank you, Pickens."

The butler's face became blank, and he took a few paces toward her. "I know you haven't asked my opinion, ma'am."

She startled and caught his gaze. "I haven't."

A part of Pickens's mouth lifted into a small momentary smile. "But I will offer it, this one time. The gentleman seems sincere. You may want to hear him out." The butler pivoted and walked back to the threshold. "Don't get so involved with your letter and forget the theater."

She waited for the door to close before pressing at the frustration that settled between her eyes. She didn't trust Ewan, and she could never ever trust him with Philip.

A noise sounded behind her. She swung, with arms raised, expecting to see her ghost lover, but saw nothing. The wind, not Ewan, had knocked over her rosebush.

She put her letter down and bent over her toppled

rosebush. With twitchy fingers, she scooped up the rich soil and filled the terra-cotta pot. The perfume of the dark, dark earth soothed her. It made her want to run out in the fields and find the spot where Mathew had claimed her. Mathew's ghost would push out memories of Ewan.

The man wasn't a caring cousin. He wanted to confuse her. He hadn't taken back his blackmail. He wanted her to sell Tradenwood, even as he'd danced with her in the fields.

She sat the pot up but couldn't take another second to enjoy it. New fear filled her. Ewan wanted to see Philip. That couldn't happen. She needed a husband now more than ever. Someone she could trust to keep all the people who could hurt her son far away. She picked up the baron's letter. With a prayer on her lips, she popped the seal. She scanned the lines. Her heart stopped, but not in a good way. She was mortified.

To love children is good, for a wondrous mother, the virtue understood.

It sounds as if you are a mother filled with love, but what lies lie in your heart? What falsehoods flow from your lips to aid your sleep? You don't have to answer this missive. You very well can be dismissive, but I'm seeking a life with a wife whose heart and actions are beyond reproach. Are you the woman I seek? If you are, tell me your greatest regret. Into your life, let me peek.

Another question? One sentence acknowledged her heartfelt response? How could he ask about personal regrets and not offer the same?

There was no way to unread what the letter said.

This would-be suitor, her newspaper groom, was all rhymes. How dare he want to know her deepest secrets, that hated R word?

The letter had to be a joke.

Someone found out about her trying to find a husband or maybe the baron liked games. Why hadn't she seen this before she struggled to pen three paragraphs to his last letter?

She started to pace, back and forth, patio tile, to parlor hardwoods, to cobblestones. A breeze swept over the fields, bringing inside a stronger scent of rain. The cooler wind stung her freshly chewed lip. She paced back into the parlor, picked up the letter, and crumpled the foolscap within her palm. This baron was playing games. Nothing was worse than a man who played games or who betrayed one's trust.

She should've stuck with the squire. His offer looked better and better. This fine-thinking rhymer offered nothing for her peace.

No. Not a thing. She lowered her head and waited for her pulse to slow, her thoughts to order. This mystery man did offer something. He'd give her a name that was as honorable as Mathew's and the hope that someone who asked such challenging questions would be a strong champion for Philip.

She wiped a horrible tear from her eye. Why was she crying? She didn't know this man, but she had foolishly put her hopes in him. She wanted someone stronger than Lester, than Ewan and all the Fitzwilliams. Then she wouldn't have to be strong all the time.

Theodosia had R's, big ones, ones that she lived with every day, ones she couldn't right. If she dared to pen one, would the baron use it to control her like Lester, like everyone else did?

Caged in her skin, she started to run. Anger at this new suitor boiled inside. She had labored long, writing and rewriting, surviving two Ester edits for the baron, being as transparent as she could about motherhood without saying the words—*my baby is almost deaf. And it's my fault.*

It hadn't been enough.

Her greatest regret was hurting Philip.

His deafness was her fault. All caused by her foolishness and pride. Theodosia's fingers shook. Her stomach churned as if she'd vomit. She needed peace. She needed to think. She needed to feel safe, like when Mathew had lived, or the night Ewan had sheltered her in the storm.

Not caring about her slippers or the hem of her dark mourning skirt, she trudged deeper into the field. The satin became damp in the fresh mud, but she didn't care. She stuck the paper against her heart and kept moving—all while the baron's reply repeated in her head.

Are you the woman I seek? If you are, tell me your greatest regret. Into your life, let me peek.

He toyed with her. Why? What was to gain from the baron laughing at her pain?

She stopped and looked up into the blue-gray sky. What if sharing the deepest part of her heart was the price to pay to gain a champion?

Was the cost too high or was her pride too much?

She was sweating, caught between crying and shouting.

Mathew had challenged her and so had Ewan, in different ways, but each had always made her think. Maybe this frustration was another way to challenge her. She swiped at her eyes, mopped at her temples. If the baron was moved at all by her letter, he would make a much better match than the dry squire.

Crumbling the paper, she stuffed it in her pocket. *A wife beyond reproach.* Could she ever be that woman, to any man? Mathew had understood her past, well, the parts she'd shared. Would he have counted her as beyond reproach?

Theodosia couldn't think anymore. She trudged deeper into the fields. Before she knew it, she was waist deep in lavender and couldn't move any further. Why was she tormenting herself? She should accept the squire. He had been the second response to her newspaper advertisement. All the lies, the regrets of the past would be put away if she married him. She rubbed at her arms, raised her face to the storm clouds. "I give up."

Horse's hooves pounded from behind.

She whirled to see who was coming toward her. With a blink, it was six years ago, and it was Mathew riding out to inspect his fields. He'd caught Theodosia picking flowers, stealing them, the week prior, but had then given his permission for her to take from his fields. He'd even had baskets waiting for her to carry away more than she could wrap in her skirt. It had been so welcome and unexpected. The Fitzwilliams had banned her from their land, but she'd had to earn some money to eat. And the low pain from the swell in her gut, the little one, had needed food, too.

She blinked again and was back in the present. She choked from the dust the rider kicked up as his mount almost trampled her.

The horse neighed like thunder. She was paralyzed in a cloud of horse sweat and dirt.

Laughing, the thick man jumped down and pulled tight on the reins, forcing the horse to obey. "You don't frighten easily, do you, Mrs. Cecil."

It wasn't Mathew's ghost but a very lively Lester hovering over her.

But she *was* scared. She shoved her shaking fingers into her pockets. All she could muster was, "Hello, Lester."

He leaned to the side and pushed his top hat back on his coal-black head. His narrow, pale eyes roamed as he gloated. "You do look a little scared."

Righting the hair starting to tumble down her back, she had to pretend to be strong. "You could've killed me. Was that your point?"

"Come on, boy." Lester tugged his silver horse. The horse neighed violently but submitted.

A moment of sympathy for the stallion swept over her. "I'm owed an apology and an explanation."

He tipped his brim. "I like to inspect what's mine, Mrs. Cecil. What are you doing so far from Tradenwood?"

She put a hand to her hip and lifted her chin. "Like you said. I am inspecting what is mine."

He chuckled in his typical menacing way, full throated and deep. "Well, our land. Yours, mine, and that mulatto of Cecil's—one big happy family."

Gall rising, she continued to glare at him. "Is there something you wanted?"

He grabbed her hand and clamped his hard palm about it. "There are many things I want from you, but for now I will settle for cooperation. Have the Fitzwilliams been bothering you?"

Lester had never showed concern for her before. And he couldn't know what Ewan planned with his play. Could he? She squinted at him. "Why do you ask?"

"They are a tricky lot, land grabbers. They may try to confuse you into signing things. When in truth, it's all to get their mitts on this place."

She wanted to say she read very well now, but it might be better to let Lester underestimate her abilities. "They haven't sent any new offers."

"Good. You'd show me, wouldn't you? I know I've been boorish to you, Theodosia, but viewing you now with the sun dancing upon you, I can see why Cecil took you as his mistress. You are built well. Your voice is pleasant. Yes. I see your appeal."

If this was a compliment, the squire had certainly run on with his praise, that is, with his mouth closed. "Thank you." That was all she could muster without laughing or spitting. It wasn't safe to engage the bull in a field alone. "I'm going back to the house. Continue riding like a mad person."

She turned away, but he seized both her hands. His rough gloves chaffed her palms, as he kissed each. After a nod, he jumped onto his horse. "Let me know what they are about, Mrs. Cecil. We keep this farm productive, we can own all the land. Land is what matters, and we should work together to win. Working together will be more pleasant. Don't make me an enemy. It won't do well for Philip, to see us at odds. Perhaps, the three of us should go away on my trip—the one that you set up but won't go on with me. He can help celebrate our wedding."

"I haven't agreed to marry you."

"Then perhaps I'll take the boy all by myself. It is my right to do so. In Holland, he will like looking at the bulbs, Of course, if he can keep up... Hate for him to fall, fall behind on my trip."

A tremor went up her spine, but she willed herself to stay put, not shaking. "Don't—Don't threaten him. Or me. Cecil wouldn't appreciate that."

"He's gone, Theodosia. Buried in the family crypt. I've been patient, but that all ends at the end of the month with your honorable time of mourning. Tell the boy I asked about him."

Would he take Philip to Holland without her? She hadn't planned on that. Dumbfounded, she watched Lester ride off. Her time of half mourning would be up in a few weeks— right after the festival. The fiend wouldn't be stopped by the mention of Mathew's name. Lester would be ruthless and abusive. She wouldn't have any recourse. She'd have to comply to keep Philip safe.

Breathing heavily, she headed to Tradenwood when another shadow fell upon her. It reached for her hand and steadied her, and this time she very much wanted to see this ghost.

Ewan was at her side. He held her hand gently as he had in the field with Mrs. Gutter. "What's wrong? Did that man hurt you?"

Everything was wrong. Every hope was being pulled from her, making her dizzy, and so unsure. She shook her head, but couldn't make words come out. Instead, she pressed their linked hands to her bosom.

With his grip tightening upon her fingers, he pulled her slowly and brought her close. "I'll kill him if he hurt you."

That didn't sound like Ewan. It was his voice for sure, but with a resolve she hadn't remembered him possessing.

He brushed her cheek. His thumb traced her neck before lowering his hand to her shoulder. "I mean it, Theo. I will."

Before she could stop herself, she fell into his arms. She needed something bigger than herself. Something to pin her hopes upon, even for a moment. And Ewan was here. His arms were tough, his chest solid, and his hold, everything she wanted when everything seemed wrong.

She stopped thinking. Didn't want to be challenged or scared anymore. She molded into her ghost and let her every fear absorb into him and disappear. Isn't that what ghosts did?

"I'm here, Theo. I saw him come at you. He meant to scare you." He kissed her temple. "I won't let him hurt you."

Her ear met the raised scars on his chest. They could be felt through his shirt and silky waistcoat. She looked up into those blue, bluer-than-the-sky eyes and saw an anchor. But anchors sunk to the bottom of things. Theodosia couldn't go lower. She couldn't have more regrets. "This isn't real. It's a daydream to replace my nightmares. Let me go."

His arms became heavy about her middle, his fingers kneading the stiffness of her back. "I'm here, truly here. I watched that big man coming at you. Who was he?"

Her ghost sounded as if he cared. Why? With the jitters caused by Lester draining away, she tried to step back, but his fingers met the nape of her neck and she became more breathless, more dependent upon him. "You've..."

She sounded strangled, but found some forgotten air in her weak body and pushed it out. "You've been watching me?"

A dimple popped on his lean cheek and the scent of him, sweet-like-cloves, haunted her nose.

"That's what ghosts do. And old habits in these fields are hard to break. And you've always been prettier than these flowers." His tone stiffened, hinting of possession. "The man who upset you? You haven't said who he was. Not a suitor gone wrong?"

She didn't owe Ewan an explanation. He was an enemy, right? With a determined shove, she broke free of his arms. Letting distance cool her racing pulse, she turned and started the slow walk back to the house.

"Who was he, Theo, I mean, Mrs. Cecil?"

At this she turned. She felt her face getting heavy in wetness, but didn't care. Who would Ewan tell that he found her crazed and weak in the fields? His father who hated her, the family who had pretended she didn't exist until they wanted to buy her land? "Mr. Lester is the man I am to marry, if my newspaper suitor doesn't come up to scratch. I will have to give up the only name I've ever had, one that is honorable and decent, beyond reproach."

He fished into his pocket and whipped out a handkerchief. "Here, Theo. I can help. Let me help."

"Don't make promises you can't keep." She mopped up more tears than she thought she had left. She felt him coming near, but held a hand up to stop him. "It isn't proper to be in your arms. You're not a beloved memory, only another man trying to convince me to do something." With a final swipe, she tossed the wet cloth at him. "Good day, sir."

He clasped her arm. "Sign Lord Crisdon's deal, Theo, and give us a reasonable lease. I'll protect you from everybody who is truly trying to hurt you. You know I don't want you hurt."

"I don't know anything about you, except that you are given to threats and careless dreams. And what do you know of me? I can tell you every memory of every dream you ever had, but what of mine? No, I was your secret little fancy. Good day, Mr. Fitzwilliam."

"Did Cecil trick you into becoming his mistress?"

She turned toward the house. "No more than you did."

He reached for her arm, and she shared his strong, alive pulse. "Theo, you loved Cecil? Did you love him more than me?"

She pulled free and then kept walking.

"Did he coerce you? Or compromise you? Did you go to him the moment I left or after you thought I died? I need to know why you didn't stay true to me, unless you never loved me at all."

Over her shoulder she saw him following, but she was done. No more explanations of her complicated world to a ghost or a baron. "If you knew me at all, you'd know the answer."

When she didn't hear steps trailing, her breathing returned to normal, in and out, in and out. That was good. If her ghost learned her truth, her deepest regret would make the hauntings worse, much worse.

. . .

Ewan watched Theo until she was safely on the patio at Tradenwood. He'd plodded through these fields every day, looking for an opportunity to catch her, to find a moment where she'd tell him what happened with Cecil, her child, or her health. It had become a sport, catching her here or there. Yet, each moment was a wonder. He'd seen the girl who'd been so shy caring for her tenants. He'd caught the number-wonder, bartering and calculating—she was as sharp in mathematics as ever.

Then she'd disappeared. She'd become the ghost, until today. That had saddened him more than it should. He swatted at his wilted cravat, crushed by the heat of her, and searched his mind for a memory, a word about her past. She'd mentioned her mother only once in passing. She'd then led Ewan by the nose into his favorite topic, himself. It had been far too easy to do for the attention-starved outcast. Pigheaded and selfish, that was what he was. He kicked a rock, wishing it was his head. He knew her, but not like he should've.

"Whoa there." Jasper had ridden up so close that Ewan's rock skipped right in front, almost hitting the pewter-colored horse. "Brother, you look like you lost your best friend. How could that be, since I am right here?"

"How did you sneak up on me?" He straightened his collar. "Where have you been? The coaching inn's tavern hasn't opened up yet."

"How droll." Jasper jumped down from his mount. "Been to Town meeting with glass makers. The hothouse ideas at Tradenwood. That's what we need here, but I must figure out how to convince Father, despite the expense. If only he'd let me run this place. I could do so much. *We* could be doing so much."

Ewan nodded, happy something captured Jasper's interest that wasn't brandy. "I'm sure you'll convince him. He might listen to your unpolluted opinions."

Jasper's face blanked, but he took some items out of his saddle. "Playwrights need to be direct or more generous in their statements."

It was unkind to drag his brother's nose in his liquor habits. But he couldn't think straight. Against his will, his mind locked on Theo and the boor who had nearly ran her down. Ewan looked down at his scuffed boots, the fresh mud from Tradenwood fields, the same darkness seemed thick on Jasper's boots. "You had a good ride? Tradenwood seems popular today."

"Yes, I examined one of our neighbor's hothouses. Funny thing. I caught a loving couple in the fields," Jasper said with a cocked brow and a smirk. "Interesting negotiation tactics. Do you intend upon seducing the enemy or was she leading you back into her web?"

"That's not what happened."

"You should be more discreet. You and the good widow or the good Jezebel, the one you wrote in your play. Is that how you intend to get her to sign the lease, beating her at her own game and bedding her? Maybe stash a bottle of ink by the pillow?"

Ewan felt his stomach fill with heat. His chest tightened, as did his fist. "Don't talk about her like that."

"Then tell me what you are doing. We were *close* once."

The way Jasper said "close" reminded Ewan of the other losses spurred on by his leaving for war. His brother was dear to him. They'd once been able to share everything. By accepting his father's ultimatum, Ewan had lost Theo, the fortune he would've inherited, and his brother's confidences. "I wasn't here to support you in the loss of Maria. I didn't come back. I stayed with my regiment. That's where I belonged."

"You belong with family, no matter what. And don't go seducing the widow and then blame us when things don't work."

Was that what Ewan was trying to do? Less comforting cousin, more carnal cretin? He shook his head. "'Twas no seduction. Mrs. Cecil has another enemy. That Lester character. He threatened her. I couldn't leave her, not until I knew she was safe. She needed defending. What do you know of this man?"

"Yes, that embrace looked quite defensible. I don't think

anything could get to her—beasts, air..." Jasper went around him and gave the reins to a groom. "Give my girl a good brushing."

The servant nodded and walked into the stable with Jasper's magnificent horseflesh.

When only the two siblings remained in the courtyard, his brother poked Ewan in the shoulder. "You be careful. You and Father are beginning to reconcile. You are back here at Grandbole. Don't destroy that for a fling."

Gritting his teeth to avoid snarling, Ewan thought of an apt way to phrase what should be obvious. "I was a gentleman. I have no designs upon her, and she has none for me. A gentleman has obligations to protect a lady. You're thick in size, not brains."

"But is she a lady? Father says she's a harlot who set her charms on the Fitzwilliams and then Cecil."

Unable to stop, Ewan reached out and jerked Jasper forward by the revers of his jacket. He shook the big man. "She was a girl, innocent and shy before I claimed her. If there is a harlot, it is me. Now this woman is a widow to my mother's cousin. She is family." He pushed him with all his might, forcing Jasper back two steps.

Ewan drew himself up, readying for another strike. "She's a lady, even if she's too dark for your tastes."

Jasper's smile faded but he didn't buck forward. Instead, he folded his arms. "I never said anything of tastes or hues. I don't know her, only the rumors, and after reading your play where you maligned everything about Theo the Flower Seller, I didn't think she still meant something to you. Thought you smartened up about her, her true character."

Ewan had been angry and hurt and had written his farce about Theo for all that loving her had cost. But every interaction he'd had since his return had proved her demure, very much the same woman who had drawn him years ago.

Guilt ridden, he stuffed his hands into his coat. "I think I was wrong about her, about what happened."

His brother folded his arms and leaned in. "Isn't this the moment in your play where the hero realizes his undying love, then breaks out in song?"

"I don't write operas. All I know is Mrs. Cecil, my cousin's widow, is alone and unprotected."

"Father has called her every uncharitable name under the sun. She still threatens our water."

"She hates everything Fitzwilliam and I'm not sure I blame her. I hated everything Fitzwilliam for years, and I have the earl's blood. I can't quite imagine what it would be like... How he would treat someone he hated with different blood, with black blood."

Nodding, as if he could understand, Jasper pivoted toward Grandbole. "Father is ruthless to enemies, all races, all classes, even peers."

"Brother, if you could find happiness with someone different than what the earl or anyone else wanted, would you risk it?"

Shrugging, Jasper stomped his boots, one after the other, knocking off the mud. An odd dance, oddly in rhythm—for him, almost graceful. "I'm not you, Ewan. You've always bucked everyone and everything for what you wanted. But if I had the chance to be that happy again, I'd forget everything, take that woman in my arms, and promise her tomorrow." He stopped, smoothed his jacket, maybe a little surprised at the strength of his argument. "Don't you have an appointment in Town?"

Surprised at Jasper's stunning advice, all he could do was nod and hope to not let his jaw drop to the dirt. "Yes, I need to get cleaned up to see Brown again."

"And borrow my gig. This is your big day. You may sell that play in which you malign your cousin, the lady."

With a nod, Ewan sighed. "He wants to see me after the curtains open on his current play, Shakespeare's *Taming of the Shrew*."

Shoulders shaking with hollering laughter, his brother doubled over. "You're joking."

"I never joke about play openings." Ewan started up the stairs, but stopped. "When everyone thought me dead, did the earl take revenge on Theo? It was his bargain, for me to go away. I agreed to serve a year and prove I was a man. Then he'd allow us to marry with his blessings."

"Why did you need his blessings?" his brother asked. "It's not like you needed it any other time."

Ewan wasn't going to answer that. It didn't matter anymore. "Thank you for the use of the gig."

"Father's waiting for you on the patio off the library. Go see him. Give him a chance to tell you his side of things. Then make up your mind about who are your enemies."

"I think I know."

Jasper smoothed his sleeves as his frown deepened. "Father became unhinged when he thought you'd died. Your mother, too. It didn't get better when news came of you recovering but not wanting to return home."

"This isn't home for me. It hasn't been since I was given an ultimatum, one I was too weak to walk away from. That's your answer. I was a boy, too weak to say no to my father, the Earl of Crisdon. I accepted his offer and have lost everything since. But tonight, I win. I will sell my play."

"Your widow cousin is not going to appreciate that, but maybe your hold on her affections will allow her to forgive you."

Theo still had a hold on him. The frightened woman in his arms, the one who had drawn close to him, so much so he'd heard her fevered heart—that was the girl he remembered, the one he'd pledged to marry. Could he forgive her, if the truth was that she went to Cecil even before the false announcement of Ewan's death, that she wasn't faithful, not even a month? "I want to be done with her, Jasper, but I'm not."

"You're thinking of forgiving her? What about Father? He felt guilty for sending you to war. The loss of you ruined the sentiment that your mother had for him."

For a moment, maybe a half second, Ewan felt empathy for the earl, for his mother didn't seem to want to return to Grandbole. He rubbed at his face. "You've always seen a side of him I couldn't, but what if *he* drove off the woman I was engaged to toward Cecil? What if he made her life so horrible that she needed help? Whom would she seek? She has no family, not even a father's name. Would she have turned to a kind stranger? Could that be how Cousin Cecil caught her?"

Jamming his fists into his coat pocket, Jasper shrugged. "Sounds like something to find out, but you're a Fitzwilliam, Ewan, not just your mother's son. Find Father in the library. Ask him what he did to the woman who is now our enemy. Then forgive him."

Forgiveness? That wasn't a Fitzwilliam trait. Maybe if he had more of the stuff from his mother's side, that good spirit that everyone claimed Cecil had, then maybe it was possible. "I don't know about either. How does one forgive a hole bigger than his footfalls?"

His brother shrugged. "When you find the answer, let me know. Go clean up for your Town meeting, but see Father before you do."

Ewan walked slowly toward his room. Maybe his raging thoughts would catch him. He'd hear the earl out, maybe Theo, too, but in his heart, he knew neither would tell him anything he wanted to hear. That's why he liked writing plays. He could make his characters say the best things and know when they lied. An impossible task with either Lord Crisdon or Theo.

Chapter Nine

Trust & Thunder

Ewan shuffled with slow, small steps down the long hall, as if he'd been summoned by his commander. Being summoned by the earl was almost as bad.

A low grumble sounded. A storm brewed and filtered in through the window. It made the air feel moist. The wet heat of the air reminded him of sultry Jamaica. He'd recovered enough to keep his enlistment and journey to the other side of the world. He'd done well. The playwright soldier had turned into a useful man. Would the earl ever see him as such?

With a breath and a prayer for peace, Ewan popped his head in the library. Unfortunately, Lord Crisdon was there.

"Fitzwilliam," has father said and bounced up from his desk. With a wave of his knurled fingers, he ushered Ewan inside. "Been waiting for you…Son."

Though the voice sounded pleasant, Ewan knew better. He stood at attention and waited for review.

The man didn't move, and his lips went flat. Disapproval surely radiated. He moved to the patio. "Come, I have tea and biscuits waiting."

Hesitating for a moment, Ewan took another breath and pushed forward. "Thank you, but no. I'm journeying into Town shortly."

His father nodded and took a seat at the table.

A luncheon for two? "Sir, I see you are waiting for someone. I'll leave you to your privacy."

"This is for you...Son."

Ewan's gut knotted three times over, a silent prayer to the Father, the Son, the Holy Spirit—anything to protect him from the fresh hell awaiting from the earl.

"Please sit."

Unable to think of a plausible excuse, such as Grandbole in flames, he puffed his scarred chest to the maximum. That way he'd still have something inside when his father's dressing down made it impossible to breathe. "I'll stand."

The earl stretched in his chair. His stylish coat and bottle-green waistcoat floated about his thin frame like kingly robes. With his nose lowered, he spoke over his glasses. "Have you solved our problem? Have you convinced the widow to lease the water rights?"

Ewan leaned against the balcony. "Nice day, Father. The weather seems to be turning. It may storm tonight."

"You have seen her?"

Deciding that looking down upon the man wasn't working, Ewan took a seat. "Yes, I've seen Mother."

"Not that her. The widow Cecil. Have you reasoned with her? Do we have a deal?"

Ewan chose a very brown and crispy biscuit from the platter and popped it onto his plate. "I did one better. I threatened her. I told her I'd ruin her if she didn't reconsider."

His father's eye grew large, the white part drowning out the beady blue dot one would call an iris. "Son, I didn't think you had that in you."

A smile crept over the man's typically annoyed features and a part of Ewan hated to destroy it, since signs of approval were rare. "Don't get too pleased. That only gained a slap, and it may have pushed other things into being. Do you know a Mr. Lester?"

The earl didn't blink, but his biscuit crumbled in his fingers. "Yes. Cecil's aggressive steward. He's a conniving devil."

"Well, he intends to marry Mrs. Cecil."

His father turned all shades of a rainbow. "We can't let that happen. He'll ruin us for sure. Cecil and his mistress-wife have run things equitably until now. Lester must be influencing her. He must be the reason for the change. If he marries her, he'll control her. You must do something."

Chewing his treat that he'd amply spread with cream, he tried not to laugh at his father's belief that it was in Ewan's power to change Theo's mind. Until today, they hadn't been exactly civil. "What do you think I should do? How am I to stop her? She doesn't work for us. Maybe you've forgotten this."

The earl grabbed his hand. "You're clever. You can have anything you want. You have to put your mind to it."

"Like gaining your approval over my choice in professions. Yes, I seemed to have done well with that these past six years."

The man drew back and through gritted teeth, he said. "Ewan Fitzwilliam, you wanted her once. Go have her now. Take her and the land that would've been yours."

His father had told him what to do and where to go many times, most hadn't been pleasant, but never this. Ewan brushed a handkerchief to his mouth. "Not that I want or need to have your blessings to go seduce the widow, but I need clarity. You are giving me permission to court her, to bed, or even marry her? Am I correct?"

"You and the wench gave a good show six years ago about being in love. You've done your military service, my only requirement. Go take her, with my blessing."

Yes, Lord Crisdon had lost his mind. Fear over his money drying up with the water rights had pushed him to the edge of insanity. "You've been in the sun too long, old man. You should go inside and rest."

"You've done what I required, now pick up where you left off. And wear some of the fine jackets and dressings I bought. You'll have to beat Lester to catch her eye."

"I thank you, but I'll borrow a room for now. I have my own things." He wanted to shove the words, "I'm my own man" down his father's throat, but this might be his father's only way of showing kindness.

Ewan softened his tone. "You are giving me your blessings to attach to Cecil's widow. We must be in serious trouble."

"Lester will be the death of the Crisdon Farms. If sacrificing you to the Blackamoor is the answer, I'll pay that price."

Well, that wasn't a compliment, yet being reminded how expendable he was to his father's plans was normal. Ewan stood up and folded his hands behind his back. "Six years is a long time. I'm not sure what I…"

The blank look in his father's eyes, the thinning of his lips to a pale line, told Ewan that no logic would sway him. "I'll consider your thoughts, but tell me, does Mrs. Cecil have a right to hate us, you?"

His father looked out toward the fields as he jammed a biscuit into his mouth. "Yes" came out with crumbs.

"Why?"

"I was very cruel to her. I had no sympathy for her when I thought you dead. Her cart vanished, and I banished her from working our fields. I wanted her gone."

His father's tone held steady as he recited how he had given a flower seller a death sentence. Getting to town on foot was almost impossible and a guarantee to be robbed or assaulted. And what would you bring to Town? Twigs? She couldn't pick the fields. "So you made her life difficult."

"Yes. Your loss made things unbearable. Your mother blamed me, but your wench did us all one better. She went after Cecil and now she's taking her revenge."

Ewan worked the knots in the back of his neck, the new ones that the truth imparted. The villain of his life was not a Circe. Theo was a woman, grieving her lost fiancé and made destitute by his vengeful father. "She has every right to starve our fields as you did her."

His father grimaced and dipped his chin. "But I've made up for that in my offers, double market price."

"She wants twenty times."

Lord Crisdon snorted his tea. "No. That's outrageous. You must stop her. Go down to Tradenwood and convince her to relent."

"I know you prefer to snap your fingers and make problems and flower sellers disappear, but that's not going to happen. Do you think it easy to fix six-year-old damage? You ruined things."

The earl looked up with eyes that showed no remorse. "I know. Your mother will never forgive me. Even after learning you lived, she refused to come back to Grandbole. Her Tradenwood is lost to her. I've ruined this place for her."

"I'm sorry for you, Father. I saw Mother. She said to tell you she agrees with you."

Lord Crisdon's brows raised, but he said nothing.

Looking at his freshly polished slippers, Ewan stepped toward the railing. "Do what you can. Love is too much to let go of without a fight. Or so I am told."

Again, the man nodded in silence, as if he couldn't

fathom what Ewan said or couldn't talk to him about things held close to his heart. Either scenario did nothing to fill the void in Ewan's chest. "I'm going to Town. I'm meeting with a theater owner. I'm hoping he'll want to produce my play.

"Sit, Son. Tell me about it... I want to hear about this passion that drives you. I'd like to help."

Like one of the characters in his play, Ewan began to recite generic lines about his play, the same ones he'd use to sway Mr. Brown the theater manager. His father nodded and smiled his crocodile smile. But in Ewan's core, he knew Lord Crisdon's actions were pretend. The earl needed his spare to win the rich widow. Money trumped race. Money made the man feign interest in his second son.

"Very good, Son. Your mother is proud of such creativity, too."

Ewan let his lips form an upside-down frown. He could pretend, too, and took his time relishing in the false praise, pretending each word, each labored syllable of his father's, carried enough heft to outweigh old disappointments.

Thunder crackled in the distance. He lifted his gaze to trace the lightning. He missed where it hit but became entranced by one of Tradenwood's chimneys, remembering Theo's passion.

His father moved from his chair and headed to the library doors. "Son, you seem lost in your words. Maybe you should rest and think about swaying Mrs. Cecil to our cause. Family is most important."

The man left and Ewan returned his gaze to Tradenwood's chimney. The sturdy dark brick offered puffs of white, seemed like it reached for something. Theo should reach for something. For a moment, Ewan wanted to be the person she reached for, even if it was merely for friendship. Maybe that would make up for his father's evil actions. Then they could see whether she'd be reasonable with the lease.

As a peace offering, he would change the name of his Circe without her signing anything. Flora sounded better, yes Flora the Flower Seller sounded much better. Would that be enough for her to trust him as she had years ago in a thunderstorm?

Lightning crackled above and he slapped the rail. *Reach for me, Theo.*

"Sir, the gig is pulled around and ready to go."

A groom had poked his head through the threshold. "Lord Hartwell wants you to leave early to beat the storm."

"Thank you." Donning his top hat and gloves, he climbed onto the driver's seat and took the reins—pondering if Theo would ever trust a ghost, a Fitzwilliam ghost, one who came to her, still doing his father's bidding.

• • •

Theodosia adjusted her gloves, creamy satin wonders with silver threads that shimmered in the dim light of her carriage. Sliding the cuff up and down, she tried to ignore each rumble of thunder. The rain had stopped before she could use it as an excuse to beg off. And the clouds had disappeared in the dusk. She shouldn't be nervous. This night would be over quickly, her friends would be happy, and Theodosia could return home to Philip.

The fear of Lester snatching up her boy tonight diminished. He wouldn't come harass her for a couple days, not after giving her a fright and a warning to think about. But he'd be unstoppable the minute he suspected her of plotting against him, and once he discovered that Philip was becoming deaf, he'd use his illness to make her do anything. She quivered. For a moment, she didn't want to be brave. She wanted to sink into the darkness of the carriage and hide. Against her will, her thoughts turned to Ewan. She'd heard the concern in his voice, felt the comfort of his arms, and had melted from the heat of his bluer-than-blue eyes.

He'd held her as if he cared. He'd pledged to protect her, as if she were special to him. That's how it had been so long ago, him seeming to care for her, and he had pushed her to new experiences, to depend upon him, to dream with him. She had wanted to elope and be his. Those eyes. It would be too easy to fall back into the caring, the holding, the needing of him.

Thunder clapped at the same time a tap pounded her door. Both made her sit up, shivering straight.

Her footman poked his head inside. "Mrs. Cecil, it will be only a few more moments. The entrance is being cleared."

She nodded. "Thank you."

When the man left, her knuckles balled, ready to rap the ceiling and signal to her driver to head back to Tradenwood and Philip. At least her boy wouldn't be upset by the noise. The flashes of light might even make him giggle, if he lay awake. Of course, he wouldn't be scared like her. You must hear thunder to be upset by it.

With Mathew gone, stormy nights sent her skittering. She'd scoot down the hall, scoop up her son, and tuck him into her big bed. It made the storm tolerable, knowing he lay safe beside her, and she by him. Snuggling in her arms, with his toothy giggles, Philip looked happy falling asleep, his bluer-than-sky-blue eyes slowly closing.

Goodness, she loved her boy, and she needed so desperately to be strong for him, but it was so hard with Lester counting the days to the end of her widowhood. And Ewan, pretending to care, only to get her to sign papers. Men. Maybe they could be bribed, given something to go away. Lester and bribery seemed a good mix. But what of Ewan?

She pressed at her temples, trying to push her fears to the back of her head, maybe into her tightly braided chignon.

Lightning flashed in the distance. She gulped then counted the seconds before hearing the low moan. The storm could be right over her fields.

Hoping for rain, she opened the door a little and stuck a hand out. Nothing. Not even a tiny droplet, nothing to justify returning home, locking the doors, and sending the girls a note of apology.

The door swung and she froze until the face of a footman became clear. "Miss Burghley says to come, ma'am. Follow me. The crowds have moved inside. Your entrance is clear."

Girding up her strength, she banished her frets to the place she'd banished Lester and Ewan for the night. Fluffing the hood of her cape, almost hiding beneath gray fringe, she noticed the crowd had shrunk. Only a few stragglers stood at Theatre Royal, Covent Garden's main entrance on Bow Street.

The young man helped her down and guided Theodosia to the west side of the building. They would pass the king's entrance, and she prayed the Prince Regent wasn't there. She wanted to blend into the dark and not be seen by those looking for royal blood, not a mixed-up mongrel's.

Theodosia wanted to strike at her own temples. Such thoughts, such fears. That wasn't who she was, but insecurities always invaded during thunderstorms, when memories became inescapable. She picked up her skirts and paused at the door the man opened. "Are there people waiting inside this way?"

"A few, but this way is private. The duke makes sure of that."

Frederica's father was amiable. Theodosia had only met him once. He had looked at her strangely but was polite. Hopefully, the womanizing duke didn't see what she saw sometimes in the mirror. Bits of her mother. She dipped in her reticule and pulled out a coin. "This is yours if you lead me to the box."

The fellow dimpled as the shine of the bright pence often lent itself to creating love. "Yes. ma'am."

Doing this, going out in public without being on Mathew's arm, made her nerves tingle. It was harder than she thought. And tonight, after being in the fields with Ewan and Lester—it reminded her of how alone and unprotected she was.

The young man led her into the darkened stairwell. Thunder rumbled. It echoed along the walls that seemed to close in. *Just a passing storm*. She followed and tried to stop chewing her bottom lip, but that proved more difficult.

They climbed and climbed and climbed some more until they reached a landing that led into a nice-sized room.

The footman pointed and then continued inside. "Not much further. And you see, this lobby is empty. Always on dark money night."

She filled her lungs, in and out. Gladness from being out of the stairwell overcame her as much as finding this lobby empty, but she chose to ignore his phrasing of her outing. He wouldn't steal her peace. This is how things were in London and far better than what it could be, if you had no money.

Theodosia straightened her shoulders and strode across the carpet as the proud widow of a good man. Enough of ghosts, slurs, and Lester. She wouldn't let anyone stir up anymore uneasy inside.

Then a zigzag of light sailed at the window. The noise would come soon.

She froze, her feet unable to move. Not until she heard the sound.

"Ma'am." The footman tapped her elbow. "Your box is waiting."

It hit and she panted. She should turn from the window, the swords of light dancing and fighting. The next rumble shook the building and everything in her chest. It wasn't safe to move. No one said it was safe to move.

"Mrs. Cecil. All is well. Come with me, Mrs. Cecil."

That soft voice sounded like Frederica's. "Come along. The duke's box awaits."

Pearl-colored gloved hands claimed Theodosia's and unwound her fingers from the tight clasp she had about her arms.

Shaking, she stood next to Frederica.

"See, we only need to go a few more steps. Then we are in papa's box." Frederica, in lockstep with Theodosia, held on to her waist and marched her inside.

Before the black velvety curtain closed behind them, Theodosia stuck out her palm with the shiny copper penny. She gave it to the footman. "Thank you."

It wasn't his fault she let thunder scare her, but her word was good. Always good. Shamed, Theodosia drew deeper into her cape. "I'm sorry. I've made a spectacle of myself."

Frederica gave her another hug. "No one but a footman saw you. We are not in front of the theater, and in a few more minutes, Ester will be engrossed by her actor. The man took the stage, and she set down her book."

Ester offered a smile, then a giggle. "'Tis true. Mr. Bex has a lovely voice."

Still embraced by Frederica, she moved to the seats. Four chairs were pulled to the rear. Ester sat in the one closest to the corner with her crimson satin overdress swishing about pearl slippers and a pink skirt. She cupped her hand to her face and became engrossed by whatever happened below, the music and a baritone's direct address. No one would see them unless they made a scene. If the orchestra kept playing over the thunder, no one would know it was dark money night.

Sitting, she pulled off her cape and tucked her neat silver slippers beneath her. When Frederica nodded and smiled, she knew her gown, with dark silver cap sleeves and a misty gray bodice and skirt was a success. "I am so glad you came. You need something different from mourning."

"This gown is still half mourning. My Mathew is still honored."

As she took her seat, Frederica's face lost its natural glow, not upon her smooth skin but her eyes. They dulled in the dim light. "You can live and still honor him. That is what he would want for you and Philip."

Theodosia clutched the girl's gilded glove to her bosom. "I know he's honored by the friends I keep. I am honored to be here."

Frederica gave a nod and half a smile. She was a sensitive type of girl, but did she know how much of a struggle it was for Theodosia to be away from Tradenwood and Philip on such a horrible stormy night?

With no more cheer to offer, she closed her eyes and sighed inwardly, setting her hopes on hearing the dramatic lines and the swirl of the violins—all while wishing the storm would end and free her from fear.

• • •

Ewan stood in Mr. Brown's office at the Royal Theatre, Covent Garden. It was quiet now, most of the actors were on stage. The play had begun. He listened for Shakespeare's words to be recited in direct address. He closed his eyes. Oh, for that day when his play would entertain crowds.

How much would they love his current creation—Theo, as a saucy Circe? Or would they prefer the version bumbling about in his mind, the one about the woman whom he held in his arms, the one who needed him? Theo had changed. She'd never truly showed herself vulnerable, only scared of thunder.

Today, she had been different. And yes, his wary chest

had puffed up in pride when she'd turned to him. Yet, how long could a peace between them last? A day, a month, a year?

The roar of thunder blended with clapping. The first act must be over. The footfalls of the actors sounded, as did a violinist. The intermission between scenes—had Petruchio accepted his fortune by marrying Katherina? The farce made of Shakespeare's boastful idiot and his shrew bride was a sight to behold onstage or in Ewan's mirror. Yes, he was a boastful idiot to be thinking of Theo returning to his arms.

The storm boomed and rain pelted on the ceiling with a heavier rhythm. It was like a gong, echoing and cleansing him of wanting her. It helped him refocus on his purpose of being at the theater. He had come to sell his play without the earl's assistance or his blockage. Now, at least, his father wasn't using his influence to stop Ewan's plays. He hoped.

The door opened and Mr. Brown, a portly fellow with thick glasses and balding head, entered. "Sorry to keep you waiting."

"No problem at all."

The man flopped on a well-worn leather chair.

A hint of tobacco touched Ewan's nose. The man's delay, had it been a vice? There were flecks of rain on his coat. "You've come from outside?"

"We're making some dark money tonight and had a bit of trouble."

The term sounded odd. He felt his brow wrinkling. "What is that? Dark money?"

"The Duke of Simone pays me a little more to allow his by-blow and her Blackamoor friends to set up in his box from time to time. They usually sit quietly, not upsetting anything. Nothing harmed seating them in the highest box with the private staircase. If notable nobles sat in their boxes, they'd go unnoticed."

Ewan's gut twisted at the disdain coming from Brown's alliteration and his garish laugh.

At least when Jasper had asked of Theo, his voice sounded of curiosity or brotherly probing. This man's tone bristled with condescension, perhaps even masked hatred, like the earl's.

Ewan rolled his shoulder to allay some of the tension tightening his neck. "But tonight was different. What happened with the Blackamoors?"

The man scratched his chin hairs, then leaned back in his chair as if set to spin a long yarn. "Seems one of them, the one with slant eyes... She had a fit caused by a little thunder. The footman thought she was going to start screaming or crying." Mr. Brown rummaged through his desk, as if he hunted for something.

Ewan braced to keep his own composure. His pulse raced, then slowed, as he glued his low-cut boots to the ground. Could Theo be here?

Brown chuckled, then slapped his desk. "You should see them all gussied up like regular women."

"But they are women, sounds like women with means."

"I don't care what they are. If the duke is paying and none of my other patrons are aware, I keep the money, dark and lovely."

How money changes things. Theo, the rich widow, was now an acceptable choice of brides, to even the earl, but Theo the Flower Seller was not. One could be in the theater like *normal women*, if the price was right. Ewan soured immeasurably, wanted to walk away, but respectable theater was small. If he couldn't get his play here, there would be no chance at the Royal Theatre, Drury Lane. "Well, hopefully, there will be no more complaints and your guests get to enjoy this play."

"I must say, the duke's by-blow could be mistaken for a

lady if not for the thickness of her lips."

He obviously didn't know the joy of kissing such plump wonders. Ewan wondered if Theo's were still extraordinary.

The man stretched and laughed. "The one with the slant eyes, she could be a looker, too, if she wasn't so dark."

His pulse ticked up. "With straight onyx hair?"

Brown guffawed, then shot up. "Fitzwilliam, did you see her?"

"Yes." A thousand times in his dreams. There was only one Theo, with beautiful almond-shaped eyes, afraid of thunder. "She is some looker."

Brown shuffled more paper as Ewan leaned against the door. Theo was here, away from Tradenwood on a night like this. Why? She was so different, a ball of compelling opposites that drew his attention like no one else.

Thinking of her, feeling that old draw, made Ewan impatient. He twisted his hat within his palm. "So you've had a chance to review my play?"

Brown sat again. He searched his desk and finally settled on pages at the bottom of his pile. "I did. Outrageous. I think it will be the talk of London. Theo the Flower seller is outrageous."

"Well, I'm working on that character's name. I think Flora the Flower Seller."

"Don't change a thing. I like it."

"Well, I'll... keep that in mind, if you are going to buy the play, or Cleo the Flower Seller will bring in the allure of Egyptian culture."

"Perhaps. I do want to buy it. This will sell lots of tickets, but Fitzwilliam... How do I ask this without sounding condescending?"

With all the things he'd said about Theo and her friends, did it matter? Ewan stiffened his stance, all but locking his knees as he'd done in the regiment. "Say it. Shoot, then reload."

Brown started rocking in his chair. He tapped his fingertips together, as if he were praying, but this man didn't seem the type to have been to church in years. "I do a great deal for my wealthy patrons. I don't like getting crossed or my license to be threatened. Does Lord Crisdon approve of this? Your father can make everything difficult, difficult with tradesmen and creditors, if you cross him.

"I'm my own man. I can handle the earl. He'll be no trouble to you."

Standing, Brown stuck out his hand. "Then you have a deal. How soon can you get the final draft to me?"

Ewan shook the man's hand, pumping it with vigor and a sense of accomplishment. "A fortnight."

"Good. I can start planning. Work on getting the earl here for the opening?"

That would be a miracle. One with strings from the devil, no doubt. "I'll see what can be done, but this deal is based on the merits of the play. Nothing more."

Catching the man's sneer-like smile, Ewan donned his hat and pivoted to grip the door handle, but turned back for a moment. "A fortnight for the final play. Have the contracts ready."

"It's a good play. We stand to make a lot of money. And I still like that name, Theo, Theo the Flower Seller."

"It will be Cleo, Cleo the Flower Seller in the final draft."

Nodding, Ewan closed the door behind him. His moment of success felt a little slimy. He wiped his palms upon his jacket. This was the theater. Some wore masks and costumes. Others showed you who they were. Mr. Brown, as his father would put it, was a *necessary means* to accomplish Ewan's goals.

Thunder crackled loud and hard as Ewan exited the theater. The rain had slacked to a light pelting. The next hoarse rumble in the sky didn't make him dash to the mews for his brother's gig. No, Ewan turned the corner and sought out the lone stairs that led to the highest boxes. He trudged through puddles, sloshing cold water on his formerly buffed boots. It didn't matter. He needed to see if the story being written in his head was correct. That the heroine of his heart was misunderstood. The earl's wrath had made her vulnerable, easy pickings for Cecil. A grieving soul was easy to mislead by a rich predator or made a villain in a farce by a playwright who needed a villain for his own bad choices.

Six years ago, that strong, opinionated girl had become frightened by the storm. They couldn't elope, not in such a deluge. So, they had holed up together in the carriage house. It was the first time they'd ever been alone. Except for a holding of hands, a shared laugh in a thick grove nestled behind the carriage house, or a gleefully stolen kiss near Grandbole, he'd never fully given himself to her, never felt so much love in her dark eyes. Not until that moment.

Knowing how his father was, why had Ewan believed the lies and made Theo a gold-seeking mistress? Anger pained his breath as he pried the stairwell door open. He'd written the wrong fiend.

It wasn't a feeling of accomplishment for selling his play that drove him up those treads. It was that small lump in his scarred chest that tightened, thinking Theo was near and frightened—thinking of her clinging to him again like she had today made him take the stairs by two.

Chapter Ten

Night at the Theater

Theodosia shifted in her seat. The actor's voice couldn't drown out the thunder or the memories. She'd paid attention to the horrible story, wondering why Ewan could think this Shakespeare so fine. Fighting, complaining, tricks, and starvation—that felt a little too familiar, too Fitzwilliam.

A boom moaned above. The storm sounded as if it were gaining force, coming for her again. She shivered and pulled her wrap tighter about her arms.

The world around her rumbled. It sounded ghostly, as if it whispered her name. She pivoted in time with the next crash and caught the dark curtains swaying. The storm had to be atop her. Her gaze became glued to the velvet. It shrouded this box as it did the space she had hidden inside at the brothel. *Mama told her to be quiet, but how could she, trapped by the storm?*

A hand grabbed hers and she almost screamed, but she was too scared. And Mama would be angry.

"Theodosia, are you well?"

The voice wasn't Mama's, so Theodosia didn't move. She wasn't supposed to, not till she heard the signal. She hated the coal scuttle within the brothel wall and how it made every violent pound of thunder echo.

A gloved hand slipped onto hers, but she couldn't say anything; she hadn't heard Mama's knock. "Theodosia. You don't look well. Dear?"

The tones, the concern… It sounded like Ester, but why would she be here? Good girls like Ester wouldn't be in a brothel.

"Theodosia."

Something shook her by the shoulders, and she tensed. Blinking heavily made the world right. Frederica's arms were about her.

Disgusted by her fears, she shook free, not wanting to be touched, even by a friend. "I'm not feeling well. I need to go home."

Ester frowned deeply with her lips pressed tightly. "No. The new actor, the one who's all the rage. He hasn't come back out yet."

Frederica's fun face seemed blank, but she nodded. "This isn't any fun for you. I'll signal a groom, and we'll get you to your carriage."

She'd ruined her friend's evening out. Theodosia's insides hurt. "Stay. I've done enough to disrupt what should be a fun occasion. I'm ashamed…to do this to you two. I wish to make myself invisible."

Wrinkling her gown, Ester crouched down, pried off a glove, and applied the back of her hand to Theodosia's forehead. "You don't have a fever. Listen to me. There is nothing wrong with being frightened."

"Yes, nothing at all." The man's voice, the one that haunted her soul, introduced himself. "I'm Mrs. Cecil's cousin. I'll see her home."

A little damp, with a dark curl plastered to his forehead beneath his beaver-skinned hat, Ewan stepped fully inside. "I'm here for you Th— Mrs. Cecil. I'll get you safely to your carriage."

Why? Why was Ewan haunting her outside of Tradenwood and on a stormy night? Theodosia stood up and stared at him. "Not you."

Gripping her hand and not letting go, Frederica stepped toward Ewan. "This is a private box. You have no business here."

The grin on his face looked triumphant. Would he shame her in front of her friends by bringing up their tawdry past? Oh goodness, would he tell them of the loving, the leaving, and the lies? With lips pressed shut, he bowed. "Miss."

"Miss Burghley." Frederica kept her voice soft but her chin high.

Nothing intimidated her, but shy Ester had skittered to the side in the corner.

"Ladies, I'll make sure Mrs. Cecil gets home safely." He lowered his voice to a whisper. "From what I recall, she doesn't do well with storms."

Theodosia's cheeks heated. She'd fan her face but that would let Ewan know she was weak.

"No." Surely not understanding his reference, Frederica didn't move. She stood as an equal to the son of the earl. "I will send her to her carriage. You may leave."

But Ewan didn't move, and the heat of his steady gaze made Theodosia's pimpled arms feel warm, too. "My cousin can trust me."

With a brow raised, Ester came out of the shadows, looking back and forth between Ewan and Theo. "Frederica, why is your cousin here? Does he know the duke?"

"No, Ester, he means me. He was my Cecil's cousin. This is Mr. Fitzwilliam."

"Yes. We are cousins by marriage. My family is Mrs. Cecil's neighbor and sometimes business rival." He extended his hand again. "It is my pleasure to assist you."

Frederica smoothed her gloves. "Fitzwilliam," she said in a voice not as strong as before, "as in the flower rivals, as in up the hill from Tradenwood."

Theodosia forgot about the new rocking of thunder and focused on getting Ewan away from her friends. Signaling that she conceded, she nodded to her conquering ghost. "Yes, he is the second son of Lord Crisdon. He is my late husband's cousin."

"Guilty." Ewan's smile grew with bigger dimples, evil I-shall-now-embarrass-you-more dimples.

She braced for his worst and that made his grin worse.

He tapped the edge of her chair. "As her cousin by marriage, it's my duty and honor to be of service."

Frederica squinted at Ewan as if there was some sort of recognition firing in her brainbox. "The man from the patio. Seems you not only do night deliveries, but pickups, too." Frederica drew Theodosia's palm up to the small diamond necklace hanging about her neck and the creamy gold ruffles of her bodice. "If you wish to leave with your cousin you may. Ester and I will be fine. We'll have to do better with weather on our outings. The Cecil Festival must have perfect weather. I will put all my hopes on that and you."

The look in her friend's eye, the love and reassurance filled that spot in Theodosia where all had drained. With more confidence in herself, she determined it would be better to go with Ewan than to expose her friends to whatever tricks her ghost had planned. "It will be perfect, just as Cecil wanted. I'll accept your offer, Mr. Fitzwilliam."

Thunder crackled as she took his hand. The glint in his bluer-than-blue eyes surely meant she'd done what he wanted her to do. That was almost scarier than the noise.

The crowd below erupted.

Ester's mouth gaped, but then closed. She nodded and turned back to the stage. Maybe her dream actor had arrived.

Frederica bounced in front and drew the curtain open for them. "You make sure your cousin gets to Tradenwood safely, Mr. Fitzwilliam."

"Ladies, I'll see you Monday for the final preparations," she said, counting seconds after the latest streak of lightning.

"It will be my duty to see she's handled with care," Ewan said. "Evening, ladies."

Free of the box, Theodosia dropped his hand, adjusted her cape, and walked past him. "Good night, sir."

"Not so fast." Triumphant, smiling, and too handsome for words, Ewan clasped Theodosia's hand, pinning it to his arm, as if she'd escape. "Don't want you to fall. It's treacherous tonight. The stairs might be wet."

No, it was more dangerous to have her hand in his, to be nestled next to the scars upon his chest. Pulling away had to be done at the right moment to leave Ewan stewing. Patience, as Mathew would say, would win, or at least retain, her peace.

He laced his fingers with hers. "Not too much further."

They stood about halfway down, moving farther and farther from the lone window that let in light and stars, if there were any. She squinted and could see the exit, the door she'd entered. "Thank you for helping me out of here."

"My pleasure. Ghosts can be helpful, especially those bent on apologizing."

Without responding, she took another tread. Truthfully, she'd let horrible Napoleon help her out of here, if it meant getting her more quickly to Tradenwood.

"Theo, I remember how storms make you nervous. I'm remembering a great deal."

His voice purred against her ear, but she didn't have the luxury of swatting him in public. Who knew how much the slap would echo in the stairwell. "Ewan, no games. Please get me to my carriage like you said you would. Your word is good?"

"As good as yours, my grieving widowed cousin." He moved slower and held fast to her hand.

She tugged but he didn't budge. "Is something wrong?"

"I was wondering if you enjoyed the play? *The Taming of the Shrew.* Maybe the storm kept you from paying attention."

"I followed. A woman marries a beast who starves her. I didn't enjoy that."

He chuckled and hummed, but his hands tightened about hers, keeping her next to him all the way down to the last step. "Yes, Petruchio wasn't nice to Katherina. Perhaps he didn't understand how to get past her anger."

"I'm no shrew."

"I'm the shrew, Theo. I was so angry at you; I couldn't see past my anger. I forgive you."

A flash of light from the window above made the dark passage glow, framed his face with what looked like truth, but she didn't want that now. Too many things needed to happen to protect Philip without her growing weakness for Ewan putting things into jeopardy.

"I said I forgive you, Theo. Have you nothing to say to me."

"What do you want from me, other than a lease for your father?"

"I'm not sure, but I'm duty bound to find out."

Another bone-jarring thud of thunder groaned, and he slid her into his arms. Like in the fields, she hid against his chest. The world moaned outside, echoing in the darkened shaft, and she shook. When he pulled her closer, she didn't resist. She needed the storm to go away. She needed to believe that something sturdy could hold her up. Right now, Ewan served the part.

But wasn't he a part of her bondage? Initially, she'd kept her heart from Mathew by mourning Ewan. That time couldn't be returned. She'd wasted it on a love that hadn't been pure.

The thundering wouldn't quit and she drove her nails into Ewan's arm.

He didn't squeal; he merely flattened his palm atop her squirming digits. "I have you, Theo. Don't be afraid."

Nobody had her. "There is much to fear. It's called tomorrow. I can't face its revenge again, when minds are changed and promises are broken." She bucked up her spine and moved backward, away from him. She pushed open the door and went into the night.

She bristled beneath her cape and for an instant she wished she still stood sheltered.

"I don't disappear that easily, Cousin." Ewan came alongside her. "Now, where is your carriage?"

"I need no help."

"Of course you don't. This assistance is to keep me honest. I said I'd get you safely back to Tradenwood."

Rain drizzled overhead and began seeping into her hair. She chided herself for standing around like a nervous hen. She would ruin her expensive gown because of Ewan. He was too near, being too nice, talking of forgiveness, reminding her of the dreams of happy-ever-after that had led her astray.

He tugged her arm. "Your carriage is over here."

She chided herself but kept pace with his larger strides. The sooner he put her into her carriage, the sooner this haunting would end. Then, she'd be rid of her ghost and all the annoying butterflies twisting in her tummy.

"I should've asked you to stay in the stairwell until I retrieved your carriage. But then I wouldn't have you at my side."

Again, he tucked her close, as if he cared she felt fragile.

Any thought of protesting died, drowned with a flash of light and thunder crashing about them. The night smelled of rain. London smelled fresh like the fields of Tradenwood.

"Easy, Theo. Like I said, I remember."

She froze for a second, her mind swept back to six years ago, when a boy and a girl thought they'd found love. She'd held on to the sweetness too long before giving it up to find contentment with Mathew. She bit her lip, gnawing it raw. "When will this end?"

He raised his head and looked about. "This storm isn't done. Neither are we."

Her stomach dropped even lower.

Ewan leaned down, within nibbling distance of her ear. "Not much farther, Mrs. Cecil."

She looked out in the blackness. The link boys had settled down and huddled underneath overhangs. Cupping her hand to her face to focus, she finally spotted her footman at the front of the mews. "There it is. My driver must've known I might not stay. I debated upon turning around several times."

He steadied her as they traipsed to her carriage. He waved off her footman. "Easy now, Mrs. Cecil. We'll have you home in no time."

His expression hurt her heart, making her chest thump at the sparkle of determination visible in his eyes.

Now her feet felt cold and she fretted about how he'd found her at the theater. His play. Was his scandalous work about her going to be performed in Frederica's favorite theater?

She stiffened as his arms went about her, but she couldn't stop him from putting his hands on her hips and lifting her inside.

"Skittish? Six years too late, Theo?"

She sank back against the tufted squab of the seating. "Thank you, and good evening."

When she pulled at the door, he caught it. "Driver. To Tradenwood."

"Yes, sir."

She heard the words and almost released a sigh of joy, but then, Ewan barged inside. The door banged shut and he sat next to her. "I'm going to see you home, like a good cousin."

It was too dark to be alone with him. She bent and lit the carriage lamp on the floor. The light made things worse. It let her see how strong and virile he looked and how near he sat, with lips that were in want of a kiss.

She pushed at her temples hoping to free them of ridiculous ideas. "Get my driver to let you out then go away, cousin ghost. I'm in no mood for your haunting. The storm has upset me enough."

"I don't think you should be alone, and we are headed in the same direction. It's best to be at your side. Just a pleasant ride for Theo and her ghost."

The slow-moving cabin felt hot, and sitting so close to Ewan made her skin warm with anger. She dropped her hood to her shoulders, but it wasn't enough to cool down, not with molten temptation a hug away.

The last thing she needed was to become faint because of him staring at her. She drew her arms about her as if to add another layer of protection. "I didn't ask you to accompany me into my carriage, only to take me to it. You've completed this promise. Don't you have a flat in Town? Some other relative to bother?"

"It's less than two hours to Tradenwood which is practically next door to Grandbole. You can abide two hours, no? Much shorter than a month."

She stared at him and hoped her face didn't show how unfair that was, but it was better he thought her disloyal than know the truth. No, the truth remained hidden, buried with Mathew.

He took off his hat and sidled to the other side of the bench.

Thunder growled and he smiled a little. "Let me be helpful. This storm still has plenty of strength."

Trapped with him in a storm for two hours. Her fear would addle her. What if she accidentally admitted to things? The delicate balance she shared with her ghost would be eroded even more.

Her mind went to the embrace on the stairs and the one in the fields. Each felt more natural, reminding her of the stolen embraces of six years ago.

"So Theo, do we share? Or do we argue all the way to Tradenwood and share by default?"

Ewan, the Fitzwilliams—they were against her. She pushed at her brow. "Enemies don't share. You came into town some way. You can most certainly return to Grandbole the same way. I'm stopping this."

She reached up to tap the roof, but he caught her hand. He'd removed his gloves and pulled off one of hers. Bare hand to naked finger, he stroked her wrist, forced her to feel his lively pulse. It was too strong, too fast, like hers.

"You can't be here," she whispered.

He kept her hand and moved nearer. The dim light danced upon the angles and planes of his lean face. The set in his jaw tightened. Self-possessed. Strong. A determined Ewan was a dangerous thing. And unfortunately, it was catnip to Theodosia, making her voice purr his name. "Ew-wan, let go of me."

Why did she have to sound stupid—breathless and stupid? She pushed away.

That disarming smile that had made him so handsome six years ago grew. "Methinks, you are afraid of ghosts, too. Do you fear me or the truth, as much as you fear thunderstorms?"

Yes, to both. But the words never left her tongue.

He claimed her hand again and put his mouth to her wrist.

In a blink, he slid off her other glove, then kissed each naked fingertip. The motion soft, tender—bad, determined ghost. "I need to tell you something, Theo. My play will be produced."

His eyes radiated joy. Part of her was happy. He was living his dream. The other part, the sane side, boiled. She snatched her palm away from his coercion, his seduction. "Good for you. Slander looks good on you."

He took her by the shoulders, forcing her reflection to swim in his eyes. "I'm taking your name out."

She'd been holding her breath when he touched her, and when his words started to make sense she gasped. "What?"

Nodding, he stroked her palm. "It wasn't right to threaten you like that."

The anxiety of what the play would mean to her reputation eased. Her chances at the Court of Chancery for Philip's guardianship improved. A sigh fled. But this was Ewan Fitzwilliam, and her heart tamped down to a near normal rhythm. "You're being kind to me? In exchange for what?"

The clap of thunder made her shiver, almost as much as when his finger slid under her cape to her shoulders. "I have you, Theo. I'm not ready to let go."

Trying to wriggle away made it worse. Her cape slipped, allowing his hands to be free. The heat of his palms wilted her cap sleeves. It was as if he stroked her skin.

"I still need my family protected, but that has to be done without hurting you. I don't want to be one of those people in your life who push you to do things. I'd rather be someone who you can turn to."

"And this is why you're in my carriage? With your hands on me?"

The pressure of his palms disappeared, but he never

let go of her gaze. "Was your skin always so soft? I don't remember."

"Leave."

"When you turned to me earlier...it reminded me of something I'd missed. Our friendship. I sold my play, Theo, and there was no one to share it with, no one who truly understood the meaning. No one else has ever heard my dreams and encouraged me, and I have no one to take care of, no one to make sure she didn't work so hard that her ride and her burdens were easier."

Those big eyes of his, which looked even larger and more soul penetrating than ever, made her nod, made her remember, too. "I'm happy for you. You can stay until we reach the fields. Then out you go."

His arm moved to her back and slowly drew her closer, inches from his chest. "That's a poor congratulation. Can't think of a better way?"

"It's all I have for you or anyone."

His gaze lowered. "I know you are in trouble. I'm here now. I'm not going anywhere. I'll talk nonsense and make you laugh, like before."

He used to tell her nonsense about plays and Greek theater things. His face had been full of vigor...and love. Like now.

She gulped and looked away. The seam on her cape became safer and more fascinating.

Thunder shook. She shook. "We'll be getting to St. Martins Lane soon."

That arm of his tightened about her. As much as she didn't want to, she found herself pressed against his chest. The memories started. The laughs, the dancing, the joy of how special it felt to be near him returned. "We'll be getting to St. Martins Lane soon."

"You said already that, Theo."

Hating her weakness, she focused on the loud thud of his heart. His alive heart.

"Why do you hate thunderstorms?" He made his tone low and dipped his chin onto her forehead. "You know everything about me. But I know so little about you."

Fearing too much would be said, she tried to push on his chest to put distance between them, but her thumbs tangled in his cravat, skirting over his thin shirt, scraping his scars, deep and long scars. She froze, thinking of him suffering, almost dying, all while knowing her choice to keep living.

But no one would've suffered if he hadn't left her. Growing too warm, too hot with memories, and those *R* things, she moved his arm and sat back against the seat. "You know enough. Can't give you another thing to use to coerce me or blacken my name. That's the Fitzwilliam way. Is Fitzwilliam Greek, meaning to crush Theodosia?"

"Were you always this funny?" His lips pushed together for a moment. "Here's something that you won't hear a Fitzwilliam say and mean it. I'm sorry, Theo. I was so angry at you for not mourning, I wanted you to pay, but I was the shrew. I thought nothing but the worst of you. I raged and wrote. But I forgot how young we were and how easy it was to let fear affect us. You've been in my thoughts—some of them have been focused on revenge, some quiet like now, remembering what we had. I never once forgot you. Look at me. See the truth."

She didn't want to look up. It was too easy to become lost in those eyes. She shook her head. "I can't believe you."

"If I can admit regrets, can't you?"

No. She couldn't. To do that would steal Mathew's legacy, the man who had saved her, who had given her so much.

"I have regrets, Theo. Deep ones."

*R*s. He had them? Couldn't he see the turmoil churning in her stomach? Against her will, her face craned up to his.

She put a shaky finger to his lips. "No. No more of this or you can leap out and find your own way to Grandbole."

His mouth opened. With his teeth, he raked her finger, shooting lightning down her skin. "I'll be brave and say it. I regret you thought me dead. I regret that my absence made you vulnerable and made you prey for others. I regret you weren't awaiting my return."

He leaned closer to her face. She could feel his breath, warm, sweet-smelling like sagebrush. The heat of it fell upon her cheekbone. "Don't you wish things had been different?"

That stupid part of her heart took over. She let her ghost, the man who symbolized the first kindness she had ever known, the first love of her heart, brush his lips against hers.

He took her face within his palms. "Well, I wish things were different, even if you can't admit it. I'll be transparent. I suppose that's what ghosts are good for. See through my misgivings. Know I've missed you, Theo."

His eyes had surely put her into a trance, for her palms were too weak to plant upon his chest to stop another advance. He angled her face then branded her mouth with his fire. He stole her peace, her sense, her air, as he took a second and then a third deep kiss.

Panicked and panting, she fell into his chest and let years of tears puddle in her eyes. She had loved Ewan, more than herself.

Ewan mopped her sobs with his thumbs. "Do you remember loving me? I remember."

He gave her no chance to respond to his whisper. His passion began again as his hands became more urgent.

She remembered his love and measuring everything against it. If she fell for Ewan again, there would be no Mathew to catch her. "No."

Her voice sounded small and weak and stupid. Why had she let Ewan into her carriage? Why had she given him room to tempt her?

His pinkie tugged a lock of her hair. "Is *no* what you want?"

Swatting at her stinging eyes, she sat up straight. "No. I—I can't do this. I'm a proper widow. I won't sit in the dark clinging to the past."

His head tilted toward her. The inches of separation she'd recovered disappeared. "Then cling to a future. I'm here, and I'm not scary." He took her mouth, tasting that raw lip that she'd nearly chewed off. "Trust me, Theo." The whisper was cool upon her jaw. Then nothing separated his kiss from hers.

With her resolve crumbling like a fallen flower vase, she bloomed, opening for him. She let him kiss her for yesterday, today, and tomorrow.

His hands went under her cloak tracing the lace of her tucker, sizing and squeezing, taking inventory of her shape, testing her lack of resistance.

He'd always been a good shut-up-I-can't-think kisser, but this was wrong and thoughtless. Anger at herself began to boil in her gut. Her desire waned. Reason, the better R word, came into her head, and she caught one of his hands.

That stopped one, but not the other. It took over, smoothing and tickling that patch behind her shoulders or that spot along a rib that made her sigh.

His fingers tugged at a ribbon holding her sleeves.

She broke from his kiss, shoved at his hands. "What do you think you are doing?"

"Exactly what you think. We are starting over, or where we left off. Father's not standing in the way this time. You only have to sign the leases to finish the peace."

He'd used her weakness to coerce her? "No, you bounder!" She drew up her cloak, hating how breathless and alive she sounded. "Seduction with Daddy's blessing? That's a new trick."

He undid his now-mangled cravat. "Theo, we've been apart six years, but I know you. I know you to be a headstrong beauty who'd rather chew nails than admit to faults or regrets. But I know desire even better. Etched in my brainbox is the way your eyes burn when you want more of me. You haven't changed. You need me. Does that scare you as much as thunder?"

"Yes."

Shrugging, he set his open palms on the seat. "Theo, I know my father did something that made you scared. You were left vulnerable, which went against everything he said he'd do while I served. I know you well enough to know that somehow Mathew Cecil came upon you in your time of need and took care of you, ingratiated himself upon you. If you weren't in trouble, my beautiful strong Theo would've never been snared by an old man."

"What? Who told you this? Your mother?"

His brow squinted then smoothed. "No one had to tell me. I figured it out. Tell me I'm wrong. Then tell me you don't desire me."

"This is what you figured out and now this story makes everything that has happened matter less."

Ewan nodded, and her insides erupted in raw, hot venom.

She forced her voice to a purr. "You want to know desire, tell the driver to go to Beaufort Wharf."

His eyes widened and crinkled as a smile exploded onto his face. He knocked on the roof, stopping the carriage. He stepped out and then returned like a flash of lightning. Soon they were moving.

Ewan held her hand, drew her fully into his embrace. "We're both too stubborn, but I will say it again, I have missed you, Theo."

She didn't respond, and kept his hands locked upon hers where she could see them.

When she peeked out and saw the familiar buildings near the banks of the Thames, she climbed up onto the seat. Her knees sucked into the tufts of the squab and she tried to look happy and wild, while not losing her balance. "You are right. Why fight this feeling bubbling between us? Let me show you my desire."

She threw her arms about his neck and kissed him soundly, pretending that nothing mattered but emotions.

His fingers were in her hair, knocking pins, forcing her chignon down her back. "This hair. Silky and strong. The slight curl, not delicate. I still dream of it, of you and me."

Righting herself on the seat, she pulled up her cape, restoring her hood. "Let's continue inside. Help me down."

He jumped to wet ground, his low boots kicking up a splash. "Yes, I want to see you in the light, Theo, how time has sculpted you to perfection."

When he turned and reached for her hand, she held onto the door. "Go inside to Adams Four, to room four."

He looked about. His face became more painted with questions. "A dark road? Dingy docks? Theo, not here. My flat is nicer. You and I—"

"Go in. Look for the crawlspace behind the curtains. It should still be there."

"Theo, I don't understand."

Scooping up his hat, she tossed it at him. "You wanted to know why I'm afraid of thunder. Because the sound is so much louder if you have to hide in a tight coal scuttle, as you wait for your mother, the harlot, to finish with the man who bought her for two bits."

He jammed on his hat, his face clouding in the shallow light of the moon. "I'm so sorry, Theo. I didn't know. We don't…. Let me get you home." He tried to climb back in, but she put up a hand in protest.

"Don't come back in here or come anywhere near me.

You have your play. You're a handsome man. A Fitzwilliam. You shouldn't have any problems finding a bedmate."

"Theo. I shouldn't have—"

"Go on with your life, Ewan. That's what I've done."

"What if that life should have you in it?"

"No more lies or twisted truths. You made me a harlot once, by bedding me, then no next-day wedding. You changed our plans."

"But you agreed. You said it was the right course, given my father's offer."

"What choice did I have?" She wiped at her face, but held fast to her resolve. This mixed-up passion for a man who could never be all she needed, ended now. "Tonight, I changed your plans. Pity your only consequence is finding a street hackney for a ride. And hear this from me. I chose Mathew Cecil. He didn't trick me. I decided to become his mistress. I came to him. I lay at his feet. And I offered him whatever he wanted."

Ewan's mouth dropped open. He wrenched at his neck as if that would make her statement of wantonness easier for his pride. "So you went after him?"

"Yes. I am everything that you wrote in your play."

"No. That's not true." He put his large hands on the door and pried it open. "Let me come back in. We can discuss this."

"Why? So, you can have another go at me? I don't want to be in your next play. My regret…is you. You said we were running away to marry, but the storm happened. And we had to wait it out in the carriage house. I was so in lo…dazzled by you. I believed you, I gave into feelings I didn't understand. Then your father caught us, and you told me to wait for you. Can't you hear your mother's laughter? You truly thought a harlot, the daughter of harlots, would wait for you? You are as big a fool as I am."

"Theo, that wasn't what it was. We weren't like that.

Theo?"

She waved her hands wildly, pushed away his fingers, then slammed the door again.

He pried it open an inch, but she clung to the handle. "Please."

She wasn't letting him back inside. Angry tears flooded her throat, but she swallowed the itching fire. He needed to hear her, and she needed to be released from the second biggest regret of her life. "I'm no longer like my mother. I'm not going to be bedded like one 'cause of a storm and nice-sounding lies, you manipulative man. I'm an honorable woman because of Mathew Cecil. He married his mistress and gave me a true name. Go on with your life, change all the names in your play back to Theo the Flower Seller, for that girl doesn't exist."

"You're hysterical." His voice fell softer. Maybe he could feel the anger she'd hidden in her bones for him not standing up for their love.

"I have regrets, too Theo. Even if you can't or won't admit to them, I will. Let's talk. Let..."

Regrets? Is that what he called leaving her unprotected to a family that would have her starve to make sure no black blood mixed in their bloodline? "No more *R* words about what we had, Ewan. That love vanished into thin air. It's a ghost to me." Theodosia tapped the roof and the carriage started moving. The door whipped shut, barely missing his fingers. He didn't hold on. Maybe her words made him not try.

She sank into her seat. Blanketing her cape tightly about her shoulders, she waited for her heart to stop pounding, for her lips to stop vibrating from Ewan.

Hopefully, he hated her enough now that he'd release her from his hauntings and his heart. For a determined ghost would destroy the only thing she valued: the honorable name of her son.

Chapter Eleven

The Depths of Hope

Ewan climbed down from his borrowed gig and stowed it in the carriage house at Grandbole. The morning sky had cleared, but the ground and air still smelled of yesterday's heavy rain. He stretched his stiff limbs, being dumped in the middle of the docks had left everything sore, including his heart.

With a shake of his head, he unhitched his horse and handed him over to the groom. The young boy looked as if he still had sleep in his eyes. "Thank you."

He headed to the door but stopped and examined the place, the heavy oak planks forming the walls. The old building might be the oldest on the family property. The loft was piled high with bundles and gear, but maybe there was still room up there for two.

He took another breath, gazing at the opening above and the hooks decorating the walls with harnesses, reins, and wheels, but he turned to the ladder leading to the loft, the quietest place to read and dream. Six years ago, he and Theo had waited out a storm up there. They had talked gibberish of what they would do when they married. Then they'd purposed to elope and they had decided, no, it was better to wait out the storm in the carriage house.

Touching the knurled ladder, he remembered the shy girl, the one so overcome by his telling her of his love, that she had allowed him every liberty. He hadn't coerced her. They'd been in love. Had Theo forgotten that?

Fisting his hands about the pole, he almost climbed the ladder but his legs weren't steady. Up all night, walking off a lifetime of anger, and even beating up a welcome footpad would make anyone unsteady.

His knuckles were raw, but he'd been thankful, ever so grateful, for something to thrash. Pounding his own skull wasn't the best option. No, Theo had done that enough.

One minute loving, alluring, responding to his touch. The next, tricking him out of her carriage. Accusing him of misleading her, of using her fear to take advantage of her.

She thought him a bounder.

But it was worse listening to her admit that she'd harlotted herself to Cecil. She hadn't grieved Ewan's alleged death not even a month before taking up with the rich man.

His father had been right. She'd become the Circe of his play, Theo the Harlot.

Yet. It still didn't feel quite right. How could the shy girl he'd once loved go on to another man so soon?

Jasper strolled through the door, his arms filled with cut flowers. "So this is where you spent the night. You look awful. Must not have gone well at the theater. Sorry, Ewan. I thought the play—"

"No. Mr. Brown wants to buy my play. I need to bring him the final copy. He's excited for it."

Nodding, a clear-eyed Jasper sniffed at the big bouquet in his arms. "Well, you look like you've had a rotten night."

The groom walked past them, yawning, and left. That left the brothers alone in the carriage house. This was bad, for Jasper had the questioning look upon his face with his happy, lopsided smile, his bright eyes searching for the right matches to set the Ewan tinderbox ablaze.

"Did you get caught in that wicked thunderstorm last night and take shelter here? Is it more comfortable here for successful playwrights? Not too drafty."

"No."

"Did the widow meet you here? I hear she came back late, very late. I was at the tavern this morning and heard some odd things."

"Tell your drunk friends she went to the theater, then returned."

"Seems one of her chatty footman talked of a lover's spat. Very unusual, since the woman has been cloistered in black and gray for months. She's been a monk, as far as they know." His brother's amused gaze disappeared. His pupils narrowed and fixed upon Ewan's hands. "You haven't been out carousing, as Father puts it. You've been in a fight, Brother. What happened last night? Did you have to defend the Blackamoor beauty from a bounder?

"No. Can we stop this conversation, Jasper?"

"Did you have to stop someone from attacking her, angry at her race? I'd assume with the Abolitionist movement starting, a buffoon might have the wrong idea. I hear they call slave mistresses fancies in the Americas."

Hot, blind rage crossed Ewan's eyes. Pulling his bruised hands to his back, Ewan spread his feet apart and prepared to strike his own brother. "Don't call her that around me. There's an unlucky footpad who stumbled upon me looking for money. He caught the bad end of my fists. I am unharmed."

Jasper's grin disappeared. "Sorry. You look mostly unruffled on the outside, but that's the outside."

Foolscap, on reams of paper, that was where Ewan wrote of his black insides. Not accustomed to talking things out with anyone anymore, he shrugged. "You look like you're getting ready to go court someone. Have you given up on your letter-writing widow? Going to try it the old-fashioned way? A matchmaking mama or my matchmaking mother taking the reins?"

"No. And no. I can wait to see what the widow answers. These blooms are for Father. He's going into Town to see your mother. He said it was your suggestion."

With a shake of his head, Ewan tried to dismiss an image of the old fool showing off his scowl to his poor mother, the gentle, sweet woman. Yet, Theo had lumped the lady into her list of complaints. Why? He rubbed his brow. "So the old earl is going to see her. Maybe there's hope of someone reconciling."

"Maybe he'll bring her back to help with the girls, but they've kind of scared her out of that grandmotherly role." Jasper moved from his post at the door, his head swiveling and studying, as if he'd never come to the carriage house before. "So this was where you secreted away, you and your flower seller before you were caught."

Ewan glanced at the loft and thoughts of Theo rushed his soul. He could still hear her laughter, her shattered breaths from his kisses.

So much like last night. He hadn't expected to rekindle things, but he hadn't expected to have her in his arms. Or that she'd dump him on the road, as if he were a blackguard. He swallowed the awful lump of gall filling his dry mouth. "Jasper, you have flowers to deliver. Don't let me keep you."

His brother came closer. Not a hint of brandy was in his breath. "We used to be able to talk. We used to see things the same."

Ewan touched the flowers, swirling the reds and pinks.

"That was before you left for your grand tour, before you married, and before I took up with someone of another race. A Blackamoor. I loved her, Jasper. Maybe as much as you loved Maria."

The pronouncement startled him as much as Jasper, but it was true.

"Father said he caught you two here. He said he called her every evil name he could conjure up but you stood up to him, even more so than what you did with me. She had to be special."

"Aye. But then I did the unthinkable. I agreed to the earl's demands. He said he'd give his permission for us to wed if I served a year in the militia. I served, and I lost her. But the earl was right about her not being faithful. That she'd be ruinous to me. She admitted last night to seducing Cecil and becoming his mistress. I wasn't cold in the ground a month."

Jasper lips thinned. The big man swirled a long rose as if it was one of his swords. "Interesting. Why would Cecil marry his mistress? With a mistress, you get the benefits of the milk and cheese for which you've paid. One doesn't have to own the cow and put your name to it."

"The widow is not a cow."

"Ewan, I think there are answers you need to figure out."

"Why?" Ewan looked at the ladder, which led to loft. He climbed the first rung but stopped. She hated him, such awfulness had flowed from those wondrous lips. "What good would it be to hear the reasons? It wouldn't change a thing."

"Perhaps, perhaps not. But maybe she needs to hear why you agreed to the earl's demands. You loved her. You said she loved you. The two of you were set to elope, but then you agreed to the old man's demands. Why?"

The old reasons of wanting his father's approval had cost him. Ewan rubbed at his neck. "I wanted the old man to not hate me for loving her. I didn't want him savaging another play like he'd done with my first. But it doesn't matter anymore. I couldn't have made Theo happy. She once mentioned wanting to own a flower store. She has the money for several, but she's purchased none. Her dreams have changed. She's changed. It doesn't matter now."

His brother strode over to him and hefted the floral arrangement into his hands. "Maybe you can use these more than Father."

Ewan squinted at the big hulk of a man. "I don't understand."

"You've beat someone senseless over her. You've used your muse to write a play about her. Until last night, not a hint of scandal about Cecil's widow. I suggest you go to Tradenwood, apologize for everything, and tell her you want another chance."

Every bit of the frustration from last night still boiled his blood. It pumped and burned and stung every organ. Head down on the ladder, Ewan dropped the flowers, then jumped down upon them. "She called herself a harlot for loving me. She condemned herself and me for giving into passion."

He kicked the pile and sent more petals flying. "She is done with me. Maybe you should go to her. You both are widows. She seems to like neighbors."

Jasper bent and picked up a few of the undamaged buds. "Maybe I should go court one of the young women your mother has foisted upon me at her parties. Seems newspaper advertisement number four hasn't written back."

"Good. You don't need anyone who can't admit regrets."

"But what of you, Ewan? You're besotted with Cecil's widow but won't go down to Tradenwood because you don't want to admit your own regrets."

"You mean go down there and say anything to have her sign away the rights to the waterway? Maybe you're more like the earl; her money now makes the neighbor acceptable."

Breaking stems in his hands, Jasper made a bigger scatter of red bits on the dirt floor. "I won't lie. I want our land protected, but I also want you happy. I know what love feels like. I know it. And I've watched it die. If I had a chance to regain that feeling I would, but you have to be brave to do that."

"I went to war. I am brave."

"On the outside, Ewan. Admit to her why you accepted Father's offer. You were set to elope, but then you changed your mind. Why?"

A sober Jasper meant all his acumen came full bore. His aim was deadly accurate. His brother shook his head. "Admit the regret, the one that made you turn from the woman you obviously loved."

"I didn't think I could support us against the earl's wrath. He'd threatened to make sure all my plays would never sell. How would I bring bread to the table? How would I be enough for her?"

Jasper lifted Ewan's hand and shook the scabbed thing. "With these. You've stood up to me with every slight I've thrown. You beat someone to a pulp last night, because of her. You should fight for her as you told Father to do for your mother."

Ewan blinked and he was on his sick bed reading the earl's gloating letter about Theo running off with another man. Dormant fury erupted. Knuckles stinging, he drew back his hand. "It doesn't matter now. That was a long time ago. She doesn't want me and I'm not so sure I want my cousin's mistress turned wife."

Jasper's face blanked. The man never showed any other emotion than humor, except when that long fuse tempering his anger was spent. He looked as if he'd explode, too. "It does matter. We all have pasts, but what about a future? What about being made new each day, because we are given a new day?"

"The elder brother holds the land not the role of a vicar. You're more loveable when you are less ministerial."

"I'm stating the obvious. Neither of you have resolved your feelings. You're both stuck in yesterday. I doubt if either of you know how to forgive."

"I forgave her when I thought she was a victim."

Jasper folded his arms, looking every inch the older, wiser brother. "Maybe it was easier to forgive your duplicity in deflowering her, thinking you died. The score sounds pretty even, in a tit-for-tat kind of way." His lips thinned to a line. "And if you don't get the widow's agreement before Father returns, he *will* coerce her. And you know how he is. It won't be pretty. Get the widow to see the light, before it is too late."

Hadn't the earl's dealings set Ewan and Theo onto this hopeless path? Ewan dropped his still fisted hands to his sides. "What did he threaten this time?"

With a shrug of his shoulders, Jasper turned. "Nothing specific, but I don't want to find out. Fix this, Ewan." Head hanging low, his brother walked out of the carriage house.

Alone again, Ewan felt a knot tighten in his gut. Theo was about to face the earl's vengeance a second time.

A sober Jasper, a fearless Jasper, not wanting to see the earl's schemes, meant the old man prepared for war.

How could Ewan get Theo to compromise when it seemed being compromised was the root of her anger at him? What Jasper had said, to tell Theo why he had changed their plans six years ago felt valid. Maybe things would be different if he'd told her then. Maybe things would be different now.

He bent and scooped up a single rosebud. Snipping off a bruised petal revealed a perfect flower. Maybe under their scars, the same could be said of the playwright and the widow.

Yes, there was a woman down the hill who needed to give him one last audience.

• • •

Theodosia stared out the balcony of her bedchamber at the sunny sky. The sun was high, casting short shadows over the rail. The morning had fled. It had to be past noon, maybe two or three o'clock, and she'd only written two words, *Dear Sir.*

She'd tried to prove Ewan wrong, that she could admit to the *R* words, but she'd failed. It was too hard to admit her greatest regrets.

A knock sounded on the door.

Theodosia pushed up from the writing chair, the one she'd taken from Mathew's adjoining room, and smoothed a drooping curl back behind her ear. "A moment."

Listless, she pulled back the flowing cream curtain around her bed. Her shawl lay there and she'd need its comfort. She was still drained from arguing in the rain with Ewan.

What if Pickens needed her to go to outside to the fields to check decorations for the festival? Her heart lunged forward then slapped back into her chest. Ewan would be there. She felt it. Pickens said he'd stopped by three times yesterday. *Oh, let this not require going outdoors.* She couldn't face him again. Not now, and never alone.

Another knock.

Resigned, she slogged forward, but before her fingers turned the doorknob, in popped Frederica. "Mrs. Cecil? Are you well? The butler said you haven't budged from this room except to check on Philip."

Pickens followed and his frown could've touched the floor. "I tried to stop her, ma'am, but I was busy dissuading Mr. Fitzwilliam."

Oh no. Ewan had come again. Why wouldn't he give up? "It's fine. Have Miss Burghley's room ready. She's here early."

Still frowning, Pickens left, closing the door with a gentle thud.

Frederica leaned against the threshold connecting the bedchambers. "What has occurred?"

Theodosia pulled at her shawl and shrugged. "I'm not in the best spirits, and you've arrived early. You were to come tomorrow morning. Is everything well with you?"

With her hazel eyes squinting, her friend slipped off her dark blue gloves. "I had a feeling you might need me." Frederica sashayed to the balcony and back. Her sleek indigo carriage gown looked like a uniform, with military fobbing and buttons about her sleeves. Was she coming to battle?

"Well, you are alone in here. There goes one of my ideas." A giggle fell from her lips, then her tone sobered. "So what happened with your *cousin*?"

Shaking her head, Theodosia backed up to the post of her canopy bed. "Nothing."

"The way the man stormed away from Tradenwood, something happened. Why is he desperate and why won't you see him?"

"How mad was Mr. Fitzwilliam?"

"He looked like he'd breathe flames. Confess. What is going on with him, with you?"

Theodosia glanced down and folded her arms about her middle. She couldn't run from the truth. Now she didn't want to. "I deserved his wrath," she said. "I angered him."

"No one can be angered by you, dear Theodosia. You care too much for others."

"Oh yes, they can be. And Ewan Fitzwilliam has the right to be mad. I led him on, then dumped him without a care onto the side of the road. I knew it was wrong, but did it, anyway."

Frederica's mouth fell open and not in a snack-on-a-bonbon kind of way, but in a wide gape. "But you...you jest. I saw him at the door, here, applying to enter Tradenwood. Where did you leave him? At the gate? The edge of the fields perhaps?"

"I left him outside my mother's old brothel, the one I was born at near the docks. A most dangerous part of London."

Silence.

Frederica's eyes grew bigger.

Shame, almost as bad as the day she had been turned away from Grandbole six years ago, rocked Theodosia. She had gone there to seek help and had been reminded that she was no better than her mother. The angry taunts rang in her head. She was filled with shame. Shame at her mother's profession. Shame at begging for a crust of bread to save her unborn child. "I wanted him to feel desperate and tawdry, like I had."

"Why would you?" Frederica's fair cheeks were ashen. "We never talk about the brothels...your mother's or mine. We don't."

For a moment, Theodosia closed her eyes, hoping to forget the hurt stirring in Frederica's irises. "This is why I hate talking of regrets. They are horrid and they remind people of their worst pain. I won't say it again."

"It's us. The lucky by-blows. The ones who escaped that life."

Theodosia rushed to her friend and lifted her chin. "I needed Ewan Fitzwilliam to see what happens to the unlucky ones. They have to go to brothels and sell their souls when men leave them unprotected."

With a nod, Frederica moved away, opened the balcony doors, and pulled back the gauzy curtains. "So you and this Fitzwilliam? He was a beau?"

"Yes. Then he went to war and died. I was left to figure out how to survive, me and my baby."

Frederica spun to her like a top. "Philip?"

"Only Mathew knew the secret, and he told me never to tell. My husband adored my son and loved him as if he was his own."

"I always thought Cecil was too old, but with Philip being so sickly—"

"Philip is sickly because I starved while I carried him—all because of the Fitzwilliams. They never approved of me and made things worse when they thought my beau, their son, had died in Spain."

Shock didn't look good on Frederica. Her features were made for lightness, nothing heavy or foreboding.

But Theodosia had to tell someone. As if to keep herself intact, she wrapped herself deeper in her shawl, the light cream wool bandaging over her gray widow's garb. "I regret believing my lover's lies, but not Philip."

Eyes growing larger, Frederica came near. "Fitzwilliam doesn't look dead now. He obviously still likes you. Maybe he could be the husband we need."

Turning her head like a mad woman, Theodosia said, "No. No. No. I can't trust him. He won't fight for Philip, not against his family."

"But you, and especially Philip, are his family, too. You should give him the opportunity to choose. The Peninsula War ended some time ago. He may have changed, and I saw how he looked at you when he assisted you from my father's box."

Refusing to agree, Theodosia shook her head faster. "That was lust. It will pass."

"But I saw your face and how you clung to his arm." Frederica paced from the bed to the desk and back, with her arms pinned behind her back, the picture of a barrister. She stopped at the desk and fingered the letter from the newspaper advertisement baron, then Theodosia's measly attempt at a reply. "Admit you still like Fitzwilliam. He's more interesting than the squire. Hopefully, he's as clever with words as this baron. Can't you see it in your heart to forgive your cousin?"

Theodosia took the notes from Frederica's fingers. "Forgive and forget? I don't know anymore. I idolized him. I made our love seem so perfect and tragic. That was a farce, like that shrew play we watched. And poor Mathew. It took him too long to get through to my heart, because I kept comparing my dreamer to practical Mathew. I'm a fool. I had a perfect man who loved a child that wasn't his, while I wrongfully held on to lies."

"But Cecil won your heart. I saw you two. You loved him, and he knew it."

"Yes, but how many months, years, did I deprive him of my heart?"

Frederica wrapped her arms about Theodosia and held on tight. "You loved him, and he loved you. Don't you forget that. He chose you. He gave that boy a name, but Cecil wanted you happy."

"Mathew would want me to protect Philip. Maybe Philip and I need to leave here. I could take Philip and the means I could quickly garner and go. Do you think the waters of Bath will help him?"

Frederica tightened her embrace. "You can't leave. You haven't left because of Lester's threats, but this Fitzwilliam makes you so scared you want to flee? He can't hurt you. Philip was born during your marriage. He's Cecil's because he claimed him."

That was true but it didn't stop the fear of the Fitzwilliams figuring out ways to use the secret to hurt Philip or to steal him away as Lester had threatened. Biting her lip, she straightened and pried out of Frederica's hug. "I can't let them put out nasty rumors about my son. If I don't run, I must marry. The sooner I marry, the safer Philip will be."

She put her hands onto Frederica's shoulders, spun her around, then steered her to the door. "You go settle into the guest room Pickens has for you. I promise to clean up and dine with you tonight. And we can talk about any nonsense you want, any *other* nonsense."

"Will there be bonbons?"

"Of course, so many we can forget what I've said."

Frederica stopped dragging her low-cut boots, but paused at the door. "Cecil had a look in his eyes that told me how much he loved you. His cousin has that look, too."

She opened the door and gave Frederica a light shove. "Bonbons. Now go on."

Her friend smiled and headed down the hall.

Closing the door, Theodosia took a long breath. Alone again, she felt lighter, maybe even motivated. She'd told her regrets and the world didn't crumble. She returned to her desk and picked up the cut of foolscap she'd started with *Dear Sir*. Her fingers tapped the smooth surface of the small pine desk. This was the ideal setting, tucked in the corner of her bedchamber, different from her business desk in the parlor. Through the billowy curtain covering the balcony, she could enjoy the sweet air rising from the fields, her fields.

Regrets didn't smell so fine. How did they look on paper?

Another knock sounded.

Frederica again? Did she think of another question to ask?

Two knocks sounded. The second echoed as it came from the lower part of the door.

Philip?

Pulse throbbing in terror, she rushed to the door and flung it open.

Her heart started to beat again as she saw her son standing in his blue pinafore next to Pickens. Then it stopped again. He was holding his ear. His pretty eyes were sad, filling with tears.

"Ma—ma."

Not caring about her dignity or station in front of her

butler, she dropped to her knees and grabbed the boy. She massaged his head, the way that brought smiles once the pain went away. "It will be all right. I'll make it better, Son. How long has he been hurting?"

Pickens bent and picked up the boy and took her arm, helping her to stand. "Only a few minutes. The governess came to me."

The woman should've come to her directly. Philip's well-being was the most important thing. She scooped up her son and took him fully into her arms. "Can you have some hot tea sent? And send for the doctor."

The man's lips thinned. "Mrs. Cecil, the doctor will be here tomorrow at the festival. He won't do any better than what you do for Master Philip."

Why did Pickens have to be right? Why couldn't the answer be different for once? Couldn't any of the doctors do something to save her son? She spun from the butler, taking Philip with her, sailing almost half into the room before she faced the man again. "You say that as if there is no hope. Is that what you want to hear?"

Her butler stood in the threshold. His face was unreadable.

She clutched her son more tightly to her bosom hoping that the feel of her, the smell of her lavender would let him know that she was close, that she'd never stop hoping, never stop loving him.

Philip let go of his ear and hugged her neck. "Make—go away."

"Get the laudanum, Pickens. It will help him sleep until this passes. That's what all the doctors have done."

The butler nodded. "Master Cecil used to say hope was everlasting. That it lifted his head as he walked in the fields. He never feared, ma'am. Hope was on his side."

She looked down at the boy her husband had claimed for his legacy and snuggled her face against his shiny black mop.

She'd never give up on trying to make her son whole.

As she rubbed his temples, she watched him breathe. He was small for his age and looked so delicate, but love overwhelmed her. He was the best part of her.

The need to gain the best advocate for Philip renewed. She'd wait for the medicine to take hold as he slept in her bed, then she'd return to her desk and answer the baron.

She wouldn't be afraid anymore. Her son needed her to be strong. She'd found a champion once, a kindly gentleman farmer, Mathew Cecil. Maybe she'd be that lucky again. Hope still existed for her and Philip. It had to.

Chapter Twelve

The Flora Festival

The noise, *tap*, *tap* made Theodosia snuggle in her blanket. Frederica would have to wait for a decent hour to hear more gossip.

Tap.

It was too early for her chamber maid.

The rhythm continued. She sat up, pulling the bedclothes to her chin. Her eyes slowly opened to the ebony darkness. She struck a match and lit a candle. Gazing at Philip's sleeping form, her pulse slowed. He lay still beside her, hopefully enjoying pain-free dreams.

Before she could tuck the covering about his shoulder, the noise started again. This time she heard the *ting ting*. It was something hitting the balcony door glass panes. Something outside wanted in.

Blinking, Theodosia squinted at the curtains. Through the parting of the fabric, she spied an outline, a ghost, no a man. *Ewan?*

Like a cat, she sprung up, closing the sheers to her bed,

hiding her sleeping son.

Fear pumped through her, her ghost…too near her boy.

Holding her breath, she pulled on her robe and cinched it tight. Starting to the doors on tiptoes she stopped. Philip wouldn't hear. Only if he were looking at you and concentrating could he make out noise with his good ear.

Sad and sighing, she stood at the glass doors, staring at the frowning man on the other side.

His hands were on his breeches. The man bent, half-hunched over, gasping air. "Theo. Open up."

"Go home." She hoped he'd heed and not wake the house, but the fire in his gaze said no. He wouldn't be moved. "Please."

"Not until we speak." He punched at the glass while still gulping like his lungs weren't working. "Not with this between us."

Unbelievable. Ewan rapped against the door, wheezing like an old fool. What did he expect climbing up here? And he could've fallen. Her chamber sat high on the second floor.

He banged this time, harder. "Let me in." His voice sounded louder this time.

Philip might not hear, but the rest of the house would. She couldn't have more whispers about her conduct, not after the footman had witnessed the argument outside the brothel. Resigned, she unlatched the door and pushed onto the balcony. "Be quick."

Ewan strutted forward, like a peacock, a panting peacock. "You don't look sick."

His shortness of breath filled her with unwanted concern. "You do. Are you very winded?"

"It will pass. It always does." He pressed at his chest in the spots where she'd felt his scars. "Overexerted myself climbing up here. Not quite the same as when Jasper and I did it as children."

"You shouldn't have done that, Ewan. It's too dark and dangerous to balance on my tree. Did you step on my clematis blooms to get here?"

Bright moonlight streamed about him, making his shoulders seem broader. He chuckled and leaned against the rail, dusting his hands. "Fretting over flowers? No regard for me falling?"

She folded her arms to keep from shoving him over the rail. "You chose to climb. No one made you. Why are you here? What if someone saw you sneaking in here?"

"From what I remember of our time together, you were consumed with lavender, not clematis."

"Good night, Ewan."

She reached for the doors, attempting to close them upon him, but this time he was faster and both his large hands covered hers.

Warm, rough, and alive. The heat of his skin seared her flesh, made her knees weak. "Leave me, Ewan. Please."

He opened the doors fully and sauntered inside. His brows popped up as his head dipped, then raised, as he circled her. "Creamy white silk is much better than dark, heavy mourning robes."

The glint in his eyes made her pulse race. His touch brought that dangerous, swirling, out-of-control feeling. It engulfed her, but she folded her arms about her middle like a shield. No matter how weak she was for him, he wasn't going to make her rash. "Say what you have to say then over the balcony and out of my life."

He leaned on the doorframe. "I have been trying to see you for days. I'm tired of waiting. You should understand that, Mrs. Cecil."

She refused to respond to his baiting and held all her retorts that it was *his* fault she'd needed Mathew. Ewan needed his say, if only to make it right that she'd dumped him at the docks. Nodding, she said, "Continue, but be brief. I have a long day tomorrow. The festival begins."

"Yes, the Flora Festival. Pickens said you've exhausted yourself in the planning, but I've come with an ultimatum from the earl. He'll triple his offer. He will pay three times the previous amount for the water leases."

"Triple? And just for leases. Not to buy all my land." She tugged on her robe sash, almost turning toward her canopy bed but stopped. "Not my requested multiple of twenty?"

His eyes squinted. He pulled a folded paper out of his pocket and pushed it between her fingers. "This is reasonable. And take hold of it. Read it for yourself. I know my notions hold little weight, but this is a valid offer to continue the water use. This will bring peace between neighbors."

"But Lester won't let me agree. He wants…" She took the paper, and curled it within her fingers. "Even if what you say is true, I can't sign this yet. It will force my hand, literally." She moved to her desk and lit a candle. Using the light, she scanned the pages. It said what Ewan stated.

With heavy steps, he followed. She felt his breath on her neck before she turned.

"I can read it to you as in direct address. You used to like me reading to you, Theo. You used to like me."

She glared at him. "I don't want you haunting me anymore."

"Yes. You made that quite clear in your carriage. But I must resolve this before the earl does. I don't want him to hurt you."

The concern in his voice was palpable, heart stopping, and she had to remember that this was the same man who'd left her in fear of his father's wrath. "I'll manage."

His hand lifted, and she tensed, as if he were going to touch her.

Frowning, he grunted something then leaned past her and

picked up her letter from the baron. "Oh, how droll, teasing you about regrets. I suppose you'll tell him how I misled you, poor innocent you."

He tossed the paper to the desk, then curled his palm under his chin. "Do be kind when you tell him how you never responded to my kisses, not even the ones in the carriage. No, that would be a lie, like saying, 'I'll wait for you to return from the Peninsula,' when you obviously didn't."

Breathing heavy in short bursts, as if he had touched his lips to hers, she slipped to the side of him. "I wish for you to take your mocking and seductions and go."

A smile lit his face and he moved to her again. "Seduction only works if the object is in the mood to be swayed. I'm no bounder. I've taken no liberties, nothing that wasn't freely offered."

"I never said you took anything."

"Theo, you made a great performance of it in your carriage. That kiss, the sizzling one that sent me flopping out the door like a happy puppy about to feast on the cook's soup bones—that was done well. You should manage theater. The production was quite fine."

"I was wrong to do that, but you used that storm to try to…confuse me. That was wrong, too."

He rubbed at his neck. "I didn't mean to take advantage. I remembered how you hated storms and meant to be of comfort. But I can't help my attraction to you. That doesn't make me nefarious; it makes me a man. I'm not seeking to ruin you, well, not like that. Admit that I'm no bounder. Six years ago, I was a man who was alone with the woman he loved."

Those pretty eyes of his held her captive, but it was easy to say this truth. "Yes Ewan, you are no bounder."

"Good. I like my sins known." His gaze raked over her.

She pulled at her lacy robe again, feeling exposed to his

hungry, hypnotic gaze. "You chose your elegant words to make me believe a lie, that you would marry me, honor, and protect me. I forgave you when I thought you'd died. I only tried to remember the good, not that you'd abandoned me when I needed you. But now, I see the truth, how you will use your elegant words to ruin my reputation."

In slow motion, he put a palm to her elbow. "I took your name out. I will not put it back in because we are fighting."

"What of the carriage? Ewan, you're not in love with me, but you kissed me like you are."

He walked around her again, lowly humming to himself. "I'm still a man, Theo, and a little weight looks truly well on you."

"Haven't you ever seen a robe before? Or a mature woman?" She wanted to add that she'd had a baby, but she didn't, not with Philip sleeping a few feet away.

His grin returned. "Yes. But since I've returned, I've only seen you in dark billowy garbs. Sheer looks good upon you, and you're not pregnant."

What? Not ashamed of her curves, she lifted her chin. "Thank you, I think, but why would you..." She shook her head, knowing his new conspiracy would take today's peace. "Mathew Cecil thought me very pretty. You've delivered your message, but you being here is not proper. Someone could catch you. They'll think—"

A snore whistle sounded. Soft at first, then loud.

"We're not alone, Theo." Anger etched his jaw as it tightened. "Here I am trying to protect you." His voice deepened. "Thinking this Lester fellow is bad and he's trying to force his way into your bed, and he's already here. Let me congratulate him with my fists."

"No. Ewan stop."

Unable to grab him, he sprang over to her big bed and drew back the canopy curtain.

Theodosia came upon him and caught the shift in his face, the slacking of his jaw.

Ewan saw Philip.

But did her poor boy see Ewan?

Another sleepy snort whistled.

Philip didn't even awake with the commotion.

Relief sweating through her pores, Theodosia pulled Ewan's hands away and yanked the curtains closed. "Stop before you wake my son."

Ewan took another peek before turning to her. "I'm sorry, Theo. You make me cork-brained."

"I can't make you anything."

"Yes, you do. I've never been a jealous man. I'm a second son. I missed titles and wealth by the virtue of birth order." His palm curled about the knurled post of the footboard. "I lost this estate to Cecil by the premature reports of my death. None of this deeply cut, not until I found out he had you. And you have born him a son."

He looked as if he'd go back to Philip.

Against her resolve or even better judgment, she reached for Ewan and rubbed his forearm. "I'm sorry, but he's a good boy."

"Little comfort, Theo. I'm envious, stewing inside. Cousin Cecil married you. From all accounts, you two seemed happy and you have a boy. If I'd stayed, if you hadn't thought me dead, he could be my son."

Gulping in her guilt, she fought the urge to shout to him, *Yes, Philip is yours!* The truth dangled upon her tongue but so did the fear of what would happen next. More fussing, and Ewan would steal her boy's honorable name and not defend him to the world. His Fitzwilliam family would come first, not the flower seller's. She'd rather die than allow anyone to call Philip the names she bore, the names her dear Frederica had to endure. With a yank, she stole back her hand and clasped her elbow. "We can't look back."

"Well, now I know why Cecil married his mistress. He wanted his boy to have a name. Someone he could leave a legacy." He punched at his hand. "Blasted Cecil, you standup fellow."

She looked down at her robe and scooped up the sash. "This is for the best. You think your father would want a mulatto heir? I know he wouldn't. Your mother wouldn't want that, either."

Ewan ran his fingers through his hair. "My mother would love my son. She's nothing like Lord Crisdon. But it matters not what anyone thinks."

"It matters to you, Ewan. I remember how it tormented you not to have their blessing."

He frowned. "All I know is my cousin was the luckiest man." Ewan chuckled as if he'd gone mad. "I truly hate him."

She followed behind him out of the house and into the night, watching those broad shoulders sag. His emotions had to be as raw as hers. The man had seen his son. He said he was jealous of Mathew's claim to Philip. Even now, tears threatened at the costs Ewan bore. Once upon a time she was the one with whom he'd shared dreams. And she'd treasured those moments. Now, she was part of his nightmares. She put a hand to his shoulder. "I am so sorry. What's done is done."

He turned it and clutched her hand to his chest. "Is it? Or is it to be repeated. I can't deny my attraction to you is still alive."

"I'm a threat to your Fitzwilliam family, remember? You wrote me as a villain in your play. Go home. Maybe read some more of that foul Shakespeare you're so fond of."

"You remember?"

"Yes, Ewan. I remember. I remember everything. I did like you reading to me."

He didn't release her hand and swung her until the big

bright moon seemed reachable. "Well, we are on a balcony. Come, gentle night; come, loving, black-browed night. Give me my Theo; and, when I shall die, take her and cut her out in little stars, that will make the face of heaven so fine. All the world will be in love with night."

It was hard to breathe. The cheek he touched burned as if branded. "You and your fancy words."

"They're foul Shakespeare's from his *Romeo and Juliet*, a forbidden love from opposing families."

"We're the same family now, sort-of-cousin."

Ewan lips brushed her forehead. "Let me make this plain. I still want you, Theo. And you should admit that part of your kisses were true. You still feel something for me."

Her heart stopped, and it would never beat right again if she started believing in him, if she again gave in to that desperate-for-her look in his eyes. She stepped backward. "You have your play. Once I'm married, I'll sign the papers you brought. Your father will be proud of you handling this."

"That solves his problems, Theo. Not mine."

With a slow step, he stood within inches of her, but kept his hands to his side, not wrapping her in those arms that would make her wilt against him like a lily lacking water. "Choose to kiss your cousin."

For a moment, she imagined pressing into his arms and waiting for him to take away her breath. In the carriage, Ewan had proved his kisses were the same as six years ago, dangerous and wild.

But she couldn't think of herself, only Philip. He needed a champion more than she needed to be held in arms that wanted her. Taking another step back, she shook her head. "Go home, Ewan."

"Theo. Everything has been frozen inside of me."

"You don't know me anymore. I still hate thunderstorms, but I'm different. I have a son who needs a mother he can respect. And I mourn a husband who made sure we were safe. He didn't care one whit about what others thought. He was our champion. I knew I was completely safe. His promises never changed."

"I was young. I had to be able to provide for us, and I didn't think we could survive with the earl against us. I should've believed more in us. He stopped my first play from being sold. That's the only reason I agreed. He never changed my mind about you. I left for war, thinking it would be a quick year and you and I would be free, with nothing to stop us."

She wanted to believe him, but too much was at stake. "We can't go backward. And it's not proper for you to be in my bedchamber or meeting me in the fields saying such things. Please, as your cousin's widow, if you care anything for me, go back to Grandbole as quietly as you came."

Standing erect, he reached for her hand and kissed it. "Then it's time to move forward." Gripping her palm high he spun her again, as he had at the beginning of his fine speech, as he had on the hill, as he had so many years ago. "I will court you again."

On the balcony, he twirled faster and faster until she clasped him tight to stop the world from spinning. He dipped his head atop hers and held her.

"I am Fitzwilliam. You know that makes me determined to win you. I will not be deterred. You need a husband and father for this boy or you wouldn't have placed an advertisement for one. Let it be me. Let me tend to you, Theo." He bent his head. His mouth neared hers. "Like it should've been before. Let me be the one. Turn to me."

His heart pounded in her ear and the scent of him—tangy sagebrush mixed with sweet oak from the tree he'd climbed—enveloped her. Right or wrong, she parted her lips, wanting to swirl away, lost in him.

"Open your eyes, Theo." Ewan pushed her shoulders and

eased her rising tiptoe stance back down. "The right way this time. With a minister…and a bed, a wide bed. Let's elope now."

"Ewan, my husband's festival is tomorrow."

"Late husband, remember. You're querying for a newspaper groom. Do I need to respond to your advertisement?"

It was good he didn't kiss her. One kiss might lead to another and tomorrow would disappear. She could feel herself falling for his teasing, but would he be there to catch her? "Ewan, we were young and not smart enough to keep our love. I must tell you. Something that I don't think you will forgive."

"It doesn't matter. It's the past, backward."

"But what I must say will ruin things. I must tell—"

He did kiss her this time, cutting off her words, her reservations, even the power to reason. His palms molded her against him and took possession of her breathing. He became air and she savored how he filled her chest with love. She levitated in his arms, so high, so fast that tomorrow didn't have to appear.

"No, sweet Theo. Not until the banns are read, then you'll be mine completely." He put her feet back onto the balcony and held her until his heart stopped racing. "Consider this a verbal application to your advertisement. I want equal, no, *all* of your consideration. We will elope after the festival. I'm not taking no and if I have to kiss you all the way to Scotland and back I will." With a safe kiss to her brow, he turned and threw a leg over the rail. "See you tomorrow, Theodosia Cecil, soon to be my bride."

He said her name, her whole one. "Fitzwilliams don't come to the Flora Festival."

"This one is. I'm coming to honor my cousin and his widow and formally meet his son. I am to be the boy's new stepfather tomorrow. He should meet me and get used to me. I will be around this time because we elope once the festival closes."

Her traitorous lips didn't say no. She watched Ewan lower himself into the tree and disappear into the night.

Going inside, she closed the door and leaned her head against the panes. The determination in his eyes was different than it had been six years ago. That scared her more than anything. How was she going to keep Philip safe, safe from angry in-laws, horrid business partners, and out-of-control passion?

She'd tell Ewan the whole truth tomorrow. Then he'd know why she couldn't marry him. Ewan would either despise her again or understand why she wouldn't expose Philip to Fitzwilliam hate.

If she couldn't marry Ewan, she still needed a husband. She dropped into her desk chair, pushed aside Ewan's lease paper, and began penning her greatest regret to the baron: she'd been so focused on the memory of a lost love, that she had fallen prey to hard times and almost starved to death, hurting her child. She'd send this note off tomorrow. If the baron dared to write back to newspaper advertisement number four, then he was the man who would stand by her and defend her to the Court of Chancery. If not, she'd marry the squire, anyone whose name wasn't Fitzwilliam.

A man who could be counted upon was who she needed, not a ghost who suddenly wanted to live again in her heart.

· · ·

The musicians could be heard all the way up to Grandbole. Ewan had his youngest scamp niece dressed and ready to join the fun below, the Flora Festival. The air held the tart smell of fresh-cut hay.

They hopped all the way to the patio and spent countless minutes numbering the gathering crowds. The parish church bells rang and gonged in symphony with shepherds, who set and pitchforked hay bundles on the edges of Cecil property. It was medieval and wonderful.

Little Lucy tugged on his hand. "Anne and Lydia would like to come, Uncle."

"Well, they shouldn't have exchanged my ink for mud, dear."

"They didn't mean it."

The child's father came onto the patio, bent down, popped Lucy's drooping chin up with his finger. "No, they didn't mean to get caught." Chuckling, Jasper straightened, clear-eyed, energized. He reached out and thumbed Ewan in the chest right atop his deepest scar. "Literally, they've tried to scare him so much they'll give his weak heart pains."

"My heart's not that weak, just scared and cautious. Girls will do that, won't they, Hartwell?" Ewan swung his niece, her white dress floating about her short legs. Absolutely cute.

The wistful look in Jasper's light blue eyes concurred. "They've tormented your uncle Ewan enough. Missing the festival is fitting punishment. Besides, it'll take the two of us just to keep you from mischief."

Setting down the girl, Ewan looked down to Tradenwood. "Seems quite a show."

"One year, Cecil had chimney sweeps on his roof, dancing and singing with their brooms. They wore gilt paper and masks. It was a sight to see. Cecil had a fondness for extravagance and made his festival like a May Day celebration. It's crowded and noisy, perfect for an afternoon of ridiculousness."

Ewan scooped up Lucy and pointed to the fields. "Look at the milkmaids. I guess it's them with the wide skirts of red and gold."

"Uncle, they have huge pyramids on their heads." She put her hands above her head like she balanced something, too. "I want to do it. Mama used to make us paper hats, but with regular paper, not the gold stuff."

Jasper's countenance soured for a moment. "Maria did that? We never went. I didn't know she…" He took his dark top hat and popped it atop Lucy's bonnet. "You can use this."

The giggling girl put it on for a second then handed it back. "This is round."

Impatience winning over humor, Ewan started down the steps. "Let's go see the pyramids and all the gilt paper. You never went?"

"No, your mother hated it and pretty much convinced everyone it was low class and a travesty to Tradenwood. I'd never heard her scream before my oldest brought up going. But Maria liked fun and music. I should've known she would go."

Mother…screaming? Ewan shook his head, but realized Theo wasn't the only one mourning a legend, a mate who seemed more perfect than life. Was love possible again for one who had loved and lost so deeply? Ewan thought about his own heart and what he believed he had felt for Theo six years ago and now. There was a chance for them now. Right?

He had to get her to elope…in his brother's carriage. What type of man did that make Ewan? Shrugging inwardly, he picked up his pace. "I'll not tell Mother we are going. Can you keep that secret, Lucy?"

"Yes, Uncle. Now hurry. I hear a violin."

"I'll not tell Lady Crisdon." Jasper caught up and took his laughing girl from Ewan and put her onto his shoulder. "Perhaps, I should blend in. Maybe borrow Father's other title again, Lord Tristian."

"No." Ewan lowered his tone and plastered on a smile. He didn't want to upset the letter-writing widow. She'd be humiliated and think he was up to tricks. She'd never trust Ewan, and her trust was important. He tugged his niece out of the way of a parade of toe-tapping musicians who rammed through the thick crowd, making their own path. "I think you should be your lovable viscount self. In fact, stay long enough to attest to our family only wanting the leases, nothing more. Not her land."

Jasper nodded. "Can you attest the same? Nothing else you seek?"

There was more, but Theodosia had to come away with him first. "Let's get to Tradenwood before all of London arrives."

Ewan let Jasper and Lucy lead the way as he followed behind. The rhythm of the musicians hit him first, the laughter, and buzz of the crowds. Then the heady smells of cooked pork called to his spirit and the breakfast he'd skipped. If it had the tart tamarind like the dishes of the West Indies, he'd dance himself dizzy. He'd missed that taste since his regiment disbanded.

His hungered spirit leapt when he saw Theo. Her hair was curled and pinned high, leaving her neck free for nuzzling. Yet, she stood on the portico wrapped in gray. Distant, lonely gray. She needed music and Shakespeare. She needed lightness.

With rainbow colors for paper patterns and bright pink table linens surrounding her festival, shouldn't she come alive with an emerald ribbon in her silky hair?

Staring at her like a schoolboy couldn't be done, so Ewan parted from his brother and niece as they became more interested in the hot air balloon hovering above the blooms. He headed to the food tables, slipping through the crowds separating him from Theo.

A wild cart owner pushed his wares too near his toes, so Ewan bounced out of harm's way and stood behind a man and older woman awaiting their turn at the carvers.

"Old Cecil would love this," one said.

The other sneered over her yellowing teeth. "The darkie got it right. The perfect amount of garish and finery."

"If you feel that way, Millie, why did you drag us here?"

"I wanted to see what she'd do and if she'd taken up with someone else. A rich widow is still rich, no matter how black."

"Stop it, Millie. She's a fairer vendor than Lord Crisdon, and you'd never see the likes of us invited to anything with their name on it."

"I hate the name of them."

Stepping away, a myriad of emotions swished into Ewan's throat like hot gall. It wasn't the insult on his family that burned, but the ones to Theo. These people ate her food, drank her wines, and did business with her, but still talked about her badly...

As he had in his play.

His gut twisted a little more. Theo wasn't stupid. She knew to the penny the cost of each morsel. She knew their sentiment. Yet she'd committed to this fair, all the trouble and expense. This Theodosia was indeed different from the girl he knew. He hungered to know her more.

He spun and glanced at Jasper running after Lucy who had Maypole ribbons. Lucy pattered up to a lady trimmed in a fine bisque bonnet and pale peach-colored gown.

Taking another look at her fair features, the indeterminate shade of brownish gold curls, she looked like one of Theo's friends from the theater. He cupped his hand to his eyes and looked again. Was that the Duke of Simone's daughter with Jasper and Lucy?

Mulatto or not, the woman and his niece had his poor brother twisted up in pink ribbons. Yet, Jasper was laughing, a full-bodied, belly-shaking laugh.

Jasper deserved to be happy. If only he could find a way

to stay that way. Then he wouldn't be chasing after a bottle, a newspaper bride, or inadvertently, Theo.

Looking to the left and then to the right, Ewan saw revelers, and people pushing food carts, but where had Theo gone? Searching, his gaze fell upon Theo's son, a little boy with an ashy tan complexion. He played near the bottom of the steps of the portico. An older woman sat at his side. Maybe she was his governess.

The woman came closer to the boy right in front of his face. "I'm going to get us lemonade. Stay here," she said in a loud voice, before kissing his head and leaving him to play. The child was alone, a perfect time for an introduction.

Ewan's chest had no more room for what-ifs: what if he'd stayed, what if she'd waited for him, what if they'd married... instead he'd fill them with would-be's. She would accept him, he would be her lover, her husband, a stepfather to her child, and father to another babe. Well, he would enjoy trying for that one.

"Cousin?"

He turned at the sound of Theo's voice. Tipping his top hat to her, he bowed. "Is everything fine?"

She bit her lip for a moment then said, "I didn't think you'd really come. Fitzwilliams never attend."

Extending his arm to her, he waited for her to take it, but she didn't move. Disappointed at how wary she seemed again, he dropped his palm to his side. "I'm here and so is my brother, Lord Hartwell, and my niece. You should meet them, Cousin, as I am going to meet your son."

As he stepped toward the boy, she came close and took his arm. "He's playing, enjoying the fresh air. You can meet him later."

"Why? You're coddling him? The boy's still in a pinafore, even with his little knobby knees exposed."

Her fingers tightened about his elbow. "They're not so

knobby, but he is little."

Ewan's gut was at odds. He liked her being so near, her holding on to him with the scent of lavender making him want to dip his head to her neck and inhale all of her. Yet, she was only touching him to keep him from her son. He pried at her thumb to be released and took two more steps to the boy. "Your son, he must be young or he'd be breached and in a full pair of pants."

A wince washed across her countenance. "He's not six, but I suppose your father tried to make you boys men as soon as possible. I want my son to enjoy every minute. I've no expectations of his growing other than health."

She had mistaken his fishing for an age as condemnation. He must have sounded judgmental, very much like the earl. He gazed at the boy again. He seemed frail as he rolled the hoop back and forth between his palms. Remembering Theo's first response to the newspaper advertisement he and Jasper had penned, about a sickly child, Ewan wanted to smack his stupid gut. The boy suffered and Ewan felt even more the blackguard.

"There's something I have to say." Tears were in her voice as she seemed to choke and sputter. "I need—to tell—"

"Let's go somewhere private." She couldn't accept his proposal between jugglers and musicians. No, it had to be in private, where he could kiss away any sadness. Her bold confession about wishing things were different, that she still felt love for him, that she wondered if they could start anew would be applause-worthy. Except, that would be the line he'd pen for one of his heroes.

Her other friend from the theater, the shorter girl with a pearl-laced bonnet, came to her side. "Mrs. Cecil. There's a young woman who says she must see you."

Theo raised her head. Her countenance cleared and his hope of her coming to her senses disappeared, too. "Take me to her, Miss Croome."

He clasped at Theo's hand but she slipped away. "But our talk?"

As soon as a dray cleared the path, the ladies started to move again, but Theo stopped. Over her shoulder she said, "We will, Cousin, after all is done."

He let her ominous tone sink in as he watched her walk away. Didn't sound like a confession of love was forthcoming. Was she going to reject him? No, he felt in his bones that this was right for them to wed. Something else was amiss.

Whatever it was, she would have to release it, forgive him, forgive herself, and then move forward. He'd tell her it was fine. No more guilt for what had happened. Things were finally on the right path. He was going to be a successful playwright, and this rivalry between the flower farms would be done as soon as Theo signed the papers. Everyone had a chance for peace, if they seized it with both hands and never let go.

Scanning, he found Theo again. Miss Croome had led her to the patio and up to the terraced gardens. The elegant negress with her creamy coffee complexion left Theo with a young blonde.

The girl's hand swung wildly.

His chest beat faster. He feared for Theo.

Something had to be amiss. Before he could stop himself, he started moving. He dashed to the side as a wobbly dray rumbled in front of him, nearly missing his leg.

Not waiting for an apology or acknowledgment, he moved closer to the gardens, navigating around a food cart. Everything was chaotic, like his beating heart. He raced up the terraces, past the laughing crowds, and stopped at the knee wall of the patio. He was within earshot of Theo.

"All can be made fine," Theo said. "You'll come work for me now."

"I'll take what you've given me and go to the country and have this babe. I have a cousin who'll help."

"If that's what you think is best. You have to keep this babe safe. You have to eat a lot, even if you don't want to." Theo's voice sounded weepy.

Ewan fought the urge to come out of the shadows. Something was dreadfully wrong.

"Mrs. Cecil, I should've listened to you when you came to Burlington Arcade. I shoulda listened. You said not to be his mistress."

Theo, giving mistress advice? Ewan rose from the wall and stared at them. He didn't care if he was discovered. He had to hear things correctly.

Theo had the girl in an embrace again.

The young woman snapped up, kissed Theo's hand, and fled down the terrace levels back to the revelers below.

Pivoting toward Ewan, Theo frowned deeply, her beautiful face marred with sadness. "You're supposed to only haunt me, not my guests."

He came closer and lowered his voice to a whisper. "Giving advice about not being a mistress? After we marry, I'm not sure I want women coming to you for the dos and don'ts of this business."

How was it possible for lips to disappear even more? She shook her head and dabbed at her eyes. The almond-shaped pearls quivered.

His gut froze with instant regret. Before he could take his boot from his mouth, she slipped past him. "Excuse me."

He should've reached for her hand, and apologized for the poor joke, but they both had pasts. He had forgiven her last night for not grieving him long enough, for letting her heart move on to his cousin. He had no choice. Unlike her, he hadn't forgotten her, hadn't stopped lov—

"She's too nice, you know."

Ewan lifted his head to see who watched him.

It was Theo's friend, the duke's daughter. She stood near, with her fan moving, frowning almost as much as Theo had. "I see how you are watching her. You care for her, more than a cousin should."

"Miss?"

"Miss Burghley." She crossed her arms. "If you don't intend to stick around, don't trouble her. Her heart's too big. It cares too much for others. It's too easy for her to be hurt."

"I'll keep that in mind."

"Miss Burghley." Her lips pouted, as if he should've repeated her name. "Why are you here now? Your cousin died almost a year ago."

"Seems your dear friend has been silent on things. Perhaps you should be asking her questions."

He turned to go back down to the party, when she swatted him with her fan. "She's silent on things and people who hurt her. Maybe that is why I hadn't heard of you until the theater."

Ewan hurting Theo? What, for a month? "I believe—

"Oh, no, that Mr. Lester fellow has her cornered. I don't know who I need to protect her from more."

As the musicians started again with a loud high-spirited tune, he turned to see where the blackguard had Theo, ready to pummel somebody like he had the night of the theater, but he spied something worse. "Move!"

Leaving the woman with her mouth open, Ewan shot down the terrace levels as if he'd become a bullet from a discharged flintlock, heading straight for a runaway cart. The big, barreling object made people jump out of its path and flee in all directions.

Everyone moved but one.

Theo's son.

"Move!" he yelled again. Ewan lengthened his stride,

trying to become as fast as a racing horse. He huffed and puffed like a steaming tea kettle. The timing of Ewan snatching the boy had to be right or they'd both die, smashed by the cart. Mouthing a prayer, he leaped, clasped the child in his hands, and raised the boy high over his head—knowing the cart would hit him square in the chest.

Blam.

Something crunched inside as the cart exploded against him as the steel balls of war had done six years ago. The impact flung them like a rag doll. Sailing backward, he still clasped the boy about the ankle. He held on even as his own eyes began to dim, but he fought the pain.

Tucking the squirming boy into whatever remained of his chest, Ewan slammed into the grass, his head bobbing up and down. The boy wrestled free but stuck his face over Ewan's.

That's when he saw it.

Mother's irises, the same crystal blue, the same as his.

He tried to fight the darkness but lost the chance to see once more the light, the light in his son's eyes.

Chapter Thirteen

The Ghost House Guest

Theodosia paced outside of the bedchamber she'd had Pickens and Lord Hartwell put Ewan. Navigating the few chairs she had brought to sit on the deep burgundy carpet, she kept remembering the screaming, the impact of the cart, falling to her knees upon Philip's and Ewan's still bodies.

Everything inside her was torn up and grieving. She had almost lost her son today. Philip couldn't hear anyone's warning. And Ewan had risked everything to save Philip, and now he could die. He could be dead and not even know he'd saved his own son.

She stopped a few times and touched the door. It felt like six years ago as she'd waited for a shop owner to read the letter the earl had tossed in her face. The man had only gotten out the words "killed in battle" before the weight of losing Ewan had collapsed upon Theodosia. All her dreams had died, a day or two after she had discovered she carried his babe.

But now, Ewan wasn't far away.

Frederica came up the stairs. In her hand was a tea cup. She held it out. "Here, drink this and then go sit. You're pacing so much you'll wear your slippers clean through to the soles."

Pulling up her hem to make sure she hadn't already done so, Theodosia lowered her head. "I've been barefoot before. It doesn't matter. Why must women be stuck outside, waiting? Shouldn't I be with him? Or maybe I should go hug Philip again?"

Ester came from her son's bedchamber. When she closed his door, the lights of the hall sconces danced. It was a hopeful sparkle, something Theodosia needed to keep her fears away. "Is my son awake? Does he need another hug?"

"Hugging Philip is always a good idea," Ester said, "but you've done that twice already. He's sleeping soundly. The jerking him out of the way and crashing to the ground, made him ache."

"But he didn't get an earache. And that jerking around had to be done. Mr. Fitzwilliam was the only one to risk his life for my son."

Dearest Ester came closer, stepping around Frederica. Her sprig muslin skirt held grass stains, as she had been the first to reach the accident. She took Theodosia's palms. "He's not some strange cousin, is he? I saw the look in your eyes when he came to the theater. It's worse now. How long has something been going on between you."

"Six years. I knew him six years ago."

Frederica put her palms over Ester's ears. "Does she need to know it was in a biblical sense?"

Ester swatted them away. "I heard, and I've read all the passages of Solomon and even romance novels. You don't have to—"

"Stop, you two." Theodosia wrapped her arms about herself, trying hard not to shake to bits beneath her shawl.

"Yes. I knew him in every sense of the word. We were going to elope when his father convinced him to go to war. A report came back saying he'd died in the field."

A puzzled look crossed Ester's brows. "Six years ago. But you were Cecil's mistress then, right?"

Yes and no and yes. None of it mattered. She turned again and touched the door. "It's too quiet. He can't be dying in there, not knowing."

Ester stepped to her. Candlelight shone in her eyes, as bright as her joy in finding solutions. "Not knowing what? That you're still in love with him?"

Bowing her forehead against the wall, Theo resigned herself. The truth burned in her throat. It needed to be freed. She'd said it to Frederica. She could to Ester, too. With a forced swallow, she nodded. "Something worse than that, but how do I tell him with the doctor, Lester, and Lord Hartwell, who is the heir Crisdon, keeping me away?"

Frederica came to her side. She clasped Theodosia's arm and forced her to turn the knob. "You go in and tell him. Make everyone leave, then tell him. You're not a waif or a servant but the owner of Tradenwood. Lift your head and say your truth. A man needs to know. He needs an opportunity to claim what is his, to take responsibility, even for a few seconds, of what is his."

Knowing Frederica's pain with her father, she knew her friend was right. Nodding, she opened the door. "Please don't leave, stay here to help me put the pieces back together."

Ester put her palms on Theodosia's shoulders. "Of course, we will. And Frederica is correct. You are Mrs. Theodosia Cecil, a free woman equal to any in your domain. This isn't the public or a private box where we must hide. Go see about your guest. You are strong enough not to crumble, and smart enough to fix things, if you break."

She gave Theodosia a push inside and closed the door.

The doctor, Pickens, and Ewan's brother looked up at her then returned to gazing toward the bed. Lester paced in the corner. He didn't glance her way at all.

The scent of sickness, tangy, and singeing mustard filled the room. The familiar perfume of laudanum hit next, as the doctor's fanning wafted it to her. She hated these smells—they always foretold pain and death.

Feet feeling like cold bricks, she forced them forward. "Gentleman, I must know how my cousin is doing. I owe him a great deal. He saved…my son."

The doctor harrumphed. "Couple of broken ribs. He's not breathing well. Can't tell if a lung is punctured. So much scar tissue."

She came closer and saw the valley and plains of the jagged lines upon Ewan's chest. They'd meshed about his heart and ran down half his stomach. Could they have been like iron to protect from the hit of the cart? Could they now keep him bound on this side, away from the hungry shadows of death?

She wanted her ghost to live. Ewan must. He had to recover. She stuffed her hands in her pockets to keep the trembling fear from showing. "Has he awakened at all?"

"He has, ma'am," Pickens said, as he shuffled to her side. The wrinkles of his face folded into deeper lines, thick like the night Mathew had died.

Pickens brushed her arm. "The doctor has given him a great deal of laudanum for pain. He'll have to be a guest for the next few days. Mr. Lester objects."

She felt her head nodding *yes* before any words could come out. "Of course, he will stay. Lord Hartwell and your daughter, too. You're welcome here."

Lester surged from the corner, almost running into Pickens. "No. None of the Fitzwilliams can be here."

He whipped past Theodosia and stood, feet apart from

Ewan's brother. "Take him up the hill."

The fool looked ready to fight. In her house? In front of Ewan and his brother. The viscount said nothing, only stared ahead.

Her butler straightened his silver-colored livery and moved to the doctor on the other side of the room. "Sir, he'll need to be a guest. He's very ill. Repeat your prognosis, sir. Mr. Lester may not have heard."

The doctor moaned again as he wrenched at his back. He sat back on the chair pulled close to the bed. "This man is not going anywhere, if you want him to live."

Visibly wincing, Lord Hartwell came from the footboard of the bed. His face seemed blank and he seemed a little lost. "My brother is horribly injured, Lester. Surely, even *you* can see that moving him would have dire results. Business is business. This is different."

Wanting to offer a hug to reassure Lord Hartwell, Theodosia raised her hand to him, but then lowered it as she approached. He was in a bad way and having her comfort, a Blackamoor's palm on a peer, couldn't be done, even if she offered humanity.

She looked down at her slippers, dusty cream kid leather with green stains, like the ones on her skirts from falling on her knees atop Ewan and Philip after the crash. Courage and fear, both demanded sacrifice. She chose courage and took a step toward him. "Mr. Lester has forgotten this is my house. My house. Mr. Fitzwilliam shall stay, if Lord Hartwell agrees."

Ewan's brother lifted his chin. His light blue eyes widened as he ran a hand through his rumpled blond locks. "Thank you, ma'am."

"No," Lester said. "Mrs. Cecil is not thinking clearly." He approached and manhandled the bedpost in his sweaty palms. "Nearly seeing your son hurt has addled you. You're vulnerable. Philip doesn't need to see you like this, so out of control."

The only one who sounded hysterical was Lester, but there was no telling that man anything. And his voice. So harsh, it sent her brainbox spinning with fire, but she held her anger. She needed him to comply. "Lester, I appreciate the concern," she said, then swallowed gall. "You can stay, too. If you are so fretful."

"You know I leave for Holland tomorrow. I thought you and the boy would come with me. It would be good for Philip. Maybe he should come with me, since you will be busy with guests."

How dare he try to manipulate her when a man's life was at stake? She stopped twiddling her finger and made sure that her bottom lip was bite-free. "No. My son will stay. If not for Mr. Ewan Fitzwilliam, my Philip would have been killed. And you know what dear Cecil said about hospitality. *When I hungered, you fed me, when I thirsted, you gave me drink, and when I looked strange, you took me in.* There is no more need to discuss this. Fitzwilliam shall stay until he is able to leave on his own two feet."

She turned again to the silent viscount. "I have more than enough room. Your daughter is now in the nursery."

Lester spun her by the shoulder as if she would change her mind, but she wasn't a spinning top searching for direction. "They are our enemies, Theodosia. Lord Crisdon wouldn't do the same for you."

No, Lord Crisdon wouldn't. He'd shun her, like he had in the past, but she wasn't that evil man. "I have been blessed by unexpected favor. How could I ever be sucked into pettiness with my Philip still alive?" Knocking his hands away, she sidestepped out of Lester's reach. "Mr. Fitzwilliam is not the enemy, Lester. He's Cecil's cousin. Surely, my boy's guardian can see that? Today, we are indebted to the Fitzwilliams."

Lord Hartwell moved near, towering over Lester. "Bear this intrusion for now. We can go back to being enemies, fighting over water rights, after my brother recovers."

Lester's eyes grew big, and he looked like a cornered rat. With a shaky palm smoothing his wilting cravat, he swung his head toward the bed, then turned his glare her direction. "You have too many guests. I'll take Philip with me until this all settles down. He can go with me to Holland. Then you can join us."

"No." She stuck her hand against her bosom to keep her heart from bursting. "Don't take him. He was almost killed. I need him here."

Lord Hartwell put his hand on Theodosia's shoulder. The touch was light, comforting, everything she had wanted to do earlier but had been afraid of insulting him. "Leave the boy, Lester. My brother's been moaning for him. He'll need to see him safe and well when he awakens. I'm sure that viewing his little Cecil cousin will make him heal faster."

"This is none of your business, Lord Hartwell. You rule up the hill, not down here."

The large man started to laugh and slipped into the space between them, forcing her nemesis to move backward, one step closer to the door. "Lester, you don't look the wet-nurse type. The young boy should stay with his mother, if you want the Fitzwilliams gone sooner. Unless you enjoy seeing Mrs. Cecil in distress."

Lester rubbed his chin, as if he hadn't thought any Fitzwilliams would come to her or Philip's defense. "Fine. I shall stay, too. I'll delay the trip."

"Stay tonight, if you must, Lester, but this trip has to go as planned. Holland is business. The first time I trust you to gain new advances for Cecil's fields, you disappoint me." She stared him dead in the eyes. "You know how much it cost to arrange: ten guineas for passage, eight pounds for a new suit for you to represent the business at your best, and now you will not go? I thought that you wanted the business to dominate. I thought I could trust you. You're costing me money."

His eyes darted as if she'd frightened him. "You are a mercenary when it comes to figures."

The man's greed and the need to one-up all the other growers was something Theodosia had counted on, plotted for. This trip would take exactly five weeks, long enough for banns to be read or an elopement to be done with a newspaper groom before his return. Well, that had been the plan, but now she just wanted him gone. She put a fist to her hip and glared at him like her knees weren't knocking. "You know I am right."

He nodded, but before she had a chance to enjoy the victory of him relenting, Lester tugged her hand, leading her to the door. His hot whispered breath scorched her ear. "Don't sign anything and don't forget where your loyalties lie, where Philip's loyalties lie."

She didn't push free, but she stood still and glared at him with every ounce of courage she possessed. He wasn't stealing her son today or hurting Ewan. "Go home, Lester. All is well here. Take care of *our* business."

With a little push, he released her fingers then nodded. "You win. I sail tomorrow for our business." The skunk stormed from the room.

The doctor closed up the sheer curtains. "Fitzwilliam needs to rest. All of you should leave this room until morning. I'll sit with him through the night."

"I will, too, once I check on my girl. Where is she, Mrs. Cecil?"

"The governess and my friends are keeping her entertained while my son sleeps."

"Take me to her. I'll tell her that her uncle is faring

better."

Theodosia didn't want to leave the room, but she had to aid Lord Hartwell. With Ewan unconscious, it wasn't the time to have that private conversation about his son. She pulled the door closed once Lord Hartwell stepped through. "Funny."

The big man shortened his stride and walked in step with her. "What is funny, Mrs. Cecil?"

"Your daughter, she kept saying she didn't do it, like a small child could get that cart moving."

Hartwell stumbled, nearly bumping into Frederica. He recovered quickly and bowed. "Sorry. Of course, Lucy would not be responsible."

His brows and forehead squished together, as if he were doing math or numbering something, then he shook his head. "Again, excuse my clumsiness, Miss."

Frederica nodded then swept to the side. "We haven't been formally introduced, sir, but it is Burghley and you are excused. Your exit was nothing like Mr. Lester's exit. He almost ran into us like—that cart." Her face seemed half ready for a laugh, half remorseful. She covered her mouth for a moment.

So many formal rules. Theodosia couldn't think of them all at a time like now, but she needed to consider them, as Tradenwood would be crowded the next few hours, the next few days. "Lord Hartwell, this is Miss Burghley and Miss Croome."

Dipping a chin to each, he relaxed his shoulders. "It is a pleasure, but I wish the circumstances were different."

Different? So many things should be different. Theodosia rubbed her cold hands together. "We must manage as best we can, but time is no one's friend."

With wide eyes, Frederica grabbed her arm. "Is Mr. Fitzwilliam?"

Theodosia patted her fingers. "He's unconscious. The doctor and Pickens are still with him. It will be a long night. My lord, this way to the nursery."

"We'll show him, so you can go back to the less crowded room. Right, Miss Croome?"

Ester nodded and stuck her novel behind her back. "Yes."

"No, ladies," Theodosia said. "Go settle into one of my guest rooms. You all must be tired. You've already done so much to close the festival for me because I was with Philip and my cousin."

They smiled at her with waggling brows, probably hoping she'd spill what happened in the room and why Lester had bolted like a maniac. Not now, not with Lord Hartwell eyeing each of them like he compared them to invisible notes. Well, how many rumors had been started about them by Lord Crisdon or cruel people like him?

With a shake of her head, Theodosia started for the nursery. "This way."

When they entered, the governess was tucking a blanket around the little blonde girl on the chaise. "She just fell asleep," the woman said. "Philip is still sleeping soundly. I've checked on him every hour. No pain tonight. I will turn in myself. Good night, ma'am."

The woman swept past and closed the door behind them.

Lord Hartwell came closer to his daughter. He let his finger smooth the child's curls. "Is it not too much trouble? Having us here? I could take this bag of bones up the hill."

It was a sweet sight, this large, burly man being so delicate with the tiny girl. She turned to Philip's bed in the corner. "There has been enough trouble today, but you have to be here. Your brother may call for you."

"You are kindness, ma'am."

She'd like to think so, but fear gripped her windpipe and squeezed. Too afraid to touch Philip's face and find him a ghost, she stared at her son. A minute or two went by. She'd counted two hundred breaths, Philip's breaths, then heard his snore whistle. Nothing in the world was as sweet.

With her fingers, she swiped back perspiration that the laudanum sometimes brought, then put her pinky on Philip's cheek, his solid, warm cheek. He was a miracle, this time delivered by Ewan.

"Your son. He's not well?" Hartwell had moved near. He'd probably watched her show of weakness. "The governess talked of pain."

She bit her lip, but decided answering wouldn't harm anything or put her more in jeopardy. "He suffers from severe ear pains, but the governess said he was good tonight."

He drew a handkerchief out of his pocket and handed it to her. If there were tears in her eyes, she hadn't noticed. She was too busy being thankful.

"May I ask why Mr. Lester would threaten to take a sick boy from his mother?"

"He's my son's guardian. His opinion apparently holds more weight than the boy's mother. He also thinks you are the enemy."

Ewan's brother scratched his chin. "My girls are my world. I couldn't be parted from them if they'd had such a harrowing experience. Your cousin, Ewan, didn't hesitate to help your son. He knows the difference between business and personal."

Theodosia did, too. It was the distance between safety and danger and what lengths she'd go to keep Philip well. After another swipe to her cheek, she bent and kissed her son's brow. "Lester's gone. And you, your daughter, and Mr. Fitzwilliam are staying. I can have tea and sweets brought up to the bedchamber."

Lord Hartwell smiled and turned back to his daughter. "Good. That will help the night pass."

Not feeling afraid to leave her miracle with Lord Hartwell, his uncle of sorts, Theodosia headed into the empty hall. 'Twas going to be a long night. Somewhere in the hours or days to come she must find a way to tell Ewan the truth.

What would he hate more, her becoming Mathew's mistress or not telling him Philip was his? She counted on her fingers, divided in the air but the sum came back the same. He'd hate her for everything.

. . .

Light filtered into the room, sinking into the hairline cracks that were Ewan's eyelids. Everything hurt. It hurt to move, to breathe.

A look to the right, he saw a balcony and doors. Was it the one he'd climbed in his youth? He was at his uncle's Tradenwood.

He closed his eyes again, hoping that he'd dreamed everything, six years spent away from family, losing Theo, his rights to this house, had all been a nightmare. Perhaps he awakened with the world righted.

Yet, one push at his chest told the truth. Scars never lied. Nor did bandages and bruises.

A cough rattled in his lungs. The sputter made things feel like they worked.

Memories of Theo and the festival returned.

Then Philip.

The child, the one with crystal blues eyes—he'd saved him from the cart.

Could the boy be his? He wanted him to be his.

With nothing more than the raw desire to see those eyes again, those eyes like his mother's, like his own, Ewan pushed and tugged but the bedsheets held fast. With a mighty thrust he craned up, but the pain made him flop back upon the mattress. His fingertips brushed leathery ivy.

English ivy?

Had he died or gone insane?

He poked at a dark emerald leaf. The rubbery shape was true, but Ewan might still be crazed. He might have even imagined seeing the boy with his eyes.

"You're awake." Jasper's voice. Was he here in this dream, too?

Ewan turned his head to the left to see his brother, stretching then brushing sleep from his eyes. "Seems the same could be said of you."

Dropping a thick book upon the bed, Jasper shuffled his feet then rose from a chair that had been pulled close. "Resting comfortably?"

Ewan tugged at the strips of ointment-soaked cloth tied across his ribs. "As much as possible."

Jasper moved to the door. "I'll tell the doctor and Mrs. Cecil. They have been attending you without ceasing these past three days."

"Wait. Don't move. Three days?"

Releasing the doorknob, Jasper pivoted. As he came closer, the dim light revealed shadow on his jaw and rumpled clothes. Had he been sitting here, waiting all three days? Guilt and warmth danced inside. Ewan had not lost everything. He still had a brother's love.

"Why do you want me to wait? You are awake. Everyone's been anxious. I can get you back to Grandbole."

"No."

"What? Explain?"

He looked up at his brother and weighed the impact of what it would mean to say his hopes aloud. Another glance at Jasper and his withered cravat convinced Ewan. "My son may be here. I don't think I merely saved a distant cousin on my mother's side of the family, but her grandson. I think

Cecil's boy is my son."

Frowning as if he'd eaten a tree of lemons, Jasper wrenched at his back, stretching again. "You definitely hit your head. You are seeing things that are not there."

"Go look at the boy and see his eyes. They're my mother's. I have them, too."

"Cecil is a cousin, Ewan. Surely those traits could be passed along."

Those eyes, could they have been imagined? New frustration stirred. He struggled to get up and fell to the mattress. "You think it is a coincidence?"

"I don't know what to think, but I do know her devotion to Cecil can't be questioned. And why does this matter now? The child is Cecil's by marriage. You claimed to be done with her."

"What if you were a woman—"

"I'm not."

"Jasper, please. You were a woman whose fiancé died in war and you find yourself heavy with his babe. What would you do?"

His brother's frown half disappeared. "I'd go to the country to family or turn to his. Or give up the moppet to Bethlehem Hospital."

"A mulatto baby might not be one of the lucky ones welcomed at that orphanage. If Theo did go to Lord Crisdon, what do you think he did?"

Picking up his book, Jasper plopped into his chair and stretched his stocking feet onto the bed. "You're a playwright. You are making up a story to suit what you want. I should not have read you Shakespeare these past three days. Maria, she liked a novel or a Psalm when she rested."

It was awful to put his brother back into the position of nursemaid. The man was still grieving, but no one had to lose anything if Theo confessed why she had not waited.

Ewan swallowed and everything tasted of hope, bright and tart. "Only one person can confirm this. Only one knows the truth. If we stay, she might confide in me."

"She is very upset over your injuries."

"I have to know, Jasper. You have to help me."

"I don't know…"

"Her time of mourning is up soon and I asked her to marry me, but like you, she is corresponding to find a new husband. She hasn't fully accepted me. I think her hesitation is the boy. I need to show her I can be good to Philip."

"Well, almost dying for him is a good start."

"I've tried to let her go. I can't. I want her. I want the boy, even more so if he's my son. I need to know."

"Ewan? You're awake."

Theo had slipped into the room. She came closer. Her almond eyes were wide, maybe with joy. In her hands were a tray of tea and biscuits. "You've awakened."

Jasper said, "I am not sure what did it, ma'am. Between your ivy plants making him good air or this tome of Shakespeare's—all your suggestions have returned the man to us."

Her beautiful full lips seemed to tremble before she leveled her shoulders. "I'm so glad." She put the tray upon the bed table and came within an inch of brushing his brow. Instead, her fingers tucked the blanket. "You need to know how grateful I am to you. You saved Philip."

His gaze locked upon hers and he dared not blink. For a moment, he saw her eyes, dark mysterious pools opening for him, trusting him, believing in him again. If Ewan could grasp her hand, work his fingers between hers, he'd never let go. "I am glad to be of service."

When Jasper coughed, she blinked and backed away.

Their connection—it pounded in Ewan's chest—stronger than six years ago. He wished in his soul he could claim her hand right now.

"My brother wanted to know if Mathew Cecil looked more like his uncle or his own mother. I think, neither. Your son is too handsome to bear the stodgy bones."

Jasper's question couldn't have come at a worse time.

Biting her tender bottom lip, Theo moved away from the bed. "I'm not sure if they favor. I only met Lady Crisdon once. Is there anything that I can do for either of you while you stay?"

Ewan didn't quite know how to answer that. Everything ached, but a battle waged inside him. Was it wrong to want her, the boy, and to feel vindicated for believing everything he'd written in his play? But Theo, unlike others who'd confess or proclaim her innocence, had drawn deeper inside. He'd never win her if she shied away. "I thank you, Mrs. Cecil, for your hospitality. You remembered Shakespeare."

"It was Cecil's favorite. He liked the foul shrew, too."

Her smile, small and sweet—would it last for Ewan, if he pushed for the truth?

Beating her to the door, Jasper stood in her way. "Mrs. Cecil, when your son's lessons are finished, please bring him. My brother's been asking for him and, as we told Lester, it would benefit Fitzwilliam's health."

She seemed to wince, her shawl fluttering, as if Jasper's girls had performed a monstrous trick. "Later. Lord Hartwell, you have not slept in three days. Your room is ready. It's a few doors down the hall. I don't want another ill man in my house."

Almost in a full giggle, Jasper nodded. "I'll sit with the hero a little longer, but then I'll follow your orders. We are at Tradenwood."

She nodded and then slipped out the door.

Jasper put his ear to the wood panel. "Good, she's not an eavesdropper. And she seemed nervous when I asked about the boy. You may be right."

Ewan pushed at his brow. "I'm almost certain Philip Cecil is my son. She passed him off as Cecil's. She's wondering if she can trust me, but what about my trust in her?"

Jasper returned to his chair. "You must've hit your head harder than I thought."

Ewan glanced at his brother and found not a drop of humor in his stern face. "What are you talking about?"

"Mrs. Cecil nearly lost her son. That worm Lester threatened to take the boy if she didn't comply, but she stood up to him so you'd have the best care. I think you need to rest some more. Awaken and see the truth."

"What are you saying?

Jasper slumped more in his chair. "The widow isn't the enemy. I don't even think she's ever been one to our family. I think she is misunderstood."

"You defend her now?"

"You can't fake the fear of losing someone you love. I saw it in her, Ewan. Even when she knew her boy was safe, she still looked as if the world was about to end. It was the fear of losing you." He tapped his rumpled waistcoat, which showed three days of wrinkles. "It matched what happened in here."

Not knowing what to think or admit to his brother or even his own soul, he went with humor. "Didn't know you were so sentimental."

Jasper ran a hand through his unruly gold locks. "I watched the love of my life die. I remember the dread of missing that last moment, of failing Maria. I saw Mrs. Cecil pacing for you, while Lester threatened to take away her son."

"My son."

"That woman has been graceful and kind. You need to look at her through a lens that's not clouded by loss."

"What?"

Tugging at his neckcloth like it choked, Jasper gave up

and stilled his hands. "You say you don't begrudge me for being the heir. Maybe that is true. But for Cecil to inherit what would have been yours, marrying the woman you wanted, and giving a name to the boy that might be yours, I'd say you have a right to be disgruntled. But it's not Cecil's fault he inherited Tradenwood or that a woman left unprotected found someone who was willing to marry her. If this boy you saved is yours, would you rather he be a by-blow bastard and not have a name?"

Ewan closed his eyes. The anger at being denied his son dissipated a little. Maybe Theo had done what she had to do. Ewan had not been here to protect her. "A name is important, but I'm here now. She should admit it. I've been here for weeks. Why withhold such a truth?"

"From the man who left her because he couldn't stand up to his father? From the man who wrote a whole play defaming her?"

Hating the list of his wrongs, Ewan wanted to strike out. Pain swelling, he tightened his fist on the blanket. "Well, I must have been unconscious for quite a while, if you are defending her. Last time I checked you held a very different position. Something about a lesser woman, one who'd been a mistress, of a lesser race, and illegitimate to boot."

"Yes. And I've been a fool before." Jasper swiped at his face before folding his arms. "I've spent three days at Tradenwood. Only leaving for a few hours to make sure that the girls haven't burnt down Grandbole before sending them to your mother. Mrs. Cecil and her friends have been generous and caring. Very good company. I've never been around women like them, educated and funny. And Mrs. Cecil has been kind."

"You take her side? Lord Crisdon would be pleased. You *are* looking to marry a rich widow with a love of children."

"You are looking for a villain. You created one in your

play, but be mad at yourself or the folly of youth. One is not here."

The weight of truth in his brother's arguments was too great. Ewan dipped lower into the sheets, swatting the ivy as he did. "So what should I do? Walk away and not know if that boy is mine?"

Jasper picked up the book from the bed as he stood. "I think I'll finish this before I sleep; I want to read how things work out between Petruchio and Katherina. I can get the doctor to say you must stay for another couple of days. Make good use of them."

Book tucked under one arm, Jasper took a flask from his pocket and poured a bit in the tea Theo brought. "You're on the mend. The girls are with Lady Crisdon. I can relax a little."

"You didn't tell Mother or Crisdon I was hurt?"

Taking a sip, Jasper's face reddened. "I did, but when I told her we were here, she didn't want to know more. Get a bit more rest."

When the door closed, Ewan released a long breath, deflating what felt like shallow lungs. Would Theo trust him enough to tell him the truth? Was his soul ready to accept if the boy was Cecil's? In either case, could there be a future with Theo and the boy who should be his son?

Chapter Fourteen

The Lies We Love

Theodosia looked at her dressing closet, waiting for the sound of footsteps. Lord Hartwell's room was beyond her door—Mathew's old connecting chamber. With Ester and Frederica staying in the other wing of Tradenwood, she'd hear the man's boots, if she stayed quiet. Then she'd know Ewan was alone and could be told he'd saved his son's life.

Waiting, she fingered a pink gown folded in tissue on the shelf. It had stayed dormant in the closet. She'd purchased it years ago to wear for Mathew at his birthday dinner. He had liked the colors and the soft silk. But he wouldn't like Theodosia disclosing the secret he'd worked hard to bury.

Bam, bam, swoosh. Those sounds—they were a man's boots, followed by the sound of a closing door.

It was time. Shaking loose her doubts, she prepared to leave. One final glance to her mirror exposed shadows under her eyes. The angled corners were red. It had been hard to sleep, in the three days it had taken for Ewan to awaken.

She stepped out in the hall and spied Pickens coming up

on the landing. He held a tray in his hand. The bowl on it steamed and smelled of broth. Bread was nicely buttered on a plate. "Evening, Mrs. Cecil."

"Who is that for? Lord Hartwell?"

"No ma'am. I gave Mr. Fitzwilliam the last of the laudanum. He mentioned wanting some nourishment."

The perfect excuse to be unaccompanied in his room had presented itself. She approached with hands wide. "I'll take it to him."

A brow rose on the butler's face. "Yes. And the footman retrieved this note."

Her breath caught until she saw the scrawl. The squire, not the baron. "Put it in my room."

He gave her the tray but took the letter away. "Shall I come for this later?"

"Yes. In an hour. I'll yell if I need you sooner."

"Good, but I was more worried about Fitzwilliam. You have left him on your doorstep so many days since his return to Grandbole."

Theodosia wanted to smile at the man's accurate memory, but she must focus on Ewan and saying the right words to him. "He'll manage."

Pickens held the door open for her. "Godspeed to both of you."

Chin up, she marched inside. The room was darker than before, no doubt from the sun finally setting. A sole candle flickered on the bed table. It cast a warm, healthy glow on Ewan. He didn't look so pale or as pained as he had before. That gave her energy. This wasn't a deathbed confession, though it would end the truce they'd formed. That saddened her to the core. She didn't want him to hate her again.

Leveling her shoulders, she strode all the way to the headboard. "Ewan," she said as she set down the tray on a bed table. "Are you awake?"

His eyes opened. Hypnotic, bluer-than-blue, his gaze grabbed onto her as it had before, when gratitude overwhelmed her soul.

"Theo, dear Theodosia, you don't look well. Is something wrong?"

"I...brought you some broth."

With a slow, jarring motion, he raised his hand from beneath the sheets and clasped hers.

The hold was light. She could break free if she wanted. "Ewan, I brought you some broth."

"You said that already."

"*Umm.* Would you like some?"

He nodded, shut his eyes, and released her.

Her freed fingers were like ice. She broke the bread, taking a small piece and soaking it in the savory brown liquid.

She looked at his strong jaw. The grown-up version of the button nose she saw every night. She stroked his cheek as she often did Philip. "Open."

He chuckled but complied. Two pieces down, he nipped her finger, suckling it before giving her palm a kiss.

Too surprised to move, she stood there, letting him have his way with her hand, nuzzling it against the light rasp of shadow on his jaw.

With a heart beating like crazy, she still didn't move her hand. It felt too nice. The joy she should've had when she'd seen him at Burlington Arcade, she let it free, one tear drop at a time down her nose, her cheek. Ewan, her first love, the father of her son, lived. And he'd almost died again saving Philip.

Grunting, he reached up and wiped a tear from her lips. "I don't want you crying for me. Have you come only to feed me? There are questions you have to answer, like will you marry me when I can stand?"

"I have to tell you about Philip. Your son, Philip."

There wasn't any shock in his expression. Instead, Ewan smiled wide.

"You know?"

"When I saw his eyes, my eyes, right before the cart hit me, I suspected. I've lain here torturing myself, wondering if you'd trust me enough to tell me. Wondering what it would be like to hear the truth from you. Now you have more reason to marry me. I want my son."

"I'm sorry, Ewan."

Hooking his palm behind her neck, he drew her closer.

She could feel his labored breath on her nose, but he went no further. "You thought me dead. You made your choices going to Cecil. He took a mistress who soon proved to be pregnant." Ewan tilted her and towed her into a deep embrace. "I understand."

She couldn't accept his truth, not when Ewan's forgiveness made Mathew weak. Stiffening, she eased his palm from her shoulders. "You think I fooled Mathew?"

"Did he know or did he feel guilty for impregnating a mistress when he was three or four times her age?"

The scorn in his voice sliced through her. It was fine for him to think her a jade, but to make Mathew's choices sound anything less than admirable was too much. She bolted up from the bed. "Don't you dare make this Mathew's fault."

"I know it's my fault. For dying, I mean, almost dying in the war."

"If there is a fault, it is mine. Mathew was good and decent."

"Theo, you don't have to protect him. You were confused, alone, carrying my child. You wanted that babe to have a name. I understand. You have done nothing wrong. Once we marry, everything will be right."

She wrapped her arms about her waist to keep from slapping her hand across his face. "I told you about Philip because you needed to know, especially after saving his life, but I don't want this to be another thing between us to cause hurt. I don't want to always be reacting to you, to keep hurting you."

"It's fine to be reactive. It's called being alive. Not living so carefully. You used to like that."

"And what did I get for that? A ghost that hates me. A boy who can't hear."

"I don't hate you. But what about Philip? What's wrong with my son?"

She tugged on her shawl, pulling at the fringes, trying to hide, but she couldn't. The truth demanded that she face Ewan. Leveling her shoulders, she turned back to the bed. "When I discovered that I was with child, you were with your regiment. I didn't know how to write you. I thought maybe your father would send me to you. I went to him and he refused to see me. Then one day he saw me in Town and tossed a note at my head. I had a shop owner read me the most horrible news—that you'd died. I'd lost you and any hope of doing better than my mother."

"You weren't a prostitute."

"The streets don't make a distinction from a woman troubled by love or money. This baby wouldn't have a real name. Philip, the Flower Seller. How would that be? The one thing I promised myself—"

"Theodosia, if I'd known, I would've married you. I want back every moment with you and Philip."

She held up her hand to block his words. "I trusted you with everything. Then you changed your mind and abandoned me with a promise of a year."

"I'm sorry. That was wrong."

She waved him silent. "I'm not done. You need to hear me. I must say this without thunder or fear twisting up my words. I thought I forgave you, when you died. I couldn't hold on to that bitterness, I had to survive. I tried to work to save money before Philip came but bad thing after bad thing happened. Your father banished me from picking his fields, and my cart was stolen. I couldn't get to Covent Gardens to sell in the mornings. I worked as a field hand but couldn't make enough money to eat and have a safe place to sleep. I began to starve."

The horror etched on his face made her heart hurt, but she had to tell him why Philip was deaf. He forced himself to sit. There was pain on his face, his breathing sounded rough. "No one would help. What about my mother?"

"One person helped." She returned to Ewan, picked up his bare feet, and swung them back in the bed. "Mathew Cecil caught me stealing from these fields. I thought he'd turn me in. They would have hanged me for stealing. That might have been a way out."

Ewan lay back but he kept his hand on hers, clutching it to his night shirt. "It was stupid to rise, but I didn't want you so far from me."

She freed her palm, but stayed at his side. "You will when I finish. Mathew had me come to his patio and he fed me sliced chicken and bread. The first full meal I'd had in months. We talked about flowers and how he wasn't watering his lavender right. He told me his favorite place in the summers was sitting on the patio. He smiled and let me ramble on with all my nervousness, wrong words. But he was a gentleman."

"So how did you become his mistress?"

"It was your mother's idea."

Ewan's lip twitched. He blinked liked he'd become crazed. "What?"

"She caught me leaving Tradenwood. She blamed me for you having gone to war. That you would be alive, if not for me. I told her I had your babe, I put her hand on my stomach, but she didn't believe me. She said harlots weren't faithful.

She warned me to never mention your name again."

Her throat clogged, remembering her desperation. Swiping at her eye, she said, "I begged her to help. She said to starve or find a new mark. I went out into those fields and cried half the day. I wanted to die, but how could I let the only thing left of you go? I saw Mathew's carriage pass, and I thought about my mother and this babe in my body. So, I washed in the waters you and Lord Crisdon want. I snuck back to Tradenwood. Mathew was asleep on the patio. I lay at his feet."

"Voluptuous you, wet from the river, dropping at Cecil's feet. I already said I hate him, correct?"

"He woke up and I threw myself at him, tossed my arms about his neck, like I'd seen my mother do at the brothel, like I did to you in the carriage. But he didn't want me. He wondered why someone who knew how to grow lavender would do this. I sobbed as I told him about you, and you dying, and that I would do anything to have enough food to save this baby."

Remembering her desperation, she felt her eyes stinging, but she stood tall. She owned her mistakes. "He agreed. He said I would be his mistress. He moved me in to the room I sleep in now. He spent tuppence on vegetables, six pence on meats and cheese. I'd never eaten so well. Philip felt better inside. I had hope again."

"So then what happened?"

"He confirmed my story with your father and even your mother. And right before I was ready to pop, he came with a special license. He said family takes care of family and proposed to me."

"So he didn't coerce you."

"No. He was kind. So wonderful with Philip. Got him every doctor that could help. When he was born, he was perfect, but then the palsy set in. He has some hearing in his right ear. None in his left. When you were yelling for him to move, he couldn't hear you."

"Theodosia, I saw the child in trouble. That's all I thought of. I didn't want him hurt or for you to suffer. I didn't suspect until I'd saved him and saw his eyes. I'm his father."

"No. He is your flesh, but Mathew is his father."

"On paper, but that is only because I didn't know. I'm grateful Cecil aided you."

Shaking her head, she pulled his hands away. "I was grateful to him, but you were still locked in my heart. There wasn't room for Mathew. He wasn't you. He didn't like the gravel of his voice, so he hired tutors to read to me. He didn't do things like you, but when I saw how he took care of Philip, how he stood up for me, even listened to me to improve the Cecil lavender, installed my ideas about hothouses, I grew to love him. Yes, I loved him very much. I was safe, completely safe for the first time in my life."

Ewan dropped his chin, rubbed at his neck. "I didn't make you feel safe."

"No. Your mind was changed by your family. How could I ever be a safe again, when one word from your father could change your mind? Mathew didn't care what anyone thought. He gave me and Philip his name. I wasn't Theo the Flower Seller. I was Theodosia Cecil."

With his face blank, Ewan looked away. "You really did love him?"

He had to know it all, and Theodosia refused to hold in her feelings. She patted her broken heart. "I was a wife, in every sense of the word, to Mathew. He gave me honor. He loved my sickly child. He waited for me to love him. Yes, I loved him with all I had."

Ewan frowned and his eye held a light she'd never seen. "So what do we do now? I want to know my son. You haven't answered my proposal. I still want to marry you."

"You are Philip's cousin. You saved his life. You can always have an influence, but Lester is his guardian. He may not want you around. And once I marry again...things will be awkward."

"Marry me. I should never have left you."

"But you did. We are not the same people, those two stupid lovers caught in a thunderstorm. You don't know me now."

"I never thought I'd left you in such straits. You were so strong and determined. I didn't think you'd faced such things. My family should've sent you to me. I should've taken care of you."

"You didn't know what I needed, Ewan. And we should have thought of the dangers of what would happen when our love was illicit. I know you say differently, but I'll always wonder what test your family will have of me."

"Theo...Theodosia. I know my own strength now. I will fight for the dreams we share."

He tried to lay back but didn't seem to have the wherewithal.

"I don't dream anymore. I close my eyes and I see nothing. You should rest." She rose and tucked the blanket about him.

He grasped her hand. "I'm serious about marrying. We could find what we had. You loved me once."

Her heart remembered, and it beat as hard as it had in the carriage the night of the theater, or the balcony, but that would mean being vulnerable to him again. And his family. Though Lord Hartwell seemed nice, it wasn't worth the risk, even if the touch of him made her pulse soar. "Get some rest. I'll—"

The door to the chamber opened. Pickens stood there with Philip. Her boy cried hard and held his ear.

"Ma'am," Pickens said, "the pain just started up."

She held out her arms and gathered the boy up. "Philip,

it's going to be better."

"What's going on, Theodosia?"

Ewan sounded angry but she couldn't help him. Philip needed her.

She bent and smoothed his thick black hair.

He held on to her leg. "Ma-Ma. It hurts. Hurt so bad."

"*Ssh*. It will be better. Pickens, the laudanum?" Her heart exploded. "We're out of laudanum."

"I sent a footman, but it will be hours. Perhaps there is some at Grandbole?"

"No. Nothing from there." She capped her mouth, then released it, and then scooped Philip up. She'd do anything for Philip but beg at hateful Grandbole, but she couldn't leave her son in pain. "If I can't get him calm. We'll ask Lord Hartwell."

The mattress creaked from behind. Ewan had sat up again. "Get an onion. Warm it, cover it in cloth. Put it on his ear."

Her face surely showed every fret and concern her mind could conjure, but he slapped his palm on the bed. "Trust me. It's an old soldier's remedy."

Pickens came to her side. "Ma'am?"

Not knowing what to do, she decided to listen to the only person who sounded calm and reasonable. "Do what he said."

Pickens nodded and left the room.

Ewan heaved and waved. "Bring him to me. Bring my son here."

She stumbled a bit, bouncing Philip against her shoulder, but she brought the tear-stained boy to Ewan and laid him out on the bed. As usual, he cried in silence like the quiet world he was becoming a part of.

Her heart broke again.

Ewan ran a hand over the boy's chest, his little jaw and nose. He mumbled something, a prayer, a wish.

Theodosia clamped her palms onto the bedframe to keep them from trembling. She was afraid for her son, afraid of how content Ewan looked comforting Philip, afraid of the way her heart pounded at the sight of them together.

It was too much, and her fear too great. The letter from the squire might be the answer to keeping Philip and her heart safe forever.

. . .

Ewan passed another quiet week in Tradenwood. He spent the early mornings reading to Philip. The warm onion helped the first night and the two other times the boy had ear pain. It was hard seeing the little man suffer. And poor Theo, every time, she looked as if she'd fall over from fright.

Swinging his feet out of bed, he sent the English ivy jiggling. Whether it made good air or not, it showed Ewan that Theo cared. She never stopped his request to see the boy, but rarely did she stay. The woman was simply too stubborn or too afraid to admit the obvious, that he could be a good father to his son, and that they, all three of them, could be a family.

Why deny the attraction that was as sweet as the lavender in the hand lotion she used? Maybe she needed more convincing. He shrugged as he pushed aside the foul Shakespeare that he'd read to his son today. Philip was a lovey child, well-mannered but quiet, very unlike his nieces. Unfortunately, the few words the boy spoke had a heavy lisp.

To think, this boy might've been more perfect, hearing out of both ears, if he hadn't left for war or if his father had showed some compassion. And what of his mother? She had known Theo had his child and had turned her out to starve. He expected such cruelty from Lord Crisdon, but not Mother.

Tired of languishing even with Shakespeare, he rose and

slid into his breeches. It took a great deal out of him to stand, but solitude was bringing him no closer to convincing Theo to trust him. And though he'd rewritten his play with the name Cleo and had made her Egyptian instead of a mulatto, it wasn't enough of a sacrifice for her. What would be?

He managed to head down the stairs, clinging tightly to the banister with each step. The exercise felt good. His lungs didn't sting as badly as they had before. Maybe he'd have enough strength to kneel and propose.

At the bottom of the treads, he huffed and repacked his chest with the savory air of a roast of some sort. Music and laughter carried through the hall, and he turned his head to its source, the blue polished drawing room.

Peeking into the opening, he saw Jasper sitting close to the pianoforte. One of Theo's friends, the duke's daughter, played a jaunty tune vigorously on the grand instrument.

He heard clapping across the hall in the parlor. As stealthily as he could, he backed up and craned his head to spy inside. Theo's other friend read a book on the chaise. In chairs, holding glasses of wine were the doctor and a new older man, one with a receding gray hair line. A second glance didn't return the man's name to Ewan, but Jasper had so many physicians visit, it was hard to keep the names straight.

The last confirmed what Theo had said about Philip. He was going deaf. He didn't think it possible to be more angry at himself. If he'd stayed, all could've been different.

Leaning against the wall, he sighed and sucked air through his nostrils. Where was the lovely hostess?

She wasn't with the boy. She'd come for him and had put him to bed at his typical time of seven.

Then it hit him, the one place she would be. The place she seemed to love the most, the patio.

Not wanting to interrupt the music or get mired in small

talk, he left the house and made his way around to the terraced gardens.

The wind stirred but he could still hear the lively tune of Miss Burghley's. In time with the beat, he cupped his hand to his face and craned his neck, scanning left and right.

There Theo stood, a beauty in a gray gown. Though he hated the mournful color, he loved how the bodice melted against her form, how the lacy cap sleeves showed forearms that held onto things with her strength and delicacy. Right now, he understood her.

She must've heard him and turned in his direction and started to descend, moonlight hitting her here and there, all the right places. A few steps away, her hands folded as if she wore a shawl, but no amount of wool could hide her loveliness. Her dark, shiny hair was coiffed in ringlets and sculpted her long neck. "Why are you out of bed?"

He took a step and came out of the shadows. "I needed to see a real flower. Mrs. Cecil the prettiest rose in Tradenwood or Grandbole."

She looked at her patio, hers and Cecil's place, as if she would flee, but didn't. "I thought you gave up haunting."

"How could I when it leads to a moment alone with you? Theodosia Cecil, may I have this dance?"

He held an arm to her. "It's not thundering. I'd like your hand given to me in trust. I won't let go."

A hundred seconds passed but she took his hand.

Slowly, he twirled her. She bit her lip then smiled.

He moved her farther from the steps. Nothing need interrupt them.

When the music slowed, she leaned her head upon his shoulder. "I always liked your height."

"I always liked you."

She reared back. "Don't talk like that. Be my good cousin."

He strengthened his hold, pushing her closer to the bruises on his chest. "Is that all you want, a good cousin? You had dreams. Remember owning your own flower shop? You were going to make blooms for my actresses."

Her face lifted and her eyes widened, beautiful pools of fine teak. "You remember?"

"I hope I wasn't always self-absorbed. Of course, I remember. What do you want now?"

"I want Philip whole, Ewan. I want him to have a full life."

"You and Cecil have done well. He's a great boy."

Her smile widened as he twirled her again. He kept at it, conserving his energy until she collapsed into him. Panting, she clung to him.

He ran a hand along her chin. "I dream, too, but mostly of a kiss. Just one. One without the fear of being tossed out at the docks again. One that you give because you trust me."

"Be serious, Ewan. What if we are caught?"

"I'll kiss you again in front of the voyeur. Indulge me, Theodosia. Your heart has moved away from me. And you have every right after how I left you, but I will praise you, for you are fearfully and wonderfully made. I marvel at how you've worked these fields, all the variety of flowers that you have bloomed. When I am with you, I know my soul is right."

She pushed at his hold, but he didn't have the strength to keep her, not if she wanted to go. "Please."

"I hid you. I made you keep our love a secret. That was the lowest, but I know that your pretty almond-shaped eyes saw my substance, how imperfect I was and you loved me still."

This time she pulled away and put her back to him. "Is that more Shakespeare?"

He approached and placed his palms on her exposed elbows, the beautiful skin freed of gloves. "No, a little King

David, a great poet for only the best women. Lead me, Theo. Tell me what it takes to win your trust."

"I thought poets spoke of love."

"I know I have your heart, Theodosia. It's been in my breast pocket next to my scars. I know the truth about us. Trust, the lack of it, keeps us apart."

She looked down. "Your hands, they are light next to mine. You need sun, then maybe they wouldn't be so different."

"Theodosia. It's night. The moonlight doesn't show much difference. You married Cecil, a man whose age alone would make him paler than me. What is it?"

"Your father thinks we are too different. I won't put you in the position of having to choose. I remember how you needed your family's approval. Even now you've haunted me to get the water agreement."

Theo was sticking with all the old arguments. None of it mattered. She needed to be that daring girl, the girl he had once believed fearless. "Then kiss me good-bye. I will keep Philip's secret and be his good cousin. I want one kiss as payment. You know costs. You'll feel good paying. Then, we are done."

With a shake of her head, she turned to face him. "It's not right to kiss you tonight."

The music played but not louder than his heart. It thudded against his sore ribs, "My mind, my soul, neither has moved from that day you said you loved me. It's been that way since I saw you in the fields. Since you listened to my foolish dreams. If you are saying we are done, release me with one kiss."

She slipped her hands about the revers of his nightshirt. "One kiss good-bye?"

Maybe she was reaching up to kiss his cheek, but he intercepted the offering and tasted her lips. She was delicate and sweet like cloves. So vulnerable, in ways he'd never imagined. It made him want to bundle her up and hide her safely in his chest.

Pushing away, she took a half step but was still in the circle of his arms. "This must stop. You can't haunt me anymore. No more trying to get back to what could've been."

"I don't know how to rid myself of you. Teach me." He dipped his head to hers again and whispered good-bye across her mouth.

Like a wildflower, she bloomed. She stood up on tiptoes and kissed him. The passion was light, safe. If that was all she could give, he was prepared to accept, but then his Theo returned.

She grabbed hold of his collar and kissed him more deeply, demanding to cross the invisible line he'd allowed her to erect.

Her hands clasped about his neck. She held him tightly and searched him. She needed to find in him whatever she needed.

He clung to the curves that burned his soul.

Nothing tentative, nothing reserved in her response to him.

He cocked her head back and tasted her jaw, nibbling along her throat, the tender flesh exposed above her pearl necklace. "I love you, Theodosia."

He held his gaze upon irises so dark, so large and wonderful. "I have always loved you, always will."

She leaned up and took his kiss again.

Arms tightening, he lifted his chin above her head. He had to get this right. "Marry me, Theodosia. Let's take Philip and go to Scotland tonight."

Stumbling backward, she tore away and began righting the pins in her bun. "That kiss was good-bye."

"No, it wasn't. Unless you are sending me to war again. That kiss said 'marry me and have at me'...in that order."

She dropped her head in her hands. "You make me out of control. I won't do the wrong thing for Philip."

"You know I'd never harm him. I would die before that happened."

She drew her arms about herself. "Mathew taught me to reason. There is nothing that tells me this time will be different. Your mother and father will never change. I accepted my squire's proposal tonight. We are engaged. Once the banns are read, we will marry. You and I will be formally done. Mathew would approve of him, and he has no family to please."

He saw it now as clear as the night sky. Theo was afraid and used the memory of her late husband as a shield. "Theodosia, there is still a ghost haunting you. Mathew Cecil. Do you think if you choose me, he'll disapprove from the grave? You're still in half-mourning garb, when your time has passed. He's not coming back. You can't earn his approval."

"He was a great man."

"He was much better than I. But he wouldn't want the woman he loved to live in fear."

Theo patted her lips, then smoothed her gloves. "You do. You want me to live in fear. How long before your father makes a new ultimatum, or how will you deal with a snub at one of your mother's parties, that is, if she even dared to invite me. I can't go back to that. I won't. Yes, let Mathew haunt me. I have to keep Philip as safe as he would want, and I hate to have to bear another name than Cecil to do it. Lester is Philip's guardian. Only a man, a new husband, will be someone the Court of Chancery will respect, and the Fitzwilliams won't be able to hurt us again."

It was suddenly very hard to breathe. Her truth had sapped his strength, made everything heavy.

"I can live without Lord Crisdon's blessings," he heaved. "But not your touch. I won't convince you. You have to see we've both changed, enough to make the love last this time."

He started back into the shadows, but turned and took a final look back.

She brushed at her face. Maybe she even cried a little for their loss. "Good evening, Cousin Ewan. I wish you happiness."

"If you truly did, you'd marry me."

He trudged back to the side door. He'd had that type of trepidation six years ago when his father had caught them in the carriage house. Being a soldier had given him the time to become brave, to learn how to live without Crisdon's blessing. But how could he live without Theo? Was there a way to change the family she feared? Well, he must work fast. Banns only took a few Sundays, then there would be no more time for Ewan and Theodosia.

Chapter Fifteen

Unveiling Truth

Ewan let Jasper help him down from their carriage as they arrived at Grandbole. Convincing his brother to leave Tradenwood seemed a more difficult task. Perhaps, he enjoyed the short holiday away from the girls, with them staying in Town with Mother.

Jasper held up his arm, though he didn't need it. Ewan was determined to leave the place as soon as possible. "You're very quiet. Not jealous of Mrs. Cecil's new company?"

"I am jealous. That is her fiancé."

His brother stopped halfway up the stairs. "Did you ask her to marry you?"

Ewan heaved heavily as he took another step. "Yes. I laid out my hopes and she trampled them like the runaway dray."

"No wonder you've been out of sorts since the good widow had that squire to dinner. You want to go back and put up a fight. I'll get my sword."

Even if he wanted to watch his brother change from his normal lumbering self to a fleet swordsman, how could

Ewan spend another minute witnessing Theo accept another man, and a stiff colorless one, at that. One who probably did not see her beauty or humor. One who wouldn't appreciate her number calculations or her biting wit, though he would taste that tender lip she bit when nervous. "She doesn't trust that I will protect her or the boy's interests. She thinks they will become Fitzwilliam pawns. I haven't figured out how to convince her otherwise. Would Father swearing an oath to her help?"

Jasper nodded. "Father swears a great deal sometimes, but I doubt Mrs. Cecil would want to hear that. Maria weathered everything with grace. I hadn't thought of how his attitude would make things difficult."

As the footman opened Grandbole's door, Hartwell walked in first, tossing his hat and coat on the side table. "I'm sorry. Truly sorry."

Ewan didn't even know what happened to his hat. Being laid up in Tradenwood, he hadn't even thought of it. Theo would think of the cost of it. "It's done for now."

"Done?" Lord Crisdon stood at the center of the hall. "What is done? Did you secure the lease or something more?"

Bracing his weight on the show table, Ewan shrugged. "Nothing was accomplished."

Jasper tugged off his gloves. "Well, Widow Cecil did assure me she will sign our lease. We won't run out of water."

His father harrumphed and strutted past a portmanteau. It sat alone near the end of the stairs. He must've returned from town. Yet with no sign of large ones or lots of maids, it meant his mother hadn't returned. Lord Crisdon had failed to convince her. "Mother's staying in Town?"

"She has other ideas and is trying to reform the granddaughters."

His voice sounded sad, sadder than he'd ever noticed. Ewan had sympathy for him. Trying to convince a woman to trust you after disappointing her was a hard task. Theo would marry someone else while he stood by, alive, desperately in want of her.

"Why the delay in signing? You two have been down at Tradenwood for two weeks. Lying about?"

Ewan looked at Jasper, hoping his brother had something to say to stop the earl's accusations.

His brother only chuckled. Then with a fold of his hands, he launched into a Cheshire cat-sized grin. "Well, Widow Cecil is busy preparing for a wedding."

Lord Crisdon rubbed his chin as a smile of half-scrunched lips erupted on his face. "So you got the Blackamoor to agree. I suppose I'm happy. Not that my son will marry her, but that Tradenwood will be back in our control. Oh, the sacrifices."

Anger and humor bubbled up from Ewan's gut, threatening the air in his lungs. "I'm not the one she's marrying. She doesn't want the sacrifice of being a Fitzwilliam. We are beneath her."

His father blanched. All the color drained from his disapproving cheekbones. "You're not engaged to her?"

"No." Tiring, Ewan headed to escape up the stairs.

"Wait." Crisdon stormed ahead and planted a foot on the first step. "That goat Lester beat you to her bed this time?"

Gripping the banister, as if he could wring it like a neck, Ewan glared at the man. "No one's in her bed. She's an honorable woman who has accepted an honorable proposal."

"Son, you were under her roof and couldn't entice her. You did a better job six years ago with the harlot."

Not wanting to fight, Ewan swallowed the itch in his throat, the gall of the fool. "Pretty hard to be seductive while ill and fighting to breathe. I'm better. Thanks for asking."

The man paced back and forth. He seemed unhinged. "So someone else will get her fortune. Why on earth did I put faith in you?"

That statement hit Ewan worse than the wagon, maybe even worse than receiving his father's letter so many years ago about Theo taking up with another man. "You brought me out here as bait. It wasn't about being a family. It was about a chance at reclaiming Cecil's land."

"If your uncle hadn't thought you dead, Tradenwood would've been yours. Your mother won't come back here until I get back what's ours."

"Ours? You mean yours. Everything is about you. If I had gone through with my original plans to elope, instead of taking up your bargain…maybe Tradenwood would be mine, but I'd have a wife and a son—"

"So now you'll let another man play father to the boy?"

He knew. The earl had known. Every last illusion in his head broke, ripped and tossed like edits to the page. Ewan grabbed the man by his coat. "You turned her away when she came for help. You could've saved my son such pain."

"Ewan," his brother said. "Let it go. It's done. Six years done."

Jasper's hands were on Ewan's trying to break his grip, but nothing could stop him from shaking the truth out of Lord Crisdon.

"I need you, Father, to say it. To be a man like you've called me to be. Say you tried to kill my flesh. That your hate made my boy go deaf."

Jasper let go and stepped down. "No. Father, tell him no."

Crisdon struggled but he couldn't break free. He caught Ewan's gaze. "Yes, I knew. Your mother told me. She wanted her run off, and I did what she wanted, everything she wanted."

Ewan tossed the man back. His hands shook with unspent anger.

A sneer started in Lord Crisdon's eyes and trembled down to his drawn mouth. "I didn't think you had it in you to finish me." He rubbed at his neck. "I don't target women, but your mother insisted on getting rid of her. I had to make it up to Lady Crisdon for sending you away. She virtually left me when the harlot got the benefit of her family's wealth. She won't come back until it's fixed."

"That's a lie, old man. Mother is not like you."

Lord Crisdon chuckled and righted his emerald-blue waistcoat, his freshly tailored coat. "We were united in getting it back at any cost, even sacrificing you for her Tradenwood."

Was Mother guilty, too? No, this had to be another convenient lie. He rubbed at the pain in his neck and moved to the door. "The bait failed. I'll tell Mother myself about failing tonight. Oh, and Mrs. Cecil wants twenty thousand pounds a year for the rights to water. Have fun paying that. I'm done with you."

Ewan couldn't tell if it was the absurdity of the number or the fact that he mentioned going to Mother's, which sobered the man, but Lord Crisdon ran to him, sputtering no.

Ewan turned his back on his father. "Jasper, I'm taking your carriage indefinitely. I'm going back to Town."

"No, Fitzwilliam," Crisdon said, "Stay. Your mother might come back to Grandbole, if you lived here."

He leaned upon the door and stuffed his shaky hands into his pockets. "Then you are both out of luck."

Lord Crisdon harrumphed and swung his hands desperately. "Stay put or your play will never be performed. I was busy in Town, too. The manager at the Covent may buy it, but the committee won't approve it. No one will ever see it."

If he'd blinked, Ewan could've sworn it was six years ago. He'd just consummated his love with the woman who understood him better than any, but to curry his father's fleeting favor he had agreed to join the fight in Spain.

He turned back to Lord Crisdon and fluffed the cravat

he'd mangled. "This is one offer I refuse. In fact, I will never darken this estate's threshold again, not until Jasper's made earl. And don't fret, old man, I need to confirm Mother's hand in this sorry affair, then she won't see me again, either. I did die six years ago. I'm a ghost to you."

Maybe the earl was shocked at Ewan's resolve, for his stone face broke a little with his lips poking out as if he'd swallowed pebbles. "An idle threat. You don't have it in you."

"I can be mercenary, too. There's some vengeful Fitzwilliam blood in here. Good day."

Crisdon shuffled about him. "Leave your mother alone. She's entertaining tonight. You can see her tomorrow."

Ewan kept moving. "She'll answer tonight."

His brother caught him by the shoulder. His big palms squeezed out Ewan's air, but he didn't know that only death would keep him from the truth. "You're both not rational. We should reason this out. Father say something. Don't let him leave like this."

Still ashen and pale, the earl groused and fisted his hands. "What are you soft, too, Hartwell? That's why you can't run this place without me."

Jasper turned from the earl and stared ahead. "Be the bigger man, Ewan. Don't separate from us again. The girls need their uncle. You can't be gone again."

"If you had to choose between Maria and this place, which would you choose?"

The shimmer in Jasper's clear eyes brightened; he pushed past Ewan and held the door open. "Take care of my horses. My gift. And get as far from here as you can."

"I'll borrow the horses tonight, but see me in Town, old boy, bring the girls, if they promise not to burn my flat to the ground."

With a final rap upon his brother's thick knuckles, Ewan strode out of Grandbole. The clean, free air hit him. If only he'd done this six years ago. *If only.*

Climbing into the carriage, he grunted, then motioned to the driver to head to Town. There was a countess he needed to see. His hope was that she was innocent or misunderstood, not duplicitous. He would not jump to conclusions or write the story in his head as he had with Theo.

With eyes shut tight, he lay back and took one long breath, then another. The memory of Theo's last kiss kept his mind right where he wanted it, centered on the rage building in his chest.

The two-hour ride to London seemed like minutes. Music could be heard outside Lady Crisdon's townhouse. Every window was bright with burning candles. He tugged his wrinkled coat, swiped at his missing hat. The musty smell of ointment and carriage leather would turn heads, but Ewan did not care. He hobbled up the steps and pushed inside.

At the top of the interior grand staircase, he saw three moppets. Dressed in fashionable ivory and pale salmon pink ribbons, they looked like Dresdens. His mother's work made them look perfect—perfectly trapped.

Lucy smiled at him. Then returned to her statue-like pose.

He nodded but he wasn't here for them. "Where is Lady Crisdon?" he asked Mother's butler.

The man dressed in a shiny satin blue coat pointed him to the big drawing room. "But I should announce you."

"No. I am her son. I'll do it."

Ewan didn't wait for a response and stepped inside. Tables were strewn about with the finest silverware and crystal. Even the gilded trim of the room sparkled. The fashionable ilk sat at the tables chatting over their dinner, something that smelled of fowl. They hardly noticed him.

When Mother lifted her head, her pretty blue eyes widened. "Ewan?"

"I came to see you after staying at Tradenwood."

She rose quickly and came to his side. "Dear boy, you didn't have to come tell me of your engagement. I have a party. We can discuss tomorrow."

"I need to know something now."

She took his arm and smiled as she giggled at each of her guests.

When they finally were alone in the hall, the joy faded. "Ewan, you could have waited, and you could have come more suitably attired. I keep different standards than what you may be used to."

"I have to ask you one question. You need to hear me."

She went to a console mirror and fluffed a curl, fingered the giant ruby necklace at her throat. "Yes, Ewan of course, but go refresh yourself, then join me—"

"Mother, did you go after Theodosia when I left to join my regiment? Did you turn her away when she asked for help?"

She lowered her gaze and picked at the folds of her fan. "Is that what she told you? They lie you know. I wasn't kind to her, but I suppose that is to be forgotten with you marrying her."

His mother played coy, and she could be as stealthy as the earl when it came to secrets. He straightened and offered her rope to hoist her canard. "So you will accept her and my son with the return of Tradenwood."

"Of course, dear." She put her satin hand to his cheek. "You've restored our loss, what was wrongly taken."

She didn't hesitate. She said everything in a calm tone, as if she were deciding menus.

He sighed, the sting to his gut worse than a mule's kick.

"And you've broken my trust, Mother. You knew, too. You knew Theodosia carried my babe and yet you turned her away."

Her breath caught, and she started fretting with the lace on the handle of her fan. "I was grieving, and it was her fault you were sent away."

"No. It was *my* fault I went away." He folded his arms and sought the right words to make her feel his loss. "There is no wedding. You will never have Tradenwood. You don't deserve it. Probably why Uncle didn't leave it to you when he had the chance." He pivoted, leaving her with her mouth falling open.

"Ewan. Ewan?" Her voice was loud enough for guests to hear. "Wait."

"Mrs. Cecil wants nothing to do with us. I don't blame her at all."

He marched out the door and didn't stop. The family he wanted to belong to had ruined the family he could have had. How would he survive so many cuts? No play, no father, no mother, no Theo. He put a hand to his chest. His story wasn't going to end like this. He was a cousin to a little boy who liked Shakespeare. He'd not lose access to him, no matter what.

· · ·

Theodosia gripped Philip's hand as she and Frederica ventured into the Burlington Arcade. Four weeks had passed since Ewan and his brother had left Tradenwood, and this was her last week as the widow Cecil. The final banns would be read Sunday. She and the squire could marry ahead of Lester's return. Her plan had worked. It had worked so well, she cried herself to sleep each night. When the picture book Ewan sent for Philip came in the morn, she cried all over again. She choked up when Pickens told her Ewan had left Grandbole, never to return. He'd broken with his family, something she hadn't wanted to happen. What pain this must be causing him?

Was it terrible to want her ghost to return and haunt her one more time?

Yes, it was. Engaged women couldn't have ghosts or regrets.

Frederica, dressed in a pale blue walking gown, strolled a few steps in front of them. Her head was high. Not a care in the world must be on her mind, but with all the colors and sights of the shops, who could blame her?

As if she knew Theodosia's thoughts were upon her, Frederica stopped and half-turned. "Why are we here again? Bonbons? You rarely come to Town unless on business. And I don't like the openness of this place, not without the duke."

Readjusting Philip's small hand within hers, Theodosia attempted a smile, but found her lips too heavy, or she'd moved to biting both the top and the bottom ones. "I needed to pick up a few things, maybe seek a designer for a wedding gown. Maybe check for a letter."

"You've accepted the squire, but you are rethinking the matter? Good. You shouldn't grasp at crumbs, when a bonbon might be on the next platter."

"Men and food? Well, one could never say your mind is fixed upon a single path. I want to see if the baron ever answered. With so much happening with the banns and my cousin, I forgot to have someone check. If the baron wrote, I need to tell him I'm no longer looking for a husband. I want to finish this advertisement business right. Correct. Rightly."

She shook her head. "That Fitzwilliam cousin of yours. He was scrumptious, a fine piece of bonbon. Now that he's returned to health, you haven't mentioned him."

"He's gone from the fields."

"Yes, you seem sad about that. Philip, too. During his convalescence, I awoke unfashionably early and found Mr. Fitzwilliam reading to his...your son. What exactly happened?" She pulled closer. "We've been friends a long time. It's fine to fancy him again."

Again? Have I ever stopped? "I don't know what to do. I marry the squire in a fortnight. Philip will be safe. The squire will represent me at the Court of Chancery."

Frederica's lips pulled into an uncharacteristic frown, all sour-lemon-puckered mouth. "You could go. You could do it. You're an honorable woman. You don't have to rely on a stiff bore. Stop selling yourself short. You know numbers. What value do you put on you? Pences or sweet pounds?"

The squire wasn't exciting. He seemed honorable and quiet, but hadn't Mathew taught her that quiet was better, better than uncontrollable fire. Irresponsible blazes burned and hurt too many. "I'm not a duke's daughter. The courts will look at me worse than how these shoppers eye Philip, trying to figure out which one of us is his mother."

Whipping her head from side to side, Frederica allowed her smile to return. "Or they are waiting to see if we have a pet monkey following our unusual entourage."

Theodosia cringed at the memories of selling flowers on the streets to ladies like Ewan's mother. They'd parade a Blackamoor page and exotic pets behind them on shopping days. "I want to scream at them to stop looking, but that would get us kicked out."

They passed the soap store and Theodosia peeked inside. Only the horrible manager was there, dusting his green glass vials. A smile rose inside. Sally was in the country, and Theodosia had given her enough money to feed herself and that baby to come. She bent to her own baby and straightened his coat. "I've saved one shop girl. Maybe I should be a reformer, too."

Philip cupped his hand to his ear as if he wanted to funnel in all the sounds. Theodosia wished she could put all the sounds in the world in a bottle for him.

"You rescued a desperate girl. You are bold in business dealings. Why not be that in the rest of your life?"

Theodosia couldn't answer, not when a thunderstorm could reduce her to a quivering mess. Instead she leveled her shoulders and tightened her grip on Philip's small fingers. "Let's go see if there is a letter from the baron and then leave. This will be done. My newspaper search for a groom will be over."

As they rounded the corner, their path intersected with Lord Hartwell. "Mrs. Cecil. Miss Burghley, Master Cecil. How are you this fine afternoon?"

Her mood lightened as she saw the smiling man. Ewan's brother had been an amiable guest and so loyal at Ewan's side. He stuffed a paper into his jacket and came toward her. "Doing a little shopping?"

"Yes, picking up a few things. And Philip has never seen such architecture. He enjoys it as much as Miss Burghley."

Chuckling, he stared at her then turned to Frederica. "Yes, I can see her hazel eyes sparkling." His gaze lowered to Philip. "There is nothing quite like Burlington Arcade, is there, young man?"

Panicked that her son couldn't hear to answer Lord Hartwell, she stepped forward. "How is your brother faring? I haven't seen him in the fields." She bit her lip, realizing how stupid she sounded, admitting to looking for the man she'd rejected.

"I'll tell him you asked. I am dining with him tonight."

Frederica tugged at her gloves as if she'd suddenly become bored. "Where will you dine in Town? Maybe somewhere rife with intrigue."

Wanting to tap her friend and make her stop man-

bubbling, Theodosia edged forward. "I suppose he is busy with his play."

"No, Mrs. Cecil. It's not going to be purchased. It seems the theater manager… His mind was changed."

"His play was rejected?" Her heart broke a little more. No. He was too good. Ewan must've said no. Could he have done that for her?

As if Frederica had read Theodosia's mind and read it wrong, she shook her head. "So sorry for Mr. Fitzwilliam. Was it not good enough?"

Lord Hartwell's brow rose. "It was quite excellent. The best I've read."

"It had to be excellent," Theodosia said. Her voice carried and more people turned and looked their way. Thinking of Ewan losing another play made her not care how loud she sounded. She stared straight into Lord Hartwell's eyes. "The theater owner couldn't see that?"

The man tapped his fingertips together. "Our father doesn't want a playwright in the family. And suddenly the offer for my brother's play disappeared."

Theodosia couldn't breathe. Somehow this had to be her fault. She swallowed and held onto Philip a little tighter. "He must be devastated."

"No, ma'am, something else had already bitterly disappointed him."

The look in his light blue eyes, wistful and sad, made her sadder. Ewan had surely told him of her rejection of his proposal, but it was for the best. "Your father has been known to have his way. Is there no way to appeal?"

"It would take hundreds of pounds and persuasion. That's a mighty sum while we are in the midst of this water war. Fitzwilliam says twenty thousand pounds is your sum."

She reached into her reticule and pulled out one of her cards with her mark. "I have given you my word on resolving the matter. There's a number that we can agree upon, I'm sure. After my wedding, I am sure there will be lot of things that can be agreed upon."

Lord Hartwell frowned. "All depends upon who you marry."

She'd said too much. Her hurt for Ewan clouded her judgment. She held out her palm and offered her card. "Take this and tell the theater person I will cover what is needed to get his play performed."

Frederica had that devilish grin on her as if she'd eyed the last bonbon. "I see you decided on pounds. Yes, Lord Hartwell, be her errand boy. That should be fun for you."

Something sparked in his eyes, and he turned from Frederica back toward Philip. "You are persuasive, Mrs. Cecil, but I don't make the best errand boy." He folded his arms. "You do know his play disparages a young woman, a flower seller who some might think is you."

She stuck her card in his face. "I know. But he deserves to have this play."

This time Lord Hartwell took it. His face reddened, and he coughed. "You have distinctive handwriting, Mrs. Cecil. Yes. I will take this to the manager and do my best to get the play purchased." He stuffed the card into his breast pocket. "Are you prepared for the excitement and gossip a play like this may bring?"

"Pounds worth. I'm not what people say I am. I am who *I* say I am. Your brother deserves to have his vision on stage. Please say you will take care of this. A Blackamoor woman may not be able to negotiate it, but I can definitely pay for it."

Jasper tipped his hat. "Character trumps a great deal of things, even rumors."

A crowd of ladies passed by, staring and giggling.

Frederica seemed above it all, as if they couldn't possibly be the object of their scorn.

But Theodosia knew. She felt it in her bones. "Not everyone can see that. And it doesn't matter how much strength one possesses. It's still in the same package. A woman needs a champion."

Frederica pulled closer, as if she tired of being ignored. "Yes, a champion to do her bidding, now go on, good little viscount."

Lord Hartwell's dimples popped as if he suppressed a laugh. "It's been a long time since someone's teased me or called me little, but I will handle this. I'll make sure Fitzwilliam gets what he deserves. Mrs. Cecil, Miss Burghley. Good day. The errand boy is leaving."

The grin on Frederica's face almost made Theodosia laugh. Her friend enjoyed tweaking everyone, but teasing a man. That was better than her beloved bonbons.

As they entered the stationers, the humor fled and Theodosia's fingers became ice-cold. She had to admit to herself, that she hoped for the baron to write. Truly, she didn't want to marry the dry squire. With Philip cupping his good ear as his head bobbed from side to side, they waited for the clerk.

Frederica played with the lace eyelets on her fan until the young man came forward. "Mrs. Cecil. There have been no new letters."

Even as the clerk moved and went to another customer, Theodosia found herself stuck in place, hoping that a mistake had been made.

But she had no such luck. The baron had never sent a response to her reply. Her letter of regret didn't pass his muster or perhaps her sin was too great. It didn't matter. The imagined romance was done. "Let's go."

After winding back through the arcade, Theodosia heard humming. Not her classical pianofortes but something the fiddlers had played at the festival. Lively and in beat, as if she skipped around a Maypole, Theo sang, "So no baron, no playwright, but a squire, a boring squire. He will save the flower seller."

"You think this is funny?"

Frederica gripped her arm. "Your plan to get you a husband from the advertisement worked. But my plan to use it to get you to meet men and dream again didn't. You stopped dreaming when Cecil died."

No. Six years ago. But she'd had a waking vision of Ewan on her balcony, asking her to trust him again. "Frederica, I don't know what to do."

"You don't need a new husband. You need an errand boy and a good solicitor. Let's pay for a man to fight your cause."

"What?"

Frederica bent and scooped up Philip. "Yes. Let's find a man and pay for his services. We can even have a solicitor draft paperwork to buy off Lester. He has a price, too."

The girl had lost her mind, or maybe the lack of bonbons for the two-hour drive had reduced her to nonsense. She followed behind her flirty friend who spouted nonsense. "I accepted the squire. Why risk it all now?"

"Because you are worth the risk. If you could see the look on your face when the clerk said 'no new letters,' you'd know I speak the truth. You don't want the squire. You deserve the dream of what our riddle-writing baron offered. Let's go to my father. He can get you a solicitor. Then Ester and I will help you craft a rejection letter for the squire. This is one *no* I can't wait to write."

One of the most infuriating things about Frederica was her ability to transcend from silly to wise in mere moments, but she was right. She didn't want the squire. "Can this be done? Paying a man? What would that cost?"

"Less than what you paid for the play for your playwright cousin. You and I, we are daughters of women who were paid to entertain men. I think it quite fitting for you to buy one."

Frustrated, Theodosia picked up her pace to the carriage. Her thoughts whirled inside. A solicitor would still be representing a Blackamoor to the Court of Chancery. That hadn't changed, but buying off Lester was an idea. "How much would that cost again?"

"Less than selling all your hopes to the squire. You are strong, Theodosia. Mathew Cecil found you when you were in a bad way and needed protection, but you forgot about the girl who fought living on the streets. The girl who escaped brothel life without a duke's pity."

Theodosia spied herself in the shop glass. Older, cut in finer clothes, but where was that fighter? She'd made Mathew listen to her and now the Cecil farm grew the best lavender in the world. She'd made Ewan listen to her, and he had respected her decision and abandoned his haunting. Today, she had implored a viscount to do her bidding. If she could get three men to listen, was it so impossible to get another, like a magistrate, to side with her? She took a breath and counted her fingers, numbering every word of encouragement that Mathew and Ewan and her mother had ever poured into her, even the things her own mother had done to hide her from sin. "Yes. I will try. I will fight."

Frederica gripped Theodosia's cold fingers. "You will win, as easy as you do with math calculations and prices. Let's go buy a man."

After settling Philip in the carriage, she looked up at the blue sky and then down into his bluer-than-blue eyes. She could fight for Philip. She had to hope she was heard, not dismissed because of her race or her humble start at a brothel by the docks.

Chapter Sixteen

My Own Man

Ewan sent the toy horse across his desk one last time. The thing buzzed and rolled across the well-worn surface, almost loud enough to drown out the impatient knocking on the door of his leased rooms. He'd bought the toy the other day on one of his walks in Cheapside when, as now, he couldn't think of what to write. Where was the freedom words had always given him?

The knocks continued. It had to be Jasper. His brother had faithfully come each week to sup. It was something he treasured, but the man probably needed a respite from his daughters and Lord Crisdon.

Corking his bottle of ink, tweaking the position of the horse to his quill, Ewan sighed. "Coming."

Pulling at his rumpled waistcoat, he rose. His walk to the door held its own lethargy. When he unbolted the sliding lock, he was stricken by something worse than lightning—pure shock. "Mother?"

Lady Crisdon stood fidgeting, as if trying not to touch her

white gloves to his threshold. "You haven't come to see me."

She had never left her salon all the time he'd been back. Now she stood at his entryway.

Mother sauntered inside, in her dark crimson carriage dress with gold fobbing, making him miss his uniform.

"Ewan. Your father says you won't return to Grandbole."

He shut the door and leaned against it. "Well, I suppose it's something we both share."

"That is different. I like being in Town for the Season, but you, you should be there, not here." Her pert nose lowered as she said, "On this side of Town."

"Why? Did you need me to make another go at widow bait?"

"You liked her once. Your father caught you bedding her. It didn't take too much of an imagination to think there could be hope—"

"Hope of what? Making my family whole or gaining Tradenwood?"

"Do you hate hearing the truth? If you hadn't been thought dead, Tradenwood would not have gone to the Cecils. It wouldn't be in the hands of that…"

"Woman. Is that the word you seek?"

She squinted and her face turned mean, diminishing her fair features. "Usurper. That is more fitting."

"But wasn't it you who told her to go to Mathew Cecil? It's rather cruel to castigate her for following your instructions." Going over to the door, he held it open. "Good day."

She didn't take the hint and moved to his desk. Picking up the carved toy, she traced the rounded lines of the horse's mane with delicate nails.

A new sense of anger hit his gut, swirling, tightening. How could she touch the toy he'd bought for his son?

She even spun the heavy wheels. "You don't care that this creature has what belongs to you?"

No charity remained in his soul, for it was clear Mother had never cared that Theodosia carried his child. He pried the toy away from his mother. Safely tucked in the crook of his arm, he released his breath. "She does have something that belongs to me, but because you didn't care six years ago, I'm rejected now."

She looked at him as she played with the fingers of her silky gloves. "I'll apologize to her, if that will make things right."

He smiled at her and leaned down. "Go whisper your apologies to the boy, Philip Cecil. Do it soon; he's going deaf. Seems starving makes for long-term problems, ones begrudged words can't make go away."

Her mouth opened, then closed, then opened again. "I'm a good person. There are charities that could've helped."

"Yes, I'm sure there are plenty waiting to help a Blackamoor carrying a mulatto baby." Fingers shaking with repressed fury, he put the toy down, whipping his hand to the door. "Good day, Mother."

"I'm sorry, Ewan."

Pointing again at the door, he watched her pout and sigh, reminding him of how she used to make him think Lord Crisdon had been cruel to her. "Go back to Father and make amends with him. You two are of the same mind. Use his money and buy the widow off. I want peace, and it can't be had caught in your struggles. Theodosia was right to not want to be a part of this family."

"Ewan." Her lips thinned and she poked at his sparse chair. "I wanted nothing of the usurper. But that was a long time ago."

"I love words; Shakespeare's the best. 'To thine own self be true, and it must follow, as the night the day, thou canst not then be false to any man.' To be true to me, is to know the truth of your cruelty. It cannot be forgotten. I wish I could choose to be a Cecil, not a Fitzwilliam."

"We are not all bad, Brother." Jasper strolled inside and headed straight for the toy. Moving it about as if he tried to avoid eye contact, he pushed the horse back and forth. "For Lucy? And am I interrupting?"

"No and no. Mother was leaving."

She wiped at her mouth and walked to the door, as if her short heels were mired in mud. "Lord Hartwell, you send the girls to me any chance you get."

"Will do, Lady Crisdon."

She grasped the revers of his brother's coat. "Convince him of what he owes to the family."

"Of course. Ewan, you must support...which side again? The Fitzwilliam side, the one that leads to bickering, or the other, like good old Cecil, who supported family. It's a tough choice."

Mother frowned and released him. "Remember who will help your horrible wee-ones get ready for their come-out."

"Good day, Mother. This is a threat-free dominion." Ewan took her palm and placed it on his heart. "Go in peace."

Head drooping, she traipsed away. She might be angry now, but Ewan didn't think it formed from the right things. That made him dour. He shut the door. "You are early to this side of Town. My neighbors must be curious to see such comings and goings."

"I had a busy day. Was a bit of an errand boy. How are you feeling?"

He leaned over his writing desk and again positioned the toy about a thumb's width from his papers. "Good."

Jasper tossed his hat on the chair and snaked off his gloves. "You don't look good, but I have some news that might uplift your spirits. I had a nice conversation at Burlington Arcade."

"Burlington Arcade?"

"Yes. I checked my box. It had a reply from my widow. You sure you are feeling well?"

Ewan spun around to see his brother hovering a bit close.

"I said, yes."

"Good." Jasper reared his fist back and belted him in the mouth, knocking him flat. Ewan fell, barely missing the desk.

The man wiped his knuckles with a handkerchief from his pocket, then extended a hand, lifting Ewan from the floor. "You deserve that."

Rubbing his stinging jaw, Ewan nodded. "You still pack iron in your fists. Glad you went for the face, not the chest."

"Well, I do want you recovered."

"Sorry, Jasper, but I tried to keep you from the widow Cecil. It didn't seem right."

"You are not very Fitzwilliam. That's why you did it wrong. The conniving is supposed to advance things. Not waste my time or the good widow's. And we left the poor girl without a response for weeks."

He nodded, all while exercising his jaw, opening and closing his teeth. "So she sent a letter of regrets. Did she rail on about me seducing her, then leaving her in dire straits?"

Jasper's face lit up like bright candles in a chandelier. "No. That would have been more interesting. No, she said… Well, maybe you should read for yourself."

Ewan took the paper and scanned the lines. It said nothing of her complaints from the carriage. It read:

I have no clever rhyme, just truth. I grieved so long and hard over my first love, carrying him in my heart that I missed the joys in front of me. I live with the guilt of not being enough help for my child.

Something lodged in his throat. Remorse and a judgmental nature made for difficult mouthfuls.

I feel the weight of a sorrow-filled heart finding new love when I thought it closed. I feel so heavy.

"That's what she wrote."

His brother took the letter back and pointed at the last lonely sentence, a swirl of black ink on the very ivory paper.

"The guilt of a surviving heart is mighty heavy." Jasper's eyes dulled. He pulled a flask from his pocket but then pushed it back inside. "She closed with: *If you can understand these regrets, I look forward to meeting with you and the mutual acceptance of our proposal.* That is bold; she's not even waiting for you to kneel."

"Not me. That's not my letter."

"You dolt. She is saying that she was in love with you. And she, like me, clung to sentiment too long. She has expressed her fears, yet she still reached for you, us."

Ewan couldn't give in to hope. She was engaged to another. He flipped his head side-to-side. "She has refused me to my face."

Jasper shook his head. "She refused the man who threatened her with a play and who originally left her in order to gain the old man's approval. She doesn't know the new Ewan, the one who's stood up to his father and, it appears, his mother, too."

Optimism started filling his heart but leached out. His lungs must still have holes. "Why can't she say these things to me? Not a letter."

"That is a minor concern, if you love her. You do love her, don't you?"

What did his feelings matter? He craved a dream so much he'd bought a toy for a boy he could never father. He shrugged. "She's made her choice. It wasn't me."

"Sad. That would make the errand I ran for her silly."

He stared at his brother, all while daring his own heart to slow its rush, a tiny bit of hope stirring it. "What did she have you do?"

"I've come from Covent Garden. She gave me her mark to pay any fees to sponsor your play. She charged me with spending up to a thousand pounds for a play that disparages her, for a love she can't forget."

"What? She can't fight my battles."

"Perhaps, but Brown is waiting to see you. The widow Cecil was right. He's open to bribes to withstand Father's threats. Go settle things with him and then go answer your newspaper bride."

"My play has to stand on its own. I couldn't let you bribe him. I can't let Theo—Mrs. Cecil pay my way, either."

Raising his arms to stretch as if he tired of being a busybody, Jasper yawned. "So are you going to go fight for the play? Our newspaper bride?"

If he could get this play sold, despite Lord Crisdon, and despite Theo's offer, that would be the way to prove his merit to himself. "Take me to Brown. I am selling a play today. Then you are buying me dinner."

"What of the widow? She isn't married yet."

"She has chosen her new husband. Perhaps, I should let her have her peace."

Jasper seemed downtrodden again, but he donned his hat and started to the door. "Perhaps, she'll get to that wedding day and change her mind."

Ewan spun the horse toy again before following his brother. If the good widow was ready to spend money on Ewan's dreams, maybe that was a signal that she was ready to trust him again. He'd haunted her to change her mind, but would she come to Ewan and bewitch him with her changed heart?

· · ·

Holding his breath, Ewan stood at the side of the curtain. He mouthed the line in silence as the actress said Cleo's infamous line, "The price to my heart is a banknote you can't pen."

The actress did it, head held high, then strutted off the stage with her hips swaying. The audience erupted. The laughter and claps shook the place. This was the third week of the play, but the moment felt like the first time.

Brown came up to his shoulder and chuckled. "This play is a hit. I must admit, you coming to Covent demanding I buy this play for a measly fifty pounds was a gamble I was willing to take."

All smiles, Ewan tugged his coat. "I knew these words were gold. I knew how the audience would love them. Admit it, Brown, this was a great deal, only cost you a few more author's benefit nights."

"Yes. It took the fear out of me crossing Crisdon. He hasn't made a peep of problems. Yet, with this being the third night of your author's benefit to a packed crowd, minus my fees, you stand to clear a tidy sum. What are you going to do with this small fortune?"

He hadn't thought about it. *A bigger flat? A gig of my own, instead of borrowing Jasper's?* "I don't know, but I'll have to make it good."

"Well, maybe you should take some time and start thinking about your next play. I'll want it. You even got the old Duke of Simone to come, dark money and all."

Ewan's pulse raced, thinking of the last dark money night. That night when he'd first given in to his attraction, when he'd believed Theo would be his. So many things he hadn't known about her, hadn't thought to know about her.

She had trusted him in that moment and he'd taken the opportunity to seduce her again. What a foolhardy thing for a man in love to do. But if she were here seeing his play, the least he could do was thank her. If not for her trying to help him, he might not have pressed Brown. He wouldn't be living the dream of his heart, seeing his play performed. "I'm going to see if the duke has brought all his special guests."

Not waiting for the final act, he spun and was out of the theater, heading to the private stair before Brown's gobsmacked mouth closed, releasing cigar-tainted breath.

Conquering one tier of steps, then another, Ewan stood tall on the final landing.

What if she'd changed her mind, come to see his play, but the shy girl lost her nerve and couldn't tell him? That's how he wrote it in his head. His heart pounded as he made it into the lobby. A few people lingered, but most were in the packed boxes. He headed to the final one, Simone's box.

As he approached, Ewan heard laughter and hoped there was that one off-note in the tones, caused by someone biting her lip. Impatient, he pulled back the curtain. The duke's box was crowded, but to the back were two beauties, Theo's friends. Two, not three.

His heart dropped. He backed out, closing the dark curtains.

Disappointment wrapped about him like the shroud to this box. Of course, she wouldn't come. The stubborn woman was probably off with her squire on a wedding trip. She hadn't changed her mind.

Before he could turn and go back down, the curtains parted and Miss Ester Croome came out. She had a hand to her mouth as if she struggled to say something, but nothing came out.

"Yes, Miss Croome."

She took a breath. "Mr....Mr. Fitzwilliam, I thought that...you're well?"

He put his hands behind his back. "Yes, and you look well. How is Miss Burghley?"

"She's fine. She'd come say hello, if she wasn't afraid of disturbing her father. It's rare for him to come...with us."

Shifting his weight, feeling foolish, he nodded. "So I hear."

She waved her ice-blue fan that perfectly matched the lace on her long gown and crisp bonnet. "Your play is very good. Your Egyptian character Cleo. She's nothing like a certain friend of mine."

"I know. Your friend was never this character. Tell the new bride that, next time you see her."

Miss Croome's brows rose. "You don't know. She didn't marry the squire. She begged off. Miss Burghley and the duke, they helped her get a solicitor. They drafted things for Lester to sign, but he won't. Now she's fighting him at the Chancery to change the guardianship."

Ewan didn't know what to react to first, that Theodosia didn't marry or that she was fighting for Philip. His heart answered both. "She's still unmarried and she's in court. Did she get it done?"

The young woman looked to the floor. When she raised her head, he saw fear in her chestnut eyes. "She hasn't heard yet, but it doesn't look good."

Anger heated in his bones. He scrunched up his fists. "Can't they see Lester has no interest in the boy?"

Miss Croome yanked off her light gloves, exposing her smooth chestnut skin. "It's difficult for the courts to rule against a man for someone less-than. Lester has even used the accident at the festival against her. Mrs. Cecil is desperate. She's sending the boy abroad tonight, and she's selling Tradenwood to the Earl of Crisdon…your father, tomorrow. Then she is leaving for good."

He started backing up. "I don't think she's taken into consideration what her cousin thinks of this plan. Excuse me."

Ester rushed forward and hugged him. "Keep my friend and her son here."

"I'll try my best." He started down the stairs, only stopped at the office to collect his benefit even before the play was done. He had to hire his way to Tradenwood and haunt his cousin one more time. She needed to see he was his own man in need of the right woman. Surely, she'd let him prove he'd fight every hell to save their son.

Chapter Seventeen

Getting Love Right

Theodosia tried to remain calm, but the maids couldn't pack fast enough. The Court of Chancery would rule any day now, but the solicitor she'd paid for, who had even hired a barrister—all said the same thing—no hope. Cecil's will was like iron, specifically naming Lester as Philip's guardian. A new husband might equal him, but now there was no time.

At this point, Lester would have to sign the solicitor's carefully drafted papers to give up his position. Why would he, when his goal was to control her *and* the Cecil fortune?

She went down the hall again, touching walls and trim. She hated leaving. Tradenwood was Philip's home. But at any moment Lester could come take the boy. He was so angry at her for refusing his proposal. If not for Pickens, he would have struck her when he learned she'd nearly married the squire.

All pretense of tolerating her was gone. He'd hurt her or Philip to have his way.

Wandering into the nursery, she saw Philip sitting in the middle of the blue rug.

"Ma—ma." He smiled then went back to flipping pages in the picture book Ewan had sent him.

The governess must've been careless, leaving things where he could pull them down. Yet, as she came closer, she noticed it wasn't that book, but foul Shakespeare. Philip must still remember Ewan reading it to him in those days he had recovered at Tradenwood.

"You miss him. You miss him, too."

Arguing, cursing sounded from below. Lester. He had barged into the house, again.

Scrambling, sliding in her slippers, she scooped up Philip and looked for a place to hide. Under the bed? A table? The closet? The dark closet.

Swallowing hard, she ripped open the door. "I'm so sorry, Philip. This has to be done." She put him up on a high shelf. "Stay quiet." Her voice sounded like her mother's and she didn't mind. "It's for the best."

He nodded as she moved a blanket to block the view of him. Watching the darkness cover her child—his blue eyes squinting as she closed the door—broke everything inside. It might as well have been a coal shuttle.

The footfalls on marble pounded like thunder. She froze for a moment then moved far from the closet and stood near the window.

The door to the nursery opened, slamming against the wall.

Lester stood at the threshold. "So, it is true. Portmanteaus everywhere. You are running. You actually thought you could take the boy without me knowing."

"Yes. I should've left yesterday." But she had wanted to see her friends one more time and hear how they had enjoyed Ewan's play. She shook her head and tried to push past him and lead him from the room. "My comings and goings are none of your concern."

"But the boy is."

She was still mistress of Tradenwood tonight, and she needed to bluff him out of the room. Chin high, she said, "You need to leave. You are not welcome."

"As his guardian, I should know his whereabouts, which means knowing your whereabouts."

She tried to pass him, but he blocked her. She huffed her frustration. "You were not invited in this house. You don't get a say."

"Yes I do. When will you learn to heel?"

"I'm no dog, Lester. Get out of my way."

He chuckled, hard and heavy, as he forced her back into the room. "So the dog is trying to run. You act so brave. I almost bought it. You're nothing but a lucky wh—"

"I am more than you will ever be. I have honor. Strength that you can't touch. Things vermin like you will never understand."

The sneer washed from his face. He gripped her hand and tugged her to him. "You've been nothing but trouble. And I'll inform the Chancery of your neglect. Shouldn't you be making me offers, not guff?"

Theodosia slipped from him, leaving her gray widow's shawl in his meaty palms.

She stood up tall. Didn't dare bite her telltale lip. "You and the Chancery are too late. He's gone. Your threatening ways are over."

Dumping the wool, he looked under the bed and the table. "You didn't have time to get rid of him."

She tapped her chin, playing the part of a conniving shrew. "How long ago did you last see Philip? When was that? Yes, before I tricked you into going to Holland—weeks ago?"

Fists balling, he charged toward her again and wrenched her arm. "Philip, come on out here before your mother is hurt. You hear me, boy? I'll break her arm."

He tugged on her elbow until she screamed, but Philip made no sound in response.

"Break it off, if you must, but my boy is safe from you. He's gone."

He tossed her to the ground and sputtered an obscenity. She landed hard on her backside, the floor stinging her hip. "Take my offer for money. You don't want me as a wife. You want money to buy your own lands. I'll give you ten thousand pounds."

"You think you can buy me off, you slut? Why settle for a slice? If I control you, I can control it all." He yanked her up from the floor. With a hand to her neck, he pushed her against the wall. "Where is the mulatto?"

She tried to buck free, then stilled, looking him dead in his eye. "Hit me if you must. But you'll never have my son. You'll never control me. I'm not afraid of you."

Lester cursed, spitting in her face. "You should be."

Theodosia closed her eyes to blunt the sting of his arm coming for her, but nothing came. When she opened her eyes, she saw a scuffle, flying fists. Ewan and Lester traded blows.

She blinked to make sure she wasn't dreaming, then ran to the door and screamed, "Help! Lester has lost his mind."

Evil Lester blunted Ewan in the back, smashing him against the closet door.

It shook, and her heart nearly stopped.

Nothing stirred or sounded. Philip had to be fine. He had to be.

The wind seemed gone from Ewan. He gasped and gasped, but he reared up. "That all you have?"

"No." Lester took a run and aimed his fists straight for Ewan's chest.

Ewan groaned at the blow, then he turned his head her way, and laughed. "He has to do better. Ghosts are hard to get rid of."

Lester shook out his fingers. He moved again toward Ewan, but two grooms barged into the room.

"Get Lester," she said. Her shaky voice surely sounded pitiful.

The men grabbed him and kept him from moving.

Ewan came and took her palm. "Did he hurt you?"

Lester twisted and tugged but couldn't get free. "Theodosia, get them from me. I will make you pay. I'll get legal action on you for shipping off Philip."

Ewan's blue eyes clouded.

Would he judge her again and believe the worst?

He released her hand and her heart fell, crumbling past her stomach.

Wrenching his neck, he pivoted to Lester. "You are a pest to my cousin. What will it take to make you go away?"

"Why do you defend her? All the Fitzwilliams hate her."

"She's the only one of us beyond reproach. A caring mother and an honorable widow. If she sent him away, it was for his good." Ewan stalked over to Lester. "Mrs. Cecil, your grooms can let the man go. I think he is in control. Perhaps even reasonable."

In her head, not a doubt remained about Ewan keeping her from harm, but to let Lester go? A second glance at Ewan and his encouraging nod, she motioned to her footmen. "Let the fiend go."

Lester smoothed his dusty brown lapel with his red fingers, then he splayed them in the air. "What's in your coat, Fitzwilliam?"

"Scar tissue, my boy, can be quite hard. Or was it the blade in my pocket?" He whipped it out, a long knife with a pearl handle. He made circles with it, before putting it away.

"The witch sent the boy away. I am his guardian. I have rights to know his well-being."

"Theodosia, is my little cousin well?"

"Yes."

"See, Lester. All you had to do was ask." Ewan started to laugh and winked at Theodosia. "There's a benefit to scars. They make you harder. More dependable. Perhaps they make one shrewd. Tell me what you need to go away."

"The Chancery will know that she denied me my rights. And running away won't do anything."

"The courts will be happy that Mrs. Cecil has packed her bags. She's eloping. Young Philip will have a new stepfather."

She wanted to object, but to do so would allow her enemy a foothold. So, she stayed quiet and nodded like a fool. Maybe she was one. She was depending solely on Ewan.

Lester's face broke. The shock made his chin drop to the floor. "What?"

Ewan came again to her side and lifted her hurting palm. "You were right, Lester. I have a tendre for my cousin. She has finally agreed to marry me. We are eloping." Ewan waved her letter to the baron in the air.

She felt her mouth pop wide, but she closed it and bit her lip. Something untoward had occurred, but the look in Ewan's eyes, one of *trust me*, made her nod again and say, "Yes. I did propose. You know the solicitor said the court will favor Philip having a father, more than a guardian. And Mr. Fitzwilliam doesn't have a conflict of interest. He's not trying to wrestle away Philip's fortune. Unlike you, he simply wants to love the boy. Who do you think the courts will side with, you or the son of a peer?"

Lester rubbed his hands together. He paced a bit. "Then I'm left with nothing."

Thinking about how Mathew would do things, she decided to allay the bull. "No, you are not. Sign the papers in the parlor, and I'll still give you ten thousand pounds. You can buy land. You take all the knowledge you've gleaned from me and Cecil and have your own. That's what you really want."

Lester paced some more. "I have to think about it. You wouldn't offer if you had no doubts of winning."

Ewan stepped in front of him. "The widow is trying to help you save face. She wants this over. For her peace, we'll offer a sum of twenty thousand but only if you agree now, and only now."

That was blackmail payment. Ewan had gone too far. She wanted to box his ears, spending so much. "That's too much. It's not—"

"To have him go away, so you can be free, the Fitzwilliam side of the family will repay this amount." He turned to Lester. "It's only a deal, if we do this now. Take your chances at the Chancery and get nothing. What say you?"

Lester's head swiveled from left to right. He flexed his fingers. "Yes." He sneered and pivoted to the hall.

"Follow him, Ewan. The papers are in my desk in the parlor. Then send him from my house."

"Theodosia, I will make sure he never harms you or Philip again. Where is my son?"

When her gaze went to the closet, Ewan shot there, too. He opened the door, sent a few blankets sailing, and brought out her sleeping boy. He kissed his forehead then handed the boy to her. "Stay up here until this is over. I'll come back for you this time."

She waited until Ewan had left before letting her sobs free. As his footsteps faded, she hugged Philip tighter. "You were so good. I'm so sorry."

Tear after tear released, but she couldn't fully breathe until Ewan returned. Philip wasn't safe until those papers were signed.

"Don't cr-cry, Ma-Ma."

But she had to.

She'd hid her child from ugliness in a dark space, but he

couldn't hear the ugliness. That was a blessing.

Something deep inside her opened, and she took a full portion of air. So many years ago, her mother had done the same thing, closeting away her babe in a coal scuttle. Today, she became her mother in a very good way, like she had six years ago, to protect her child.

The front door slammed, followed by more footsteps.

Ewan returned, he came inside the nursery and lifted her up. He put Philip on his shoulders and lifted her palm. "You are safe from him, Theodosia Cecil, but not from me."

She reached up and smoothed Philip's pinafore. "I'll take my chances with you."

His brow rose. "Why? Am I not so scary?"

She dried her face with her hands. "You should fear me. You overspent ten thousand pounds. You have some explaining to do."

As if she hadn't spoken, he spun and cooed at Philip. "I will buy you the best set of breeches. This year to come. You will be six then."

Waving at him to stop, she tried to step in front of him. "Don't make promises. It is so hard to keep them."

He shrugged and spun faster. Philip tossed his head back and laughed. "Your mother is being stubborn." He moved closer to the boy's good ear. "I promise to fill you up every day with words. I'll make up for the years I've missed." He caught her gaze. "I can do the same for you, too, Theodosia."

She bit her lip, then followed him down the steps, giving chase all the way to the parlor.

Signed and blotted on the desk were the renouncement of Lester's right as a guardian and the contract giving him twenty thousand pounds. Her figure of ten had been crossed out. "Ewan, do you know how much one can buy with that amount?"

"I'm sure you do, Mrs. Cecil. The point is, he's gone.

Lord Crisdon will pay."

She had planned on the earl paying Lester's portion tomorrow when she sold him Tradenwood, but that was tomorrow's trouble. Ewan had done it. He'd saved Philip. Smiling, she picked up the papers and held them to her bosom. "Thank you, Ewan."

The man wasn't listening. He was too busy taking Philip to the bookcase and having him put his fingers on the spines.

Pickens entered the room. "Ma'am, I made the arrangements for Philip's passage with the governess, but the footman said there had been some commotion while I was out."

A quick swipe to her eyes, and a check to her chignon, she turned to her butler. "It's over. Lester is gone."

A smile filled the old man's face. "May I start the unpacking?"

She shook her head. "No, Pickens. I'm still selling."

Ewan frowned as he lifted his lips to Philip's ear. "Maybe I can change her mind, or at least delay her, Pickens. Mrs. Cecil is eloping tomorrow. Make sure she is suitably packed, her and the boy. One bag each should do."

Her mouth dropped open again, wide enough to gulp all the air in the parlor. She recovered, tugging on her short gray cap sleeves. "Leave us. There is much to discuss."

Swiveling his head between them, Pickens backed to the door. "Will you require anything?"

Hugging Philip as if he were a delicate China doll, Ewan approached Pickens. "See that no one disturbs us. I want the widow to compromise me in privacy. But do bring some tea and biscuits."

Smothering a laugh, Pickens bowed and closed the door.

Setting Philip on the chaise, he motioned to her. "Your word is good, Mrs. Cecil. Is it not?"

She didn't move. "Yes."

He took a step to her direction. "You proposed to the baron?"

She squinted at him, but answered the truth. "Yes."

"Then you proposed to me. I answered your advertisement, initially giving my brother assistance. He's looking for a bride."

"So Lord Hartwell is a liar, too? Pity, he seemed nice."

He strode a little closer. "Lord Tristan is one of my father's lesser titles. He borrowed it. He is truly seeking a wife of convenience through newspaper advertisements. By happenstance, he stumbled upon yours. I do find it odd, that you'd attract another Fitzwilliam, but we are attracted to unforgettable women."

The things she wrote, thinking she'd found a kind stranger—it had been Ewan. She clasped her naked arms, hunting for her missing shawl, as if it would keep her from feeling so vulnerable. "Then it was him who I proposed to, not you. Did you like this joke? Did it give you both a good laugh?"

Ewan put his palms lightly to her elbows. "There's no laughing at you, but I did use the letters to test you. You passed. You astounded me. You exposed more and more of your heart in your responses. It frustrated me, tormented me, actually, that you couldn't be this free in my presence."

She dipped her head as her soul warred between disbelief and anger. "Those were private responses meant for someone else. Or at least the notion of someone else."

He closed the distance between them. "It made me jealous and crazy to know you couldn't say the same to me. I didn't understand before. I failed you in the worst way. Your letters gave me the chance to know you." He turned toward Philip. "Is it fine with you if I kiss your mother?"

The boy didn't lift his head. He picked up a book from the table and was turning pages.

"I'll take that as a yes."

She tried to move or duck but he engulfed her in his solid arms. He kissed her chin and worked his way to that spot on her throat that made her knees buckle. Weighing the cost of returning his passion or running, she clung to his lapels.

He stopped and held her. "My love will consume you, Theodosia. But I'll burn until you are sure. I want you only as my proper wife. Elope with me. I don't want to wait another moment to wed."

Breathing so hard from the air he'd stolen with his words, she shook her head. "This is reckless. We can't survive your family. Not six years ago, not now. You've freed me from Lester. That's all I want. Let me leave here with Philip."

"So you promised to marry me in a letter, will you compromise me in this closed room with a minor's supervision, and then leave?"

"You're twisting things, Ewan. I'm not a playwright so I won't try to best your words." She moved from him and headed to their son, but he clasped her shoulder, the one still smarting from Lester's cruelty. "Ouch."

He turned her, taking care to massage her arm. "I was fooled by or hadn't paid attention, to the fact that you act a great deal braver than you are. One of us must be brave enough to stay. Let me spend the rest of my life filling you with the words I should've six years ago. That you are loved. I believe in us, and I'll never leave your side."

He stroked her face. "You care so much for others. You're smart. No one can match you with numbers. You even let a fool save face."

"Mathew taught me to not let a bull run mad."

"I'm talking about me. You let me go to war, because you thought that's what I wanted. This fool didn't realize I should've put what you wanted first. I'll deal with my family, but my priorities are right here, you and Philip."

She grasped the revers of his deep chocolate coat. Too hesitant to draw near, too scared to turn away. "I can't put my hopes on something that will vanish. I won't have Philip caught in another war."

He patted her fingers and led her to the chaise. "Then trust me, a little more each day for the rest of my life. Don't let me haunt your memories. Let me be present every day with you and my son."

Whether she agreed or not, she was nodding yes between his kisses. His arms fit snug about her. Secure in his embrace, she didn't want to be released.

As his hands started to wander, he stopped himself and sat next to Philip. "Tomorrow won't be here fast enough. I'm going to sit here and read. This overnight stay should be enough to ruin my reputation. Then you'll have to make an honest man of me."

"But Lord Crisdon is coming then."

Ewan reached for her hand and eased her into a comfortable spot beside him, even propping a pillow behind her head. "We'll keep the meeting, then elope. If selling Tradenwood is what you wish, then do it. We need to be together in a place where I can write and get Philip the aid he needs. But I want you to keep Tradenwood. Cecil meant it for you and the boy, not the Fitzwilliams."

She closed her eyes. Maybe morning would never come. Philip was safe sitting between her and her dreamer. That memory she'd tuck into her heart. It surely made it hurt less than waking up tomorrow to lose Tradenwood and Ewan to the Earl of Crisdon.

• • •

Sunlight filtered into the room through the open patio doors. Morning had come. Ewan blinked and stretched. Philip slept in his lap. He fingered the boy's dark straight hair. Knowing that he helped keep him safe from Lester—that had to right some of the wrongs done to the boy.

He eased him onto the sofa and stood. Reaching up, he relieved that tense knot in his back. Then it hit him. His fiancée had left without giving him a morning kiss. He searched the room but his chaise mate had abandoned him.

Scratching the light scruff to his chin, he wondered if she had taken to her bedchamber. Pride built in his chest. She trusted him with Philip. That made up for her less-than-wholehearted endorsement of eloping.

Theo wasn't one to be rushed. He wanted her to love him as deeply and as completely as he did her. Thinking of her, of what she liked, it came to him where she'd be. The patio.

She sat upon the knee wall. Wrapped again in her trademark shawl and yesterday's gray gown, Theodosia didn't quite look rested. Crinkles set under almond eyes. Her smooth bronze face held a frown. What a travesty for such a tasty mouth. "I know why you bite that lip. It's quite ripe."

She smiled for a second but stared at something.

He turned and saw the wonderful blooms of the clematis, sweet in purple and rose. "Why are you sad in such a place?"

"Mathew built this arbor. We planted the vines together. He was very happy here."

"We will keep it going, if you don't sell Tradenwood."

"Will we?" She shrugged. "Your mother hates it. Calls it weeds."

A few steps closer and he saw fear settling into the black pools of her eyes. "Go upstairs and dress. Get Philip dressed, too. Wear any color but gray or black."

She took his hand and held it to her heart. "I'll be ready before Lord Crisdon comes."

He almost wanted to check and make sure she didn't escape out the front door. Theodosia wasn't convinced of his resolve but the walls, the curtain between them, had to fall.

He went to her desk, pulled out a quill, and began to pen corrections to the legal documents she had in a pile, including the bill of sale he'd found yesterday. Not deterred, he purposed to win. If they eloped today, and she made him a proper husband, he knew they would. She had to agree.

Within the hour, the sound of a carriage arriving rumbled through Tradenwood.

Pickens announced the Earl and Countess of Crisdon and led them to the parlor.

"Son?" Lord Crisdon asked, raising his head. "I didn't know you would be here. I no longer need your assistance. The widow is selling."

Mother rushed to him and wrapped her arms about him. "I've missed you so, Ewan. Your play is wonderful. I've seen it twice with all my friends. I told you, Crisdon, he would be great."

"Yes, you did, my dear. A Fitzwilliam, the talk of the town." Lord Crisdon folded his arms, wrinkling the sleeves of his pristine charcoal coat. "A Fitzwilliam in theater."

Lord Crisdon turned toward the hall. "There could be worse things."

Theodosia stood at the threshold of the room, holding Philip.

Ewan's breath caught, overpowering the anger boiling in his gut at his father's sneer. She'd changed into a fresh gown of blush. Bright and beautiful, with her silky hair way up in a shiny black chignon, she could be one of the pretty flowers on the trellis. And Philip, he wore a crisp white pinafore and sat safe and secure in his mother's arms.

"I see you are here, Lord Crisdon," she said, "I didn't think you'd come, too, Lady Crisdon."

His mother looked her way for a moment, then took a few steps Theodosia's way. Maybe she had to see the boy's crystal-blue eyes.

Lord Crisdon took papers from his pocket. "Here is the paperwork. I'll have my bank draft the amount."

Brow raised, Theodosia took the papers from him and handed them to Philip. Carrying the boy to the mantel, she pointed to the flames. "Philip, toss this rubbish into the flames. Lord Crisdon, we will use *my* paperwork, and you were to come with the banknote or there will be no deal."

"Crisdon," his mother said, in a voice that sounded weepy. "Don't cheapen out now. She's going to sell."

Ewan shook his head. "I have a better deal for you all to consider, and it will only cost twenty thousand pounds."

"Speak up, my boy." Lord Crisdon moved toward Ewan. "I am assuming, since you are here that you've already married her, and the land is ours."

"No. I am here to see about Mrs. Cecil and her son's best interest. I edited a few pages of the bill of sale to a lease, of sorts."

Theodosia bit her lip. She came to him and took the papers from him. "Ewan, this is not what I—"

"Trust me, Mrs. Cecil. Trust me now, or never."

With a nod, she handed the papers to Lord Crisdon.

His father took them and pressed his beady face close to the pages. He harrumphed. "Twenty thousand pounds to lease the water rights? How is this good? It doesn't give us Tradenwood."

Ewan took Theodosia's hand within his and she smiled, a big true one. "The widow is eloping, but I will make sure her affairs are in order. Sign this, pay her, and make Jasper master over Grandbole. Then this lease is perpetual. You will never suffer from water rationing again; no further payment after this."

His father groused. "A lease that can be changed annually? Why would I ever do this?"

"You can simply pay a one-time fee and abide by the terms, or you pay annually. What was the amount each year you wanted, dearest?"

"It was twenty thousand pounds per annum," Theo said, turning Philip away from Lady Crisdon's slow advance.

Ewan took his son from Theodosia. He wanted Mother to see him, to feel the loss that he'd lived until yesterday. "Mrs. Cecil, if the Earl of Crisdon is late in his payments at 4 percent interest, what would that be?"

Theodosia didn't blink and said, "That would be another eight hundred pounds."

With Philip squirming, he leaned down and kissed her forehead. "She's a dream with numbers."

Lord Crisdon guffawed as he paced back and forth. "That's blackmail. Son, you are very sure of yourself."

"Never been more, my lord, never more."

The man smiled at him. "Didn't think you had it in you, my boy."

Catching Theodosia's gaze, he gave her hand a little squeeze. "I didn't either, not until I lost the one person who believed in me."

Mother sat on the chaise and pulled out her fan. "But what of Tradenwood? I thought she was going to sell it back to us?"

Lord Crisdon went to the desk and dipped the pen in the ink. "No. Fitzwilliam has come up with a good plan."

Tears welled in his mother's eyes, and she fanned faster. "No. This was my home. I was born here. She doesn't—"

Philip fidgeted more, so Ewan set him down. The boy took the old book of Shakespeare from the table and climbed up onto the chaise, next to Mother.

Fanning harder, she looked straight ahead. "Do something, Crisdon."

"Mother, he *is* doing something by taking Mrs. Cecil's

deal. If not, he knows Ewan Fitzwilliam-Cecil will personally ensure not a drop of water will flow to Grandbole."

Theodosia looked up. Her trademark lip bite had bloomed into a perfect smile. "Ewan, you would change your name, for me?"

"Yes. Cecil will be the name celebrated in Town, and it allows you to keep the only name you've ever known."

She gripped his arm tighter. "Thank you."

Something passed over his father's gaze. He pulled his note from his pocket and made the sum twenty thousand pounds, but he made it out to Ewan Fitzwilliam-Cecil. "You win. Lord Hartwell will now have full control of Grandbole, and I will join your mother in London. Come along, my dear."

Mother rose. "So you are marrying her? You will be master here?"

"It's none of your concern. I love you, Mother, but you are not welcome."

Her big blue eyes widened to a point of almost popping. "I'll say sorry. Have you no charity for your old mother?"

Ewan moved to the door and held it open. "My loyalties are to Theodosia and Philip. Maybe we'll visit you in Town at one of your fabulous parties, but not here."

Her jaw trembled. She clutched her husband's arm and left the room. Lord Crisdon paused for a moment and grasped Ewan's hand. "Hold on to what is yours. And congratulations. You bested me."

"Father, I made things right."

The man nodded and left the room.

Theodosia came to his side and put a palm on his arm. "I am so sorry, Ewan." She hugged him tight. "I never wanted you to choose."

Ewan scooped her up, pulling all her weight against him and spun her. "A man has to choose."

"I can't believe." She was winded, tearing up so much,

but the last wall separating them had to be released. "Your mother looked so heartbroken."

For a moment, he cradled her against his silk waistcoat, against his scar-filled chest and restored heart. Setting her on top of the writing desk, he grabbed a handkerchief from his pocket and mopped up every droplet trailing her flared nose. "We have one thing to resolve. Now, that you've compromised me with this overnight stay, forced me to change my name, you must decide if we wed."

She hiccupped and furrowed her brow. "I thought you had decided."

"No. You need to ask me and mean it. Now, I am not opposed to you thoroughly ravishing me, if that will bring you assurance of my affections." He kissed her palm. "I need you to be very sure."

"I'm scared Ewan. What if we end up hurting each other again?"

Wiser than before, he shook his head. "That won't happen. My love for you is stronger than anything."

"But I'm not strong, not when it comes to you. Ewan, I'm weak. I'm fragile. I fear you walking out of my life, out of my son's life, and this time no miracle will bring you back."

"Love means being brave. There is no one braver than you, Theodosia." He put his hands to her waist, lifted her in the air, and twirled her until she clung to his neck. "My love means you can put your weight on me, all of your burdens. I love you, sweetheart." He set her back upon her slippers and took one step from her. "The strength of my feelings could overwhelm you. I could sweep you away in a wave of emotion so thick, that you'd float. I have enough love and patience to wait for you, until you are sure. You are worth everything to me, but I need to know if you want to be with me for the rest of your life?"

Swaying a little, she twisted her fingers. She stilled and

put her hands to his face. "Ewan Fitzwilliam."

"Fitzwilliam-Cecil."

"Ewan Fitzwilliam-Cecil, will you marry me?"

He said nothing and stared at her.

Her forehead filled with lines, and she put a hand to her hip. "Well?"

"Was that it? What about the part about loving me forever? Your note said something about keeping me in your heart. I want to hear that aloud. A direct address is important. And do it loud, so Philip will hear."

Theodosia's lovely mouth opened but nothing came out. She shook as if she'd received a shock.

Maybe this was too hard for her. Maybe it was too much to expect after all they'd been through. Loving her more than himself and his ego, he decided to make it easier for her to accept him. "I'm teasing—"

She put a finger to his lips. "*Shhh*. I need to say this. Be patient or I won't get the words out. You know I struggle with words. That day so long ago in the carriage house, I should've said the words, *don't leave me*, or *take me with you*. I should've begged you to not to part from me. I was so afraid of your father and so shamed for my own actions. I let fear steal my voice then; I can't let fear take it now."

He wanted to tell her he understood, but he knew her well enough to know she had to say her peace. "I'm listening."

Biting her lip, she stopped and grabbed ahold of his gaze. "Six years ago, an ignorant flower seller lost her heart to a dreamer, but what that wonderful man needed to know was that he was her best dream. Ewan, my heart crumbled when I thought you died. I wanted to die, too. Then I found I carried your babe. That part of you had to live. I had to keep alive any piece of you and the love that burned so brightly it scorched my soul. Know that even when you were dead, or far away, you were in my heart, haunting my memories with an everlasting love. When I couldn't grieve anymore, when I thought my soul was dry, you were there in my tears."

He took her hand and kissed it, then wove her palm against the scars on his chest. "I should have been here to dry those tears. I will never ever let you be far from me again. I'll never be parted from you, Theodosia. I love you more than anything."

Trembling, she fell into his embrace. "Mathew rescued me and Philip. I loved him for that, but I have always, always been in love with you. Not a day, not a moment passed without you being in my heart, and this time, I know you won't let me go. I can trust you with all of me, with the best of me, with our son."

He claimed her lips, whispering his love in each kiss, taking her mouth with a desire to assure her he felt the same, that she was a part of him, too—the only part that had worth.

She brushed at her eyes. "So, yes, Mr. Playwright. I love you. Marry me. Make me Mrs. Ewan Fitzwilliam-Cecil, a new name that I will love above all else."

"Yes," he said, hoping she heard the promise of forever in his tone. "We should be going. I want you to have our name as soon as possible."

Slipping from him, she went to her desk and rummaged inside until she pulled out her satin reticule. "That name, it's better than Flower Seller."

"You will be Theodosia Fitzwilliam-Cecil, the flower girl who made two men love her. For my vanity's sake, I'd like to think of the first husband as a placeholder, the one you needed until I grew up."

"Mathew wasn't—"

"I know." He brushed his lips against hers. "It's my goal, to make you secure in my love. I want to be your preferred husband. I hear it's difficult to beat a true ghost."

"You were my first love, Ewan, and now my last."

"Time for new memories." Grasping Philip in one arm, he clasped her hand and headed to his rented carriage. "It's time to go elope."

Pickens stood at the door, the one he'd stood guard on the many nights Theo had kept Ewan at bay. His smile was big. "Godspeed."

"Tell Lord Hartwell and my fiancée's dearest friends to have a wedding supper ready here when we return, in three days."

He settled his family inside the carriage and tapped the roof. As it started down the drive, Theodosia settled Philip onto his lap. "We could've taken one of my carriages. This is a long trip for a squirming child."

"No, I like it quiet and intimate here. Forces you to be near."

She frowned up and looked out the window. "I should go get medicine or an onion for Philip. He might have pain."

"I thought of it. It's in my stowed bag. I must be prepared to live life with you."

"That's a half a penny for the onion. At least ten shillings for the laudanum. That's a lot of money."

He reached for a bag on the floor and pulled out the little wooden horse and put it in Philip's small hands. "Well, this playwright will use his simple means to be of use."

"You are. You make me happy. We will be safe with you, Ewan. This time, I truly know it."

Blessed beyond measure, he waited for Theodosia to settle beside him. It was the place she belonged, next to his heart.

Epilogue

Theodosia yawned as the sounds from the first floor of Tradenwood, a pianoforte and laughter, finally started to quiet. Her open balcony door let the sweet smell of clematis inside her candlelit room. She sat at her vanity, staring at the gold band Ewan had purchased for her at Gretna Green. Simple, elegant, easily encompassing her finger. Her heart warmed at the sight of it. This meant security for her and Philip.

What a whirlwind the past three days had been. They'd journeyed to Scotland, only stopping for a meal or to water the horses. They'd arrived for a simple ceremony with a blacksmith whose coal-dusted hands had bested her own coloring. It all seemed too quick, and too short of a service to support the guinea Ewan had left the man.

Yet, maybe it was worth the stares they'd received. They did look different from other couples venturing to marry. Nonetheless, once Ewan had kissed her dizzy, she'd stopped paying attention to villagers and the footman. His love made the world disappear.

The door connecting their rooms opened, and Ewan

came inside. The burgundy-colored robe draping his shoulders made his outline look royal, kingly, but the scars showed him as blessed.

Barefoot, he strode to her, took her hand, and spun her to Frederica's pianoforte tune.

"How is Mrs. Fitzwilliam-Cecil this evening?"

She looked in his eyes and didn't know quite what to say. Happiness spilled from her heart, but so did nervousness. This was their first moment alone since the wedding.

He twirled her again. "Philip's tucked in bed. Your friends, Miss Burghley, Miss Croome, and Miss Thomas have assured me that they will take care of him, should he need assistance. And my dear brother is also in charge of making sure my theater friends don't stay too long."

Ewan stopped midstep. "I may have tasked the wrong man to chaperone. He's enjoys a good party."

"Lord Hartwell is quite capable. He chose my advertisement, after all. I feel quite confident in him."

"Yes, he does seem to have good taste, as does Miss Croome. She's beguiled by the actors. Maybe she has a future in the theater."

Theodosia muffled a giggle, thinking of her dear friend. "No, she's too shy, but she has a serious liking for Arthur Bex. She adores his voice."

Ewan tugged free the bow of Theodosia's nightgown. "He's a great actor, but she should take care. He's fighting something, not sure what, but something."

"Little Miss Croome is big with plans but too nervous to carry them out. You saw how she was mouse quiet through supper."

He spread the thin fabric of her robe and wove his hands underneath, cupping her shoulders. "Sheer does look good on you."

Her face heated and she took a half step backward. "I

haven't changed too much. It's been six years since you saw—all of me."

"Shyness is one of your enduring qualities, too." Ewan scooped her up. His eyes, those bluer-than-blue wonders, glittered with candlelight. He carried her to her wide bed, separated the curtains, but allowed the gauzy fabric to sweep her face. "One of many and finally a bed, a wide one."

Soft and gentle, he laid her upon the mattress. He dipped out, blew out most of the candles, then entered from the other side of the canopy.

The music below faded. The beating of her heart overtook his. Six years since she'd been this close to him. Maybe she was dreaming, a wicked, delicious dream of the man who knew her soul, who was finally free to love her.

The sweetness of his gentle caresses almost distracted Theodosia from his fingers slipping off her robe, his thumbs flicking pins from her hair.

He splayed her locks between his palms. "You are the most beautiful woman. Six years have served you well."

She sat up with her hair dripping down her arms. She bit her lip and waited.

Smiling, he reached over, grabbed all the pillows, and turned back down.

"What? Ewan?"

He fluffed one and adjusted it underneath his neck. He worked a spot in the bedsheets smooth before stretching. "Good night, my love."

She hovered over him and shook him. "But technically this is our wedding night."

"I'm not rushing you, Theo. I made my father pay a large dowry for me, which cancels out the payment made to Lester."

"Yes, that was clever of you, but what does that have—"

He trailed his pinkie over her nose. "This being my

first marriage, shouldn't I be like the new bride awaiting discovery?" He leaned up and nipped the lobe of her ear, raking it with sensations. "You know what to do to help my motivation. I remember a vixen, a saucy Circe plying me with temptation in a carriage. Where is she?"

"Hiding. Wondering how things will be with us. Six years later."

He put her hand to his chest, forcing her to feel the wild thread of his heartbeat against the scars. "We will be better. We know better. We will love better."

The confidence in his voice reminded her how far they'd come. Finding joy in their strengths and vulnerabilities, she traced a circle, her unending love, for Ewan. "Perhaps, but I'll settle for love long-lasting. I just want us to be in love forever."

He eased his hand behind her neck, then traced her spine down to the small of her back. "Yes, but I will never settle, and I don't have to with you, not the way I love you." He tugged her to him. "This shyness is endearing, my sweet, but not exactly how the Circe of my play would go about enticing me. I'll have to give you plenty of direction, plenty of practice. Maybe a rehearsal every night."

She wanted to complain she wasn't anything like his Cleo character, but the playwright had abandoned words, sculpting Theodosia with his writing hands into a heroine besotted with love, one completely breathless beneath his weighty kiss.

Acknowledgments

Dear Friend,

I enjoyed writing *The Bittersweet Bride*. It was a great deal of fun and a bit of a challenge to shape these meant-to-be-together characters separated by history and a lack of trust. I hope you enjoyed their journey to forgiveness and love.

My diverse stories showcase a world of intrigue and romance, and offer a setting hopefully everyone will find interesting, and a character to identify with, in the battle of love and life.

Stay in touch. Sign up at www.vanessariley.com for my newsletter. You'll be the first to know about upcoming releases, and maybe even win a sneak peek.

Thank so much for giving this book a read.

Vanessa Riley

Author's Note

In 1819, Burlington Arcade was built by the Earl of Burlington. It is one of Britain's earliest shopping arcades. He designed it for "the sale of jewelry and fancy articles" and "for the gratification of the public." It is still in existence.

By Regency times, historians Kirstin Olsen and Gretchen Holbrook Gerzina estimate that Black London (the black neighborhood of London) had more than 10,000 residents. These were free, not enslaved, residents given to industry, mercantile, or in the service of estates around London. This population became absorbed into the culture by marriage.

During the 1800s, placing an advertisement in a newspaper like the Morning Post for a marriage of convenience was an acceptable way for single men and women to find a mate. For those new to the area or if the person had particular circumstances, like widowhood, small charges, etc., which could preclude a normal courtship, they turned to advertisements.

Editorial caricatures focused on the prevalent themes or societal worries of the times. A Woodward Devlin print from 1803, called "Advertisement for a Wife," shows a man surprised by the respondents to his marriage advertisement with one of the ladies being a Blackamoor. You can view the caricature and examples of advertisements at: http://vanessariley.com/NewspaperBride.html

About the Author

Vanessa Riley worked as an engineer before allowing her passion for historical romance to shine. A Regency era (early 1800s) and Jane Austen enthusiast, she brings the flavor of diverse peoples to her stories. Since she was seventeen, Vanessa has won awards for her writing and enjoys bringing her tales to the world. She lives in Atlanta with her military-man hubby and precocious child. You can catch her writing from the comfort of her Southern porch, with a cup of Earl Grey tea, or cooking in her spicy kitchen.

MY SCOT, MY SURRENDER

a *Lords of Essex* novel by Amalie Howard and Angie Morgan

Brandt Montgomery Pierce is a bastard—and proud of it. Despite the mystery surrounding his birth, he has wealth and opportunity, and wants nothing more. Especially not a wife. Lady Sorcha Maclaren is desperate to avoid marriage to a loathsome marquess, even if it means kissing a handsome stranger. But after the kiss turns into a public embrace, Sorcha and Brandt get more than they bargained for—a swift trip to the altar.

TO LOVE A SCANDALOUS DUKE

a *Once Upon a Scandal* novel by Liana De la Rosa

Declan Sinclair is devastated to discover his brother has been murdered, and he's the new Duke of Darington. Clues point to one man, and, he resolves to destroy the culprit. If only the killer's daughter didn't tempt his resolve. Lady Alethea Swinton has cultivated a pristine reputation. But she's willing to court scandal to help handsome Declan uncover the truth behind his brother's death. Until she realizes Declan's revenge will mean her family's ruin.

The Lady and Mr. Jones
a *Spy in the Ton* novel by Alyssa Alexander

Jones, born in the rookeries, was saved as a young boy and trained to be an elite spy. He serves His Majesty in espionage, hunting rogue spies. Cat Ashdown is a baroness. She knows every detail of every estate that commands the largest income in Britain—yet her father placed her inheritance in trust to her uncle who is forcing her to marry against her will. The baroness's battle against law and convention leads her to Jones and results that are surprising...and possibly unwanted.

A Perilous Passion
a *Wanton in Wessex* novel by Elizabeth Keysian

Determined to redeem his honor after a humiliating military defeat, the Earl of Beckport is living incognito, hunting a band of smugglers at the center of a French plot to invade England. Beautiful, enigmatic Charlotte Allston instantly becomes a person of interest to the earl...and not just in the smuggling case. Passion flares between the two. But when her attempts to help with his secret mission only endanger it, he must question where her loyalty truly lies.